# THE IMMORTAL FIRE

## THE CRONUS CHRONICLES · BOOK THREE

## ANNE URSU

**ATHENEUM BOOKS FOR YOUNG READERS**
New York   London   Toronto   Sydney

Atheneum Books for Young Readers
An imprint of Simon & Schuster Children's Publishing Division
1230 Avenue of the Americas, New York, New York 10020
The text for this book is set in Hoefler Text.
Manufactured in the United States of America
First Edition
2 4 6 8 10 9 7 5 3 1
Library of Congress Cataloging-in-Publication Data
Ursu, Anne.
The immortal fire / Anne Ursu. — 1st ed.
p. cm. — (The Cronus chronicles ; bk. 3)
Summary: As Philonecron plots to destroy the gods,
transform the Underworld, destroy humanity, and remodel Olympus,
Mr. Metos takes thirteen-year-old cousins Charlotte and Zee to join the
Prometheans, who have an age-old weapon that may help protect them.
ISBN: 978-1-4169-0591-2 (hardcover)
[1. Adventure and adventurers—Fiction. 2. Mythology, Greek—Fiction.
3. Animals, Mythical—Fiction.] I. Title.
PZ7.U692Imm 2009
[Fic]—dc22
2009008917

For Dziwe Ntaʙa,
my cousin

# Contents

# Under the Sea, Again

AT THE CRADLE OF CIVILIZATION, CLOSE TO THE belly button of the world, there is a sea like no other on Earth. This sea is unique for many reasons—the particular wine-dark color of its water, the fact that it is at the nexus of three continents, and of course because of the vast population of Immortals who call it home. Up until about an hour ago, it was also unique because on it there sailed a yacht like no other—but there is not much of that yacht left anymore, thanks to the ministrations of a rather vengeful, extremely giant, giant squid.

At this moment it is not the wreckage of this yacht

like no other that currently makes this sea unique, nor the number of Immortals in formal wear speeding away from that wreckage, nor even the body of the gargantuan Ketos that lies at the bottom of this sea a few miles away—no, what makes this sea so very, very special is the man (or something very like a man) currently inside that Ketos's belly.

And him, surely, you recognize. The black pointy hair, pale skin, red eyes, and unmistakable air of megalomania? That is Philonecron, former Underworld Assistant Manager of Sanitation, grandson to Poseidon, would-be usurper of Hades's throne, brilliant schemer, beautiful dreamer, impeccably clothed, paragon of good taste, victim of vile villainy, endlessly persecuted, but always resilient, able to rise from the ashes of ignominy better and more diabolical than ever. And something very special has just happened to him.

For, what is that object in his hands? Mighty, mystical, and decidedly misplaced? That couldn't be the trident of Poseidon, one of the artifacts fashioned for the three sons of Cronus in their epic war against their father for control of the Universe? Its magic—great and terrible—is dependent on the presence of Poseidon himself. Or, it turns out, someone who shares his blood—if that someone happens to be an evil genius.

And isn't it fortunate that Philonecron is?

Philonecron certainly thinks so. It is quite something to have your destiny made manifest to you in an instant. To the uncultivated mind, his presence in the belly of the Ketos at the very moment his grandfather's trident happened to come sailing inside might seem to be the greatest of luck. But Philonecron's mind is nothing if not cultivated, and he recognized in the incident the white-gloved hand of Fate. Fate—so judicious, so clever—who truly understood the Universe's greatest problem: that he, Philonecron, was not in charge of it.

Now, perhaps there have been times in your life that you have been presented with the object of your heart's most fervent desire, and perhaps in those times excitement overtook you to such an extent that you may have behaved in a way that one might, in retrospect, call rash. And if so, you will understand all the things that happened next.

Let us just say, hypothetically, that you'd been trapped inside the stomach of a Ketos, tossed around in its stomach acid a few times, and that stomach acid was currently disintegrating your lovely silk cape. You'd also been anticipating an escape through the creature's digestive process that was sure to be the most unpleasant thing you had experienced in a life that had recently been quite full of unpleasantness—and then, suddenly, the creature died on you and suddenly digestion did not look so bad compared to spending an eternity where you were—and then you were presented an object that was capable of granting your every wish? What would you do?

Well, you explode the Ketos from the inside.

Afterward you find yourself standing on the floor of the Mediterranean Sea, and you recall how very much you do not like being wet. You are also now covered in Ketos-goo, and technically you have no one to blame for that but yourself. Nonetheless, you are quite uncomfortable. And so you do the natural thing.

You get rid of the sea.

Afterward you find yourself standing in a vast cylinder surrounded on all sides by a wall of swirling sea, and you are so happy to be dry again and breathing air—which, while not as good as the dank darkness of the Underworld, is a great improvement on water—though there are still bits of Ketos on your tuxedo.

It is at this point that you notice that you are not alone in this cavern in the sea. For some distance from you is a tangled mess of chariot and some very cranky-looking horses, and emerging from that tangled mess is the owner of the trident.

He looks confused at first—perhaps wondering where the sea went—but his expression changes when he sees you.

"Grandson," he breathes. "My trident, you found it. Give it to me!"

Now, you are nothing if not methodical. That is the point of being an evil genius—one doesn't just follow one's impulses wherever they might lead. One *considers*. This is what you do, you *consider*. You ponder your goal, meditate on all the options, deliberate on the ramifications and/or permutations. This is why your plans are always so very, very brilliant.

Sometimes, though, sometimes there is not time to meditate, ponder, or even deliberate. Sometimes you are standing in the muck covered in Ketos-goo while the second most powerful god in the whole Universe is staring at you, and he wants his trident back. And so you do the only thing that is really possible at that moment.

You aim the trident at him.

"What, this?" you say, purring slightly. "You want this?"

And this seems, suddenly, a very good time to get a few things off your chest. Because when you don't let these things out, they build up inside you, and that's simply not healthy for anyone.

You take a step forward. "Do you know, Grandfather, that you are really quite tacky?" you say, your voice like silk. "You think your taste is so very well developed, but really you are the most vulgar creature in the Universe. Truly, I don't think you deserve this trident. I think it belongs to someone who can use it to make a better world." A slow smile spreads across your face. "Don't you?"

Silence then, while you watch the dawn of comprehension on your grandfather's face. It takes some time, as he is really quite stupid.

And then he roars and charges toward you. "You can't use that," he yells. "It's worthless to you."

And you say, "And that is just another failure of imagination on your part. Would you like to see?"

And then it seems there is nothing to it but to act. And in a few moments, Poseidon, Lord of the Seas, second most powerful god in the whole universe, has vanished, and in his place is a small blue sea cucumber. A shiver of great portent passes through you as you stare at the creature's small body as it flaps tackily in outrage. Then you look down at your trident—your beautiful, brilliant trident—and you cannot help yourself. You give it a hug. Finally, after all your searching, you've found love.

"That," you coo, "went rather well, don't you think?"

# PART ONE

---

## Water

CHAPTER I

HOLES

A FEW DAYS LATER, HALF A WORLD AWAY, ONE ordinary eighth-grade girl was lying on the couch in her den, stroking her cat and feeling sick. There was nothing too extraordinary about this situation; this girl stayed home from school, and if you looked at her you would not be surprised. For Charlotte Mielswetzski (you know how to pronounce that by now, right? *Meals-wet-ski?*) was covered in gross yellow bruises and small cuts and wore her wrist in a splint and generally looked as if she had had an unfortunate encounter with a very large falling piano.

But Charlotte's sick feeling had nothing to do with her injuries, at least at the moment. It was caused instead by the most extraordinary images on the television screen in front of her.

Her mother entered the room and looked from her daughter to the television. She watched silently for a few moments, and then shook her head.

"Have they figured out what caused it yet?" she asked Charlotte in a grave voice.

"Uh-uh," Charlotte muttered. On the screen in front of her, helicopters circled around the all-too-familiar wine-dark waves. Water swirled angrily around the great hole that had appeared suddenly in the middle, as if someone had carved out a piece of the sea. The gaping blackness at the center looked like it might suck the world into it at any moment. It was so wrong, it would have made Charlotte ill to look at even if she did not suspect the cause.

"They say all the sea life in a mile radius has just disappeared," Mrs. Mielswetzski said. "Poof! Look!" She pointed at the TV screen. The image had changed to another part of the sea, near the coastline. An entire village worth of people huddled on the beach, staring at the sea in front of them. And it was no wonder why, for the waters in front of them were thick with dolphins. There must have been thousands, leaping frenetically in and out of the waters as if trying to escape. Charlotte's stomach turned, and a low, wary rumble came from her cat Mew.

"You know"—Mrs. Mielswetzski turned to Charlotte—"I looked at a map, and I think the . . . incident . . . is very close to where our ship was. If we'd been there a little longer . . ."

Charlotte didn't respond. There was no doubt in her mind that the cavern in the Mediterranean Sea was just where their cruise ship had bobbed helplessly only a few days ago.

"Honestly, Char," her mother continued, "I know it sounds absolutely crazy, but sometimes I wonder if something really . . . strange is going on. After what happened to us . . ."

Charlotte eyed her mother. Mr. and Mrs. Mielswetzski had recently had the very strange experience of falling unconscious on a cruise ship off the coast of Virginia and waking up to find themselves on the same ship in the middle of the Mediterranean Sea. Everyone seemed to have accepted the cruise officials' completely implausible explanations, because there was no plausible one. Only Charlotte and her cousin Zee knew the truth: The ship had been transported there by Poseidon, who was planning to punish Charlotte by feeding it, along with all its occupants, to a giant Ketos.

Her parents, like most of the rest of the world, had no idea that there was any such thing as a Ketos, or that Poseidon and the rest of the Greek gods were anything more than half-forgotten myths.

"I know what you mean," she mumbled. Something very weird *was* going on. It wasn't just the half-mile-wide hole that had suddenly appeared in the Mediterranean Sea, or the behavior of the dolphins. Strange reports were coming in from the whole region. A fleet of ships from the Croatian navy had disappeared. Sharks off the coast of Rome had gone psycho, swimming after fishing boats and patrolling the beaches. A whirlpool had suddenly appeared in a shipping lane. The waters of the Aegean Sea had turned so choppy that no ship could travel on it. A several-mile-long swath in the Mediterranean had turned pitch-black and cold, as if it had simply died.

There was more, too, things that would never make it to the TV news. Someone had started a blog cataloging all the incidents, and Charlotte spent the morning pressing reload on it until she couldn't stand it anymore. There was a tiny deserted island that had somehow become cloaked in eternal night. In Rome a fisherman showed up at a hospital covered in animal bites; he babbled some story about his boat being set upon by a monstrous woman with a pack of dogs for legs. On the small Greek island of Tilos, the mayor's daughter had gone missing, and there were rumors she'd been seen chained to a cliff face above the sea. She wandered back into the town after a day with no memory, but a vague impression of being rescued by a tall, dark-haired man. The captain of a sailboat racing team was found swimming desperately for shore. He said his boat had been wrecked on a small island he'd never seen before. They were very surprised to find a young, beautiful woman living there, a woman whom the man could only describe as bewitching. When asked about his shipmates, he just shook his head and said they had decided to stay. On the isle of Rhodes, a twelve-person caving expedition had disappeared. In Croatia twenty people disappeared from a city street midday. Whoever had taken them had left, in their place, perfect stone statues of each person.

As the scene of the TV shifted to a reporter standing on the beach interviewing people, Charlotte's mother shook her head grimly. "I guess I'd better pick up your cousin. How are you feeling, sweetheart?"

*Horrible. Terrified. Furious.*

"All right," Charlotte said with a half shrug. Anything more hurt too much.

Her mother frowned at her, her face full of sympathy and concern. As far as she knew, Charlotte had woken up on the cruise ship with the rest of them, with no memory of how she'd suffered her injuries. There was no way for Charlotte to tell her they'd all been inflicted by Poseidon himself.

"Do you need anything?"

"No. Thanks, Mom."

"All right," she said, glancing between Charlotte and the TV. "Listen, don't worry about all of that. I know it's scary. But it will be okay. We're safe." She leaned in to kiss Charlotte gently on the forehead and then left.

On the TV the reporter was interviewing a white-haired, rough-skinned woman from Cyprus who was babbling excitedly in a foreign language. All around her, fish were flopping on the sand while children scurried to pick them up and throw them back into the water. A voice-over translated the woman's words:

*"It's the end of the world."*

A terrible shiver passed through Charlotte, and the woman turned to the camera and said something to it, her dark eyes a challenge to everyone who saw her. But whatever she said, they did not translate. The scene cut to the newsroom, where the reporter appeared on a big monitor next to the shiny-haired anchor. "As you can see," the reporter said, "explanations for the mysteries in the Mediterranean are in short supply, but"—she smirked—"theories abound. Susan?"

"Fascinating," said the anchor. "What did she say at

the end there, when she looked at the camera? Do you have it?"

The reporter looked at her notes. "More superstitions, Susan. 'Find the heir,' she said. 'It's our only hope.'"

"Huh. Another mystery in the Mediterranean!" exclaimed the anchor, as a banner appeared below her, echoing her words. "Thanks, Brittany. Coming up next, who says you can't teach an old dog new tricks?"

Charlotte glared at the TV and changed to another news channel, then lay back on the couch to wait for her cousin.

It was not long before Zee appeared in the family room, looking rather out of breath. He was staying with the Mielswetzskis while his parents were in London on business, and Charlotte was glad, as she didn't think she could endure any of this without him. Carefully shutting the door behind him, he whispered, "Any news?"

Grimly Charlotte filled him in on the day's events, while Zee listened pale-faced. When she was done, he sat down on the couch, looking stunned. They sat for a moment, watching the images on the TV. A helicopter had flown into the inside of the immense cavern and shot video; the sea just stopped, like a wall of water.

"I don't get it," he breathed as Mew crawled on his lap.

"I don't either. Maybe Poseidon was trying to destroy the ship by taking the sea out from under it? Anyway"—she lowered her voice more—"I guess he has his trident back."

"Brilliant," Zee muttered.

Charlotte grimaced. Zee had never even really seen Poseidon in his full glory. Poseidon had wanted to kill Charlotte *before* she stole his trident, aided in the destruction of his yacht, humiliated him publicly, and ultimately defeated him with the very timely help of her cousin. He hadn't really seemed like the type to forgive and forget. And now he had his trident back. And Charlotte would have to spend the rest of her life staying away from oceans, seas, lakes, rivers, and possibly even showers or baths. She was going to be very stinky.

"But it's everything. The shipwreck on the island— that's Circe, right?" In *The Odyssey*, Circe was a sorceress who lured Odysseus's ship to her island and turned all his crew into pigs. She and Odysseus canoodled for about twenty years while the pig-men roamed around and Odysseus's wife waited for him to come home. Men were weird. "Someone was attacked by a woman with a pack of dogs for legs—that's Scylla. The people turned to stone . . . there was a Gorgon in the city! In the city! Zee"—she lowered her voice—"they're *letting themselves be seen.*"

Charlotte hadn't even realized it until the words were out of her mouth—but that's what was so wrong about all of this, even more than the great hole in the sea. The gods had retreated because Zeus didn't want to deal with humanity anymore. And they kept it so humanity didn't know they existed. That didn't mean they didn't interfere—some gods used the mortal realm as their playground, and people as their playthings. The policy seemed to be that they could do whatever they wanted as long as no one noticed them.

Well, people were noticing them now.

The implications didn't escape Zee. "Something's changed," he muttered, almost to himself.

Charlotte looked at her cousin, eyes wide. "What do we do? People are going to get hurt." An image flashed in her mind—the woman being interviewed on TV while the voice-over proclaimed, *"It's the end of the world."* She was just a crazy person, though. Wasn't she?

The cousins looked at each other. There was nothing they could do, not by themselves. But they could join the fight. Because Mr. Metos was coming for them.

Mr. Metos had been their English teacher in the fall, but that was just a cover. He was really one of the Prometheans—a group of descendants of the Titan Prometheus who worked to protect humanity against the gods. The small mischiefs, the under-the-radar interferences, the stray monsters loose in the mortal realm—the Prometheans were there, keeping the worlds apart, keeping people safe.

And Charlotte and Zee were going to join them. It was all they'd wanted since they'd come back from the Underworld after seeing the condition of the Dead—left to fade and suffer because no one tended to them. But there was nothing they could do.

Now Mr. Metos was coming for them. Just after they came back from the sea, they'd gotten a letter from him. *I believe that you are in danger,* it had said. Since Zee had just been kidnapped by their immortal enemy Philonecron and Charlotte had nearly been killed by Poseidon several times over, this news was not exactly new. But the end of the letter was:

> There is something afoot, something
> that may affect the fate of us all, and
> I'm afraid you two are involved. My
> first priority is to keep you safe. I will
> come for you soon.

Humanity needed protection—now more than ever—and the cousins were going to help. They were going to be god-fighters.

Mr. Metos did not say when he was coming—just

*soon*. The cousins' hearts ached for him to appear, for him to take them, for them to get started. In the meantime, they'd decided they would bone up on their myths so they'd be prepared for whatever awaited them. (It had been Zee's idea; Charlotte was not prone to extra-curricular research.) Zee's backpack was bulging, and he put it down and began to pull out some books.

"I got these all from the library. There were a lot, actually. Mr. Peaberry said Mr. Metos had ordered a bunch in the fall."

"Huh," Charlotte said. "I guess he expected us to use them." She watched as Zee's stack of books kept growing. "Wow. Mr. Peaberry must have been impressed."

Zee looked embarrassed. "I told him we were in a mythology club." He glanced at Charlotte, who raised her eyebrows at him. "I froze under pressure. But I'm British; you lot believe we do that kind of thing."

He had a point. "So what did you find? Did you get a chance to look at any of them?"

"Well, there're a few collections of myths. I got some plays, too, though I'm not sure they're really, you know"—he lowered his voice—"true. A lot of them are just about mortals, really, with gods pulling the strings in the background, but this one"—he lifted up a small green volume—"is about Prometheus."

Charlotte exhaled. Prometheus made humans.

When his creations were not faring well in the world of beasts, he appealed to Zeus to give them fire. Zeus refused, because that's just the kind of guy he is, so Prometheus stole the fire that gave humans knowledge of the gods. As punishment, Zeus chained Prometheus to a mountain where an eagle would gnaw on his liver every day. The first time Charlotte had heard that story, she had thought it was particularly disgusting, and she didn't even know it was real.

"Anything interesting about Zeus?" Like directions to Olympus and ideas for devastating insults?

Zee shrugged. "Not yet. Mostly he likes to change himself into various animals and chase mortal women."

"Charming," said Charlotte. "But probably not helpful."

From downstairs came the sound of the doorbell. Mew looked around, then sprang toward the door of the room, leaping through as Zee opened it.

"Good watch kitty," Charlotte said with a small smile. Mew liked to appraise anyone who came into the house, in case they carried with them ill intent (or maybe cat treats).

"Char," said Zee, sucking in his breath. He was pointing at the TV screen, and, with a feeling of doom, Charlotte turned her head to look.

People running, carrying overstuffed bags, animals,

children. A parking lot filled with buses and vans. Dark-haired men in suits, ushering them forward. A coastal town emptying out, its shell awaiting its doom, silent and brave.

Charlotte hit the volume button. In the background a siren blared.

*"The tsunami will hit within the hour. The Italian armed services have been hurriedly evacuating the coastal villages since a naval ship called in the warning. Oceanographers are calling the tsunami mysterious; there was no seismic event in the area. For now, the cause will remain unknown. Now the focus is getting these people out of harm's way."*

"It's our fault," Charlotte whispered, tears in her eyes. "Somehow. We did this."

Zee did not disagree. They watched in silence, in horror, as the town emptied out and the wave approached.

Suddenly Mrs. Mielswetzski's voice came traveling up the stairs. "Char! Zee!" she called. "Can you come down here?"

"Just a second, Mom," Charlotte said weakly, unable to take her eyes from the TV.

"Somebody's here to see you!"

Charlotte looked at Zee and shrugged. This was not really the time for a visitor, but what could they do? Charlotte wiped her eyes.

But when they got downstairs, everything changed.

There he was, standing in the Mielswetzski living room talking to her parents as if no time had passed. He looked the same, tall and thin, with a gaunt face and messy dark hair and clothes that had seen better days. There was a time, way back before anything had happened, when Mr. Metos had seemed sinister to Charlotte. Now he seemed like the friendliest face she'd ever seen, and the sight of him almost made Charlotte want to hug him.

Almost.

Charlotte's heart threatened to leap right out of her mouth. All the waiting was over. They were going. The world needed them now, and they were going.

"Look, Charlotte," said Mr. Mielswetzski, "your old English teacher came by!"

"Isn't that nice?" said Mrs. Mielswetzski.

"Very friendly of him, I think," said Mr. Mielswetzski.

"Um," said Charlotte, her voice squeaking slightly. It was important not to show how excited she was. "Hi, Mr. Metos. It's nice to see you."

"Hello, Charlotte, Zachary," said Mr. Metos in his calm, stern voice. His eyes flicked over the cousins, and when they landed on Charlotte, they showed a flash of alarm.

"You've been injured?" he asked, his voice impassive.

"Um, yeah," said Charlotte. "I had an . . . accident."

She could feel her parents shift behind her. It was hard to concentrate, so loud was her heart.

As for Mr. Metos, he clearly had no idea what had happened to them the week before. It was strange, for once, to have more information than he did. "I see," he said, gazing at Charlotte. "Well, I've just come back into town, and I wanted to return one of your books, Charlotte." He nodded toward a book on his lap that Charlotte had never seen before. "I found it while unpacking some boxes."

Charlotte frowned. "Unpacking?" she repeated. Why would he need to unpack when they were just going again?

"Yes," he said. "I've just taken out a lease on an apartment a few blocks from here."

Charlotte and Zee exchanged a glance. "Are you . . . staying here?" Charlotte asked in a disbelieving voice.

Mr. Metos knitted his eyebrows. "Why, yes," he said. "I have some . . . pressing concerns that have brought me back. I should be here for some time."

"Oh," said Charlotte, staring at him. "Because I thought . . . I thought you would be going away again."

"No," said Mr. Metos, a note of finality in his voice. "No, I'm staying right here with you."

CHAPTER 2

Say What?

Charlotte stood there staring at Mr. Metos,
his words reverberating in her head. What did he mean,
he wasn't going anywhere? Was he lying? Was it part of
his grand scheme? Surely he was lying, surely there was a
grand scheme, surely it was a trick for her parents, surely
he'd come to take them with him.

But as Mr. Metos gazed upon her with an inscru-
table expression on his face, she realized that he was
telling the truth. He hadn't come to take them to the
Prometheans. *My first priority is to keep you safe,* he'd
written. He'd come to *protect* them.

Charlotte didn't need protection. She'd faced down Hades and Poseidon—and, okay, it was only the timely intervention of a giant squid and her cousin, not to mention the Lord of the Seas' monumental anger management problems, that had allowed her to survive her Poseidon adventure, but still. She did survive. And Zee had saved everyone in the Underworld, and ultimately saved the cruise ship, not to mention survived a week as Philonecron's Zee-bot. What had the Prometheans done?

They were kids, and thus somehow needed protecting. But it seemed to Charlotte that she and Zee had done most of the protecting of late, and lots of people were still alive because of it.

Zee was stock-still next to her, and she knew without looking the expression of disbelief on his face, while Charlotte tried hard to fight the angry tears that burned in her eyes.

"So," said Mr. Mielswetzski, "Mr. Metos, will you be working at Hartnett again?"

Mr. Metos cleared his throat. "Yes. The middle school has employed me to do some tutoring and special projects for the rest of the year. I'll be available there"—he cast a glance at the cousins—"should anyone need me. I'm in talks with the upper school about teaching there in the fall. English, of course."

"Oh, that's wonderful!" Mr. Mielswetzski exclaimed. "We'd love to have you." Charlotte's dad taught history at the upper school and was very enthusiastic about it. "Perhaps you and I could teach a joint class. I was thinking just the other day about how closely the study of American literature and American history parallel—"

Charlotte wasn't listening. Mr. Metos was going to teach at the high school in the fall? Just in time for her and Zee to start going there? And then what, was he going to magically land a job at Charlotte's college? Professor of Mythology and Ruining People's Lives? He was going to follow them for the rest of their miserable, pathetic, useless lives, while people suffered the whims and neglect of the gods.

Her father was blathering on about the Civil War while Mr. Metos listened. It was all Charlotte could do to keep her rage from exploding her from within. Now they were just going to stand here, like everything was okay, and make conversation?

"Mr. Metos," interjected Mrs. Mielswetzski, "have you seen what happened in the Mediterranean? What do you think?"

Charlotte stared at the Promethean, her eyes narrow. Yes, what did he think? Pretty scary, huh? Boy, wouldn't it be nice to talk to people who had just come from battling with Poseidon and might have insight on the situation?

Mr. Metos's face did not move, his eyes registered nothing. Charlotte had spent enough time with him to know his face only got blanker the more momentous something was. "It is . . . very unusual." He paused for a moment and then continued, "But we can be sure good people are working to solve it."

He did not look at Charlotte or Zee, but Charlotte knew he was speaking to them all the same.

"Really?" she said, unable to keep the quaver out of her voice. "Because there's a tsunami coming. People are running away. It's horrible. They're terrified." She articulated each word carefully. Next to her Zee was straight and still, but she could feel his anger and frustration in the air.

Mr. Metos turned his blank eyes to her. "Isn't it fortunate there was warning? So they could all get out in time? You can be assured the whole town will be evacuated."

Ah. Charlotte understood. The Prometheans were there. What did the blog say about the mayor's daughter who'd been chained to the cliff? A tall, dark-haired man rescued her? The girl probably didn't mention the shabby clothes because that might have seemed rude. The descendants of Prometheus, all of the same bloodline, were recognizable for their dark features, lack of fashion sense, and general cold black hearts.

So the Prometheans were in the Mediterranean. Keeping people from being sacrificed to sea monsters and saving them from tsunamis and rescuing them from dog-legged women-beasts. And still, Mr. Metos had left them to come to Charlotte and Zee. Because Charlotte was sure they could really spare people now. But she and Zee were apparently such babies that it was worth losing a Promethean to nanny them.

Charlotte blinked rapidly but could not keep the tears from her eyes. Mr. Metos's gaze fell on her, and she flushed. That's what babies do, isn't it? Cry?

"It's especially scary for us," added Mrs. Mielswetzski. "Because we were just there."

And then Charlotte saw something flash through Mr. Metos's eyes, just a flash, and then it was gone. He turned to Charlotte's mother and asked, ever so casually, "Just there?"

"Oh, yes," said Mr. Mielswetzski. "It was all quite strange. There were navigational difficulties with the cruise ship, a gas leak, and a huge storm—it's really a long story, but we were all on the Mediterranean! Except Zee, of course, who stayed here. We felt bad for leaving him behind, but it turned out he was lucky."

Next to Charlotte, Zee let out a barely perceptible noise.

"We had quite the ordeal," said Mrs. Mielswetzski.

"Well," Mr. Metos said, "Charlotte and Zachary will have to tell me all about it." He turned to them. "Miss Mielswetzski, Mr. Miller, I'm starting at school tomorrow. Would you come to my office for a meeting? I have a project I'd like to discuss with you."

"Oh, no," interjected Mrs. Mielswetzski. "Charlotte's not—"

"No, it's all right," Charlotte interrupted. "I'm going to school tomorrow."

Her mother turned to her. "Charlotte! The doctor said—"

"She said I could go back when I felt better. It barely hurts now." This was true, in a way—the pain from her injuries had nothing on her fury and disappointment now. "Mom," she added, eyes full of sincerity, "I really don't want to fall behind at the end of the year. I mean, eighth grade is important."

Mrs. Mielswetzski pursed her lips and eyed her daughter suspiciously.

"Tara, the girl wants to go to school!" said Mr. Mielswetzski.

"Fine," Mrs. Mielswetzski said. "But you call me the instant you feel any pain at all."

Mr. Metos watched this whole transaction so impassively that Charlotte knew he was desperate to talk to them. And it almost made her want to say forget it, she was not going back to school, she was, in fact, never going back to school ever again, and would spend the rest of her life in the company of her parents so Mr. Metos would never find out what had happened on the Mediterranean Sea.

And, were she not desperate to talk to him, maybe she would have.

"I will, Mom," she muttered.

"Well, then, I'll see you children tomorrow," said Mr. Metos.

Charlotte's ears burned. *Children.* That's what they were to him.

Charlotte's parents showed Mr. Metos the door, telling him all the while how nice it was for him to stop by and how glad they were that he was back and what a wonderful teacher he must be to take such an interest. Charlotte and Zee watched, silently, stonily, until her mother turned and asked, "Aren't you going to say good-bye to Mr. Metos, Charlotte?"

"Good-bye, Mr. Metos," Charlotte said as flatly as possible. And then, before her parents could talk to her, she turned and stalked up the stairs, with as much dignity as her body allowed her to muster. Which, in truth, was not much.

• • •

As Charlotte opened the door to her bedroom, she was hit by a strange rotting smell coming from the room. It seemed to match her mood perfectly. She plopped face-down on the bed. A few minutes later there was a soft knock on her bedroom door. Charlotte turned her head and mumbled, "Come in, Zee."

Zee opened the door quietly and entered, followed closely on his heels by Mew, who promptly jumped up onto the bed and hopped on Charlotte's back.

"Ow," moaned Charlotte.

Picking up the cat, Zee sat down on the floor and leaned against the wall, then gave the wall a good bang with his head.

"Ow," he muttered. His face crinkled up. "What's that smell?"

"Dunno. The decay of my dreams, I think." She groaned again. "I can't believe it."

"Yeah," Zee said.

"We should have known," said Charlotte.

"Yeah," Zee said.

"Of course he wasn't going to take us to the Prometheans. We can't do anything. We're just"—she spat the word out—"*children*."

"Yeah," Zee said.

"What are we going to do?"

"I don't know," Zee said.

Charlotte shook her head and glared off into the long shadow in the corner of her room. It seemed to flicker as she looked, take shape, a demon stalking her. She blinked and the illusion was gone.

"Well, we'll just have to convince him," she said. "Tell him we want to join the Prometheans. Tell him we can help, that he has to let us help!"

Zee nodded slowly. "We'll do it tomorrow."

Charlotte shut her eyes. The whole Mediterranean could explode by tomorrow.

"It's not going to work. He's not going to let us go."

"I know," said Zee, setting his jaw in a manner that would be best called Charlotte-esque. "But we have to try."

That night Charlotte dreamt that she was running as fast as she could, clutching Mew in her arms. A great cartoon wave was chasing her, gliding along the ground. An endless line of half-glowing shadows stood off in the distance, passive and unmoving.

Shades. The Dead. They were always there in her dreams, lingering listlessly in the background, a constant reminder of her great failure. Sure, Charlotte and Zee had saved them from Philonecron and an eternity of torture. But they were left with an eternity of dreariness. Hades ignored the Dead, let them wander the plains of the Underworld aimlessly, let them fade into near oblivion. Everyone Charlotte had known who'd died—her third-grade teacher who was always giving Charlotte books, her grandfather who did magic tricks, her grandmother who burned every batch of cookies she had ever made but never stopped making them—had gotten lost in the endless void of eternity. They were only shadows now. After they'd gotten back from the Underworld, Mr. Metos had gone off with the Prometheans; he said they would try to find a way to help the Dead. That didn't seem to have happened, and they were still down there, suffering.

They were ever-present in her dreams, a constant reminder that they were waiting for her. As she ran from the terrible wave, she could not help herself; she turned to the great line of them and called for help, but they did not move. They could not move. The wave was catching up, she could not outrun it, it was right behind her—

Darkness. Complete and total. Everything had changed, as if someone had changed the channel. Charlotte felt around and discovered she was in some kind of cage. The air around her was dank and cold, and it reminded her of the long passageway to the Underworld. She was in a cave, that was it, a cage in a cave and she had to get out, because she had something important to do.

Charlotte ran her hands up and down the bars of the cage, trying to understand her surroundings. The cage was small; she could touch both walls if she reached out in either direction. And the bars were thick and close together, much too close for her to slip through. And as she felt around she realized there was no door to the cage. It was impossible—there had to be a door somewhere. A feeling of horror crept over Charlotte suddenly—where was she? How did she get in here? And how was she ever going to get out?

"Hello? Is someone there?" she yelled.

Silence. Silence like eternity, silence like death.

Then a form appeared, one of the Dead, its soft glow seeming like the brightest light in the whole universe.

"Hello?" Charlotte asked. "Can you hear me?"

The Shade stared at her. It wanted her to do something, to know something. And then—

Light, there was light—somewhere off in the distance. It was uncertain, inconsistent, dimming and brightening like—like fire. Somewhere in the caves someone had lit a fire.

The Shade was gone. In the distance, though, a voice:

*Charlotte. Charlotte Ruth Mielswetzski. Over here.*

"Who's that?" Charlotte asked. It didn't sound like anyone she knew.

*Over here,* said the voice. It seemed to be female, and possibly young. *I have to show you something.*

And that's when her alarm went off.

Charlotte blinked herself awake, then rolled over and hit the button. "Well, I guess I'll never know what she wanted to show me," she mumbled to Mew, blinking back the image of the oncoming wave.

"Meow," said the cat, raising her head sleepily.

Charlotte lay back on the bed as the pain in her body began to announce its presence. Part of her wanted to go right to her computer to see what had happened overnight; the other part just didn't want to know.

She cast a glance at her clock and sighed. "Do I really have to get up?"

"Meow," said the cat. She climbed on Charlotte's chest and began kneading it with her paws.

"Ow," said Charlotte.

"Meow," said Mew.

And Mr. Metos. They were going to go in today, to try to convince him to take them to the Prometheans. It was going to be an utter failure, but they had to try.

"We should have just left him in the Underworld," grumbled Charlotte. Mew gazed at her reproachfully.

"Okay, okay, maybe not. But we should have at least *thought* about it."

Mew exhaled through her nose, turned around twice, and settled down on Charlotte's chest pointedly, as if to keep her there.

## CHAPTER 3

# Missing Persons

CHARLOTTE FINALLY WILLED HERSELF OUT OF BED, got ready, and went downstairs to find the rest of her family gathered in the kitchen, watching the news. She glanced at Zee, who gazed significantly back at her.

On the TV, a coastal town was being assailed by wind. A line of cypress trees bowed to one direction, their branches reaching out to the side as if trying to flee. The dark sky roiled overhead. Houses shuddered and gave up pieces of themselves to the wind's might. The air was thick with cloud and sand and debris. Not a soul was in sight; it was like not a soul existed on Earth—they had all abandoned it to the wind.

And then, just like that, the wind stopped. The trees snapped back in relief. All was calm. And then, suddenly, the debris began to stir, the wind started up again, the trees bowed exhaustedly—in the other direction.

"Whaaaa—," breathed Charlotte.

*"Because of the unpredictability of the squalls,"* said the voice-over, *"the Sicilians cannot bring in ships or planes to evacuate the island, so the people of Mozia must simply take cover and wait this strange storm out."*

"The wind's been doing that all morning," Mrs. Mielswetzski said in a low voice. "It hits, stops, and then changes direction. It doesn't make any sense."

"The people . . . ?" Charlotte asked.

"In underground shelters. Sometimes it stops for an hour and then starts again, in a completely new direction. It's like . . . it's like the wind is . . . toying with them. . . ." There was an odd expression on Charlotte's mom's face—wonder and disbelief, as if she was realizing the world was not quite the place she thought it was. Which, of course, it wasn't.

"What about the town where the tsunami hit?"

Her parents exchanged a look. "Well, they were able to evacuate," said Mr. Mielswetzski slowly. "But another one hit last night, even bigger, at the same place. There was no warning. . . . The town's just gone. They're watching for more and evacuating the nearby towns just to be safe. But it's not just there; there's a big storm brewing off Istanbul. That's the Black Sea."

"It's like it's spreading," Mrs. Mielswetzski said quietly.

Charlotte and Zee exchanged a heavy look. She was right. From the Mediterranean to the Black Sea to . . . ?

"Hey, look," said Mr. Mielswetzski, pointing to the TV screen.

All eyes turned. The image was still of the wind-battered coast, but in the distance an enormous rainbow had appeared, spanning half the horizon.

"That's . . . beautiful," said Mr. Mielswetzski.

He was right. It was beautiful. Inhumanly so. The rainbow shimmered beguilingly in the dark sky, and even the clouds seemed to hang back to admire it. The colors were so vivid that they were difficult to look at, as if human eyes were not built to take them in. It was immense, awe-inspiring, ostentatious . . .

It looked like it was showing off.

And then another appeared, a little closer to shore, its bands of color thick and discrete. And then another, pouring down from the clouds to the awaiting sea.

"What the—," exclaimed Mrs. Mielswetzski.

Even the reporter was stunned into silence. The scene

suddenly flashed back to the shore, where the trees were now bent completely to the side. The sand was so thick in the air you could barely see. And then the wind shifted abruptly, like a car thrown into reverse, and the trees all lurched to the other side. A few snapped and fell to the ground, pieces flying off into the wind. Then a rainbow burst forth from the sky, right in front of the camera, spilling out onto the ravaged beach, grander than all that had come before. The wind swirled and then the trees were pulled upward, reaching to the heavens.

"I don't understand," said Mr. Mielswetzski under his breath. "It doesn't seem possible."

Zee had sidled up next to Charlotte and muttered in her ear, "They're trying to show each other up."

She nodded slightly. That's what she thought too. In *The Odyssey*, there was some god who kept the dangerous sea winds captive on an island in the Mediterranean. Well, it seemed he'd let them out. And the rainbows—the goddess Iris was is charge of them. They were doing something—playing, battling, some kind of godly power-off. It was either spite or recreation, but either way the consequences would be disastrous. The world could not survive if enough gods decided to show off.

"We'd better go," Charlotte said, her voice flat.

"You didn't eat anything," protested Mr. Mielswetzski.

"I'm not hungry."

Her parents just nodded. There were no comments today about how breakfast was the most important meal of the day, no mention of a healthy breakfast building a healthy mind, nothing about how studies showed that kids who ate a good breakfast did better in school. Not today.

"All right," said Mrs. Mielswetzski, with a glance toward the TV. "Let's go."

It was a quiet car ride that morning, everyone pensive and tense. Charlotte could not imagine what her mother was thinking. She must be scared. She had caught on somehow—not the truth, of course, but she knew something was horribly wrong. The things that were happening should not be happening—they were impossible. Any one of them would be frightening enough on its own, but together . . .

Was it scarier, Charlotte wondered, to see all this happen and know the cause, or to wonder at the dark? She was terrified for very real reasons; Mrs. Mielswetzski and everyone else watching were scared of the terrors that lurked in the vast unknown. Would it be better, in a way, if they knew?

Mrs. Mielswetzski pulled up in front of the school and turned to her daughter.

"Are you sure you want to do this, honey?"

Charlotte looked up the stairs toward the big double doors of Hartnett Middle School and exhaled. No. "Yeah."

"How are you feeling?"

Bad. "All right." She gazed up the stairs again. "Mom? Keep watch on the news, okay?"

Mrs. Mielswetzski rested her hand gently on her daughter's head. "I promise."

Charlotte expected to find a grim school when she walked in the doors: wide-eyed students talking in low voices, half-empty hallways as frightened parents kept their children home. But no. People around her moved by, talking and laughing, going about their day as if everything was perfectly normal. Who cared that half a world away everything was falling apart, that people were huddled in basement shelters while their homes blew away?

"You all right?" Zee muttered, standing next to her.

"Not really," she said.

"Um, Char," said Zee, his voice suddenly tight. "I have to go."

She turned toward her cousin, but he was disappearing behind the doors of the school auditorium, where he had no reason on earth to be.

And then, from across the hall, a surprised voice called her name. Maddy.

It used to be that her cousin and her best friend got along really well—which was always a relief, since Zee mostly turned and ran when confronted with anything resembling a girl. But then Zee and Maddy started going out, and Zee dumped Maddy for one of the Ashleys. Maddy was devastated, and Charlotte was furious.

Except it hadn't been Zee at all—he'd been kidnapped by Philonecron, and Proteus, a shape-shifting sea god, had taken his place and apparently decided to relive his youth through Zee. Which was sort of ironic, because Zee wasn't really living his own youth.

So Charlotte was forced to tell Maddy things like, "You have to understand, Zee just wasn't himself," but of course Maddy didn't buy it, and Charlotte couldn't exactly tell her the truth, because (a) Maddy would never believe her, and (b) Proteus in real life looked like he was about a thousand years old, and some things it was just better to go through your life not knowing.

"I didn't think you were coming back all week!" Maddy exclaimed, running up to her.

"I felt better this morning," said Charlotte. "So I decided to come."

"Oh, I'm so glad you feel better. I was so worried!"

The official lie was that Charlotte had been in an accident over spring break—which was technically true, if you consider being bounced around the deck of a cruise ship by Poseidon an accident. It was a lie that her parents were only too happy to participate in, as falling unconscious while your cruise ship was mysteriously transported half a world away and your daughter suffered serious, unexplained injuries seemed careless, to say the least. So Maddy had come over on the weekend, bringing magazines and cookies and movies and all kinds of sympathy. Because Maddy was a good person, she didn't ask for the gory details about the accident, which was fortunate, since it never happened.

As they walked slowly through the hallways, Charlotte felt people's eyes on her. It was like they'd never seen anyone beaten up by Poseidon before. She could feel how ridiculous she looked—black and blue with little cuts, and walking like she was made of sand. It grew worse with every step. She had already moved more that day than any since she'd gotten home, and it was not going very well.

"Did you see the news this morning?" Maddy asked. "The Mediterranean's gone crazy."

"Uh-huh," said Charlotte.

"It's got to be global warming. It's the only explanation. Jack Liao thinks it's aliens, but he thinks everything's aliens. Oh," she said, her face turning stony as they turned the corner to where Charlotte's homeroom was. "I'd better go."

A hurt expression crossed Maddy's face, and Charlotte's heart sank. It was very awkward having your cousin break your best friend's heart, and even more awkward when it wasn't your cousin at all but a geriatric shape-shifting sea god in disguise. The two people in the world she could count on weren't speaking to each other. The purgatory of the rest of her life was already proving to be something very like hell.

When Charlotte entered her homeroom, she saw Zee huddled in the back, looking ashen. She made her way toward him, ignoring the eyes on her as she passed. Someone let out a low whistle, and she heard a whisper, "That was some accident."

Charlotte slipped into the desk next to Zee and gave him a look. This Maddy thing was going to be horrid. "I've seen you braver," she muttered.

"I think I'm going to go back to London," he grumbled.

"That's probably for the best."

"Ashley's not speaking to me either," Zee added mournfully. "Neither's the other one."

"On the bright side," Charlotte said, "the Ashleys aren't speaking to you."

Zee shot her a look, then lowered his voice. "This was on the message board for me," he said, handing her a folded-up note.

On the outside, Zee's name was written in Mr. Metos's scrawl. Charlotte's heart sped up, and she unfolded it.

*You are excused from lunch,* the note read simply.

She looked at Zee and nodded. They would meet Mr. Metos then. Now all they had to do was wait.

It was not easy. The day passed horribly slowly. It was already too much that Charlotte had to be here while the world was falling apart; it didn't seem fair that she had to go to math, too. She spent the whole time staring at her blank notebook. Every once in a while she would glance up at the board where Mr. Crapf was solving equations, but finding nothing comprehensible there, she just looked back at her paper and waited for time to move.

Gym was no better. They were doing fitness testing, and since Charlotte could not participate, it was her job to sit on the hard bleachers and record everyone's times for posterity, as if posterity cared a whit about how long it took the Hartnett eighth graders to run from one orange cone to another. At one point Chris Shapiro sidled up next to Charlotte and made some comment about how it was too bad her accident didn't make her any less funny-looking. Charlotte rolled her eyes and then added two seconds to his time.

All morning she wondered about the world and what was happening to it now. She couldn't figure out the connection between all the events—had Poseidon decided to let all the sea gods loose to unleash mischief? Was he looking for Charlotte and Zee? Was he punishing humanity for Charlotte's sins? How many people were going to suffer because of her?

And then, finally, it was time.

As the Hartnett eighth graders moved en masse to the cafeteria for their meaty goop and tater tots, Charlotte and Zee walked away from them and down two flights of stairs, where Mr. Metos's new office was. Whatever power Mr. Metos had that allowed him to keep getting employment near Charlotte whenever he needed it did not, apparently, extend to getting a decent office. They'd stuck him in a narrow gray hallway in the school basement, in between storage rooms. The sound of the boiler echoed through the hall.

"Ready?" Charlotte asked, her hand poised at the door. Her stomach churned. Everything seemed to depend on this moment.

Zee nodded.

Mr. Metos sat behind a big, old-looking wooden desk on which perched a school-issue computer. Charlotte couldn't imagine that was going to get a lot of use; Mr. Metos seemed to think calculators were too modern to be bothered with. There were three boxes of books in one corner, and a file cabinet stood in the back. The room was dark and dingy, with one small egress window in the back providing a small bit of sunlight.

Urged on by Mr. Metos, the cousins sat down in two metal folding chairs. Charlotte didn't know there was something that could make her body ache more, but the day was just full of surprises. "I am so glad to see you," he said, his voice soft. "I have to apologize. I am very sorry for leaving you alone. It was deeply irresponsible of me. I meant to keep you safe, and all I did was endanger you. I mean to make up for my failure. First, Charlotte, what happened to you? I need to know everything. It's very important. Leave nothing out."

"Mr. Metos," Charlotte interrupted, straightening, "we don't need your protection."

Mr. Metos raised an eyebrow. "You don't? So those injuries of yours, they *were* from a car accident?"

Charlotte flushed. "Mr. Metos, we want to come with you. We want to join the Prometheans."

Mr. Metos's eyes widened. "Join the Prometheans? Goodness, is that what you thought would happen?" He sounded genuinely taken aback. "I see. Well, I'm sorry if I gave you that impression. But that is no job for young people. You two must live your lives. You're young, you're just—"

"*Children*," Charlotte finished, her heart sinking.

"Mr. Metos," Zee interjected, "we can't just live our

lives now. We know the truth, we saw the Dead, we know how the gods are. We can't just sit around and do nothing, can we?"

"That's exactly what you'll do," said Mr. Metos, a flash of anger in his eyes. "I don't want you involved in this!"

"We are involved!" Zee said, his voice as forceful as Charlotte had ever heard. "Do you know what happened to Charlotte?"

Mr. Metos gazed at Zee. "That is what I am trying to get you to tell me."

Zee exhaled and glanced at Charlotte, who shrugged. As Zee got up and started pacing around the room, Charlotte told him the whole story. She told him of Zee's kidnapping by Philonecron, of Poseidon's plan to lure her onto the sea, of the Siren and the cruise ship, Charlotte's adventures on Poseidon's yacht, her efforts to get his trident in order to defeat the Siren, and the ultimate confrontation that sent Poseidon into the watery depths, entombed in the tail of the creature that he had sent to destroy the ship.

Mr. Metos came as close to a real facial expression as Charlotte had ever seen. "This is all true?" He looked from Charlotte to Zee. Both nodded. He leaned back in his seat and exhaled.

"I—" He shook his head again, eyes fixed on a point on the floor. "We learned about the cruise ship and the

Ketos, but too late. Our eyes were . . . somewhere else. I never dreamed . . . I see I was even more negligent than I thought. It's all my fault."

"No," Charlotte said. "No, you see, we don't need protection. We can take care of ourselves just fine."

Mr. Metos looked grave. "No," he said. "Charlotte and Zachary, you defied an Olympian. Word of this—" He stopped and continued, as if to himself, "I must inform the others. We may have to move up the timetable."

Zee came back to sit down. "Timetable?" Charlotte asked. "For what?"

Mr. Metos did not answer. "You really handled Poseidon's trident?"

Charlotte nodded again, even though it was not a question, really.

"And"—he eyed them carefully—"you do not know what became of it?"

"Well, it was, you know, in the Ketos," Charlotte said. "He swallowed it. I'm sure Poseidon got it back eventually. Once he, you know, extricated himself . . ."

Mr. Metos shook his head in wonder. "An object like that . . ."

"Well, it only worked for a little bit," said Charlotte. "Only Poseidon can use it. It only works for a little while once it gets out of his hands."

"I suppose that is a blessing," Mr. Metos said. "If that got into the wrong hands . . . And Philonecron, you know nothing about what became of him?"

"No. Not since we blasted him off the ship." One of Charlotte's last acts with the trident had been sending Philonecron shooting through the doorway of the ship out into the open sea. It was pretty fun.

"And Poseidon, the last you saw of him, he was being dragged under the sea?"

The cousins nodded. "Why?" asked Charlotte.

Mr. Metos looked at them, as if considering. "It sounds impossible," he said finally. "I am still not sure I believe it. But Poseidon is . . . missing."

"Missing?" the cousins echoed in unison.

"Yes. Missing. There is no sign of him. Naturally this has caused some . . . disruption within the sea realm. For all his faults, the Lord of the Seas maintained a certain . . . order. The prospect of his rage was a powerful deterrant."

"I'll bet," muttered Charlotte.

"Is that what's going on?" Zee asked. "The tsunamis, the windstorms . . ."

"Yes. Some of the gods are . . . having a little fun. While the cat's away, the mice will play. . . ."

"What about the hole in the sea?" Charlotte added.

"We don't know. No one knows. It doesn't seem

possible that it's unrelated to Poseidon's disappearance, but . . ."

"So it's only going to get worse?"

Mr. Metos nodded. "I would imagine so. All the . . . activity is concentrated around the Mediterranean now, but I fail to see how it will stay contained there. One god's misbehavior begets another's."

Charlotte's stomach tightened. "You think . . . that could all happen here, then?"

Mr. Metos gazed at her. "You can rest assured we are working on it. We are keeping watch, that is our job."

"But," protested Charlotte, "we can help. We want to help." We *need* to help, she added silently. An image popped into her head: Maddy and her parents running for their lives.

"You can help me by staying safe," Mr. Metos said, his voice on the border between firm and angry. "For once, I want you two to listen to me. What I need is for both of you to be on alert. Keep your eyes out for anything unusual, no matter how small it may seem. You must let me know."

"Are you expecting something?" asked Zee. "About us, in particular?"

Mr. Metos gazed at them impassively. "Just be on the lookout."

That sounded promising. When they left Mr. Metos's office, Charlotte and Zee walked down the hallway in silence for a few moments. "So, what do you think that was about?" Charlotte asked finally. *Just be on the lookout.* It occurred to her suddenly that Mr. Metos might have very real reasons to think they needed protection.

"I don't know," said Zee. "But we're going to find out."

Charlotte shot him a tired look. Right, Zee. But . . . "How do you propose we do that?"

"We're going to sneak in and search his office," Zee said. Charlotte stared at him, and he grinned. "When you were telling the whole story about Poseidon? I unlocked his office window."

## CHAPTER 4

# Epic

AFTER HAVING TURNED THE SECOND MOST POWER-ful god in the whole Universe into a sea cucumber, Philonecron found himself feeling a little bit giddy. Could you blame him? It was all he could do not to go storming up Olympus that very moment and take what was rightfully his.

Soon he was on top of the water, riding Poseidon's chariot toward shore. Naturally he made a few modifications, turning the chariot and horses pitch-black. It went so much better with his coloring. As he sped along on top of the choppy sea waters, moving toward shore, he noticed the water in his wake turning black. He could not help but feel the poetry in it. It was a metaphor made manifest—magnificently so, as it had always been one of his dearest wishes to spread darkness wherever he went.

As he rode along, holding the horses' reins in one hand, he gripped his trident in the other, feeling its gentle warm hum against his cold flesh. It liked him, he could tell.

The sky above him was still dark with night, and the large round moon tipped the waves with white light. It illuminated strange shapes in the water—odd debris. It was not until he saw an enormous, expressionless golden head bobbing up and down in the water that he realized what he was looking at—the head was from a statue of the trident's previous owner (and as hollow as the one it represented), and this was the wreckage of his yacht.

He could not help himself—as the blank eyes stared dumbly up at him (though no more dumbly than the god himself), he turned the trident on it and exploded it. And then, a few yards away, he saw a muscular golden torso—and *BAM*. And a few yards beyond that, a floating lounge chair—and *ZAP!*

Philonecron sped through the night, pointing the trident this way and that, as bursts of light shot from it toward the flotsam and jetsam from the yacht. He heard a gleeful laugh in the night air, and he reflected that the owner of it sounded like he must be very, very happy indeed—and then he realized it was he, Philonecron, laughing from the pure joy of it all. And then—

"Hey! What are you doing with that?"

Philonecron whirled around in the chariot to find himself looking down at the insipid form of Poseidon's son Triton, who was floating on one of the yacht's inflatable life rafts. Philonecron pulled the horses to a stop while Triton blinked at him stupidly, fingering his conch shell horn, his fish tail flapping, his horse hooves shuffling around on the raft's surface.

"Oh, this?" Philonecron purred. "Well, you see, your father gave it to me."

Triton frowned. "He did?"

"Oh, yes," said Philonecron, eyes innocent. "He was going to go away for a little while and wanted someone who would take proper care of it. He said since his own son was too worthless to use it, he would have to skip a generation, as it were."

The boy's knuckles turned white around the conch shell. "He did not!"

Really, it was worth it just to see the expression on the boy's face. Shock, horror—but not disbelief.

"Oh, all right, no, he didn't," admitted Philonecron. "You see, I took it and then turned him into a sea cucumber. And now it's mine, all mine. Isn't it marvelous?"

"I'm telling Uncle Zeus!" Triton said, beginning to back away slowly on his raft. Unfortunately for him, there was not very far to go.

"No, no," Philonecron breathed, "that would not be wise. We must be discreet, yes? For, you see, I am planning to march up to Mount Olympus and use this to overthrow your uncle, and when I do that, it's very important that he's not expecting me."

Triton gasped, as if to suck in the whole sky, and lifted the horn to his lips. But it never got there, for Philonecron swung the trident forward—he was getting really fast with it now—and where there was once was a fish-tailed centaur on a life raft, there was now just a very small, fish-tailed weasel with a tiny conch shell around its neck. As Philonecron urged the horses on, the weasel blew on the shell and it emitted a small squeak.

Forward he went, through the night, blasting yacht debris as he moved, wielding the trident this way and that, aiming at targets farther and farther away. It was a magnificent ballet of destruction, and Philonecron the prima ballerina. He began to hum a triumphant melody as accompaniment, and soon the whole sky was his orchestra—trumpets and tubas, flutes and French horns, clarinets and chimes, bassoons and contrabassoons,

snare drums, tom-toms, tambourines and timpani—and
he providing the cymbal crash. He didn't just point and
shoot; he could spin, he could twirl, and land his shots
with accuracy and panache. *Zip! Zap!* The trident was a
part of him now, part of his body, his mind, his very soul,
and he knew then that the two of them would never be
parted.

Here and there he encountered refugees from
Poseidon's fateful party, their formal wear soaked and
tattered. He had met so many of them in his time on
the yacht. They laughed at him, they sneered at him,
they taunted him—as if any of them would have fared
any better against the malevolent machinations of his
spot-faced, squeaky-sneakered nemesis. He dealt with
them all, one by one, turning them into toads and snails
and urchins and eels and pucker-mouthed sucker fishes
and sucker-mouthed fish pucks—*bim, bam, boom,* bib-
bidi, bobbidi, boo!

The sea swayed for him, the moon bowed for him,
the stars sang out, the wind whipped through his hair,
the sky opened up to its boundless infinity. Normally it
all would have seemed oppressive, but he understood,
now, the beauty in it all. It was for him, there was a
whole Universe out there, for him and the trident,
too—for *them,* together, forever—there were barbarous
giants locked under the sea, traitorous Titans holding

up the earth, murderous malcontents chained up in Tartarus—he would free them all to attend the coronation of chaos for the new king of it all. Demons and Dragons, Cyclops and Gorgons, Chimera and Hydras. Wham! Bam! Alakazam! Eternity! Infinity! Destiny! Take that, and that, and that—

The next morning Philonecron woke up to find himself lying on the sandy beach of a small island, the trident cradled in his arms. He found himself, oddly, clothed in some kind of straw skirt and wearing a short-sleeved collared shirt with a plague of tropical flowers festering on it. Around him a bevy of strange small sea creatures skittled and scuttled and writhed and wriggled. A few feet away a great Minotaur was passed out on the beach, seaweed tangled in its horns. Next to it dozed a giant Hydra, one head resting on the Minotaur's bull chest, a plastic flower necklace hanging limply around each of its necks. Two Harpies buzzed around the bright Mediterranean sky, screeching, and a Gorgon sat underneath a tree, gnawing on a large red and green parrot.

This was probably not as discreet as he would have liked.

The instant Zeus heard that Philonecron, the greatest genius the Universe had ever known, now possessed one of the artifacts of power, he would surely go into hiding. Philonecron's plan depended on the element of surprise, on separating Zeus from his thunderbolt—because while Philonecron plus trident were probably not a match for Zeus and his mighty thunderbolt, Zeus *without* the thunderbolt was almost certainly no match for Philonecron and his most special friend.

Above him, the song of the island birds rang out through the trees and with a quick flick of the trident, he silenced them. He needed to think. What he needed was distraction, distraction and a place to hide. The sea gods would help—those that were not now invertebrates. As soon as it got out that Poseidon was missing, they would start having a little fun. Perhaps Philonecron could help get things started by sending his new monster friends out into the mortal realm.

But he should probably take off the leis first.

The morning sun beat down on him, and he felt so exposed, with Zeus's sky spread out about him. Another flick of the trident and the island was in eternal night. Darkness spread over him like a warm blanket, and he sighed in relief. Silent birds, monsters roaming loose, eternal night—when he took his rightful place on the throne of the Universe, this was what things would look like, only with more torture.

Oh, he had such splendid plans. Would you like to hear them? You would? Wonderful.

## PHILONECRON'S ACTION PLAN FOR A
## BETTER TOMORROW

1. *The Gods.* Some would be destroyed, of course. Zeus he would turn into a dung beetle and squash underneath his finest Italian shoes. The rest he would lock under the Earth, where Cronus and his fellows were imprisoned, and let them spend eternity settling their interpersonal issues. He would probably give some of them a chance to pledge eternal fealty to him, and then throw them in with the Titans anyway, because that would be fun.

2. *Underworld.* Ah, his childhood home. It is true you can never go home again, but you can turn it into a demon's paradise. Back when he was going to take over the Underworld, he thought he'd throw all the Dead into Tartarus, the Underworld's chamber of eternal torment. But now that he was older and wiser, he realized it would be far better to turn the whole Underworld into Tartarus and set the Erinyes—Tartarus's creative and vengeful mistresses of punishment—free to use the entire landscape as a playground. Sometimes you just need more room, you know?

3. *Earth.* There would be only minor adjustments: He would turn the sun black and the moon to blood, dry up the seas, poison the lakes, cook up a few deadly plagues, unleash all the beasts and monsters upon the mortal populations, and then sit back and watch the slow, painful extinction of humanity.

4. *Olympus.* Soon to be called Philonecropolis. Oh, it would be the finest of everything—crafted of obsidian and ebony, velvet and silk. He would assemble a team from

the best architects and interior designers—taking hearts from a few, brains from others, a few legs here and there. He would install an orchestra pit near his throne room, calling up the world's greatest musicians to play for him. Eventually they would drop dead from exhaustion, but then he'd just grab a few more from the pit to replace them. The walls he would line with works of the great masters—and perhaps, for fun, their heads as well.

You see, Philonecron had a plan—not just a plan, but a *vision*. A vision and a can-do spirit. This is why the Universe was rightfully his. It was all there, in front of him. He was standing on the cusp of eternity—he could look over the edge and see his wildest dreams, there for the taking if only he would jump.

So what was wrong? Why was he just lying there, staring at the darkness above?

It is a terrible truth that sometimes in our moments of greatest triumph we are plagued by self-doubt. This is the consequence of the sort of cruelty that he had suffered in the hands of the midget Medusa who had been put on Earth solely to torment him. It was not enough that she had thwarted his Underworld plans, caused him to lose his legs, poisoned his precious Zero against him, plunged him into the sea, gotten him swallowed by a Ketos with major halitosis issues—no, by constantly thwarting him in all his endeavors, she had taken away the most precious thing of all, his sense of self-worth.

*It is all right,* he told himself, staring up at the black sky. This was the way of things. He was a hero, this was a hero's journey, an epic for the ages—the saga of a humble demon's long journey from Underworld garbage collector to Supreme Lord of All Creation. He never wanted an enemy—he was peace loving, not prone to conflict—but every hero had a nemesis, one as terrible as he was great. It was only literary. It was the conquest of the Universe, after all. One did expect it to be literary.

Was she still out there, lurking in her vile little lair, clad in an item from her relentless series of discount casual wear, plotting her next move in her eternal quest to ruin his life? What if—it was absurd, but bear with him—what if at his moment of triumph, when Zeus was on his knees quavering in front of the trident, weeping and pleading, what if the little mortal monster appeared—because that was what she did, she *appeared*—and ruined everything? What if, just as he was about to get what he most wanted, she came, grabbed his beautiful dream with her sticky little hands, and stomped on it with her squeaky rubber soles?

He had thought Poseidon would have killed her—in some showy and very painful way—but he realized it made no sense. It defied reason that the Blunder God, who was by no means an evil genius, could accomplish something Philonecron could not.

Yes, the more he thought about it, the more he realized that the adolescent she-beast must have survived, somehow, and was still out there, plotting his defeat. Would she succeed?

He could find her, hunt her down, tear her apart piece by piece, but what if she defeated him again? His destiny lay before him, but he could not see it.

But he knew someone who could. This was an epic quest. He must begin it properly.

It had been months since he had been banished from the Underworld, and Philonecron found he still had not gotten used to the Upperworld and all its barbaric brightness. He felt so unmoored wandering around with the great maw of the Upperworld sky gaping above him. As he made his way up Mount Parnassus, he was tempted to take the trident and sink the whole place underneath the surface of the Earth—but he was trying to remain discreet, and that, someone might notice.

And then, of course, there were the people. In the Underworld, mortals were a smoky nuisance, nothing more. But here they walked around like they owned the place. The Upperworld had become some kind of free-range refuge for barbarians and troglodytes. And Zeus ignored them, just sat back and let it all crumble around him. He cared nothing for the world and all its potential. Not like Philonecron. That was the thing about Philonecron—he cared.

As Philonecron walked along toward his destination, surrounded by a teeming mass of humans stuffed in their pleated shorts and T-shirts, it was all he could do to keep from turning them all to dust. They should at least sense something as they passed—some sense of peril, of power, of panache—but no, they just trampled around the most powerful place in all the mortal realm with their cameras and their sweat stains as if it was nothing more than a (perish the thought) shopping mall.

And there she was, the Oracle, sitting next to a stone bowl, twirling her long black hair in her hands. As he stepped up to the Temple, her head turned toward him, and she let out a long-suffering sigh.

"I suppose you're not here for the scenery," she said.

Philonecron eyed her. He had never consulted the Oracle before—it seemed rather immodest to travel all the way to Delphi just to hear that he was destined for greatness. She did not look as though she held the secrets of the gods in her hands. There was something very self-conscious about her luxurious hair and red lips and white dress that perfectly flattered her figure, and Philonecron could not help but wonder if she might be a little vain.

"Hardly," he sneered.

She exhaled again and shifted languidly on her perch. "Name?"

"Shouldn't you know that?"

She rolled her eyes and repeated, *"Name?"*

"Philonecron," he said, eyebrows raised.

The Oracle's eyes widened, and a mocking smile broke out on her face. *"The* Philonecron?" She gasped dramatically. "Careful, there are mortals about! They're after you! Run!" She threw her head back and cackled.

Philonecron's jaw twitched, and his hand quivered on the trident underneath his cape. "Adorable," he said. "Now, Oracle, shall we get on with it?"

"Okay, okay," said the Oracle, wiping a tear from her eye. "Sorry, sorry. So, what would you like to know?"

Philonecron straightened, and his red eyes looked carefully around. "You are sworn to secrecy, Oracle?"

"Yes, yes, I am bound to silence. Oracle-client privilege. Now . . ."

He leaned in toward her and whispered, "I am on a quest to overthrow Zeus. Will I succeed?"

The Oracle rolled her eyes. "Oh, boy. One of those."

"What do you mean?"

"Demon, do you think you are the first to ask me that question? Try to be original, please."

"Answer me."

"How could it be you? You are Poseidon's heir. There is a way to these things. Don't you know anything?"

His red eyes hardened. "Listen to me, Oracle," he murmured. "It would be wise not to cross me."

"Why? Will you sic some mortal whelps on me? HA!"

"No." Philonecron took a great step back and raised the trident at her.

She froze and stared at the object. "That does not belong to you, demon," she whispered, not taking her eyes off the trident.

"Oh, but it does now," he said. "So, about my question? Who overthrows Zeus?"

"I see. If you want to be that way—"

"I assure you," he purred, "I do."

The Oracle closed her eyes for a desperate moment, and then shook her head. "I am sorry, I cannot see it. The name of Zeus's usurper has been hidden from Immortals." She looked up at him, a flash of panic in her eyes. "I have never been able to see it."

"That's . . . unfortunate," Philonecron said, leveling the trident at her. Within a matter of moments, an enormous, festering pimple appeared right in the center of her forehead. The Oracle shrieked, hands flying to her face.

Philonecron kept the trident on her. "Would you like another?" he asked silkily.

The Oracle peeked out from behind her hands and stared at her reflection in the bowl, then shrieked again. "No! Wait!" she said. "Wait. I can help you." She held her hand up toward him. "It is all darkness. But this I can see: Listen to me, demon." She leaned in, looking deadly serious. *"Your enemy is your friend."*

Philonecron inhaled sharply. "My enemy!" She could not mean—

"Your enemy," the Oracle said. She waved her hand over the stone bowl, and suddenly the image of the vilest creature in the entire Universe appeared. She was alive. Philonecron shrieked and blasted the bowl with the trident.

"Hey!" said the Oracle, dusting herself off. "I need that."

"I will destroy her," he breathed. "I will—"

The Oracle held up her hand. "I would not, if I were you. You need her alive."

His eyes narrowed. "Alive? Why?"

"Your enemy is your friend," she repeated. "Your mortals are at a crossroads. If, and only if, they are taken to the descendants of the traitorous Titan within the current moon, they will lead you to your answers."

CHAPTER 5

# Breaking and Entering
# The Charlotte Mielswetski Way

Zee and Charlotte huddled in the stairwell at the other end of the hallway, waiting for Mr. Metos to leave his office. The bell rang, signifying the end of lunch, and still the office door remained closed. And so they waited, and waited, and waited some more. Eventually Charlotte had to sit in a corner, as her body could no longer support itself.

"You all right?" Zee asked, peeking around the corner at the hallway.

"Fantastic," Charlotte muttered. "Doesn't he ever have to go to the bathroom?"

"Maybe that's the big secret of the Prometheans," Zee whispered back. Then suddenly he hissed, "Char!" and motioned her back, then slipped into the stairwell. Charlotte could hear footsteps moving away from them down the hallway.

The cousins were as still as could be until the footsteps disappeared. Then Charlotte peeked around the corner. The coast was clear.

Charlotte peeked out of the stairwell. "One of us should stand watch," she said. "In case he comes back."

"Char," said Zee, looking suddenly uncomfortable, "I'm honestly not sure I can fit through the window."

"Zee, are you calling me short?" she asked in mock outrage. It was rare that there was a physical feat Charlotte could do that Zee couldn't, considering he was the best soccer player in the galaxy. But he might be right. "Okay. I'll go."

"Be careful," he said. "I'll be right outside the door."

It took Charlotte some time to drag her sorry body up a flight of stairs and out the back door, then around the back of the school, which was, to her relief, deep in shadows. She crept next to the bushes, peeking into the window wells trying to find the right one, hoping desperately that no one happened to be looking out their windows right now. Because there was nothing suspicious about this.

And then she found the right one, climbed carefully down a rusting ladder into the window well, and tugged open the window.

Here was where the plan fell apart a bit. Charlotte sat in the window well, eyeing the drop to the floor below. Normally it would be no trouble for her, but normally she wasn't walking around like she'd been squashed by a steamroller.

"Zee, you couldn't have left a chair under the window?" she grumbled to herself.

She could do this. If people were huddled in basement shelters from murderous winds, if they fled from towering waves, Charlotte Mielswetzski could jump.

And so she did.

And it hurt.

A lot.

Tears sprang to her eyes, and she clenched her teeth and groaned. Then she gathered herself and hobbled over to the office door, pressed her ear against it, and tapped on it softly.

"I'm here," Zee whispered from the other side of the door. "No sign of him. Hurry!"

Okay, then. She surveyed the office. She didn't know what she was expecting to find, exactly. But anything would be more information than they had.

She peeked into one of the boxes stacked in the

corner and was greeted with an overwhelming smell of must. That seemed promising. She reached in and picked up a glossy, new-looking hardcover book and found to her surprise that it was nothing more than a grammar textbook.

"Boring," she murmured, absentmindedly opening the cover.

But the pages before her eyes looked like no grammar textbook Charlotte had ever seen. They were old, so old it seemed they might crumble if you examined them too closely. And the contents were most definitely not grammar, at least not English grammar. On one page was solid text, all in Greek, and on the other was a large engraved illustration of some kind of very unpleasant monster. It had great dragon wings, a massive dragon tail, and the head of a very mean-looking lion. It looked at first as if there was a ram-like creature standing behind it, but upon closer inspection Charlotte realized that the ram head was simply coming out of the monster's torso. It didn't look particularly nice either. From somewhere in the back of Charlotte's memory emerged the monster's name—*Chimera*.

"Boy, I sure don't want to meet one of those," Charlotte muttered to herself.

Something about the book made her want to spend the rest of the day paging through it, but of course there wasn't time for that, and she really didn't want it to disintegrate in her hands. She carefully placed the book back in its box, then scurried behind the desk to look at the papers scattered on top.

Mr. Metos's computer sat on the desk, its screen dark. Charlotte wondered idly if he even knew how to turn it on. She ruffled through the piles of papers, but they all seemed to be school correspondence. The first and second of the desk drawers revealed nothing but office supplies. The third, though, was locked. Charlotte tugged on it a couple of times, to no avail.

Grumbling to herself, she reached around to turn on the computer, not expecting much. Her elbow knocked the mouse to the side, and to her surprise, the computer sprang to life.

"Huh," Charlotte said. Apparently Mr. Metos used it after all.

She expected to have to enter a password, but the desktop appeared in front of her immediately. Chewing on her lip, she clicked on the e-mail program and surveyed his in-box.

More school stuff—some of which looked like it might be pretty juicy, but Charlotte didn't have time for that—and one e-mail from a foreign-sounding name that Charlotte did not recognize.

Heart skipping a beat, she clicked on the name.

An e-mail popped up, and Charlotte let out a small groan. The good news was it was clearly related to the Prometheans. The bad news was it was in Greek.

Now she knew why he didn't bother to have a password.

With a nervous glance toward the door, Charlotte opened up the web browser and did a search for a Greek-English translation site. The one that popped up had space for only a sentence or two at a time, so she selected a random chunk from the middle and inserted it into the translator.

She was not, in truth, expecting much. She'd tried a number of times to do her Spanish homework this way, and the translations always ended up sounding like a poetry slam on crazy-person day.

This was no exception:

> **We can select him above tomorrow.**
> **We have prepared a place in order to**
> **we keep also him it is sure. Under the**
> **circumstances, appears the alone way.**

Grumbling, she selected another chunk of text and put it into the site. It made equal sense.

> **We will keep the hidden safe of all.**

But the next line seemed clear enough:

**The son stays secret.**

"Huh," said Charlotte, quickly highlighting another bit of text and inserting it. Just then she heard Zee's voice say, in a manner that could best be described as bellowing, "Mr. Metos!"

Charlotte swore to herself. Where was he? If he was just coming down the stairs, she still had a chance to get out without him noticing, but—

"Zachary, what are you doing here?" Mr. Metos's voice rang down the hallway. He was definitely on their floor, and coming closer.

"Oh, I just wanted to talk to you for a bit," Zee hollered down the hallway. He sounded like he was hailing a cab from a block away.

*Nothing suspicious about that,* Charlotte thought.

She looked around the office. She could hide under the desk all day until Mr. Metos left. That always worked in the movies. Or—she could go out the way she came.

This was not the movies. Charlotte closed all the programs on the computer and put it to sleep, then hurried back over to the window.

Outside, Zee was parrying the best he could. When

Charlotte first met him, he never would have been able to do this—talk himself out of a bad situation. He would get all flustered whenever anyone required him to speak at all. Now, though, he was dissembling like a pro. Charlotte liked to think that spending time with her had been edifying, but she also knew that saving the world will do wonders for your self-esteem.

She pulled a chair over to the window and slowly, painfully hauled her body up, wincing at the pressure on her splinted hand. When she got up, she gave the chair a kick and it wheeled somewhere deskward. It would have to do.

"Why don't you step into my office, Zachary?" Mr. Metos was saying.

"Just a second," Zee said. "Let me check something."

Charlotte scampered out onto the window well and yanked the window shut, casting a glance at the office door behind her. It was opening. Just as the forms of Mr. Metos and a very nervous-looking Zee appeared in the doorway, she threw herself toward the fire escape ladder and crawled up.

That also hurt.

When Charlotte escaped the well, she collapsed against a first-floor window, her heart pounding with residual fear. Her wrist was still throbbing, and her ribs and back loudly protested the entire ordeal. Somewhere below, Zee was talking to Mr. Metos and wondering what in Hades had happened to his cousin.

"That," she whispered to herself, "was close."

"Charlotte?"

She whipped her head around. Mr. Crapf was staring out the window at her. She had somehow managed to land herself right outside of his classroom. She scooted away from the window, and the math teacher raised the window and poked his head out.

"Fancy meeting you here," he said drily.

Soon Charlotte was in the principal's office, weaving a tale of pain-related woe. And a few minutes later she was on the front steps, waiting for her mother to pick her up and take her home.

"Are you okay, sweetie?" Mrs. Mielswetzski asked when Charlotte climbed into the car. "Do you want to tell me what happened?"

"I just needed to get out and get some air."

Mrs. Mielswetzski clucked her tongue. Charlotte knew she was physically restraining herself from saying she knew it was too early to go back to school. "I think we should go back to the doctor."

"Oh, Mom," said Charlotte. "It's okay." She wanted to be thinking about the words on Mr. Metos's computer, but her brain hurt too much.

"Char," her mother insisted, her voice thick, "there's nothing okay about it. You just got . . . *battered*. And you're still hurting. You couldn't even make it through the school day."

"Mom, I just needed to rest for a minute, that's all." The fact was, her mother was right.

"And we don't even know why or how you were injured. I mean, why did you get so hurt when no one else did? It doesn't make any sense."

Charlotte bit her lip. This was the sort of thing she'd hoped her parents wouldn't think too hard about. "I don't know," she mumbled.

"The doctor said it looked like you'd fallen off a mountain. Twice."

"I don't remember."

"I know, I know," her mother said, her voice softening. "I just want to make sure you're safe, that's all." Closing her eyes, Charlotte sank into her seat. *Just be on the lookout.* She was many things, but safe was probably not one of them.

When she got home, Charlotte went up to her room to check that the world was still there. There had been a third tsunami, in the same place, the biggest of all, and it wiped out three towns. The Sicilian island was still being assailed by wind, and the sky above was positively littered with rainbows. Another island was plagued by constant lightning. The gods were never ones to be subtle.

Charlotte went to the blog that was cataloging the more clearly supernatural events, but when she typed in the address, the site did not load. She tried a couple more times, then did a search for it, to no avail. It was just gone.

That was enough for one afternoon. Groaning, Charlotte dragged herself over to the bed, where—her mind reeling with tsunamis and secret sons—she soon fell asleep.

She was awoken a couple of hours later by a firm knock. As Charlotte sat up in bed, blinking and confused, the door burst open to reveal a rather frazzled-looking Zee. "There you are! I thought I was going to have to explain to your mother that you'd been abducted by aliens!" he breathed.

"Sorry," Charlotte said, rubbing her eyes.

"*I'm sorry, Aunt Tara,*" Zee continued, "*I don't know where Charlotte is. I think she's fallen through some kind of space-time vortex. Too bad, that. What's for supper?*"

"Sorry," Charlotte repeated. "I went out the window. You did a good job of stall—"

"I had no idea what happened to you," Zee interrupted. "I thought you were hiding under the desk at first and were going to be there all afternoon until Mr. Metos left. I thought maybe I'd try to get him out of the office somehow, but he caught on pretty quickly and I looked like a total git. Then I saw you weren't there at all, and I figured you'd gone out the window, but when you didn't show up in history, well, I don't know. I thought maybe you'd uncovered some sort of spell in a book and you read it out loud and a mythical beast came out and ate you!"

Charlotte stared at him. Zee was gesticulating wildly, and his words had virtually tumbled out of his mouth. She couldn't believe it was true, but—

"Zee? Are you *mad* at me?"

Zee's arms dropped to his side. "No."

"You are! You're mad at me!"

"Well, really, Char," he said crossly, "you could have left me a note on the board or something. What was I supposed to think?"

"Clearly you were supposed to think that I had activated some Charlotte-eating monster by reading a spell out loud from a book!" Charlotte had felt bad all afternoon, but now that Zee was here and in such a twit, she couldn't help but think it was kind of funny.

"Well—"

"Don't worry, Zee, if there's one thing I've learned from years of reading, it's that you're never supposed to say a spell from an ancient book out loud. I went out the window, Mr. Crapf saw me and sent me to Mr. Principle, and he called Mom."

"Yeah," Zee said, his voice softening. "She thinks you're hurt. And traumatized. She's pretty worried about you."

"Yeah," said Charlotte, guilt washing over her again.

"So"—Zee plopped into Charlotte's desk chair—"what happened? What did you see?"

So Charlotte told him about the gibberish e-mails. "The son stays secret, it said." She leaned in, eyes wide. "Zee, I think Mr. Metos has a son!"

He frowned. "Hmmm . . . I don't know . . ."

"What else could it be? A *secret* son. Why do you think it's a secret? Does that mean he has a wife?"

They exchanged a doubtful look. That was hard to imagine.

"Maybe it's some sort of past affair that he can't talk about," Charlotte continued. "Maybe it's dangerous for some reason to have been with the boy's mother. Or"— she gasped—"maybe the boy is a threat to the mother, so they have to hide him from her!"

"Maybe . . ."

"It's like Zeus, you know?" Charlotte continued breathlessly. "The Lords of the Universe always get overthrown by their sons in Greek myths. Cronus heard a prophecy that his heir was going to overthrow him, so he swallowed his babies, until Zeus was born and Cronus's wife gave him a stone to swallow instead and hid baby Zeus away in a cave and he was raised by wolves."

Zee frowned. "I don't think it was wolves. I think that was Romulus and Remus."

"Well, whatever. The point is, he's got to be secret for a reason." Charlotte's eyes widened. "Or maybe he's secret from the gods! Maybe Mr. Metos is afraid they'll harm him if they knew, like use him to get to the Prometheans. Or maybe he's dangerous to them somehow!"

"Perhaps," Zee said with a shrug.

"Zee," Charlotte cried, "maybe he's a god!"

"Mr. Metos?"

"No! The son. Maybe Mr. Metos had a son with a goddess. That sort of thing happens all the time."

"I can't really see him doing that," Zee said drily. He had a point; Mr. Metos didn't like the gods very much. "Anyway, if he did have a son with a goddess, wouldn't the son be mortal?"

"I don't know. Sometimes the descendants of gods and mortals are gods. Mr. Metos has Titan blood. He's a descendant of Prometheus. If you mixed that with god blood, that could be really powerful." As the words came out of her mouth so confidently, Charlotte was aware that she had absolutely no idea what she was talking about, but it *sounded* plausible. "Anyway, if he has a son and wants to keep it secret, we know now, right? We could blackmail him. Make him take us to the Prometheans."

"I don't know . . ."

"Come on, Zee. Poseidon is missing. The other gods are rampaging. That's our fault. Somehow. If it weren't for us, those people would still have their towns."

"Char, I know! I'm just not sure there's enough evidence. . . ."

"What else could it be?" Charlotte asked. "We can feel him out, anyway. See how he reacts."

"You're going to school tomorrow?"

Charlotte sighed. "I guess. Don't worry, if things get bad, I can just get caught sneaking out again."

Just then her father knocked softly on the door. "Oh, Charlotte," he said, "I thought you were sleeping. Mr. Metos called for you."

"Really?" Charlotte asked, deliberately not looking at her cousin. "What did he say?"

"He wanted you to come see him tomorrow before school. At seven thirty. He said it was important. Mr. Metos was quite concerned about you."

Charlotte and Zee exchanged a look. "He was?"

"Yes. He must have heard you had to leave school today. He told me we should keep you at home tonight. He wanted to make sure you knew he said that. What a nice teacher!"

"Uh-huh," said Charlotte, her heart sinking. Something was wrong, something was coming. For a while it had seemed that they were in charge, that suddenly Charlotte and Zee were going to take matters into their own hands, that somehow the situation was controllable. But it wasn't. It never had been, and it never would be. No matter what they wanted, the fight, it seemed, would always come to them. Something was in store for them now. Charlotte could feel its presence breathing down her neck, and no matter what she did, eventually it was going to pounce.

The dream came to her quickly that night. Again she was trapped somewhere dark, dank, and cold, and again she knew instinctively she was in a cave. Her hands traced the familiar cold bars of the cage, searching for a door she would never find.

And then, again, light. Just the barest trace, but Charlotte's parched eyes drank it up voraciously. She still could not see much around her—the outline of her cage surrounded by some hulking darkness, while the light flickered teasingly somewhere in the distance.

"Hello?" Charlotte asked. "Is anyone there?"

Then the Shade, standing there, waiting, watching. It wanted her to do something, it needed her to do something, but she couldn't, she was trapped in this cage.

"I'm sorry," she whispered. "I'm sorry."

*Charlotte?* The voice came out of nowhere. *Over here!*

Something in Charlotte's mind told her she'd been here before, she'd heard this voice before, and she really wanted to know what it had to say.

*Charlotte, come here. I want to show you something.*

In a blink, her world was flooded with warm, low light, and she finally could see what was around her.

She was in a cage all right, a cage with close-set, thick iron bars that was suspended from the ceiling of the cave a few feet off the rocky ground. The cave she was in was about the size of her living room, with craggy walls that were marked with several-feet-high Greek letters that seemed to dance slightly in the stale air. And standing before her was a small, dark-haired girl whom Charlotte had certainly never seen before.

The girl was about six or seven, in a white dress with long, flowing white ribbons in her dark hair. The dress was odd-looking, old-fashioned, with a white sash and stiff triangular skirt, like the sort of thing your great-grandmother might buy you if she didn't know you very well or like you very much. Odder still were the girl's eyes—a deep, strange shade of green like nothing Charlotte had seen before—eyes that stared calmly at Charlotte. The Shade stood near, watching.

Something in Charlotte's conscious mind went off—no, she'd never seen her before, but there was something familiar about this girl, something she should remember.

*Who are you?* Charlotte whispered.

*That's not important,* said the girl. *I want to show you something. Come on out.*

*I can't,* Charlotte said.

And just like that, a door to Charlotte's cage opened, a door that certainly had not been there a second ago. The girl had not moved; she still stood gazing at Charlotte through the thick cage bars.

Charlotte looked from the girl to the open door. Suddenly she could not see any ground below her at all, just darkness. The Shade watched her.

*Come on.*

*Is it safe?* Charlotte asked.

*No,* said the girl. *Come out anyway.*

The next thing Charlotte knew she was stepping out of the cage into the blackness, waiting to reach the ground that she knew was just a few feet underneath her, but then she was falling into the darkness. She fell and fell and it seemed she would never stop.

She woke with a jolt, upsetting Mew, who had settled on her chest. It was still night, completely dark. The world was absolutely silent. Charlotte closed her eyes and tried to settle herself back to sleep, but sleep would not come. She could not shake the vividness of the dream, the terror of falling, the silent expectation in the watchful Dead. And then Mr. Metos's phone call came back to her. It must have been something serious for him to call them at home, for him to leave a message that sounded so very much like alarm. They were in danger again.

With a sigh, she pulled herself out of bed and went to the window to look at the street below. There was nothing, just darkness. It was uncommonly dark, actually. She looked up—the night sky was covered in a thick blanket of clouds that obscured the stars and the moon. There were no heavens that night, no stars watching over them. The Earth was on its own.

CHAPTER 6

A Rather Alarming
Development

CHARLOTTE WOKE UP THAT MORNING FILLED WITH
apprehension and dread. When she came down to
breakfast, she found her parents engaged in what could
only be described as a Talk. Even more suspiciously, the
Talk broke off quickly when she entered the room.

"What is it?" she asked.

"Nothing," said her mother.

"Ephesus is ruined," Mr. Mielswetzski said, seeming to change the subject. "It's an archeological site in
Turkey. I'd always wanted to go there."

"What happened?"

"They don't know. It's all shattered. Like an earthquake hit, but there was no earthquake last night."

"Oh," Charlotte said.

"How are you feeling, dear?" asked Mrs. Mielswetzski. "Are you sure you want to go to school today?"

Charlotte nodded.

Her parents exchanged another look. "I'll drive you guys," said Mr. Mielswetzski. "Let's get your cousin."

As Charlotte stared out of the car window on the way to school, images from the past year flicked through her mind. Here a Footman reaches for her on a quiet street, here another bears her toward the steaming River Styx, here Hades's Palace crumbles around her, she's attacked by the monstrous Scylla, nearly drowned several times, beaten to within an inch of her life, here she's standing on the deck of a lifeless cruise ship as Poseidon comes bearing down on her from one side, a giant sea monster from another. It was a lot to happen in the eighth grade. She'd escaped death so many times, but if people kept trying to kill her, eventually one of them was going to succeed.

Charlotte thought fleetingly of her recurring dream. When she was in the Underworld, she saw the lake that dreams come from. Philonecron had used it (or bribed someone to use it, since he was exiled) to send Zee dreams to try to lure him down to the Underworld, but Charlotte had had strangely prophetic dreams as well, dreams that seemed to warn her about Philonecron's shadow-stealing servants. It didn't seem that Philonecron himself would have sent those, but the cousins were never able to figure out who had.

Whether these new dreams had been sent or were just figments of her (admittedly active, but can you blame her?) imagination, Charlotte didn't know. And whatever it was the girl in the dream wanted to show her, she still hadn't seen it—unless, of course, it was merely the feeling of plunging toward certain death, which Charlotte already knew all about, thank you very much.

There was something else about the dream, something that nagged at her. The girl seemed so familiar somehow, even though Charlotte knew she'd never seen her before. There was something in her memory about a cave, a girl, a dream, but she couldn't place it. It might have simply been that she'd dreamed about it before and the memory lingered in her subconscious, or maybe it was something she'd seen in a movie; it might have been nothing. But it might be something. Charlotte resolved to mention it to Zee later.

When they got to school, Mr. Mielswetzski stopped the car and said, "Zachary, go ahead. I want to talk to your cousin."

Zee got out of the car and glanced at Charlotte through the window of the front seat. He nodded toward the front doors and mouthed something to her, then walked up the stairs toward school.

Charlotte looked up at her father, who was regarding her gravely.

"So," he said, "what happened in school yesterday?"

Huh? Oh, that. "Oh, I was just . . . I don't know. I just had to get outside and rest. All those people, and I wanted some air. . . ."

Her father nodded slowly. "Is that all?"

"What?"

"Was there any other reason you were outside?"

Charlotte stared. Did her father not believe her? "What do you mean?"

"I mean," he said with a sigh, "that your mother and I worry about you."

Oh. Yeah. She knew. Apparently her days of respite from being thought of as irresponsible were over. "I'm very good at taking care of myself," she said stiffly.

"I know that. You don't need us anymore. But . . . that's part of the problem."

Charlotte looked at her father questioningly. That was not where she expected this conversation to go.

"Charlotte, you're just—" He frowned. "Some people in the world are destined to have quiet lives. Your mother and I are like that. We're happy, and more than that, we're *content*. And then there are people who are marked for . . . for trouble, for risk, for excitement. And you, my dear Lottie, are one of those people."

Charlotte looked at her feet. He didn't know the half of it.

"Look at the cruise ship," he continued. "Hundreds of people onboard, all without a scratch on them. Except you. You look like you've been put through a meat grinder." He shook his head. "Your mother and I know that there's going to be a lot in your life we're not a part of. And"—he looked at her pointedly—"that there already has been."

Charlotte's ears burned.

"And as much as we want you to tell us everything, we know that's not always going to happen. So we're just going to have to take it on faith that no matter what you face, you're going to come out all right. Fortunately, we have a lot of faith in you. So as you're out leading your unquiet life, think of your parents, who are worrying about you and who love you and who know that, whatever challenges you face, they have nothing on you."

Charlotte felt a lump rise in her throat. Her father knew. Oh, he didn't *know* know, but he sensed something. It was true: She had been marked for trouble—

mostly by accident, but nonetheless, marked she was. And as worried as they might be now, her mom and dad would probably go crazy if they knew the truth. Charlotte had been so busy trying to keep things from them, as if they were her adversaries, that she'd forgotten she needed to protect them too.

"Thanks, Dad," she said quietly. What had she been thinking? What were they going to do, run off with Mr. Metos and leave a note? *Went to Greece, off fighting gods, see you when I see you?* How was she going to do what she needed to do and keep her parents from losing their minds? And who was going to protect them when she did?

"All right," said her father. "You'd better go meet Mr. Metos." He reached over and rubbed her hair. Charlotte smiled weakly and started to get out of the car.

"Lottie?" Mr. Mielswetzski added as she was about the close the door. "I'm proud of you."

Focusing on a spot in front of her, Charlotte went up to the school. She found Zee waiting for her in the front lobby, and the cousins headed wordlessly to Mr. Metos's office. Maybe, Charlotte thought fleetingly, it was nothing, maybe Mr. Metos had just decided to tell them more about Poseidon. Or maybe he'd just baked some brownies and wanted to give them some. . . .

But when Zee knocked on Mr. Metos's door, there

was no answer. The cousins looked at each other and knocked again. Nothing.

"Maybe we're early," Charlotte said.

"Hmmm," said Zee, shifting.

Trying to ignore the metaphorical hot breath on her neck, Charlotte leaned against the gray wall, while Zee paced up and down the long, quiet hallway. Every once in a while he would wander over to the stairs to see if anyone was coming, but no one ever was. 7:30 became 7:35 became 7:40, and by 7:45 Charlotte was officially worried.

"I'm officially worried," she said.

"Perhaps he just got held up," said Zee, sounding unconvinced.

"Perhaps he got eaten."

"Don't say that," grumbled Zee. He knocked one more time, then placed his hand on the knob. A puzzled expression crossed his face, and he turned the door-knob, and the door opened.

It was unlocked.

Charlotte closed her eyes, afraid of what she might see.

But to her immense relief, there was nothing horrible in the office, and no sign of anything horrible either. On first glance it looked just as it had, though there were some strange things. His office chair was pushed back from the desk, as if someone had sprung up from it quickly, and his phone hadn't been placed back in its carriage well. Charlotte wondered if that was from the call to her house, or if there'd been another call later, one that had caused him to jump up in his chair and burst out of his office.

"Looks like he left in a hurry," Charlotte mumbled.

"Looks like."

It was better, at least, than the alternatives. At least Mr. Metos hadn't been taken; he had gone somewhere, urgently, maybe something to do with them—or maybe there was something even more important. (Like something to do with his maybe-son?)

Charlotte sighed. "What do we do?"

Zee shook his head. "I don't know. Maybe he'll come back."

After every period, one of them ran downstairs to check for Mr. Metos, but he was never there, and Charlotte spent her classes staring out the window, wondering what was going to befall them now.

It was a strange day. It had been sunny and beautiful since they'd gotten back, and it was no different when they'd gotten to school in the morning. But as the day went on, the sky darkened—as if too eagerly anticipating sundown. Thick, black-looking clouds rolled in and hung ominously in the air. Something was not right.

Then, when Charlotte was sitting in history, paying no attention at all to the origins of the Cold War, there was a moment when the whole building seemed suddenly enveloped in shadow. A very cold feeling passed through Charlotte. She turned her head to look out the window, and that was when the street in front of the school exploded in flame.

Somebody screamed. Fire alarms began to wail in the school hallways, and the whole building seemed to shift. The students—who had practiced lining up in an orderly fashion once every month since they'd been dropped off wide-eyed at kindergarten nine years earlier—stampeded to the door and into the hallway, Ms. Bristol-Lee shouting commands at them as they fled.

In a flash, Zee was next to Charlotte and the two stared out the window at the flaming ground, then up into the sky. There was nothing, nothing at all, and then a shadow passed over the school again.

There was a loud roaring noise, so loud it shook the foundation of the school, and Ms. Bristol-Lee screamed, "Charlotte, Zachary, come on!"

The next thing Charlotte knew, Zee was pulling on her arm, and the cousins were running through the hallways, following the chaos of a school's worth of students pushing toward the exits. Another roar shook the school, and smoke poured under the door from the gymnasium behind them. A crash echoed from some-where.

Smoke billowed down the hallways, pursuing them as they fled. In the distance was the crackling of fire and the echoing yells of their schoolmates. Into the stairwell leading to the basement fire doors they went, down one flight, then another, as shell-shocked teachers manned posts on the landings, trying to manage the chaos. Then they could go no farther. At the bottom of the stairwell, in front of the basement double doors, was a bottleneck of students trying to push their way outside to safety. Zee tugged Charlotte back into the smoke-filled hall-way, into the open door of one of the classrooms.

"Out the window," he yelled, and Charlotte, her body screaming in protest, climbed up onto the ledge and hit the lock, then tried to open the window.

"It won't go!" she shouted back.

Zee swore loudly and ran toward the door, just as another impossibly loud animal roar burst through the air, shaking Charlotte's bones. There was the sound of shattering glass, a blast of skin-singeing hot air, and sud-denly flame erupted in a room across the hall. The door hung limp on one hinge.

Fire lapped out into the hallway, toward them, and, swearing again, Zee slammed their door closed while Charlotte hit at the stuck window.

A coughing Zee joined her efforts and as smoke filled the room, some deeply buried school fire safety video replayed in Charlotte's head and she grabbed a jacket from the nearest desk and rolled it under the door to slow the smoke.

Then a loud grunt emanated from Zee. Charlotte whirled around and he was picking up one of the desks and hurling it at the window. The window shattered and in a flash Zee was at her side, urging her toward it. Charlotte climbed up on the ledge and stumbled through, cutting her hands on shards of glass. As her legs landed on the ground, pain shot up through her body, reverberating through her chest and back, but she didn't have time for that. She whirled around toward the window just as her cousin came bursting out, landing next to her with a thump.

"You all right?" Zee yelled.

Charlotte nodded and shook her head at the same time. Zee helped her up, and they hurried up the hill that lay behind the school.

"What's happening?"

"I think there's something up there," said Charlotte, pointing to the dark clouds overhead.

The sky seemed perfectly still. All the activity was coming from the school below. For a moment Charlotte thought she was wrong, the fire came from inside the building, there was nothing up there—and then, within the clouds, she saw movement.

In the parking lot off to the side of the school, the Hartnett students milled around noisily. The teachers came running out of the building, leading the last stragglers with them, as fire trucks squealed to a stop just in front of the school.

From their perch on the hill, Charlotte and Zee stared up at the sky, trying to discern what lurked there. There was another unworldly sound, and, with their necks craning upward, they began to back away hurriedly. A shape punctured the cloud above. Dark, impossibly large, dragon-like, it flickered in the air and then disappeared behind the clouds again.

The cousins gasped, and chills racked Charlotte's body.

"What is it?" she breathed.

Below them, the students and teachers of Hartnett Middle stood in awe, watching their school burn. Charlotte looked from them back to the sky and to her cousin.

"We have to go," she said, her voice cracking a little as she gestured toward the people below. Whatever that was, it wanted them. While there had been times that siccing a fire-breathing creature on her school might have sounded appealing to Charlotte, it was one of those concepts that was much better in theory.

Zee nodded and pointed to the fields above the steep hill behind them. "There," he said. "Can you run?"

No. "Sure." Charlotte nodded lamely.

Zee grabbed her, and the cousins turned on their heels and ran toward the fields that lay beyond the school, hoping the creature followed them, hoping the creature did not follow them. As the sirens and shouts of the students echoed behind her, Charlotte could not bring herself to stop and look up. And if she stopped, she didn't think she could go anymore.

Zee was pulling her along the best he could, but Charlotte's ribs couldn't seem to hold her lungs anymore, her back felt as if it would snap in two, and her eyes were beginning to see black.

There was something following them, something large and heavy, something that made the air around it recoil. And then Charlotte's legs gave out and, dropping Zee's hand, she collapsed on the ground.

A great creature exploded through the clouds, a creature with tremendous leathery wings and a long, serpentine tail that even the sky seemed to cower from. It was no dragon—its body was thick and mammalian, and its head was that of a gigantic lion, and on its torso was a snarling goat head. A Chimera.

Charlotte screamed. The beast dove toward them with the agility of a sparrow. Zee dove for her, ready to grab her, ready to carry her on his shoulders if he had to, but suddenly the Chimera had landed on the ground next to them. The goat head, with its enormous circular black horns, focused its bloodred eyes on Zee while the lion head bared its teeth at Charlotte. Then, with one mighty flick, its great tail swept over and thrust Zee aside.

"Zee!" Charlotte yelled, but before she could go after him, the Chimera had sprung toward her. She thought then that she was done for—after everything that had happened she was going to die in the field above the school; but the creature did not attack her. It leaped over her, and as it did it reached a scaly, slimy, car-size, dragon-clawed hand down and enfolded her in it, retracting its claws as nimbly as Mew. With a mighty flap of its wings, the Chimera sprung up into the air and carried her off.

# PART TWO

---

## Fire

## CHAPTER 7

# WILD KINGDOM

THE PREVIOUS EVENING, SLEEP HAD NOT COME EASILY
to Zachary "Zee" Miller. Something seemed to linger
in the darkness in the Mielswetzski family guest room,
something large and threatening, something that was
either the specter of his future or a giant Zee-eating
lion. Zee was rather hoping it was the lion.

Like Charlotte, Zee wanted nothing more than to
devote himself to working against the gods. But that
didn't mean that he wasn't a little apprehensive about
the proposition. And he would have preferred, for once,
to be the one in control of the fight, but it seemed

once again that the fight was coming to them. The giant black bear of destiny had lumbered into his room, climbed on the bed, and crawled directly on top of Zee's chest, where it curled its enormous body up and fell into a deep, lengthy slumber.

And when he did find himself drifting off despite the metaphorical zoo around him, his sleep was not exactly restful. Not satisfied with the vagueness of the threat before them, his mind tried assiduously to divine its nature by enacting some of the possibilities. In the theater of his brain, Zee saw any number of mortal threats to himself and his cousin played out, from well-aimed bolts of lightning to vindictive Minotaurs to armies of rabid snaggletoothed Munchkins. Not that there was anything particularly Greek about snaggletoothed Munchkins, but Zee couldn't be held responsible for the whims of his subconscious.

There was one dream, though, that was not like the others. It began with Zee in total darkness, darkness so complete he felt it seeping into his mind. He knew nothing, he was nothing. Then suddenly there was light, just a flickering, but he was conscious suddenly of the force of his breath, the tightness of his skin, the persistence of his own heartbeat. The light grew brighter, and Zee looked around and knew.

He had been here before. He knew this place.

He was in a long tunnel in a cave, and up ahead in the distance burned a fire. And pretty soon he would hear—

*Hey, Zee, come over here!*

—the voice. He knew the voice. He was not surprised, then, to behold in front of him a girl. She was young, about six or seven, in a white dress and white ribbons that gleamed in the flickering firelight. She was pointing toward the light, and Zee dutifully took a step toward it, then suddenly found himself in a small room inside the cave, at the center of which burned a tiny fire. Out of the corner of his eye, Zee saw shapes on the cave walls, like primitive cave drawings. It took a moment for him to realize they were moving. Then the girl appeared in front of him, a line of Dead standing behind her.

*Do you know where you are?*

*No*, Zee said.

*That's too bad*, she said.

And then he woke up.

Zee's eyes popped open, the last image of the dream still lingering in his mind. The last time he'd seen the girl, it had been just before Charlotte had left on the cruise. She had shown him this cave, and then he had suddenly seen a flash of Charlotte in danger on the sea. (Now that he thought about it, it might have been nice of the girl to warn him about Philonecron, too, while she was at it. . . . Not that Zee was ungrateful or anything.)

But there was no warning this time, nothing but the cave, the fire, and those strange drawings on the wall. Zee closed his eyes and tried to bring them forth in his mind—he had a feeling they weren't done by cavemen.

Still, as much as he struggled to clarify the pictures, he could remember no more detail. Zee sighed, and the great big bear groaned, turned around twice, and settled back in for a nice, long nap.

That morning, like every morning since their return from Poseidon's yacht, when Zee saw Charlotte he had a strong urge to order her back to bed.

It was Zee's fault that she'd been hurt. He'd been so preoccupied with getting revenge on Philonecron that he hadn't stopped to think that she might be in danger. And when he'd had the dream of her on the seas, he was so busy thinking of his own problems that it didn't occur to him to warn her until it was too late.

It didn't seem fair that Charlotte had to suffer when the whole thing was Zee's battle. And, as much as he wanted to throw himself into the fight against the gods, he couldn't stand the idea of risking further harm to Charlotte. Part of him wanted to lock her up somewhere and go off himself—but at the same time he knew he couldn't do it without her. Plus, if he did, she'd destroy him emotionally with a stunning tapestry of insults, and then break his kneecaps.

Still, that morning in the car on the way to school, as Zee's eyes fell on the sickly yellow bruise peeking out from underneath Charlotte's sleeve, he thought again about the white-dressed girl in the dream and the warning he had not heeded, and he vowed never to let anything bad happen to his cousin again.

That vow lasted through lunch. When the Chimera burst through the dark clouds and dove toward them, Zee knew—he just knew—that it wasn't coming for him. He lunged for the beast, with no idea what he would do when he reached it—and the next thing he knew something slammed into him with the force of a city bus.

Everything went black. Zee slowly became conscious of the smell of grass around him, and he fancied himself lying in the soccer field at his old school after a long practice, waiting for the rain to come cool him off, existing, for one moment, in a world of perfect peace.

Except rain clouds don't roar. The Chimera's voice rattled the ground, shaking Zee back to the terrible reality. He sat up, his head and back throbbing, just in time to see the creature envelop Charlotte and take off.

Time stopped. Everything went perfectly quiet, the giant wings of the beast moving through the air in slow motion, like some monstrous ballet. Somewhere Zee was conscious that his hands were scurrying around on the ground, that he was springing to his feet, that his arm was hurling a stone at the Chimera.

The rock bounced harmlessly off its stomach and fell to the ground. With the goat head eyeing him haughtily, the Chimera looked down, opened its mouth, and issued a torrent of hot air, and the spot where the rock had fallen burst into flames.

And then, with a mighty beat of its wings, the creature pushed itself higher in the sky and flew off into the horizon, leaving Zee standing alone in the field. His head exploded in a sound that might have been his own yelling.

The rain came then, steady and forceful, slowly quenching the fire that burned a few paces away. Zee stood, water beating down on his face, his mind refusing to reunite with his body, until a burst of thunder in the distance shook him back to himself. Sucking in air, he looked frantically at the clouds above, then turned on his heel and ran back toward the school.

Zee would have liked very much to have known exactly how to proceed, to have a vast store of knowledge as to the habits of Chimera and Chimera-like creatures, to have an arsenal of weapons custom-designed for such monsters and their associates—in short, to have any idea at all what in the world to do now. But, despite his rather vast recent experience with mythological monsters great and small, he did not. He needed Mr. Metos.

It occurred to Zee that the Promethean's absence from the school on that particular day was no accident—someone, somehow, had removed him so he could not protect the cousins from the creature. At least Zee now knew what he'd been trying to warn them about.

So focused was he on his thoughts that he did not notice the person standing at the edge of the field until he nearly ran into her.

"Zee!" Maddy exclaimed, her voice cracking.

Zee stopped abruptly. "Maddy!"

Maddy stared at him, eyes agape, rain streaming down her face. "Everyone's looking for you," she said, her voice high and tight. "They lined up by homeroom and you weren't there. You're missing."

"Oh, we—"

"Jack told me he thought he saw you guys go up here, and so I ran over, but I didn't believe it was really true. I thought you were—" She pointed in the direction of the school. Smoke billowed in the air up ahead, mixing with the thick clouds.

"I know," he said, trying to catch his breath. "The door was blocked and we went out the window—"

Maddy looked around, seeming still dazed with fear. "Where's Charlotte?"

"Uh . . . she's fine. Look, Maddy, have you seen Mr. Metos?"

Maddy started. "What? Why?"

"Oh, I just, uh, have to ask him something."

"The school's burned down, everyone thinks you're dead, and you want to ask Mr. Metos something?"

"Um, yeah, well . . . Perhaps we should . . ." He stared at Maddy, with her eyes round and full of fear and sorrow and pain. With rain pouring down on him, smoke from the school thick in the air, and the trail from the Chimera lingering behind him, his mind sharpened.

"Maddy," he said. "Look, I treated you horribly." He looked her in the eyes. "I was not myself—I was . . . barmy—and I'm really, really, really sorry. You're the only girl here I can talk to, and I hope you can forgive me."

Silence, while the air thickened and the Chimera flew farther away, and then Maddy's eyes softened. "Maybe," she said, a small smile on her face. They stood a moment in the rain, and then her eyes widened. "Oh!" she exclaimed. "We should probably tell everyone you're alive."

Zee and Maddy raced back toward the school, Zee's mind full of his cousin. She was all right; she had to be. If the Chimera had wanted to kill her, it would have in the field. Whatever its mission—and Zee did not think a Chimera had come to Hartnett Middle School by random chance—it wanted his cousin alive.

Right?

Under normal circumstances, the scene at the school would have seemed quite dramatic, but it was a bit hard to focus on when your cousin has been carried off by a lion-headed dragon, and Zee moved around as if in a fog. The firefighters, aided by the rain, were on their way to quelling the blaze, and all that remained of Hartnett Middle School was a burned-out skeleton. The students were gone, evacuated by buses to the upper school campus. Only the principal remained, watching his ship go down with all the dignity he could muster. But when he saw Maddy and Zee, he burst into a run toward them.

"Zachary! They said you weren't in there." He gestured to the firefighters. "But I'm sure glad to see you. Is Charlotte with you?"

"Yeah," Maddy said, turning to Zee. "Where is she?"

"Um, she went home," said Zee.

The principal sighed. "I suppose I should be very angry at you, but I'm just happy to see you. And Madeline—you should be with your classmates." He shook his head and gave them both a stern look. "I'll let everyone know you're safe."

A few minutes later one of the firefighters came over and gave both of them a lecture—the firefighters had searched the building for them— and despite everything else, Zee felt his ears burn. Brilliant—more people that he'd put in danger.

"Everyone is being picked up at the upper school," said Mr. Principle. "Your uncle will be expecting you, Zachary, and your mother, Madeline. I've called in to say you'll be right there. Now"—he looked around thoughtfully—"to get you there . . ."

"I'll take them," said a voice behind Zee.

Zee whirled around, letting out a great exhale. Mr. Metos was sweaty and looked as frazzled as Zee had ever seen him—and that was saying a lot for someone who had gotten his liver chewed by a Harpy.

"Zachary, where is your cousin?" Mr. Metos asked steadily.

"Um—"

"She went home," Maddy said.

"She did?" Mr. Metos gazed at Zee over Maddy's head.

"Yes," said Zee. *No,* he shook his head.

"I see," said Mr. Metos. "Well, we should reunite you."

"That would be nice," Zee said.

"Why did she go home, anyway?" asked Maddy.

Zee could only shrug, and Maddy did not press. The three of them walked in hurried silence to Mr. Metos's car, Zee trying desperately to catch the teacher's eye. He had to close his mouth to keep the story of what had happened from spilling out—though it seemed that Mr. Metos, in his Mr. Metos way, had some idea of what had passed. But did he have a plan?

That question was partially answered when they got to Mr. Metos's small car. The hatchback was open and a long, thin steel pole was sticking out. When they opened the doors, they found that the pole traveled from the trunk all the way to the front seat, where its pointed edge threatened to burst through the front windshield.

"Oh," Mr. Metos said as Maddy started to climb into the backseat, "be careful."

The front seat was filled with books, so Zee climbed into the car on the other side. Maddy was frowning at the object that separated them.

"Mr. Metos?" she asked slowly. "Why is there a spear in your car?"

CHAPTER 8

# And Now Presenting Zeus on High, Father of Gods and Men, and Lots of Other Stuff Too

When you think of Zeus—Lord of the Sky, the Cloud-Gatherer, Master of the Thunderbolt, God of Gods, Supreme Ruler of All That Is and Was and Ever Shall Be, and Even What Might Be Too—you probably have a hard time pinpointing the one quality that makes him the most greatest ruler in the entire Universe. There are, after all, so many—his strength, his good looks, his leadership qualities, his vast knowledge and experience, his highly advanced sense of humor, his skill with the ladies—but if you were to really think about it, the thing that truly sets him apart is his absolutely spectacularly fantastic judgment.

Yes, that is why he was chosen above all to be Lord of All, and that is why the Universe is thriving to this day. If you looked back on the history of the Universe since he took over, you would see one thread shining through it all—all of Zeus's awesome decisions, keeping the whole place from spiraling into chaos. Sure, Zeus listens to everyone—he's Supreme Almighty Lord of the Whole Universe, not a *tyrant*—but the decisions are his to make. That's his job. He's the Decider.

He hadn't asked for this job—it's simply what you get for being so wise and just that the whole Universe looks to you to rule it. When he led his older brothers and sisters in the War on Cronus, he thought that they would all rule together, but all his siblings begged him, "Oh, Zeus, you are so awesome, so magnificent, we need you, the *Universe* needs you, lead us, guide us!" It was the curse of greatness.

So, while the other Immortals were out frolicking and gallivanting and whatever else gods who don't have to make the tough decisions do, Zeus was busy ruling the Universe and being Lord of Justice and stuff, and it's not easy, you know. It's hard work. Finding the most perfectest, most justest solution for every problem is a huge deal.

Still, Zeus managed to do it every time.

Like Ixion. Ixion was a mortal king whom Zeus invited to dine at Olympus. Pretty great of Zeus, right? And how did Ixion show his gratitude? By casting his dirty, coveting mortal eyes upon Zeus's bride, Hera. So, after careful reflection on what was the very best way to handle this situation, Zeus decided to blast him with a thunderbolt, then bind him to a wheel of fire that would spin for all of eternity. There. Justice!

Or the whole Persephone thing. Persephone was the daughter of his sister Demeter, and Hades saw her frolicking in a field one day and was like, "Oooh, pretty!" and asked Zeus if he could have her, and Zeus—never one to stand in the way of young love— said, "Sure! Help yourself!" So Hades burst through the earth and kidnapped her (Zeus preferred to be a little subtler when courting the ladies, but he wasn't going to judge) and dragged her down to the Underworld to make her his queen. Well, wouldn't you know it, but when Demeter found out she got in a major snit and blamed Zeus—which was totally out of line because he wasn't the one who burst through the earth and kidnapped her, now, was he?—and she started sulking. And normally Zeus would say, "Fine, sulk all you want," because he certainly wasn't going to interfere with a mother's grieving process, but Demeter was the goddess of the harvest, and so nothing grew on Earth and then all the people and animals and stuff began to die. And, you know, if you're Lord of the Universe and a few species go extinct, well, *c'est la vie*—but if the whole place slowly starves to death under your watch, people are going to talk.

So Zeus—reluctantly—stepped in. He told his brother he'd have to return Persephone to her mother but promised he'd keep his eyes out for another pretty young lass Hades could kidnap. (Keeping eyes out for young lasses was, after all, one of Zeus's core competencies.) And then things got really crazy, because Hades tricked Persephone into eating some pomegranate seeds, and once you eat the food of the Dead you're bound to the world of the Dead, so suddenly Zeus was faced with what you might call a problem. A command challenge. But fortunately, he was Zeus, Lord of Justice, wise above all, and he came up with the perfect solution: The girl would spend six months of the year with her mother and six months in the Underworld, during which time Demeter could sulk all she wanted. She couldn't, after all, starve every man and beast on Earth in six months. (Probably.) It was a brilliant solution. Win/win!

And there was Prometheus. Prometheus was a Titan who had the foresight to side with Zeus in the War on

Cronus, and to reward him Zeus let him make his very own species. And Prometheus made these, like, little god-shaped creatures, which was a little weird, but, hey, whatever floats your boat.

So Prometheus made humans, and then felt bad for them just because they were starving and freezing and getting eaten by wild boars and stuff. And so, instead of doing the sensible thing, which was writing off the whole lot and starting again, he had the genius idea of giving them the gods' sacred fire. And when Zeus says "genius" he means moronic. Because the gods' sacred fire, as you might be able to discern, belongs to the gods.

Anyway, the whole thing went something like this:

> PROMETHEUS: Hey, Zeus, you know
> how the humans are starving and
> freezing and getting eaten by wild
> boars and stuff?
> ZEUS: Yeah?
> PROMETHEUS: Can I give them fire?
> ZEUS: Oh, yeah, that's a genius idea.
> PROMETHEUS: Oh, thanks, I really
> thought so—
> ZEUS: I was being sarcastic.
> PROMETHEUS: Oh, okay.

Except it wasn't okay. Because Prometheus had the brilliant idea (again: sarcastic) of stealing the fire from Olympus and giving it to humans, and suddenly the humans changed. They had been brainless two-legged beasts before, but the fire gave them knowledge of the gods, and they transformed into the sentient, needy pains in the thunderbolt they are today.

So suddenly you had all these hairless mini-yous running around making sacrifices to you and building temples and asking for your blessings and mercy, and let's just say that changes the whole god dynamic. Which was the whole reason he didn't want the humans to have the fire in the first place—it wasn't just that he didn't *care* what happened to them, it was that there were going to be *consequences*. (Okay, it was mostly that he didn't care, but still.)

So the mortals needed to be punished for Prometheus's actions. Zeus did want to be careful, however. He could, naturally, wreak enough destruction to destroy the entire planet, but he didn't want to destroy the Earth, just, you know, people. That is the thing with power—it's important that you have wisdom to go along with it, otherwise you might do something rash.

So he sent a flood to wipe out the whole population.

It was a terrible bother, of course, and he was exhausted for days afterward, but the situation demanded decisive action. Leadership. And that would have been the end of the whole thing had Prometheus not foreseen the flood and warned his son, who built a nice little houseboat for himself and his wife, and so they survived and had a whole mess of kids and there went Zeus's plan to destroy the human race.

But, as Zeus soon learned, there are advantages to humanity, particularly the female aspect of it, which is soft and pretty.

Oh, people told him to stay away. Zeus's mother warned him that someday his womanizing would cause his downfall, but you know how moms are. Sure, there were some problems here and there, mostly because his wife Hera just didn't get the concept of an "open relationship."

Like with Io. Zeus stole her up to Olympus to spend some quality time snuggling by the fire. Then he heard Hera outside the door, so he—thinking quickly, as always—turned Io into a cow. So Hera walked in and Zeus was like, "Here, Pookums, I got you this cow!" And Hera was all, "Wow, Cuddlebug, thanks for the cow, I love it! Hey, you know what I think I'll do? Set this awesome cow loose to roam the Earth and send a fly after it to sting its butt and torment it for all eternity!"

So, that's what happened. Poor Io. Zeus couldn't save her, because that would have been admitting to

Hera that she wasn't *really* a cow, you know? It pained him to see the girl suffer, and so Zeus had to find himself another mortal girl to comfort him. That was the story of things: He'd see a nice girl, Hera would find out and get all jealous, and find some way to torment or destroy her, and Zeus would have to go find somebody else. It was a big bother, of course, but hardly led to his downfall. Well, there was the one time Hera got really mad and got together with Poseidon and the pair of them stole his thunderbolt and tried to overthrow him, but Zeus just hung her by her heel from the sky for a few days, and she didn't try that again.

Sure, Zeus knew that you had to be careful with your offspring. After all, he'd overthrown his father, who'd overthrown his father in turn. But he was on top of things. Like with his first wife, Metis, there was a prophecy that if she bore a son he would overthrow Zeus. So Zeus ate her. Problem solved.

He didn't really worry about being overthrown anymore—he was so Universally beloved that all the Immortals would come to his aid, and so mighty and feared that no one would try in the first place. Anyone who came up with such a creative, brilliant solution to the Mortal Question had certainly proven why he was Lord of the Universe. Letting humans think Immortals were all some kind of myth was the perfect solution—

there were still mortals for the gods who wanted them for entertainment value or whatever, but no one had to be *responsible*. Do you know what it's like to have people praying to you all the time? Every moment of every day, there's no peace at all. Sometimes you just wanted some alone time, you know? And to tell the truth, by the end there, he'd found that mortal women were a little loath to come to Olympus for snuggles because they were worried about what Hera might do, and it just made it hard to get a date.

So it was hands-off from then on. (Though he didn't mean "hands off" exactly literally; Zeus was under a lot of pressure, and if he needed to let off some steam by going speed dating and picking up a nice school librarian or something, that was his right. He was Lord of the Universe, after all.)

It was working out brilliantly, really—the Immortals were happy, Zeus was happy, and his judgment had, once again, proved impeccable. Life was going along just fine, and Zeus didn't even have to think about mortals—except the soft, pretty ones.

And then everything changed.

It began one day a few months ago as he sat in his throne room doing his daily cogitating and snacking on some baklava, when his cupbearer came in. Ganymede was a mortal boy Zeus had kidnapped when he needed a new servant, and the boy did such a very nice job that Zeus made him Immortal so he could have the privilege of waiting on Zeus for all eternity. A few years ago, after taking a date to the Ice Follies in Cleveland, Zeus had the brilliant idea of having Hephaestus make Ganymede an outfit that looked like a cup, so now the boy wore a black leotard and tights and a giant china teacup around his middle. There were some terrible accidents at first, so after a while Zeus decided to stop putting hot tea in the cup. That was another great decision.

"My Lord," Ganymede said, giving a little half bow. "I come bearing news."

That was one of the reasons he liked Ganymede so much. He had such a nice way of putting things—*I come bearing news*. It's great when your servant says something like that, and it's even better when he's wearing a giant teacup.

Zeus bowed his head in a way that said he welcomed his news but was far too regal to actually say so. He'd gotten very good at things like this over the years.

"My Lord, a half-breed tried to overthrow Hades."

"Really," said Zeus. "Did it work?" Now, that would be funny. Next time he saw his brother, he was going to be sure to laugh at him.

"No. It almost did. The demon stole the shadows

of mortal children and turned them into an army. He destroyed the Palace, but"—the boy took a deep breath—"two children stopped him. Mortals."

Now, that was both funny and unfunny. Funny, because two mortal kittens did what his brother could not. Unfunny, because those two mortal kittens defied a god.

Naturally, it didn't take long for Hera to come sauntering in, smiling that annoying smile of hers. "My love," she said, all too casually, "did you hear about the mortal children in Hades?"

Zeus sighed. "Yes." He knew what was coming next.

"Are you going to destroy humanity now?"

He could not stop himself from rolling his eyes. There'd been a pro-Extinction faction among the gods ever since Prometheus's heirs survived the first flood. They were always sniping at him in the background, always criticizing, because that's just what some people like to do.

It wasn't exactly a coincidence that Hera was the one leading the destroy-humanity crowd. Zeus saw right through her. She just wanted to keep him from speed dating.

"No, honey," said Zeus, drawing himself upward. "I made my decision."

"I see," Hera said. "And, in your infinite wisdom, have you *decided* what we're going to have for dinner?"

He relaxed. You see, this is the way the other gods talked to him. With respect. For he did have infinite wisdom, and they all recognized it.

As for the mortal children, they were a problem and certainly demanded some justice, but he soon learned that the foiled half demon was a grandson of his nut-job brother, Poseidon, and he would surely take care of it. Sometimes you had to delegate. That's another thing a good leader does.

So anyway, all was quiet for a few months. Then, as he was sitting in his throne room one day, doing his daily cogitating and snacking on some deep-fried Fig Newtons, Ganymede came in with some more news. His nut-job brother had tried to get revenge, yes—by transporting a cruise ship of five hundred people half-way around the globe, hypnotizing them with a Siren, and setting a Ketos after them. Which was pretty much against the whole "do whatever you want, just don't let them notice you" principle. But somehow the children managed to abscond with his trident, destroy his yacht, and send Poseidon plummeting to the bottom of the Mediterranean Sea. Not only that, but—

Ganymede cleared his throat. "Poseidon is missing."

Zeus didn't blame him. If he'd let two thirteen-year-olds steal his great object of power and humiliate him in front of his party guests, he'd go into hiding too.

So of course it didn't take long before Hera came sauntering into the throne room, all "Did-you-hear," and he said of course he heard, he was Lord of the Universe after all, and she was all, "They handled the trident. That alone—" and he eventually had to get a little firm with her and yelled, in his most booming voice, "Quit nagging!"

Frankly, it was bewildering. Zeus had decided to deal with the Mortal Question by withdrawing from humanity. End of story. He had made his decision; why would he change his mind? That would be like admitting he'd made a mistake, and of course Zeus never made mistakes. He could not understand why they would even question it—the decision was naturally the best of all possible ones, because he had made it. Duh.

Well, soon after that, there was cogitating and peanut butter olives, and then there was Ganymede and something about a hole in the Mediterranean Sea and gods running around willy-nilly making storms and letting out monsters that were terrorizing mortals. Still, it wasn't like the whole world was falling apart—just a few bad apples, nothing more. Everything would be fine when Poseidon showed his big blue face again. It was his realm, after all.

And then something very unexpected happened.
Zeus was not even cogitating, but rather taking a nap
because things were getting pretty exhausting, when
Ganymede came in, hiding something behind his teacup.

"Um, my Lord?" he said, looking rather unsure about
something. "They've found Poseidon."

Ah, well. "Really? Where?"

"Well . . . here." He held up a large plastic bag filled
with water. Inside was a long, round, spiny creature that
looked like nothing more than a big fat spiny cucumber.

Oh, it was Poseidon, all right. Even as an echi-
noderm, his arrogance was unmistakable. Something
about the blue of the creature matched all too well his
brother's skin—easy to tell, since Poseidon liked to
show so much of it. Zeus was surprised it didn't have
chest hair.

"Well, bother," said Zeus. He was about to laugh—
for really it was very, very funny—when he noticed
Ganymede staring up at him.

"Can you change him, my Lord?"

"Hmmm," said Zeus. "Well, let's see. . . ." And so he
took out his thunderbolt and waved it around a bit—if
you did it just right, little sparks came out and it looked
extra tough—but nothing happened. Of course nothing
happened. He didn't have the right artifact.

"Did they find his trident?" Zeus asked casually.

Ganymede shook his head.

Well, that was that, then. So, Zeus got a large aquarium, placed it in the corner of his throne room, and put his brother inside. He decorated it with a little treasure chest, some driftwood, and a small plastic Poseidon statue, which he thought was rather a nice touch.

So there Poseidon lived, and would live until someone found the trident and they could change him back. Zeus had never thought much of sea creatures, given that his brother had made them all, but he did have to hand it to Poseidon on the sea cucumber. Now, there was a creature. It just hung around at the bottom of the aquarium and ate algae and didn't talk—which made it a real improvement on the actual Poseidon.

But as the days wore on and the trident never appeared, Zeus was faced with what you might call a dilemma. He had on his hands a whole bushel of bad apples now. Earth on the whole was beginning to go haywire, and it was beginning to reflect poorly on him. His whole perfect, wonderful plan was falling apart. But it wasn't his fault, it was the children's; that was clear. If they'd never interfered in the first place, Poseidon wouldn't have tried to get revenge. Then he never would have been turned into a sea cucumber, and the sea realm wouldn't have become an Immortal free-for-all.

Yes, he had made his decision, but circumstances change and a good leader changes with them. The children had caused all of this, and maybe humanity needed be to punished for it. Zeus hated to give Hera the satisfaction of doing what she wanted, but if those children did one more thing it would be time to make another decision. It would be a terrible bother, of course, and his world would be a little more empty without humans, but sometimes you have to suffer for justice.

They had one more chance.

CHAPTER 9

# Smoke and Mirrors

O h," said Mr. Metos. "The spear belongs to a friend who works for a museum."

"Oh," said Maddy. She glanced at Zee, as if trying to exchange an *Isn't this weird?* look with him, and he tried to pretend that seeing a giant, ancient-looking spear in the former English teacher's car didn't make perfect sense to him. He could barely take his eyes off it. Mr. Metos had a plan, all right—a plan and a weapon.

"Madeline," said Mr. Metos, eyeing the two of them in the backseat, "how are you feeling? It's been quite a day."

Zee blinked. Concern for people's emotional states was not really Mr. Metos's strong point.

"Oh, well, I'm okay," said Maddy. "It was a little scary, especially when we thought—" She glanced at Zee and shook her head.

"I can only imagine," said Mr. Metos, his voice smooth and easy. "We'll get you home as soon as we can." He paused. "I have some water bottles under the seat there. Would you like one?"

"Oh, yeah, that's nice," Maddy said offhandedly. She reached down and pulled out a bottle of water. "Zee?"

"Sure," Zee said, realizing suddenly how thirsty he was. He took the bottle from Maddy and opened the cap.

"Zachary," said Mr. Metos, his voice steady but firm. "Before you have a drink . . ."

"Hmmm?" asked Zee, the bottle poised just below his mouth. Next to him Maddy took a long drag from her water and gave Zee a shy smile. Zee looked from her to the bottle in front of him to Mr. Metos, who was looking at Maddy.

"Maddy!" Zee blurted.

"Uhhhh," said Maddy. She turned to Zee, her eyes full of fog, and then collapsed against the seat.

"What happened?" Zee exclaimed.

"I knocked her out," said Mr. Metos.

"You did *what?*"

"She'll be fine in a couple of hours."

"Mr. Metos!"

"It's harmless. Zachary, we need to talk about the Chimera. Do you want your friend to hear?"

"No, but—Couldn't we have, you know, *dropped her off* somewhere?"

"There's no time to waste, Zachary. I assume the creature has your cousin?"

"Yes, but—"

"I'm not going to have any more children exposed to this world, all right?" Mr. Metos interrupted, his voice sharp. "I have enough trouble keeping the two of you safe!"

*Yeah, fat lot of good you've done there,* Zee thought, slumping back against his seat. Next to him, Maddy slid farther down.

"Zachary, by just *knowing* about the gods, you are a threat to them, do you understand? A Chimera has just come to your middle school and snatched your cousin. Do you think that sort of thing happens by accident? Do you think all across America, Chimera are swooping down to earth, abducting schoolchildren?"

Zee bit his lip and glanced over to Maddy again.

"I knew something was coming," said Mr. Metos,

as if to himself. "I was supposed to protect you, and then—" He shook his head grimly.

So Mr. Metos thought it was all his fault. Each of them had been blaming himself, but none of it mattered, because once again it was Charlotte who was suffering.

"Do you think Charlotte's . . . all right?" Zee asked quietly, taking his eyes from the unconscious Maddy.

Mr. Metos frowned. "I hope so. I must say that it's very odd that the Chimera took her away. I need you to tell me everything that happened."

"Strange," he said, when Zee had finished. "It's all so strange. Chimera are dumb, violent creatures. When they are unleashed on a town, usually everything and everyone is destroyed. I don't understand." He shook his head. "What direction did it go off in? Do you remember?"

Zee pointed back behind the school.

"Hmmm . . . That's the direction of its nest. . . . A compatriot warned me that there was a Chimera nesting in the area, and this morning I was told it was on the move. I went to track the nest, and by the time I found it, well . . ."

Right. Zee turned and stared out the window. Rain beat down insistently on the small car, and the black clouds lingered in the air as if they were contemplating staying forever.

"The spear," Zee asked, with a glance at the weapon next to him, "is it magic?"

"It is"—Mr. Metos paused—"special. This spear is forged from parts of the spear of Bellerophon, a hero who slayed a Chimera. There are four of them in the world, and the Prometheans have three."

"Will it work?"

"It's better than nothing. It would help to have a winged horse, but you don't happen to have one of those on you, do you?"

Mr. Metos had turned off the road that led to the upper school and was driving past the shiny skyscrapers of downtown. For a moment Zee imagined the Chimera perched menacingly on top of the tallest building, surveying the city below.

And then they were driving along the river, past the new developments that had sprung up in the last five years, past the old apartment buildings and seedy shops, past the point where anyone bothered to travel at all.

"It's here?" Zee asked quietly, as he surveyed the abandoned riverside warehouses around him.

"At least it was," said Mr. Metos. And with that, he pulled off into a small alleyway, then stopped the car behind a large, crumbling brick warehouse that looked as if it might as well have a sign that said MONSTERS WELCOME . . . GHOSTS, TOO!

"Now, Zachary," Mr. Metos said, "I need you to wait here."

"What? No!"

"You don't think I'm going to let you come in, do you? That beast might be in there."

Something began to buzz in Zee's ears, and he got a very strong urge to punch Mr. Metos in the nose. It was not in Zee's nature to trifle with authority, but authority was not generally so incredibly maddening. A flood of protests readied to burst out of his mouth—and some not very nice words as well—but all that came out was a sort of strangled exhalation that sounded like the protestations of an exasperated goose.

"I can trust you to wait here, then," Mr. Metos stated as he got out of the car and pulled the spear from the back. Zee reached for the door, ready to escape.

"I'm sorry, Zachary," said Mr. Metos, turning the key in the lock. Zee frowned at him—did Mr. Metos think he was an idiot?—and then pulled up on the door lock.

It wouldn't go. He squeezed himself into the front seat and pulled the lock there, but it still wouldn't go. Zee let out a *yargh*, then, bracing himself, kicked the window.

Nothing happened. He groaned, and then climbed into the backseat, then into the trunk of the hatchback.

He did not count on Mr. Metos to be carrying around some sort of tool kit or anything practical like that—no room with all the spears. But the spare tire well had the standard-issue spare tire and what Zee needed most in the world—a tire iron.

*BAM!* One hit, and the glass of the back window dissolved into jillions of fragments. With one last glance at passed-out Maddy, Zee burst from the car.

The rain poured down on him as if in warning, and instantly Zee's T-shirt and jeans adhered themselves to his skin. Water ran along the ground under his feet, and within a few paces, his shoes were squelching with every step.

The warehouse in front of him was three stories high and about a quarter of a city block long. Large glass windows lined the walls, most of them broken. In front of Zee was a rickety iron fire escape ladder that led up to windows on the second and third floor.

Zee crept along the side of the building, cringing with every squishy footfall. There was no sign of Mr. Metos anywhere. He half expected the walls in front of him to burst into flame at any moment, but so far all was quiet. As he moved along, he passed several large windows with thick bars covering them. He peeked into one and saw nothing but darkness. As he crept by the next one, his mind registered a flash of movement inside.

He turned the corner and found himself in front of a large sliding door that must have been the warehouse's truck entrance. The door had formerly been locked with a padlock, but the padlock was in pieces at Zee's feet, and the door itself looked as if a truck had driven right through it.

Sliding over to the door, Zee peeked into the building. He could see nothing but darkness. He squinted his eyes and peered into the blackness, and that's when he realized it had no depth at all. Something very large was perched right in front of the door.

He drew back, stifling a gasp. From beneath the rain, a smell of rotting meat assailed his nose. Well, at least he knew where the beast was. He took a step backward, and his left shoe announced his presence to the wide-open sky.

Zee froze. His heart threatened to burst out of his body. For several long moments he stood there, as still as a statue, as still as prey. Finally, carefully, as if moving through glue, he bent down and took off his shoes and socks.

Studying the building, he tried to think of what to do next. Soon something would happen, soon Mr. Metos would strike, soon the Chimera would burst forth from its perch. He needed to get in before it moved away— preferably, given the beast's preferred method of attack, behind it. And then . . . well, he did not know. With any luck, he would be able to find Charlotte and get out of there without attracting any attention. Then Mr. Metos could deal with the Chimera on his own, since that was the way he seemed to want it.

Next to the service door was a long pipe that traveled up the brick wall to the roof, and next to that on the second story was a window with a big broken patch. Zee eyed the wall. The brick was crumbled and uneven—uneven enough, perhaps, to climb up, assuming his hands didn't slip off the wet pipe or the brick didn't crumble under his feet and send him plummeting to the ground. *No better way to find out,* he thought, then grabbed the pipe and started to climb the wall.

This year at Hartnett they'd done a rock climbing unit in gym, bringing in these walls that had little ledges scattered all over the place. Unsuspecting students were tied to a rather absurd-looking harness and told to scale the walls. He had thought that it was an utterly ridiculous way to spend your time—strapped to a pulley, pressed against a sweaty-smelling wall, moving slowly from one little blue knob to another until you reached—oh, joy— the gym ceiling. Zee preferred, generally, to stay close to the ground. And now, as he slowly moved from footfall to footfall, pressed against the wet, crumbling wall, using the slippery pipe to support himself while rain continued to pour down on his head, he found he had grown no fonder of the experience.

It took what seemed to be hours—days—but Zee finally made it up to the second story. Willing himself not to look down, he moved his foot to a spot a few feet below the broken window, grabbed the ledge, and pulled himself up.

He hunched on the sill, peering into the warehouse. Slowly his eyes began to negotiate the darkness, and he saw thick floorboards below the window, so carefully, maneuvering around the broken glass, he climbed through the window and into the building.

He was greeted by the smell of mildew, mold, rotting meat, and burnt fur—so strong that it threatened to push him backward. Something scurried beneath his feet. Gathering himself, Zee looked around.

He could not see much—just the floor a few feet in front of him and some lurking shapes that looked like crates. He strained to listen, but could hear nothing except the rain against the building and the *plunk, plunk* of drops falling through the ceiling. The Chimera was there—he could smell it, but whatever it was doing, it wasn't moving. With a deep breath, Zee took a gentle step forward, willing the floorboards not to creak.

The darkness lifted somewhat, and now he could see

he was in some kind of loft. Slowly he crept toward the rail at the edge and looked down.

He was above a vast warehouse room, largely empty except for some piles of crates and large, heavy chains hanging down from the ceiling. The Chimera, he knew, was right below him, but he could not see it. Nor could he see any sign of Mr. Metos or his cousin. Below and to the left was a series of tall doors that led, Zee realized, to the rooms with the barred windows. The one closest to Zee had a large crate in front of it. He studied the room carefully, and then he noticed a shape lurking behind one of the piles of crates. He stared at it and realized there was a distinctly human form crouching there: Mr. Metos.

Then, from below him, there was a great movement—he felt it as much as he heard it. The Chimera was shifting, stretching, moving. Zee inhaled sharply, and he could see the Mr. Metos-shape flinch and draw upward.

There was no time. Charlotte was surely on the lower level, and he had to get down there without attracting attention, and quickly. Off to the side of the loft, a foot or so in front of the rail, was a large chain that hung down from a pulley on the ceiling, and without taking the time to decide whether or not it was a good idea, Zee climbed up the rail and lunged for the chain.

His plan had been to shimmy down and drop quietly just out of the beast's line of vision. It was a good plan—or it would have been if the big iron pulley was not attached to a rotted old beam and if it was not just waiting for some large weight to be added to the chain so it could all come tumbling down. Which is exactly what happened—Zee made it about halfway down when there was a creak, then a snap, and then a clanging and a screeching, accompanied by Zee falling, chain, pulley, and all, to the ground.

It was only a few feet, but it seemed to Zee as if it took several hours for him to fall—enough time to contemplate not only what a terrific mistake he had just made and where this mistake fit on his all-time top ten list (pretty high), but what might await him as soon as he landed on the concrete floor, and exactly how much it would hurt if the pulley fell on him, and how much better it might be if it did. He also had time to take in the scene in front of him—Mr. Metos creeping toward the Chimera, spear poised—and to think that that was the sort of situation where one really prefers absolute quiet.

*BAM!* Zee landed on the concrete floor, pain pounding up his back. The chain clanged down next to him, followed quickly by the large iron pulley, which made the loudest noise in the history of the universe as it hit the concrete.

A roar shook the building, and the Chimera—which was sitting half a length of the building away—whipped its heads toward Zee, just as Mr. Metos, with a mighty grunt, hurled the spear at its chest. It landed just off center, and the Chimera screamed and reared back, crashing through the loft above it.

Zee narrowly avoided getting hit by one of the creature's wings as it writhed. He rolled out of the way as it indiscriminately shot white-hot breath into the air, catching a group of crates, which burst into flame.

"Zachary," Mr. Metos shouted. "Get out of here!"

The Chimera lunged toward the sound of Mr. Metos's voice, and Zee picked up a brick and hurled it at its goat head. Roaring, it turned around, whipping its tail at Mr. Metos and knocking him to the ground.

Zee was face-to-face with the beast now, as flames began to spread in the vast room. The lion head snarled at him, revealing a jet-black mouth and gleaming sharp teeth. Behind it, the goat head still writhed.

Ignoring the pain in his back, Zee took off at a run toward the back of the vast room, away from the flickering flames. Out of the corner of his eye he could see Mr. Metos lunging for the spear still stuck in the Chimera's chest. Zee stopped and picked up another brick and hurled it at the Chimera, hitting it right between the eyes.

The Chimera let out a low growl, swiveling its heads back and forth from Zee to Mr. Metos. And then something very strange happened. The beast narrowed all four of its eyes, let out a small puff of blazing breath, and then drew itself up to its full height, unfurled its wings majestically, and, knocking the spear out of its chest, took off, bursting through the top of the warehouse and off into the clouds.

Zee and Mr. Metos stared, panting, at the large hole in the roof, waiting for the creature to come crashing back down.

But it didn't.

"I don't understand," said Mr. Metos to himself.

Fire flickered along the south wall of the warehouse, and smoke began to tickle Zee's lungs. "Did you find Charlotte?" he shouted.

Mr. Metos shook his head. "You try those rooms, I'll try the crates," he called back. Zee half registered that he was clutching at his chest and working hard to breathe.

Zee ran over to the tall doors along the north wall of the building, pounding on each one and yelling his cousin's name. Then he remembered the flash of movement he'd seen and raced toward the room with the crate blocking the doorway.

"Char," he yelled through the wall.

"Zee!" his cousin yelled back.

Relief crashed into Zee with such force it almost knocked him over. "Are you all right?"

"Get me out of here!" she yelled.

Coughing from the roiling smoke, Zee called over to Mr. Metos, then braced himself against the tall crate and pushed with all of his might. Nothing. When Mr. Metos got there, he joined Zee, but they could not get it to move.

"Hold on," said Mr. Metos, and went over to the iron spear. With a grunt, he hoisted it up and brought it over. "Might you . . . ?" he asked Zee, motioning to the crate. His face was racked with pain, and it looked as if it was all he could do to hold the spear.

Zee took the spear, grunting a little under its weight, and wiggled it in between the wall and the crate. Using all his strength, he pulled back on it, using it as a lever, and finally the crate began to move.

"At least that spear was good for something," Mr. Metos grumbled, as an opening appeared between the crate and the wall. Within moments, Charlotte had slipped out and was staring at her cousin, wide-eyed, panting, and disheveled.

"Let's get out of here," Mr. Metos said, looking back through the smoke at the flames that had now engulfed the entire south wall.

When they were outside, Zee studied his cousin, who looked as if she'd been picked up in the claws of a dragon-like beast and flown several miles. Her voice was hoarse and her fists were raw, probably from pounding on the walls of her prison.

"Are you all right?" Zee repeated through a fit of coughing.

"No!" Charlotte yelled, sounding rather furious. "I'm covered in slime!"

A grin spread across Zee's face, and he felt tears prick his eyes. "Yeah," he said, eyeing the sticky substance that had attached itself to her clothes in roughly the shape of a dragon claw. "You are."

Mr. Metos, still clutching his side, motioned to them both. "Let's get in the car, children. Zachary, that was extremely—"

Zee whirled around. "Would you *stop* it?" he spat.

Mr. Metos blinked. "Pardon me?"

"Mr. Metos, we are not children. We are thirteen years old. In the past year we've gone to the Underworld and back, we've dealt with Hades and a whole army made of enchanted shadows, we've fought Philonecron and Poseidon and a gigantic carnivorous sea monster. And all the while you've been telling us how much we need to be protected."

Something was buzzing in Zee's head. The sound

grew louder and louder as the words poured out of his mouth, until he could barely hear what he was saying anymore.

"You speak of these great dangers to us, but you won't tell us what's going on, so the next thing I know I'm watching Charlotte be carried off by fluffy-the-Dragon Kitty while you're skipping around trying to find its nest!" Next to him, Charlotte sucked in air. "So there will be no more locking us in cars, and there will be no more *drugging people*. We're involved, like it or not—this is our fight just as much as it is yours. You complain about the gods not taking responsibility, but you won't let us take any. And you can't just manipulate people and lock them in places because they're in your way—it's arrogant . . . and . . . pigheaded and . . . cruel. And," he finished, "it isn't nice!"

There was a moment's silence then, while Charlotte watched him in awe, and the buzzing in Zee's ears died down. Mr. Metos blinked at him several times, then looked down at the ground and cleared his throat.

"Come on, ch—Charlotte, Zachary. Let's go."

In silence, the three of them climbed back into Mr. Metos's hatchback and collapsed against the seats, Charlotte in the front barely registering the body of her friend in back. They drove wordlessly back along the river and through downtown, Charlotte and Zee each staring out their windows, contemplating what had passed.

Everyone was so lost in their own thoughts that no one noticed Maddy when she stirred, until her foggy voice broke through the silence.

"What's going on?" she asked sleepily.

CHAPTER 10

# Maps and Legends

By THE TIME MR. METOS'S SMALL HATCHBACK HAD
arrived at the upper school campus, all the other students had been picked up and taken to the safety of
their homes, where they would be treated extremely
well by their parents, who had always operated under
the assumption that if you dropped your children off at
a school in the morning, that school was likely to still be
intact when you picked them up in the afternoon.

At the middle school campus, officials searched and
searched for the cause of the fire, but could not come up
with the answer. One said that it looked very much as if

the fire had come from outside the school, but that, of course, was impossible, and he was ignored.

As for the school building, it was, frankly, toast. There would be no more classes at Hartnett Middle School for some time, and when the media pressed the principal on where, exactly, he planned to educate his students, he could only stare at the hollowed-out shell of his former dominion and request that they ask him a little later.

It had taken some doing for the passengers in Mr. Metos's car to explain to Maddy exactly where they were (why, on their way to the upper school!), why Charlotte had suddenly appeared in the car (they'd worried about her walking home and had gone to find her), and why everyone looked as if they'd been attacked by a horde of flaming monkeys (Fire! Fire at the middle school! You remember . . . )—not to mention where she'd been the whole time (fallen asleep, must have been so tired . . . ), but she seemed satisfied. She was too glad to see Charlotte alive to ask too many questions.

When they pulled into the upper school parking lot, they found Mr. Mielswetzski and Maddy's mother standing there, looking rather frantic. Mr. Metos explained that they had gone to find Charlotte, and Mr. Mielswetzski looked as if he couldn't decide whether to be grateful or to punch Mr. Metos in the face. Zee understood the feeling.

As Charlotte's father shepherded them into his car, Zee could see Mr. Metos standing in the parking lot, watching them go. If you did not know him, you might describe his expression as entirely blank, but there was a small tightening of his eyebrows, a twitching of his mouth, a flickering in his eye, and it made Zee all the more nervous.

As exhausted as he was, Zee felt every muscle on alert, and he kept looking out the window to see what was coming for his cousin now. This is how it had always been, he thought grimly—Charlotte and Zee passive, waiting, reacting, leaving the great front door of their lives wide open and waiting to see what might waltz in. Zee was tired of it. He was tired of them being manipulated, used, followed, bruised, battered, kidnapped. If something was coming for them, this time he wanted to be there to meet it.

When they finally got home, after a thorough debriefing with Mrs. Mielswetzski, Charlotte and Zee headed upstairs.

"I need a shower," Charlotte grumbled as they got to the second floor.

"All right," said Zee. He supposed no monsters could get her in the shower, but you never knew.

While his cousin washed the Chimera-claw slime off herself, Zee paced around the room and Mew made agitated circles around the bed.

"You would have fought off the Chimera, wouldn't you?" Zee whispered to the cat, who gave him a look like she would very much like to try.

He felt like he had been stomped on by a troll. His body ached from his encounter with the Chimera tail and the fall, and his lungs still felt as if they were filled with hair balls. He smelled, too—of smoke and fire and mildew and some other things he'd prefer not to think too carefully about.

Finally Charlotte appeared in his room, looking much less slimy. She sat on the floor very gingerly, as if she were settling down on a bed of nails, and Zee winced in sympathy.

"Are you sure you're all right?" he asked.

"Sure," she huffed.

She did not seem all right. Her jaw was set so firmly it looked as if it might lock that way, and her eyes were narrow and looked like lasers might shoot out of them at any minute. Which, really, might come in handy next time they were attacked. The whole thing had the effect of almost covering up all the pain he knew she was in. Almost.

"I can tell."

"That thing," she said, her voice quite loud suddenly, "that thing *took* me. It dumped me in a room and shut me in. And I tried and tried to find a way out. I pounded on the door and tried to break the windows, and . . ." Charlotte's voice broke, and she shook her head. Zee's heart burned. He could not imagine how scared she must have been, locked in that room, not knowing what was coming next, not being able to do anything. He felt another surge of anger.

"Did you kill it?" she asked.

"Um, no," Zee said, wincing inwardly. "It got away."

"Oh," said Charlotte. "Did you at least hurt it?"

Zee's fists balled up. "Yeah," he said. "Mr. Metos put a spear in its chest." Suddenly he slammed his hand down on the bed. "We should just go. Go to Greece, try to find the Prometheans on our own."

Charlotte's eyes widened. "Are you serious?"

"Who cares about Mr. Metos? What do we need to know about the Chimera—it came after you, that's enough. Anyway, what if this is happening all over? Chimera carrying people off, people who don't have anyone to save them? Char, the monsters are on the loose. Isn't that our fault?"

"Yeah, but—"

"What are we supposed to do? Hang out here while you get nicked by flying mutant lions?"

"No, but—Greece is a big country. How are we supposed to get there, anyway? Walk?"

"We'll ask Sir Laurence. He'll give us money." Sir Laurence was the English gentleman turned giant squid who'd helped Charlotte escape Poseidon. With the aid of Poseidon's trident, she'd turned him back into an English gentleman. His family fortune had grown quite substantially in the century he spent as a cephalopod, and he'd helped pay to smuggle Zee back to the States after Charlotte had rescued him from Philonecron.

"And then how are we supposed to find them?" Charlotte asked. "Just walk around Greece asking everyone if they know the secret lair of the descendants of Prometheus?"

"We'll find them!" Zee could hear his voice getting loud and tight. "Or we'll go to Olympus. We'll find something to use on Zeus. We can't just sit here!"

"But that doesn't mean we should go running off stupidly, either," Charlotte retorted, sounding suddenly very dangerous.

"Running off stupidly is what you do, Char! That's, like, your whole reason for living!"

Narrowing her eyes, Charlotte stood up. "I think I'll go to my room now," she said coldly. And with a toss of her wet hair, she hobbled out the door, while Mew gave him a look that clearly said, *You, sir, are a stupid git.* Groaning, Zee punched his pillow.

It was a chilly Charlotte that Zee met when he came down for dinner that night. He did not understand why she'd resisted his idea—she was the one who had been taken, she was as angry as he'd ever seen her as a result, and she was the one who always wanted to go running off half-cocked anyway.

The Mielswetzskis, too, were grave and shaken as they ate their plates of spaghetti and turkey meatballs.

"I still don't understand where you were," said Mrs. Mielswetzski. "Why on earth didn't you go with everyone else?"

"Oh," said Charlotte. "Well, we had to go out a window, and—"

"You *what?*"

"It was the only thing we could do," Charlotte mumbled.

"Didn't you evacuate with everyone else? Why didn't you join everyone in the parking lot? Do you know what your father thought when you didn't get off the bus?"

Charlotte looked down. "I know," she said. "I'm sorry. We just . . . couldn't."

"I don't understand you two," she said. "Why can't

you just be more careful?" Her mother looked at the table, her eyes filling with tears.

Charlotte flushed, and Zee eyed her. Where she usually seemed defiant when her parents talked like this, now she just looked cowed.

"I'm sorry, Mom," Charlotte repeated, stabbing at a stray piece of spaghetti.

Dinner proceeded silently from there, interrupted only by Mr. Mielswetzski's attempts to force more turkey meatballs on everyone, and after it was over, Zee began to trudge up to his room to beat on his pillow some more.

"Wait, Zee." Mrs. Mielswetzski stopped him. "I forgot. You got a package today." She handed Zee a small tube wrapped in brown paper. "Must be from England. Different mailing system they have there, huh?"

Zee studied the parcel. No, the postal system worked the same in England as it did in the States, but whoever put together this mailing didn't seem to know that. Everything was just slightly off: The stamps (which certainly were not British stamps) were on the wrong side, and the address was written in one long line and seemed to have been scripted by someone who had a rather creative understanding of how to form letters. He tried to catch Charlotte's eye as she went upstairs, but she didn't seem very interested in looking at him.

Zee headed upstairs, and with a fast-beating heart began to unwrap the brown paper. Inside was a small cylinder made of dark wood with a wooden cap on it. He unscrewed the cap and found inside a small silver object and a rolled-up piece of delicate-looking paper with a wax seal.

For some reason, Zee found himself looking around, as if invisible spies might be peering over his shoulder. Sometimes that's just how getting wax-sealed scrolls in the mail makes you feel. But his room was empty save for Mew, so he examined the objects before him.

The first was a silver flattened cylinder with a cap on it. Zee took off the cap and discovered that it was a lighter, which was not exactly what he was expecting. Frowning, he depressed the button, but nothing happened. He tried a few more times, then put the lighter aside and turned his attention to the scroll. Carefully he broke the seal and unrolled the paper.

Before him was a drawing of some kind—there were some mountains, a body of water, a town—

No, no, not a drawing, but a map.

Zee sucked in air and studied the paper before him. It was a map, all right, but what it was a map *of* he couldn't tell. There was no indication of the location it depicted—making it, if you asked Zee, rather a failure of a map in the first place.

There was something specific about the mountains, though. Zee studied that part of the map carefully and noticed there was some kind of structure on one of the hills—he saw some sets of pillars, some rock formations, and a long, zigzaggy staircase.

Zee rolled up the map again, tiptoed out into the hallway and, after looking carefully for oncoming Mielswetzskis, went over to his cousin's room and knocked on the door.

"Hi," Zee said.

"Hi," said Charlotte.

"Listen, uh, I'm sorry. I don't like you getting carted off, you know?"

"I don't really like it either," said Charlotte defiantly.

Zee bit his lip. This sort of thing wasn't really his strong point. He didn't even, truthfully, feel that sorry—sure, he shouldn't have snapped at her, but his feet still itched as if they wanted to break into a run and not stop till he found the Prometheans. (Though that might require a rather long bridge.) He decided to get to the point.

"Um, I got this." Zee handed her the map. "It just came in the mail. No idea who sent it."

Her face softening, Charlotte reached for the scroll and unrolled it. "It's a map," she said in a puzzled voice.

"I gathered that," said Zee.

"But what of?"

He shrugged.

"Not a very good map, then," mumbled Charlotte.

"Nope. It came in this." Zee handed her the brown paper and watched as she studied the strange writing. "It could be a trap." Mysterious maps do not just arrive in the mail—nothing in their lives was that easy, and when it was, there was usually someone trying to kill them on the other end.

"You mean"—Charlotte looked up, smiling a little— "just because we get a mysterious map in the mail from someone who doesn't know how to address an envelope doesn't mean we should go waltzing off to find out where it leads?"

Zee grinned. "Something like that. And there's this, too." He handed her the lighter. "It doesn't work." He got up to pace around the room, while Charlotte fiddled with the lighter.

"Oh, well, that clears everything up. I suppose it's too much to ask people to tell us what's going on?"

"Come on, Char," said Zee, staring out the window. "What would be the fun in that?"

"Speaking of, Mr. Metos e-mailed me. We're supposed to come over tomorrow, whenever we can get out."

"Or we could just go talk to him now," Zee said, motioning out the window. Mr. Metos's small hatchback was parked across the street. In the darkness, he could see the form of his teacher, alert and waiting, watching over them from the shadows.

The next morning, after Mr. Mielswetzski left for school and Mrs. Mielswetzski went off to a meeting, the cousins left the house to find Mr. Metos waiting for them in his car down the block. He looked ragged and exhausted, and Zee realized he had been there all night. They drove off in silence.

They had been to Mr. Metos's last apartment a few months before, after Philonecron's servants had tried to nick Charlotte on the street and he'd gotten there just in time. He'd explained everything to them then—that Greek myths were real, that someone named Philonecron was trying to overthrow Hades with an army made of children's shadows, and that he was collecting these shadows by following Charlotte and Zee around. And Zee hoped that now, in this new apartment, he might explain everything again. Zee was ready to make him explain.

Charlotte, meanwhile, wanted to look around the apartment to try to find some sign of Mr. Metos's possible secret son. Beyond a closet full of boy-size clothes or a bunch of photos on his refrigerator—which would sort of negate the secret part—Zee was not sure what exactly that would be. He was, in truth, a little skeptical about Charlotte's theory, but he wasn't about to tell her that.

When they arrived, they found that Mr. Metos's new apartment looked quite a bit like his old one—and was decorated similarly, with a shabby sofa, boxes of books, and nothing else. Zee idly wondered where he kept the spears.

Soon the two cousins were sitting on the sofa, just as they had months before, and Mr. Metos was standing before them, his face a mask of seriousness. "I must admit, I am . . . puzzled. Chimera do not generally behave that way. They sow destruction everywhere, yet no one was hurt in this attack. And they do not place people in rooms in abandoned warehouses and trap them inside. Usually when they abduct someone, it is—forgive me, Charlotte—for the sake of their own dinners."

"Great," said Charlotte.

"I suppose it's possible the Chimera was, well . . . saving Charlotte for later."

Next to Zee, Charlotte grumbled something under her breath.

"Do you think it was . . . random?" Zee asked. "I mean, with everything that's going on . . ."

Mr. Metos shook his head. "If we were in Italy or Turkey, maybe. But the activities in the Mediterranean have not spread this far. Yet. And even if they had, the Chimera taking one of you two, of all people, is too much of a coincidence. It was coming for you. We can assume that. But it makes no sense. They are not errand runners. And unlike your friend the Ketos, who is controlled by Poseidon, a Chimera does not have any masters. At least until now."

Charlotte and Zee leaned in, as Mr. Metos seemed to be considering something.

"I have not been very forthcoming with you, and once again I put you in more danger. As I said, your adventures have not gone unnoticed. It is typical of the gods that Philonecron would try to overthrow Hades and all anyone cares about is the mortals who stopped him. I have long feared that Olympus would try to punish you. Now you publicly humiliated Poseidon—and were the last to see him before his disappearance. This is not the sort of thing they will take lightly."

Charlotte and Zee did not speak. There was really nothing to say.

"It is safe to assume that Olympus sent the Chimera to attack you, though I am still puzzled by its behavior. In a way, though . . . in a way it is a relief."

"What?" the cousins said simultaneously.

"The gods do not discriminate among mortals. We were afraid that Olympus would punish random people for your sins, or indeed . . . all of us. We had some intelligence . . ."

Charlotte and Zee looked at each other heavily. They kept trying to save people but seemed to put them in more danger as a result.

"They may still," Mr. Metos continued. "But we have a plan."

Zee's heart sped up. "What?"

"I am sworn to secrecy. I will just say we have a . . . weapon. Something that will give us leverage over Zeus. The Prometheans have guarded the secret of this weapon for generations. Keeping the knowledge of it secret and safe until it was . . . ready . . . has been our mission since Prometheus himself, and has been mine all my life. . . ." He paused and gazed at the cousins. "Though now I find I have a new one."

"What's that?" Charlotte asked.

"Keeping the two of you alive."

"Oh," said Zee.

"And apparently I cannot do that by myself, and I cannot do that while you two lead your daily lives in the open. I have made every attempt to shield you from danger, and with every attempt the danger seems only to grow. There's only one option that I can see."

Charlotte and Zee looked at each other. "What?" Charlotte asked, her voice shaking a little.

"You are coming with me. We are going to the Prometheans."

CHAPTER II

# Frenemies

AFTER HIS VISIT TO THE ORACLE, PHILONECRON made his way back to his darkened island and settled himself into a nice, dank cave. The trip had not gone according to plan. The plan had been for Philonecron to announce himself, at which time the Oracle would gasp and prostrate herself in front of him, trembling at his greatness and power, and plead for his eventual mercy when he took his rightful seat on the throne of the Universe.

In fact, that is precisely how everyone should greet Philonecron, and if he were going to be perfectly honest—and he firmly believed that honesty was essential for personal happiness—he was a little puzzled that no one did. Even—he must admit—a little hurt.

But that was not the real issue. *Your enemy is your friend,* the Oracle had said. He could not fathom it. She was not his friend, not his friend at all. Friends don't thwart each other's plans. Friends don't crush each other's dreams. Friends don't send each other shooting several hundred feet through the night air and plunge them into the cold sea.

You know what friends do? Friends help each other. Like the trident. The trident was his friend, his *special* friend; it was *there* for him. Of course it was *physically* there, since Philonecron never let it out of his sight, but it was there for him *emotionally*, too. And if he needed to turn a prying wood nymph into a cockroach so he could pluck off her legs, it was there for him then, too. Do you know how long he had been waiting for a friend like that?

*Your enemy is your friend.* Could it be? Was she there for a reason? Was Fate playing her hand again? For Fate had chosen him, Fate was guiding him, Fate had laid out his path, nemesis and all.

And then, finally, he understood. Everything was out in front of him, past, present, future. His enemy *was* his friend. For if it had not been for her, he would be ruler of the Underworld right now; he would never even have thought to cast his sights higher than that. And if it had not been for her, he never would have been on Poseidon's yacht, never would have fallen to the bottom of the sea, never would have been swallowed by the Ketos, never would have had the trident fall into his hands. His enemy, as repugnant and odious as she was, had acted all along in the service of Fate.

He clapped his hands together and gasped. Oh yes, his enemy was his friend, for she spurred him on to greater things, to more noble heights. And when he did overthrow Zeus, he would have her to thank.

But something was wrong, something was making him uncomfortable, and not just the sharp point in the rock on which he was sitting. He had gone to the Oracle to ask if he would overthrow Zeus. *How could it be you?* she had said. *There is a way to these things,* she had said. *You are Poseidon's heir.*

He did not understand. He hardly needed the Oracle to tell him who his grandfather was. He had, after all, just turned him into a sea cucumber. But there was something he was missing.

He closed his eyes and heard her voice again: *There is a way to these things. You are* Poseidon's *heir.*

How remarkable it is to be a genius, how extraordinary. Even he—modest he—stood in awe of the power of his own mind. He felt it hum and buzz, so much like the trident, as it studied the jumble of pieces before him, then one by one picked them up and began to put them together.

He would need a spy, first of all. He could go to the she-beast's lair himself—he had been there before, after all, shadow collecting—but Philonecron possessed enough self-knowledge to realize that that might not be a good idea. Despite how rational and judicious he might appear to you, he was *emotional*, too, and it simply would not do if, when face-to-face with the miniature Machiavellian monstrosity, passions overcame him and he blasted her to bits. For he needed her alive.

No matter. Using the skin of a nearby tropical crawling bat for parchment, Philonecron crafted a message, then boarded his chariot (and it was, he must admit, quite a nice thing to have a chariot) and sped across the waves toward the mainland. Soon he was in the sewers of Athens and watching a raven, his message tied to its leg, fly through a door and into the long passage to the Underworld.

Even in his excitement, Philonecron could not help but feel a wave of nostalgia as he stood by the open door that led to the home of his heart. Even as a variety of Underworld creatures flew, stomped, and slithered past him out the door into the mortal realm, he had eyes only for the darkness they had come from. Familiar smells wafted up to him—mildew and rot and festering Harpy carcass and even, if he concentrated, a bit of burning flesh from Tartarus. He bit his knuckle and turned his head away—it was all he could do not to dive through the door into the nether realm's embracing bosom.

Then, with a flapping of wings, his bird was back (or at least its skeleton). Heart aflutter, Philonecron pulled a scroll off its legbone and quickly unrolled it.

He had found his spy.

Two days later, Philonecron met up with Eurynomus. It took some doing, as the demon moved with absolute quiet, had skin the color of flies, and possessed a natural tendency to lurk in the shadows. He could even move through wood and stone as easily as air. He was the perfect spy—but it did make him hard to find in a crowd.

But then, there he was in Philonecron's cave, his blue-black skeletal form emerging from behind one of the rocks, cloaked in gloom and silence. Though it was not his appearance Philonecron noticed first. Eurynomus wore a coat made out of vulture skin and feathers that perfectly matched his flesh—but there was no accounting for taste. Or smell.

Slowly the demon gave his report: The mortals were

going nowhere. There was a man whom they'd hoped would take them away, but he had disappointed them.

Philonecron understood. The girl and poor, misguided Zero were being kept against their will by the meddling Metos, who meant to protect them from the big bad gods. (The foolish Promethean had it backward; it was the world that needed protecting from the girl.) He should have known. You get to know a lot about a person when you've chained them up and watched a Harpy gnaw on their liver. Metos wanted to keep them safe, out of harm's way—but what if he were to think they were in danger where they were, that he could not protect them on his own?

It would be simpler to just go to the Promethean headquarters himself, of course—blast through and "convince" the Prometheans to let him in on their secrets. But nothing was ever simple. Philonecron had tried to find their headquarters, back when Charon had warned him the god-fighters were onto his attempted coup, and it was as if it did not exist. It was apparently hidden from Immortals. If what he sought was inside the building, he would simply have to wait until it came out.

Philonecron had the lifespan of one moon, the Oracle had said, and the moon was waning. It was time to act.

• • •

There was not much time. The beast was stupid, bestial, indiscriminate—but that was no different from Poseidon, and Philonecron had handled him perfectly well. It would simply require a little retraining, that was all. And for dramatic impact, it truly could not be better.

The plan was perfect. The attack would look like it was ordered from Olympus—targeted at her, and only her—and yet she would somehow, miraculously, survive. She would think it was through her own cunning and skill, she would think she was in control, but behind her there was Philonecron, the glorious puppet master, joyously pulling the strings. She would escape, Metos would take them to his fellows, and Philonecron would follow. Whatever his answer was, it would emerge. Once again, his spiteful little nemesis would be the one to give him exactly what he needed on his Fateful journey.

A few inquiries made, a few arms twisted, and soon Philonecron had found what he was looking for, in a lair deep within the Polish Carpathian Mountains.

"Hello, my pretty," he cooed, leveling the trident at the great monster. "How would you like to do a favor for the future Lord of the Universe?"

CHAPTER 12

# Anger Management

FAR AWAY FROM THE WRECKAGE OF HARTNETT MIDDLE School, from the fleeing Chimera and the faltering flames, from the giant Malls and Great Lakes, is another ordinary school in another ordinary city very like this one. And in this school was a teenage boy named Steve, who appeared to be quite ordinary indeed. Sure, there were extraordinary things about him—his uncanny knack for remembering trivia, for one, which had earned him the captainship of the school Quiz Bowl team. His devotion to the mother who had raised him on her own, for another, which would have earned him some teasing were it not for the third extraordinary thing: his temper.

That third thing was the reason this teenage boy currently sat in the office of the school's psychiatrist, where he was mandated by the school to be every Thursday during lunch period. No one seemed to care that Steve was a growing boy and needed to eat lunch—a fact that made Steve rather angry. No one else noted the irony.

"How are you feeling today, Steve?" asked the psychiatrist.

"Hungry," Steve grumbled.

"Yes, well, besides that. I heard you had some problem in biology today."

Steve's eyes flared. "Mr. Ward accused me of cheating. I would never cheat! I just knew the answers, that's all."

The psychiatrist nodded.

"I mean, what kind of a place is this?" Steve continued, his arms folded tightly across his thin chest. "A kid does well on a test, and instead of saying, 'Oh, great job, we're really proud of you,' they think you must have *cheated*? He called my *mom*. Now she's gonna think—"

"Steve," said the psychiatrist. "Not every teacher is familiar with the disparity between the effort and interest you put into your schoolwork and your intelligence."

"I wouldn't cheat," Steve said, sulking.

"I know," said the psychiatrist. "And I told Mr. Ward so."

The psychiatrist studied Steve's face. He was a complicated kid. She did not know the story of Steve's father, only that he was not in the picture. The psychiatrist had seen this before—a boy who takes out his anger at his absentee father on other male authority figures, not to mention the world at large. She worried with Steve too that this lashing out was concealing something deeper: a fear that his own father had left because of something wrong with *him*, a need to be loved and accepted, and that need could lead to him latching onto the first father figure who showed him kindness.

"So he told you, too," Steve grumbled. "Does everyone think I'm a cheater? And dumb, too?"

"No. It's all right. He was wrong, and he'll apologize to you tomorrow. But you have to apologize for calling him"—she looked at her notes, then raised her eyebrows—"what you called him." Steve began to protest, and she held up her hand. "I know, I know he was wrong. He should have gotten all the facts before he accused you. But that doesn't excuse what you said, and now you might be suspended again. Remember what we talked about. When you feel yourself getting angry, take a step back, take time to calm down, think about the consequences. Okay?"

Steve tightened his arms and stared at the ground. "Step back, calm down, consequences," he muttered. And then his face contorted and he kicked the small table next to him. The spindly leg cracked, and a plant slid off the top and came crashing to the ground.

The psychiatrist blinked. "Well," she said mildly, "we can try again next week."

When Steve got home that afternoon, he burst in the door to find his mother waiting for him in the living room.

"Mom, I didn't—"

"I know you didn't," she interrupted. "You would never cheat. I know that. But what you did wasn't right either." She sighed. "Sweetheart, I know things are hard. But someday someone is going to show you what a good place the world is. And nothing else is going to matter then. And when they do, I want you to thank them, and then come home and tell me about it, all right?"

"All right, Mom," Steve grumbled. He shuffled his feet over to the big picture window and leaned against it, staring off into the distance. He did not notice the black car parked in the shadows of the tall pines across the street, nor the man in the passenger seat focusing small binoculars right at him.

"The mom seems like a nice lady," the man said

to his partner, who was in the driver's seat. "Very pretty."

"Well, sure," said the partner. "When do we move?"

"Tonight," said the first man, "when they're asleep." He patted a black briefcase. "He won't notice a thing."

# PART THREE

## Earth

## CHAPTER 13

## Good-bye to All That

As Mr. Metos's words settled in the air, Charlotte could not believe her ears. After everything, they were finally going to join the Prometheans. It was all she had wanted since they'd come back from the Underworld, all she'd hoped for, and it had seemed it would never happen, that she would be stuck in the unbearable purgatory of ordinary life, or at least math class (which was pretty much the same thing), while the Dead suffered and other people fought her fight. And now she was going to get it.

So why wasn't she happier?

Next to her, Zee was sitting wide-eyed and still, as if he, too, could not believe what he was hearing. He had been all ready to knock Mr. Metos unconscious, then start running and not stop till he got to Greece, but now they didn't have to.

Mr. Metos was saying something now about travel plans and passports, but his words seemed to blur together. There was something he was leaving out, something very important.

"Mr. Metos, what's the plan?" she interrupted.

He frowned. "I'm telling you the plan, Charlotte."

"No, I mean"—she looked over to Zee, who was staring at her with a confused expression—"what about our parents?"

"Your parents?" he repeated.

"Well, you must have some plan for them, right? So they won't notice we're gone?" She could feel a twinge of urgency in her voice.

"Ah," said Mr. Metos. He let out a long exhale and regarded her for a moment. "Forgive me, Charlotte," he said slowly, "but I am not used to considering family."

There is nothing like being carried through the air by a flying, fire-breathing, slime-clawed monster with an extra bonus goat head to make you take stock of your life, and all Charlotte could think of was her conversation with her father the previous morning.

As she was leading her unquiet life, he'd said, she was supposed to remember that they were back home worrying about her.

And she'd remembered. For she had thought, up there in the skies, with the Chimera claw digging into her back, that that was it for Charlotte Ruth Mielswetzski—after being assaulted by a Footman, nearly dumped in the Styx, set upon by a shadow army, dropped into the Mediterranean Sea, and attacked by Poseidon and a sea monster simultaneously, she had finally met her doom. Oh, she'd fought, of course— she'd kicked and scratched and squirmed and bit, but no matter how hard she'd struggled, she could not get free. (And of course, if she had, she would have plummeted to the earth below—but that seemed, on the whole, like a better fate than getting eaten.)

And what would happen to her parents? She'd almost lost them to Poseidon's monster, and the worry had torn her heart to shreds—how would they feel if they lost her? She had been so busy thinking of her responsibility to the world that she forgot about her responsibility to the people who loved her most. She wanted to save the world, yes, but wasn't there a way to do it without making her parents suffer? There had to be.

"Yes, but you've got a plan, right?" She could feel Zee looking from her to Mr. Metos.

"I'm afraid that I do not," he said slowly.

"There must be something. Some kind of spell or potion or something to make them"—and here her voice cracked a bit—"make them forget us?" Even as she said the words, a chill passed through her body. One of the great things about having parents is there's always someone who knows you exist.

Sighing, Mr. Metos shook his head. "I don't like it any more than you do. But I can't think of another way. The best thing we can do for your families is keep you safe and alive, and . . . I can't do that here."

"But . . . what about them? Who's going to keep them safe and alive? You said the gods' rampage would spread all over the world, spread . . . here." Her mom and dad didn't have any idea about the dangers of the world, the dangers that were coming. They needed her to protect them.

"Our job is to protect them. Not just your parents, but the whole world. We can ensure their safety. But right now we need to ensure yours." He regarded the two of them for a moment, and then added, not unkindly, "You chil—you two wanted to join the fight. That, I'm afraid, involves sacrifice."

Charlotte frowned. Sacrifice was, of course, the wrong word; it was not just the cousins who would suffer. What they were doing was not sacrifice, it was cruelty.

"I think," said Mr. Metos suddenly, standing up, "I have a few phone calls to make. Why don't you two wait here and discuss whatever it is you need to discuss." He got up and began to walk toward the bedroom, then turned abruptly and said, "The Promethean headquarters is shielded from Immortals. They cannot see it. I believe only there can I keep you safe. But as much as I want you to come, I cannot make you. It is your choice. If you decide to stay, I will stay with you and protect you to the best of my ability."

They sat in silence for a few moments, Charlotte staring at an unidentifiable dark stain on the carpet below. A breeze blew suddenly through the window, rattling the dusty blinds in a way that sounded to her like a clattering of teeth. She shifted uncomfortably.

"I didn't even think . . . ," Zee said finally.

"Mmmm," said Charlotte.

"This is why you were so mad yesterday."

"Mmmm," said Charlotte.

"Being carried off by that creature made you a little jumpy about this sort of thing, didn't it?" He shook his head. "Sorry. I should have known."

"Mmmm," said Charlotte.

"I suppose my mum and dad would fly back from London to look for me. They'll be terrified." He grimaced, then focused his gaze on his cousin. "Char, do you want to go? We don't have to."

Turning to her cousin, Charlotte looked at his face but, thanks to his special ability to mask all emotion, could not read it. She knew what he was thinking, though; they were standing in the middle of a road with a large semi bearing down on them, and they had to pick a direction to run. On the left side were their families, innocent and loving, who did not deserve any pain, and on the right was the terrible knowledge they shared. There was a world where Philonecron had never noticed Zee in the first place, where Mr. Metos never came to Charlotte's school, where none of this had happened at all, and in this world Charlotte and Zee knew nothing of the gods and the way they treated humanity. And in this world, the cousins lived their ordinary lives, never knowing how lucky they were that they did not have to face such choices. In that world, Chimera weren't being sent after them and in that world, the gods were not running rampant around the Mediterranean. That world was very close to this one, but not, unfortunately, close enough. All of humanity, and her parents, they all had a semi bearing down on them, too. One they couldn't even see, let alone know how to stop.

"Yes, we do," Charlotte said quietly. "We have to go."

Zee nodded, as Charlotte felt her heart twist and burn inside of her. They did not speak then, each thinking of duty and destiny and what must be left behind, while the breeze stirred up dust around them.

Eventually the door to the bedroom opened, and Mr. Metos emerged. He stood in the doorway, appraising the two of them.

"Well?" he asked quietly.

Charlotte looked at Zee, who nodded. "We're coming," she said, trying to control her voice.

Mr. Metos straightened. "That is a relief. I still need to make some arrangements, so we can't leave for a few hours. I will come pick you up tonight. I believe the best thing to do would be to leave after your family is in bed, so we are not discovered." At these words, Charlotte gulped. "You don't need to bring much—we can take care of whatever you need there. We'll go to an airfield, and a jet will be waiting for us—"

"A jet?" Charlotte was distracted out of her misery for a moment. "The Prometheans have a jet?"

Mr. Metos gave her a half smile. "Remember, our group is very old. We have always been . . . well funded." Eyeing his clothes, Charlotte raised her eyebrows.

"Do you have passports?" he asked. Zee nodded, but Charlotte shook her head no. Her overseas travel had been strictly limited to Poseidon transporting their cruise ship to the Mediterranean. "It's all right. That can be taken care of. I'll pick you up at midnight. Does that work?"

The cousins nodded solemnly.

"Good. Before then I want you two to stay inside, and if you see anything remotely out of the ordinary—"

"Like a flying, fire-breathing, dragon-butted lion?" Zee muttered.

Mr. Metos attempted a smile. "Like a fire-breathing, dragon-butted lion, call me right away. I can be over in no time."

And with that, there was nothing more to say. The three of them got into Mr. Metos's car, and they drove back to the Mielswetzskis' in silence.

The rest of the day passed slowly, with Charlotte feeling as if she were moving through some kind of strange, transparent goo. The sick feeling in her stomach only grew stronger as the day went on, and by dinnertime she felt as if anything she ate would instantly re-emerge, fully formed, from her mouth.

"Not hungry tonight?" asked Mrs. Mielswetzski.

"Not really," muttered Charlotte. Across the table Zee was stirring his fork in his peas.

"Well, that was quite a thing you two went through yesterday. I'm sure it must have been terrifying." Her mother was being kind, deliberately kind, and Charlotte knew she felt bad for sounding angry with them at dinner the night before. Her mother hadn't been angry; she was just worried.

"Mmmm," said Charlotte.

"We're just so glad you two are all right."

"Mmmm," said Charlotte, looking down.

There was a moment's pause while Zee moved on to stirring his potatoes and Charlotte chewed on her lip. She could feel her parents watching them both carefully. "So," Mr. Mielswetzski interjected brightly. "We had a big meeting at the upper school today. As long as the fire marshal agrees, it looks like the middle school students will be coming there for the rest of the school year!" He beamed. "They're going to have trailers in the parking lots too, for the overflow. So it looks like you can't get out of school that easily." Grinning at Charlotte and Zee, he added, "It will be so much fun to see you two in the hallways!"

"Right," mumbled Charlotte.

"Oh, now, your dear old dad won't embarrass you, I promise."

For the first time that evening, she looked up at her father. "You don't embarrass me," she said.

He blinked. "I don't?"

She shook her head.

His grin widened. "Even when I dance?" And with that, he got up and began to do some sort of spastic boogie. "I could come into your classes and give lessons! Kids these days don't know how it's done!"

"Oh, Mike!" said Mrs. Mielswetzski.

"What do you think, Lottie?" he asked, jerking his body around like a fish stranded on land.

"Um," Charlotte said, pushing back from the table, "I have to go." With that, she ran upstairs to her room, closed the door, and flopped on the bed. In the distance she could hear her father say, "That bad, huh?"

Charlotte allowed herself to cry for exactly five minutes. Then she punched her pillow, sat up in bed, set her jaw, and wiped her face clean. It was time to get moving. Resolutely she went into her closet and got out a small duffel bag she'd used for sleepovers at Maddy's. Mr. Metos had said to pack lightly, so she threw a few changes of clothes and some toiletries in there. They probably had deodorant in Greece, but she didn't want to take any chances. Then she put the duffel and the backpack in her closet, and sat on the bed and waited.

She could hear Zee banging around in the room next to hers, filling his bag with a few boy essentials, and wondered what he was thinking. She, at least, got to say good-bye to her parents—his had left for a few days in London a couple of weeks ago and then had called to say business would keep them there for a couple of months. They'd invited Zee to join them, but he hadn't wanted to. Charlotte got the feeling Zee had not liked living in London very much.

Around her, the room darkened slowly, and soon night had surrounded her entirely, but she did not get up and turn on the light. She watched the numbers on her clock radio change and listened to the familiar sounds of the house—her parents rattling around in the kitchen, then moving to the living room, where she knew they would sit and read and listen to old people's music. Then, finally, they turned off the radio and headed up the stairs. The bathroom door opened and shut a few times; footsteps went back and forth down the hallway, and then stopped right outside her door.

"What are you doing?" she heard her mother say.

"I want to say good night to Lottie," her father whispered back.

"The light's off. She must be asleep. Zee is too. We should let them sleep."

"Those poor kids," whispered her father. "Maybe we should try to do something fun this weekend. Take their mind off things."

"Good idea. I have to admit I always thought Charlotte would be happy to see her school burn down."

"My Lottie is full of surprises," said Mr. Mielswetzski,

voice full of pride. And then they disappeared down the hallway and into their room.

Charlotte did not move for ten more minutes, lest her parents hear her, and then she could sit no more. She turned on a lamp and began to clean her room, straightening her bookshelves and her desk, making her bed the way her mother always wanted her to. And then it was eleven forty-five. Mr. Metos would be there soon.

Before Charlotte could think about what she was doing, she had opened her parents' door a crack and peeked in. There they were, two large lumps on the bed, her father snoring steadily, her mother sleeping with her feet sticking out of the covers the way she always did.

Charlotte took a deep breath and started to close the door.

"Lottie? Is that you?" Mr. Mielswetzski raised his head.

She grimaced. "Um, yeah."

"Is everything okay?"

"Yeah, I just, um . . . I was just . . . going to the bathroom."

"It's across the hall," mumbled her mother.

"She must be very sleepy," whispered her father.

"Oh, yeah, thanks. Um, good-bye."

"Good night," responded her parents. And Charlotte shut the door, fixing the image of them in her mind, trying not to wonder if she would ever see them again.

Soon she was back in her room, at her desk, writing her parents a long note, because she simply did not have it in her to just leave. She could not make them understand, but she could try. Last time she'd done this, she'd been going down to the Underworld, and she'd told them, simply, not to worry. They'd worried. This time she would try, somehow, to explain.

Dear Mom and Dad,

Zee and I have to go away for a while. Dad, you said that a lot has happened in my life that you don't know about, and you are right. Zee and I have learned things about the world, and we have to go try to make everything okay. I don't know if we can, but we have to try.

I'm sorry I can't explain more. You wouldn't believe me if I told you. But we're safe. We're with Mr. Metos, and he's going to protect us. We'll come back as soon as we can, I promise.

I love you.

Charlotte

With a deep breath, she got out her duffel bag and put it on the bed, opening it to look through one last time. Mew sat on the foot of the bed, looking suspicious. Charlotte gulped—it was bad enough leaving her parents.

"Mew, we have to go now," she said, her voice breaking. "We have to go to be with the Prometheans." The cat stared up at her, wide-eyed. "You went into the Underworld. You saw what it was like. I'm going to miss you very much. You take care of my parents, all right? Something might be coming, something they won't be ready for. You protect them."

Charlotte picked up the cat and gave her a huge hug, then turned back to the note and added:

*P.S. Please take good care of Mew. She likes being scratched just behind her left ear.*

Mew started yowling then, loud and mournful. Charlotte looked around in a panic. "Shh, baby," she whispered. The cat narrowed her eyes and yowled more loudly. Tears welled up in Charlotte's eyes, and all she could do was grab her bag and dart out of the room, shutting the door behind her. She could hear Mew's yells through the door.

Quickly she went downstairs to find Zee waiting for her in the front hall, looking a little displaced.

"Are you all right?" he asked gently.

She shook her head. "Mew knows. She's yowling up a storm."

Pain flashed across Zee's face. "I guess we should go before—"

"Yeah," said Charlotte, wiping away a tear. "We'll be back," she added, hearing the lie in her voice. Back? After what exactly? They were going to join the Prometheans. They were going to the belly of the beast. Was that the sort of thing one came back from?

Zee nodded, and Charlotte knew he didn't believe her either. "I left them a note," she added, pointing upstairs. "Because that worked so well last time."

"I left mine a letter. I just don't want them to think something horrid has happened to us, you know?"

"I hope nothing does."

"Aw, come on, Char," Zee said with a half smile, "what could possibly go wrong?"

She gave him a small smile back. Zee carefully opened the front door, and together they stepped out of their home into the still night.

Mr. Metos was there, waiting for them in his dark car, and as the cousins approached he got out quietly, opened the trunk, and put their bags inside.

"Ready?" he whispered, holding the door open for them.

Charlotte nodded, and with one last long look at her house, she stepped inside.

## CHAPTER 14

### The Lair of the Prometheans

For much of the last year, Charlotte felt like she had been living in a book—one of those where ordinary kids are unwittingly plunged into an extraordinary world where they must struggle against unimaginable evil to save the world, not to mention themselves, except usually in those books the kids discovered they had super-special top secret powers perfectly suited to thwart that particular evil. Or at the very least the kids have been Chosen somehow, they're fated to save the world. Charlotte had no powers of any kind and was not fated to do anything except, perhaps, get a C in math.

But as they drove up to the airport hangar where the small jet awaited them, blanketed by the dark of the night, she suddenly felt that she'd fallen out of a book and right into a major summer blockbuster movie, with car chases, lots of special effects, and a very big set budget.

Of course, in movies, when you pulled up to a private jet, you were usually in some sleek black sports car or limo; you were never, ever in a dented banana yellow hatchback that looked older than you. Fate liked to keep Charlotte firmly fixed in reality.

They drove all the way up to the foot of the sleek white jet, and Mr. Metos motioned to them to stay in the car as he ran out and had a few words with the tall man in a dark overcoat who was waiting for them. As the cousins watched, the man handed Mr. Metos a manila envelope and then disappeared into the night. Mr. Metos opened the door then, hurrying them out of the car and up the stairs into the jet, but not before handing Charlotte the envelope.

"What's this?"

"Your passport."

"Oh," she said, impressed.

As Charlotte stepped into the Prometheans' jet and surveyed her surroundings, she thought that if the circumstances had been different, she would have thought this was the coolest thing that had ever happened to her. Actually, she reflected, even given the circumstances, it still was; with big, plush, leather easy chairs arranged around tables, wood paneling, thick carpeting, and what seemed to be a kitchen in the back, she felt that she could pretty happily move right in. She glanced at Zee, who was looking back at her, eyebrows raised. They had experienced quite a bit in the last year, but getting spirited off in a luxury jet was rather different from walking through the pitch-black, bug-infested, slime-ridden caves that led to the Underworld.

They sat in two cushy chairs on either side of the aisle, and Mr. Metos took a seat facing them. Charlotte looked out of her window into the night and tried not to think of what she was leaving behind.

"Mr. Metos," she asked, as the plane was taking off, "what's going on in the Mediterranean?" So much had been happening that she had not kept track. Guiltily she thought how nice it was to have that luxury.

Mr. Metos exhaled. "It does not seem to stop. We are managing the best we can. Unfortunately, one problem seems to lead to another. At first the gods seemed to be just playing, but now old rivalries are coming to the fore. The Temple of Athena in Athens was hit by a lightning bolt and burned to the ground. You know the archeological site Ephesus was destroyed? There were two giants who fought on opposite sides of the War on Cronus. One lived at the bottom of the sea, and without Poseidon to keep him there, he has gotten out and challenged his old rival to battle. You know the results. We were fortunate it happened at night. If tourists had been there . . ." He shook his head.

"There's more," he said, eyeing them seriously. "Someone's been blowing out doors to the Underworld. There are monsters escaping—and maybe getting in."

Charlotte's heart tightened. "The Dead?"

"The gods' mischief will not stay contained to the Upperworld. The Underworld gods have always ignored the Dead, but now . . ."

Charlotte closed her eyes. "Can't we do anything for them?"

"We will," Mr. Metos said. "We will. It's our job." They sat in silence for a moment, visions of the Dead haunting Charlotte's thoughts.

"But it's not just protecting people," Mr. Metos continued, changing the subject. "Keeping the truth under wraps is getting harder. There was a Minotaur rampaging through the Athens suburbs, smashing up streets. He put seven people in the hospital before we got to him. We had to leak a story about an escaped mental patient in a costume. There was even an Internet site cataloging all of the more suspicious events."

Charlotte started. The blog! "I saw that. Did *you* take that down?"

"Well, not I. That's Hector's job. The Internet has posed a curious challenge to us, it provides a place for people all over to share stories and theories. Under normal circumstances, the Immortal intrusions are few and far apart enough that we can cover them up, but if someone put all of this together . . ."

"But I thought it was your job to protect humans against the gods, not keep their secrets for them."

Mr. Metos frowned. "Well, it's the same thing."

"Why?" Charlotte asked.

*"Why?"*

"Why shouldn't people know? Shouldn't they know the truth? Especially now." Charlotte could hear her voice getting high. "People are scared. Wouldn't it be better to know? I mean, by keeping the truth from people, aren't you being just like the gods?"

She could feel Zee shooting her a look, and Mr. Metos eyed her coldly. "Hardly," he said. "There is a delicate balance that exists. We are trying to preserve it. Remember, like it or not, humanity exists at the pleasure of Zeus. We would like very much for that to continue. He flooded the world once when he was displeased. If it had not been for Prometheus . . ."

Charlotte blinked. "Really?"

"Prometheus had the gift of prophecy," Mr. Metos explained. "He foresaw the great flood, when Zeus decided to destroy humanity after Prometheus stole the sacred fire, and warned his son Deucalion, who built a boat—and he and his wife survived the flood."

"Oh!" Charlotte knew the story of Deucalion but had not remembered he was Prometheus's son. "So he was like the first Promethean."

"You could say that. He certainly protected humanity; he ensured its very survival."

"Not to mention his own," Zee murmured.

A small smile crept over Mr. Metos's face. "You could say that, too."

"Greek mythology is very big on sons," Charlotte said, trying to be casual.

Mr. Metos's eyes fell on her. "I suppose," he replied. "Listen, I have work to do. The chairs recline, and there are pillows and blankets underneath the seats. I think you should get some sleep."

And with that, Mr. Metos was up from his seat, leaving Charlotte to reflect on his reaction. It was very late, though, and she was very tired. She reclined the chair with the intention of just dozing a bit, and fell fast asleep.

In her dream, her mother was looking all around the house, searching in closets and drawers and under beds for something she would never find. *I have it*, Charlotte wanted to say, *I have it right here*—but she could not speak, she could only watch as her mother's search grew more and more desperate. The scene changed—Poseidon was barreling down on her, followed by Sir Laurence, followed by her dad on water skis, shouting, *I'll protect you, Lottie!* And again—she was running through the Underworld, chased by a giant Chimera, but instead of a lion's head it had the head of Philonecron, spitting fire at her. *I'll get you, my pretty,* he said, *and your little dog, too!* And again—she was in a cell in a cave in total darkness. . . .

Ah, this dream. The first parts happened as if she were watching them on fast forward—darkness . . . cell . . . cave . . . light . . . and then the girl, surrounded by Dead. Charlotte's heart broke at the sight of them, she wanted to reach out, protect them all. She stepped out of her cage and she was falling into blackness, and somewhere her conscious mind expected her to jolt awake, but this time she kept falling until she landed with a thump on the ground.

Ouch. Even in her dreams, she got abused. It took Charlotte a few moments to recover before she could get her bearings, but once she did she forgot all about her pain.

She was in another cave room, and in the center

there was a small but intense fire, and somehow, as one knows these things in dreams, Charlotte knew it was the source of flickering light that she'd seen from her cage. Of course, there was no opening in the roof, no way for Charlotte to have fallen inside, but that didn't matter. What mattered were the strange markings she saw on the walls.

Gingerly she got up to get a closer look. They were like prehistoric cave drawings, but much more sophisticated, and they were moving. Charlotte stared at the pictures one by one, following them from beginning to end. The girl's voice:

*Do you know what you're looking at?*

Yes. There's a great big blue guy, and some other little people running around naked. Other than that, no.

*Oh, come on,* said the voice, exasperated.

And Charlotte awoke with a start. That girl was getting on her nerves. Zee was muttering to himself in his seat across the aisle. Charlotte leaned in and heard, "E marks the spot!"

She stared. He said something unintelligible, and then she heard, quite distinctly, "Seek the belly button!"

His eyes popped open, and he saw Charlotte gaping at him.

"What?" he asked defensively.

"You were talking in your sleep!"

"Strange dream," mumbled Zee, and promptly fell back asleep. And Charlotte did too.

The next thing she heard was Mr. Metos's voice telling her to wake up. It took her a moment to realize where she was, and when she did she felt her heart tighten. Outside the plane it was light. She couldn't imagine what time it was at home, or whether or not her parents had woken up yet to find her gone.

She turned her head to look out the window, expecting to see—what? A brilliant sun, Grecian temples and cypress trees, and goats roaming free on the airport grounds? Whatever it was she was expecting, it was not what she saw, which was pretty much what you'd see at any U.S. airport—a gray sky, a big hangar, lots of black-top, and in the distance some towers. An odd noise came from Zee's direction.

"Huh," said Charlotte. "This is Greece?"

Mr. Metos turned to her. "Greece?"

"Um . . . yeah . . ."

"No, we're in London."

"What?" exclaimed Charlotte.

"Oh, brilliant," muttered Zee.

Charlotte eyed her cousin. He had never expressed a particularly strong urge to come back to his home city, and judging by the look on his face, he would have been perfectly happy to go a few more years without returning.

"Our headquarters has been here since the 1830s," Mr. Metos said. "We came here during the cholera epidemic."

*"During?"* Zee asked.

"Yes. Ares had decided to spread a little plague, so we had to find a way to stop it. And we stayed. It's always been a good place to keep your eyes on the world . . . and it's an easy place to blend in with the crowd if you need to. We do have a satellite office near Delphi, which, as you might imagine, has been rather busy lately. Now, if you'll excuse me, I'll get your bags."

After he disappeared into the back of the plane, Charlotte turned to her cousin. "You all right?"

"Sure," he said with a shrug. "I just wasn't expecting this. It's sort of ironic, isn't it? My mum and dad sent me away from here for my protection, and now we've come back for my protection. It's weird, I'll be so close to them, but . . ."

Mr. Metos came back and collected their passports. Then they gathered their things and stepped outside of the plane onto a staircase. A black car was waiting for them below. A thick layer of gray clouds blanketed the sky, and the air was cold and wet, and Charlotte regretted the shorts and tank tops she had packed. They descended the stairs, and another man got out of the car and placed their bags in the trunk.

"This is my colleague, Teodor," said Mr. Metos, introducing them. "Teodor, this is Charlotte Mielswetzski and Zachary Miller."

Charlotte straightened herself and shook his hand in her most adult-like manner. She and Zee were under no illusion that the Prometheans were just going to let them sign up for adventures, like open activity period at camp; they would have to convince them. Or else Charlotte and Zee would just sneak out and follow them. They were not going to be stopped now.

There was an official-looking attendant waiting inside the hangar, and as Charlotte and Zee climbed into the car, Mr. Metos went over and handed him their passports and a thick envelope that Charlotte had a strong feeling contained a rather large sum of money. The man left, Mr. Metos got into the car—and then they were off.

As they drove, Charlotte stared out the window, thinking of what was behind her and what lay ahead. Other than the road signs, the world did not, in truth, look that different from the world she'd just left—it just had a grayer sky and greener grass. They passed railyards and warehouses covered in graffiti and shiny office buildings and large billboards advertising candy bars and all-soccer-all-the-time channels. But as they drove on, she began to see, among all the familiar modernity, stone farmhouses, little churches, and other buildings that gave the impression of being impossibly old.

In the front seat, Mr. Metos and Teodor murmured back and forth to each other. Charlotte strained to hear. Next to her, Zee sat slumped in his seat, looking straight ahead at the seat in front of him.

"As we get into town," Mr. Metos said, turning to them, "it might be best if you did not show your faces out the window. We should not be seen together. Remember, you are missing now. If someone should happen to recognize you and see me with you . . . well, I would very much prefer not to be arrested."

"Oh," said Charlotte, thinking of the note she had left for her parents. Maybe it hadn't been such a good idea to mention Mr. Metos after all. He turned back around in his seat, and she stared at the back of his head uncomfortably.

Slowly the sprawl consolidated into actual city, and Charlotte was surrounded by jostling cars and crowded sidewalks. Double-decker buses and black cabs roared down the wrong side of the street, and tourists poured across crosswalks. They turned into a neighborhood comprised of skyscrapers intermixed with classic-looking white stone buildings, all set around thickly winding roads.

"That's it," said Mr. Metos, as they pulled up to a curb on a narrow, winding side street, pointing to the building in front of them.

It was a four-story building made of smooth white stone. If there were any sunshine at all, and if the narrow street let in any light, the white facade would actually have been quite lovely. As it was, the marble adopted the damp grayness of the street. There was a set of stairs leading to two glass doors flanked by iron railings, and on the side was a bronze placard that read, SMITH AND JONES IMPORT/EXPORT, EST. 1832.

"It's in an office building?" Charlotte asked.

"Yes," said Mr. Metos. "What did you expect?"

An underground lair. A cave with narrow tunnels, leading to a nook with beeping computer equipment and a guy wearing headphones, transcribing radio signals. A secret vault filled with money of every currency, another nook with someone forging passports, a hidden weapons chamber, a dusty library filled with crumbling maps, a dungeon full of rabid spiders, and of course a bright, shiny room where someone worked full-time getting Mr. Metos jobs at Hartnett.

"It's right out in the open. The gods really can't—"

"We have a few tricks up our sleeve. There are ways

of . . . obscuring things from Immortals," Mr. Metos said. "They cannot see this building, even if they look right at it."

Soon they had pulled into an alleyway and up to a white garage door that led to an underground garage. Teodor punched a code into a keypad and the door opened. Charlotte strained to see the numbers he was punching—you never knew when that sort of thing might come in handy—but she could not.

"New code?" asked Mr. Metos in a low voice.

Teodor glanced back at them. "Pie. First ate," he whispered back.

Charlotte raised her eyebrows. These people made no sense at all.

Before them was a parking garage filled with cars that looked just like the one they were in, sort of like a Promethean taxi fleet. Charlotte thought that if she were running things, she might vary their choice of automobiles a bit so as to be a tad more inconspicuous, but as so often happened, no one had asked her.

They got out of the car and walked toward a small elevator lobby. They passed a nondescript door marked with a placard that read HAZARDOUS MATERIALS, and Charlotte pointed to it. "What's in there?"

Mr. Metos raised his eyebrows. "Hazardous materials. Come, follow me."

The elevator looked as if it might have been established in 1832 as well. When the door opened, it became apparent that there was no way four people were going to fit inside, so Teodor murmured, "I'll wait here," and backed away.

They went up one flight, then the elevator opened onto a vast lobby, a two-story room with slick, polished stone floors, a brass-railed balcony, and ornate moldings on the walls. Some large ferns were spread along the floor, and Grecian statues in porticos lined the balcony. A doorman stood in front of two pairs of big golden doors, and at the back of the room an impeccably dressed receptionist sat at a desk, typing on a computer. She looked up and squinted at Charlotte.

"That is Phillipa," Mr. Metos whispered. "She is under the impression she works for Smith and Jones Import/Export. As you can see, we try to maintain the facade of our front company as thoroughly as possible. It's a fully functioning company."

"Does it work?"

"Yes. No one asks too many questions around here. There are a lot of undercover organizations in this area. The bank down the street is a front for a group that thinks Norse myths are real; of course they're just crazy."

He led the two of them up the big stone staircase to the balcony. "The offices of the import/export business are here"—he motioned to the dark oak doors that faced the balcony, then led them onward—"and around the corner here is the entrance to the rest of headquarters, including the offices and residences."

"And spears?" Charlotte whispered.

"And spears. The elevator leads directly up there, as well." They were in front of another door reading PRIVATE. Mr. Metos got out a key and unlocked it.

"Do we get keys?" Charlotte asked.

Mr. Metos eyed them. "There's really no reason for that, as you two will be staying in the building."

Charlotte and Zee exchanged a glance. Yeah, right.

They headed up three flights of stairs and through another door to a long, dark hallway lined with rooms. "Normally," Mr. Metos said quietly, "you would see more activity here. But we're a pretty bare-bones operation right now, with most personnel in the Greece office."

"Why didn't you take us there?" asked Charlotte. Didn't they need Mr. Metos there?

"I have no intention of taking you two so close to the belly of the beast. We aren't able to have the same protections there either. We'll be much safer here."

Mr. Metos led them down to the very end of the hall and pointed to two adjacent rooms. "This will be your home for the time being. You'll find the rooms well stocked—we've arranged for breakfast and some clothes and books for you both. There's a kitchen down the hall, and across from that is the infirmary. I am right there"—he pointed to the room next to Zee—"and if you need anything at all, you can come find me. And—"

"Metos." A man's voice traveled down the stone-paved hallway like a shot. They all turned and saw an olive-skinned man with black hair and a sharp, bony face come striding toward them. His face was lined with two parallel long, deep scars that traveled all the way down his neck to his shirt collar. They looked newly acquired.

Something passed over Mr. Metos. He nodded briskly. "You're back."

"Yes, I had to check on . . . things here."

"Zachary, Charlotte"—Mr. Metos turned to them—"this is Timon."

"Nice to meet you," said the cousins.

Timon looked from Mr. Metos to Charlotte and Zee. "Mmm," he said, his nostrils flaring. "You children have your rooms?"

"Uh-huh," said Charlotte, stiffening.

"I trust you'll stay there, then." With a twitch of his lips, he turned and left.

"Friendly chap," said Zee.

"I'm sorry for my colleague," said Mr. Metos, looking

at Timon's back. "He is . . . distracted. I have to check on something. I'll show you around later, all right?"

When Charlotte stepped into her room, she had to admit it was a lot nicer than it would be in a secret cave lair. It was spacious, with a nice big bed, fully lined bookshelves, and an attached bathroom, complete with a big marble bath. She opened the closet and found six T-shirts, three button-down shirts, and six sweaters, all different colors of the same style, plus three pairs of jeans. On the floor were two shiny new pairs of sneakers that Charlotte had no intention of ever wearing—hers had been to the Underworld and Poseidon's yacht with her, and she was not going to give up on them just because they'd stepped in a little Harpy poo.

There was no way Charlotte was going to be able to rest; she was too keyed up. She was just about to leave to go knock on Zee's door when he beat her to it. Soon they were sitting on Charlotte's bed, talking in low voices.

"So what do you think?" Charlotte asked.

"I don't know. It's so odd. My dad used to work a block away. We're in a district called the City of London; it's sort of the financial district. Lots of banker types in identical suits having lunch and buying and selling things. No one lives here."

"Are we anywhere near your house?"

"Nah, I live in Battersea, south of the Thames.

Lived, anyway." He exhaled. "Let's go look around."

"Can we start by looking around the kitchen? I'm starving."

Zee nodded. "Me too. Come on."

They had made it halfway to the kitchen when they heard loud voices coming from behind Mr. Metos's door—Mr. Metos and the man he had just introduced them to. Without a word to each other, they crept over to the room and listened in.

"Why did you bring them here?" Timon's voice was saying. The cousins looked at each other. Gee, wonder who that was about.

"We've been through this," said Mr. Metos. "I couldn't protect them by myself."

"You didn't need to be protecting them at all. We need you. We're all that's standing between the Mediterranean and total chaos. Not to mention—"

"Well, I'm here, aren't I?" Mr. Metos interrupted.

"We can't afford any distractions, especially now. Metos, we can't be babysitting."

"They do not need babysitting," said Mr. Metos firmly. "They have faced greater powers than either of us, Timon."

*Yeah,* thought Charlotte.

"Do you know how much trouble these children have caused already? Do you see the result of their interfering?"

Charlotte flushed. She did not need to be reminded that everyone suffering in the Mediterranean had her to thank.

"A Chimera attacked them!" Mr. Metos's voice rose. "Who do you think sent that, Santa Claus?"

"And that is precisely why they shouldn't be here," said Timon, his voice matching Mr. Metos's. "Here, of all places! In fact, wasn't the distraction that they provided . . . useful, now that we have Prometheus's secret?"

The cousins looked at each other again. Prometheus's secret?

"Are you suggesting that we should have left these two exposed . . . as bait?"

"I am suggesting, Metos, that you are forgetting your mission. We are here to protect humanity, not two humans."

"I have never forgotten my mission," he said coldly. "My first loyalty is to the Prometheans. You leave them to me. I will keep them out of the way."

Charlotte bristled. For a moment it had seemed Mr. Metos was ready to trust them, was on their side. But that was wrong. He'd stopped calling them children, he'd taken them with him, but that only went so far. His first loyalty was to the Prometheans, and Charlotte and Zee would be kept out of the way.

CHAPTER 15

# The Writing on the Wall

To Charlotte, it was just like she was home and grounded all over again. The difference was, her parents had had no idea that she'd saved the world, whereas Mr. Metos knew perfectly well, had seen it with his own eyes, all the Protheans knew it—and yet here she was.

They should have been *glad* to have them, she thought. They should have a whole Promethean retreat where they all gathered and listened wide-eyed to Charlotte and Zee's stories of their encounters with the gods. Mr. Metos should stand in front of the group, beaming, and say, *I would like to introduce someone very special,* and then they would all burst into spontaneous applause, a few would even stand up and cheer, and that would move the rest of them to their feet, the whole room hooting and hollering for Charlotte and Zee and all they had experienced, all they had accomplished. Then there would be a question-and-answer period. *So, Zachary,* Teodor would say, *what's the best route for getting to Hades's Palace quickly?* And Timon would ask, *Charlotte—may I call you Charlotte?—how can we use Poseidon's temper to our advantage?* And afterward there would be a great reception with toasts to them, and cake, really delicious thanks-for-saving-humanity cake.

Then footsteps approached from behind the door. Charlotte motioned to Zee. They scooted backward so it appeared they were coming down the hall—as opposed to being pressed against the door, listening in.

As the Prometheans left Mr. Metos's room, Timon saw the cousins and shot them a suspicious look. "Out of the way, huh?"

"We're allowed to eat," Charlotte muttered under her breath.

Just then a ringing came from Timon's pocket. He took out his cell phone and listened for a moment, then stalked off to the stairs. Mr. Metos watched him go.

Charlotte took a step toward the kitchen. "Excuse

me," she said, inching around Mr. Metos. "We don't want to be *in the way*."

Whether or not Mr. Metos got her point, she could not tell. "You must forgive Timon," he said, looking in the direction the Promethean had gone. "He has a singularity of purpose that can be . . . frustrating at times. But know, he was the one who spotted the tsunami, he was the one who started the evacuation. If it hadn't been for him . . . Still, it would be better if, while he is here, you stayed out of his way. I'm afraid your position with us is precarious. Timon must believe you are not a distraction."

They nodded, Charlotte looking back at him steadily.

"He will not be here long," Mr. Metos continued. "He is needed in Greece. The situation there—"

"We could help," said Charlotte defiantly.

"You will *stay safe*," Mr. Metos said, a note of anger in his voice. "The Prometheans have been protecting humanity for millennia. We continue to do so now. You must have faith in us. We will make everyone safe. We have a plan. Now, if you'll excuse me . . ." Mr. Metos took a step toward the stairs.

"Ah, Metos!" a clear voice rang out from behind a slightly ajar door. "Are those the cousins? Send 'em in!"

Looking distracted, Mr. Metos motioned them

toward the room. A young man who looked no older than a college student was sitting at a desk, staring at his computer. One of them, anyway—the room had three different computers and was littered with computer books and equipment.

"Hey," he said. "I'm Hector. I've heard a lot about you guys."

That was more like it. The cousins trotted into the office, Char shooting a dirty look back into the hallway. Not that Mr. Metos saw it, but it made her feel good.

"Aw, don't mind him," Hector said. "He's worried about you. You wouldn't believe how he fought to bring you guys here. Everyone's just stressed. There's a lot going on." A flash of something passed through his eyes.

"So I hear," Charlotte muttered.

"Come on, help me out on something. How does this look? No one here's very web savvy." He turned his computer monitor to them. "The trick is to make it look amateurish, but convincing. You want to make something to attract the crazies."

On the screen was a web page that looked like a newsletter, with white text on a black background. The headline blared:

REVEALED: ALIENS IN THE MEDITERRANEAN!!!

It looked amateurish, convincing, and crazy.

Scattered on the page were grainy photos, mostly

things Charlotte had seen on the news—the dolphins, the flopping fish, the sharks swarming in shallow waters, an aerial view of the hole in the sea. Then another Charlotte had never seen—a fuzzy, glowing image at the bottom of the sea that, if you squinted enough, looked like a UFO.

"Photoshop," he said proudly. "Things have gotten a lot easier since Roswell. They had a devil of a time staging that after someone unleashed an automaton in the Nevada desert. And look at this. This is the kicker." He scrolled down to another photo. It took a moment for Charlotte to make sense of what she was seeing, but something about it made her feel sick. Then her mind began to put it together—it was a chunk of something floating in the water, and in the middle of that chunk was a massive, glassy, pig-like eye.

Charlotte gasped. "That's from the Ketos!" Her stomach turned in revulsion.

"Yup. They found some pieces of it in the sea, near the hole."

"Do you know what happened to it?" Zee asked.

"Nope. They're examining some of the pieces. That's not my department. But"—he leaned in and whispered, eyes glowing—"there's a Hydra in a cave in Dover."

"Dover!" Zee said.

"Sure. The monsters have been getting restless, and

this one settled here. I get to go kill it tonight! My first Hydra! Wish me luck!"

They obliged. Then, after taking some crackers and cheese from the kitchen, they headed for Charlotte's room. Zee poked his head into her closet. "Mine's the same way," he commented. "I've got the same shirt in every color of the rainbow." He closed the closet door and sat down on the floor. "At least one of the Prometheans is nice," he said, nodding in the direction of Hector's door.

Charlotte grunted. "He must be adopted. Anyway, I think he just felt sorry for us." Which made two of them.

"At least Mr. Metos defended us."

"Yeah, but if that's his attitude, he might as well be *babysitting*. After everything we've been through, you'd think he'd trust us."

"Well, what did you expect, Char? Remember, he thinks he's protecting us. That's the only reason he brought us here. We were kidding ourselves. We can't just expect adults to throw us at Zeus and say, 'Have at 'em,' can we?"

"No, but . . ." He had a point. How many times, exactly, was she going to let Mr. Metos disappoint her?

Zee was right. As much as she would like things to be different, no one was going to treat them like adults until they actually were (assuming they made it past their thirteenth year). It was strange; the only one who really gave them any credit at all was Philonecron, who seemed to think there was nothing strange at all about his mortal enemy being a thirteen-year-old girl.

It didn't matter. They didn't need Mr. Metos. They'd done everything else by themselves. All they had to do was figure out what the Prometheans knew. And if they had some kind of weapon that could be used on Zeus, well, Charlotte and Zee would find it and use it themselves.

Charlotte lowered her voice. "So, Prometheus's secret . . ."

Zee nodded, wide-eyed. "Yeah. It's the weapon, don't you think?"

"It's got to be. But what is it? None of the myths that I know of say anything about Prometheus having a weapon."

"I think we have to read more. I brought some of the books from the school library."

"You did?" Charlotte was impressed. Somehow it had never occurred to her that anything that came from school could be useful.

"Yeah. They're in my room. There's that play about Prometheus, and a couple other books. I'll take a look."

"Okay. We need to lie low anyway. Maybe we can read for a while, and sneak around when it's dark."

Zee agreed. He went out the door and came back in a few moments with a couple of thick books, then disappeared back into his own room while Charlotte started thumbing through them, trying to find some clues.

She read everything there was on Prometheus, but she didn't find out anything new, except more information about his power of prophecy. Prophecies played a big part in a lot of myths. Like in the story of Cronus, Zeus's father. He was a Titan, and he ruled the universe after overthrowing his own father. Cronus heard a prophecy that his son would overthrow him in turn, so whenever his wife had a baby, he swallowed it (gross). This went on for five babies, but finally, when Zeus was born, his mother hid him away and gave Cronus a rock wrapped in swaddling clothes to swallow instead (Cronus being, apparently, not very observant). Zeus was raised in a cave, and when he had grown up, his mother gave Cronus some herbs that made him vomit up his brothers and sisters, and together they overthrew their father. Then Zeus, Poseidon, and Hades divided up the world—Zeus getting the skies, Poseidon the sea, and Hades the Underworld—and thus began all of Charlotte's problems.

In later myths, a lot of prophecies were made

through the Oracle at Delphi. The Oracle told people things like they were going to kill their father and marry their mother, which led them to do all sorts of really complicated things to avoid killing their father and marrying their mother—things that ultimately resulted in them killing their father and marrying their mother.

It hadn't occurred to Charlotte until that moment that, like everything else, the prophecies were all real, the Oracle of Delphi was real. In other words, she could go to the Oracle and ask about her fate—meaning she had a fate. So if she had gone a year ago—which would have been rather silly, because she wouldn't have known it was real—the Oracle could have told her she would go down to the Underworld, she would face Philonecron, and she would narrowly escape his shadow army. It would have told her to stay away from the sea—but of course something would have happened and she would have found herself on the sea anyway, because it was fate, after all.

In the quiet of her room, Charlotte lay there, thinking of fate and all it might portend. Somewhere out there, someone knew what was going to happen to her. And whatever she did, whatever she chose, it wouldn't matter. Because it was her fate.

Charlotte felt suddenly very helpless. Nothing she did mattered at all—her future was already set down before her, waiting for her to dutifully follow along its path. And nothing she and Zee had done—rescuing the shadows, stopping Philonecron, saving the cruise ship—really meant anything, because they were destined to do it.

Sighing, she flipped through her book, looking at every reference to Prometheus, but could find nothing else significant. Her eyes began to droop. Her body felt strange and soft, her muscles ached, even her brain hurt, and it occurred to her that it was night. The words in front of her began to blur, and Charlotte gave in, setting the book aside and closing her eyes.

She was in near darkness, in a room lit only by the soft, eerie glow of the Dead that lined it. They had no faces, but she could feel their attention—unwavering, intense, almost pleading. Something had changed in the Underworld; it was not right. They needed her, they needed her to do something, they needed her to understand.

"What?" she said softly, her voice cracking. "Please, what can I do?"

Then—the Dead were gone, replaced by firelight. She was in the same cave room as before, the small fire in the middle, the drawings on the walls. She went over to look again—the blue man, something in his hand, something that seemed to flicker. She felt the presence of the Dead again, watching, waiting. The small, naked figures huddled, running in fright, starving—all pleading for something, someone to help them. Everyone was counting on her. Charlotte stared at the pictures one by one, following them from beginning to end, and suddenly she knew what she was seeing.

*That's right,* said a voice in her head. It was the girl. *Now do you know where this is?*

*No,* said Charlotte.

The girl let out an annoyed sigh. *Do I have to draw you a map?*

Jeez, Charlotte thought, some people are so sarcastic.

She sat up in bed as the sun streamed in her window. It could not be a coincidence. There was no way she just happened to keep having this dream—it was too vivid, too significant. She had to tell Zee.

She got out of bed and went to the door, opening it cautiously. There were loud voices coming from the kitchen, and a man was disappearing down the other end of the hallway. Looking carefully for signs of life (or at least of Timon), she crept to Zee's door and knocked softly, and soon she was sitting on his floor.

"It's probably nothing," she said, "but—I had a weird dream. And I keep having it."

A strange expression crossed Zee's face. "Char, what is it?" he asked.

"Well, I'm in a cave, and there's a girl, and—"

Zee closed his eyes for a moment and let out a long sigh. "Black hair, white dress, white ribbons, bit of attitude?"

Charlotte stopped. "You know her?"

"I've been having the same dream," he said flatly. "There's a cave, and a fire, and pictures on the wall—"

Charlotte swore. "I suppose it's entirely random that we're having the same dream," she grumbled. Why hadn't she mentioned it to Zee earlier? In a flash she remembered why the girl seemed so familiar to her—Zee had described her before. She had warned him about the cruise. Charlotte groaned again, awash in her own stupidity.

The cousins sat for a minute in silence, reflecting on what they had just learned.

"It can't be Philonecron sending it," Zee said after a time. "He's banished."

"No, I don't think it is," said Charlotte slowly. "But I think I know what it means. Have you looked at the pictures?"

Zee shook his head. "I can't really make them out. There's some people and a big blue guy, and"—he frowned, as if trying to call it up—"he's giving them something, isn't he? But I can't see it—"

"*Fire*, Zee," Charlotte said breathlessly. "He's giving them fire."

Zee gasped as it dawned on him. "Prometheus!"

Yes. On the cave wall the pictures were telling the story of Prometheus—first there was an image of him, the great blue man-like man, creating humans from clay; then one of a man starving, another freezing, and another being chased by a fierce animal; then Prometheus arguing with Zeus; then presenting fire to man; then man looking up into the heavens and seeing the gods.

"Why would someone want us to see that?" Zee asked.

The cousins stared at each other, waiting for inspiration that did not come. Zee shook his head, bewildered. "You saw the pictures better than I have," he said. "Was there anything unusual in there? Anything new?"

"I don't think so. It just seemed to tell the story. . . . There's something we're missing." Charlotte rubbed her eyes. "I think the girl would say we were being very stupid."

"Well, she needs to be a little more explicit, doesn't she?" Zee grumbled, leaning his head back so it hit the wall with a loud thunk.

Just then there was a commotion from the hallway. The cousins peeked out of the door to find Teodor and another Promethean carrying a stretcher down the hallway, heading for the infirmary. A young Promethean walked with them, holding up an IV that was attached to the person on the stretcher.

Charlotte and Zee stood in the doorway as they passed, and Charlotte's heart sank to see that on the stretcher was Hector, looking green and weak. As he passed, the young Promethean turned and gave a small wink. Charlotte exhaled.

The trio disappeared behind the door, and soon the other Prometheans had come out again. Charlotte and Zee exchanged a look, then went to the door and knocked on it.

*"Entrez!"*

They entered slowly, unsurely. Hector was lying flat on a hospital bed. When he saw them, he smiled.

"What happened?" Charlotte asked.

"Ah, the blasted thing stung me," he said, his speech slightly slurred. "It's all right."

Charlotte felt a wave of relief. All right was good.

An older man in scrubs poked his head out of a side room. "Out!" he commanded them.

The cousins nodded. The doctor disappeared behind the door, and Charlotte smiled at Hector. "I hope you feel better soon."

"Oh, I will," he said. He blinked. "Hey," he said, lowering his voice suddenly, "come here for a second." He began to fumble in his pocket for something. "Come visit

me later, all right? I want to hear all about Poseidon."
When Charlotte approached, he grabbed her hand and
looked at her intensely. "Listen," he said, his voice quiet.
"Don't do anything hazardous, all right?"

The doctor emerged, carrying a large syringe. He
glared at Charlotte and Zee. "Go!"

And they did.

"He didn't look so good," Zee whispered when they
got to the hallway. "I bet that was an antidote the doctor had. What was that at the end there?"

"He gave me something." Charlotte knew what the
cool object Hector had pressed into her hand was without looking at it. She opened up her hand and showed
it to her cousin.

A key.

"To what?"

"I don't know. But let's find out."

"Now?" Zee blinked. "I thought we were going to
wait to look around until nighttime."

"Ah, who cares. Anyway, it's Mr. Metos's job to keep
us out of the way, right? So really," she added brightly,
"if we're out wandering around, it's his fault, not ours.
They can't keep two teenagers locked in their rooms,
there are *laws*. Come on!"

## CHAPTER 16

### Behind Closed Doors

The hallway was empty, and most of the doors that lined it were shut. Charlotte tried the key Hector had slipped her in a couple of the locks, to no avail. They passed by one that was open a crack, so Charlotte peeked in to find a bedroom that looked very similar to hers. "I bet they're all like this," she said. "Come on, let's see what's on the other floors."

They headed up the stairs and opened the door off the stairwell to find themselves in an immense, extremely well-stocked gym.

One wall was lined with a long series of large weight

machines. In another section was some gymnastics equipment—a vault, rings, and parallel bars. There was a rock-climbing wall, and in front of that were some archery targets, next to which was a ten-foot-high dummy with javelins sticking out of him. Charlotte thought it was probably a good idea to avoid rock climbing during target practice.

In the far corner of the gym, a man in sweats wielded a sword and battled an unseen foe, wearing what seemed to be virtual reality glasses. He jumped, ducked, and even did a backflip before lunging forward, striking his nonexistent quarry.

"Brilliant," Zee breathed.

"As long as nobody makes me use it," Charlotte grumbled. She'd gone a long way to escape gym.

They closed the door and went up another flight to find themselves on another narrow, marble hallway lined with offices. The offices all looked similar—small, wood-paneled rooms filled with big desks, bookshelves along the walls, and computers. Charlotte popped into one, Zee standing guard. It was impeccably clean. The books (all in Greek) were all lined up perfectly on the bookshelves. The chair was pushed neatly against the desk, the trash was empty, the desktop was shining. Charlotte tapped the space bar on the computer, but nothing happened. It didn't seem like anyone had used the office for a while.

"Mr. Metos said everyone's in Greece," said Zee, clearly having the same thought.

Charlotte looked into the next office and caught a weird shape out of the corner of her eye. She turned to find the head of a Gorgon mounted above the fireplace, with a gleaming golden sword above that.

"Cool," she murmured.

The next room was much larger than the rest. One wall was lined with buzzing radio equipment, and another with GPS monitors like Charlotte had seen on her cruise ship. There was a giant control panel in the back of the room. In the center was a large glowing table, the size of a banquet table in a castle. The cousins peered at it to find the top was an enormous monitor with the entire Earth displayed. There were little blinking green dots all over the map, from Brazil to north Africa to eastern Europe to New York, but most scattered around the Mediterranean. There was a small concentration right in the center of London, and a much larger one off the southern tip of Greece. And then, as they studied the screen, that one suddenly disappeared.

"Huh." Charlotte shrugged, looking at Zee.

Zee shrugged back, then went over to the radio equipment and put on a pair of headphones. He listened, frowned, and shook his head. "Not English," he whispered to Charlotte.

They moved around the room, studying the various monitors, and then moved on.

Across the hallway was another series of glass windows that looked in on a dark, sterile-looking room. A man in a white hazard suit was leaning over a table on which a large spotlight shone. As the cousins watched, the man moved away from the table to reveal the disembodied head of a Cyclops, its one eye staring dully at the cousins.

"Ew," Charlotte whispered.

"Let's go," said Zee, grimacing.

Across the hall was a large glass-paneled room, this one brightly lit. The cousins peeked in to find Mr. Metos, Timon, and two other Prometheans sitting around a big table looking serious. The doctor from the infirmary was talking to them. Pulling quickly out of view, Charlotte leaned in as close as she could to the wall but could hear nothing. It was dead silent. She looked at Zee and shook her head.

"Soundproofed," she whispered.

"I'm sure they're not saying anything we'd want to hear," he muttered.

Charlotte was about to move on when she surveyed the group and noticed something. She whirled around and hissed to Zee, "They're all men!"

"Huh," Zee said, as if she had told him she really fancied some cabbage.

"Huh?" she repeated. "Huh? I say they're all men and all I get is *huh?*"

Zee blinked at her.

"Everyone we've met, they're all men! Women aren't any good for protecting humanity? They're just there to answer phones?"

"Well," Zee said, "maybe it's a bloodline thing. They're all descendants of Prometheus, right? So maybe it's carried along the male side, you know?"

Charlotte narrowed her eyes. Honestly.

Just then the stairwell door burst open and Teodor appeared, looking wild. He did not even seem to see the cousins as he pulled open the meeting room door and rushed in. There was some commotion as the door closed behind him, then all was quiet.

"Late for the meeting, I guess," Zee said. "Come on."

The topmost floor had just three doors. The cousins headed for the first one, only to pull back as soon as they looked inside the doorway. There was a man sitting in there with his back to the door, watching a bunch of TV screens, a steaming mug at his side.

Zee was ahead of Charlotte, so, pressing himself against the hallway wall, he looked into the room, then turned back and mouthed, "Security cameras." He looked back again and studied the monitors while

Charlotte waited. After a couple of minutes he looked back and motioned her forward. They snuck past the doorway, Charlotte wondering how the man with all the security monitors failed to notice the two kids spying on him.

"Were we on there?" Charlotte asked.

"No," Zee said, looking somewhat puzzled. "It's all the parking garage."

Charlotte frowned. "Maybe it rotates?"

"I thought so, but I kept watching and it didn't change. The parking garage and one bedroom somewhere."

"A bedroom?"

Zee shrugged. "Yeah, just somebody's room."

"Huh." She shrugged and looked around. They were in a small nook in front of a door that read STORAGE. Zee tried the doorknob, and it opened.

"I wonder what the Prometheans store," Charlotte said. "I mean, do they have, like, mops, or—"

She was interrupted by a loud intake of breath from Zee, who had stopped short in the doorway. Charlotte looked inside and gaped.

Before her was a vast room filled with weapons—spears, bows, swords, axes, a small trident, whips, shields, staffs. The cousins stared, wide-eyed.

"Want to invade any small countries?" Charlotte whispered.

"Yeah, in 300 B.C.," Zee responded. He had a point—they were a couple of chariots away from being perfectly prepared to make their run on Alexander the Great.

They moved into the room slowly, looking around in wonder. "I guess this is where Mr. Metos got the spear," Zee muttered. Charlotte couldn't help but wonder how exactly Mr. Metos got the spear from England—overnight shipping? And wasn't the delivery guy a little suspicious?

The cousins walked around the room, studying the bounty before them. Some of the objects seemed impossibly old, and Charlotte had distinct flashbacks to the Ancient Worlds exhibits on museum field trips in elementary school.

"Do you think one of these is Prometheus's weapon?" she whispered.

Zee shook his head. "I don't know." The cousins moved through the room, studying the weapons with no idea what they were looking for. There were so many different things, but none of them looked any more special than anything else. Chewing on her lip, Charlotte studied a wall of swords. She didn't know what she expected to find—a note taped to a battle-ax with the message, *Charlotte and Zee, it's this one!!!! Hugs!*

"It's hard to imagine they'd leave something like that out in the open like this," Zee said with a shrug.

"Maybe not," said Charlotte. "Anyway, even if it is in here, we're not going to find it unless we know what we're looking for." She picked up an arrow and examined it. The tail was a rich blue and teal and seemed to be made from peacock feathers. The head came to a point so sharp it almost hurt to look at. Unthinkingly, she touched it with her finger and let out a yelp. A pinprick of blood seeped out of her finger.

"Careful!" Zee gave her an are-you-crazy look, which Charlotte had to grant was fully deserved. "I wonder what these are for," he added, pointing to a glass cupboard. Inside were three very small, very sharp-looking daggers. Charlotte grimaced.

It wasn't just weapons in the room. On one shelf sat a small, glimmering harp with strings that looked like gossamer. Next to it was a pan flute made of reeds that looked as if it would break if you breathed on it. There was a glass jar filled with rotting, pointy teeth, each about the size of Charlotte's hand, and another with an apple made of gold.

Suddenly a string of curses came from Zee, accompanied by a very loud bang. He had pulled a small bronze shield engraved with the image of a Gorgon head off the shelf, and immediately it fell to the floor, dragging his arms with it.

"Heavy," he explained sheepishly.

Along one wall were some shelves filled with small vials of herbs, roots, flowers, liquids, and powders. Charlotte moved over to the shelves and looked at the contents carefully. "Wolfsbane, borage, eyebright, fennel," she said, reading the labels aloud. "flax—hey, my dad puts that on his cereal. Garlic, nightshade . . ." Each label had a drawing on it—some had a medical symbol, more than a few had a skull and crossbones, and some had illustrations of a part of the body. On one was a drawing of a head resting against two hands. POPPY AND AGRIMONY, the label announced.

"Hey, look," she said to Zee, who was tinkering with a bow. "This one makes you sleep. Maybe that's what he used on Maddy."

Putting down the bow, Zee came over and read the label, then shook his head slowly, muttering, "I just don't think you're supposed to go around giving middle schoolers poppy. Anything interesting?" he asked, motioning to the wall of herbs. She shook her head.

They looked around the room for a while more, hoping that some secret would reveal itself to them, until finally Zee whispered, "We should go. There's still another room."

"Well, at least we know where to go if we need to break out of this place," Charlotte said, motioning to the weapons.

The last door in the hallway led to a vast library, filled with books from top to bottom. It looked as if it had once been very well organized but someone had stopped trying—there were piles of books, scrolls, and maps on tables, in carrels, and on the floor. Charlotte walked around the shelves, studying. "They're in all kinds of languages," she told Zee, who was looking through one of the carrels. "English, French, Spanish, Greek, Arabic, and lots I don't recognize." She picked up a Spanish book and began flipping through it, wishing suddenly that she'd paid attention in class after the first week.

One section was devoted entirely to books on the Underworld. Picking one off the shelf, Charlotte flipped through the pages, frowning when she saw an illustration of Charon, the Ferryman of the Dead, staring back at her. He was much better dressed in the picture than in real life. She skimmed the page. "See," she said to Zee, "it doesn't say anything here about his love of Fruit Roll-Ups. That's the sort of thing we could teach these people."

"Perhaps you should make a note," Zee said. "I'm sure thePrometheans would like us writing in their books."

There was a whole section on different gods (*Persephone's Promise*), and another on monsters (*The Riddle of the Sphinx*), and a wall of books about herbs

(*The Gifts of Gaia*). And then Charlotte found herself in front of a large section with books on Prometheus. She motioned to Zee, her eyes skimming the spines. It was too much to hope that there was a *Prometheus's Weapon for Dummies*, she mused—but then she noticed something that made her stop: On one of the spines was an illustration that looked very familiar.

"Zee!" she whispered, taking down the book and handing it to him. "Notice anything?"

He looked at the book and gasped. "That's the cave painting!"

The cousins stared at each other. On the spine of the book and again on the cover was an exact replica of the symbol of Prometheus holding a torch from their dream, above the title: *La légende de la flamme de Prométhée.*

"It's in French," Charlotte said. She might not know any French, but she was also not an idiot, and the words were easy enough to read. "Does that mean . . . ?"

Zee nodded slowly. "What it looks like," he whispered. "*The Legend of the Flame of* . . . I assume that's Prometheus . . ."

Zee trailed off, as the cousins exchanged a momentous glance. "The Flame of Prometheus," Charlotte repeated. "Prometheus's fire . . ."

Zee opened the book and began concentrating hard

on the page before him while Charlotte looked on, her heart racing. "I think . . . it's the fire that Prometheus gave to humans, the actual Flame," he said. "There's a legend that Prometheus hid it somewhere, that it's still going, and this book is about someone's attempt to find it."

"Did he?" Charlotte breathed.

"Um," Zee said, flipping to the back of the book while Charlotte waited, listening for approaching steps. "No. He says it's just a legend; it doesn't exist."

Charlotte closed her eyes. She was so close to understanding everything; the truth was right in front of her, if only she could see it. She called up the image of the cave wall from her dream, the story of Prometheus told in pictures, unfolding under the flickering firelight—

She gasped. "Zee," she said, "what if it does exist? What if what the girl is showing us isn't the cave paintings at all? What if it's the fire?"

A chill passed over Charlotte. She was right, she just knew it. The whole dream hadn't been about finding those paintings at all—it was about discovering the fire.

Zee had bowed his head again and returned to the book, brow knotted in concentration. "It says the fire of Prometheus would give humans knowledge of the gods again," he said, translating slowly. He stopped reading and looked up at Charlotte as the import of what he had read sank in.

"That's the weapon," she whispered, her voice thick with excitement. "That's Prometheus's secret. The Prometheans must have found it. And they're going to use it."

Silence while the cousins took this in. Charlotte could not believe it—what would happen if everyone knew about the gods again? Well, it was clear, wasn't it? They'd know them for who they were: criminally irresponsible toward the living and the dead at best, murderous at worst. There were so many humans now, led by the Prometheans, that they'd put up a good fight. They'd have a chance at least, unlike now.

Still, something was nudging at her, some inkling of doubt. There was something wrong, something she was missing.

"Do you remember what Mr. Metos said when he told us about the weapon?" she said, speaking slowly, thinking aloud. "He said they had something that would give them *power* over Zeus. What if they're not planning on using it at all? What if they're planning on, like, holding it over Zeus or something?"

Zee frowned. "How could they do that?"

All this thinking was making Charlotte's brain hurt. What did the Prometheans want? Mr. Metos had said that their mission was to protect humanity from the gods—did that mean they would overthrow them if they got the chance? Or something else? What would they do with power over Zeus?

"We should ask Mr. Metos. Tell him we know what the weapon is. Get him to tell us what they're going to do with it. And if they're not going to use it, well"—she took a deep breath—"we will."

As she said the words, she was hit with the weight of them, and she felt something shift inside of her. For so long they had been passive, reacting to events, waiting for the next step in their story to unfold. They had had all the will in the world, but no ability to act, no knowledge about how to proceed. Until now. They'd wanted something to fight with. Well, now they knew what it was. Not the Flame, but all of humanity, by their side.

At that moment they heard a loud yell coming from the hallway. Charlotte peeked out of the door to see Timon in the doorway of the room with the security console, talking seriously to the man inside.

"We better go," she whispered.

But just then Mr. Metos emerged from the stairwell. There was a very odd expression on his face. Charlotte ducked her head back. Now was not the time to get kicked out—not when they were so close to the truth.

"Come on," Zee whispered. "There's an emergency exit at the end of the hallway."

Softly the cousins crept out of the library and ducked around the corner. Charlotte grabbed the emergency exit door, and they slipped inside the stairwell.

"Let's get back to our rooms," Zee said. "We can pretend we were sleeping or something."

Charlotte nodded, and they hurried down the two flights of stairs to the floor with the residences. But when Zee pushed on the door, it wouldn't open.

"Locked," he mouthed to Charlotte, whose heart sank.

"I don't suppose . . ." She got out Hector's key and tried to put it in the doorknob, but it didn't even come close to fitting.

It didn't seem likely that any of the other doors were unlocked, and when they went up to the office level they had no better luck. They ran back down the stairs, trying each door as they passed it. And then finally, at the very bottom, one opened.

"This should either lead outside," Zee said, "or . . ."

He didn't need to finish. They emerged into the parking lot underneath the building, the exit door closing behind them with some finality. Charlotte whirled around and tried the knob, but it wouldn't open.

"Great," she said.

Zee exhaled heavily. "There must be a way back in," he muttered.

"Yeah, because the reason they leave everything unlocked up there is so people can wander in whenever they feel like it," Charlotte muttered.

"You know, you're awfully sarcastic sometimes," Zee said.

Sighing, Charlotte banged her head against the wall. "I suppose they'll come looking for us."

"I suppose they will," Zee said darkly, pointing at a security camera on the wall above them. The camera was moving slowly back and forth.

Charlotte swore. "Think it saw us?"

"I'm not sure," Zee said. "I think we can duck under it, though. Come on."

Charlotte, feeling altogether like an idiot, bent down and moved underneath the camera's gaze, toward the alcove that held the elevator.

"I guess we could go up to the lobby," Zee said, "and see if there's a way in. . . ."

Just then they heard a pinging sound from the elevator, and the door began to open slowly. Zee grabbed Charlotte and they ducked out of the alcove and pressed up against the wall outside the elevator lobby, next to the door marked HAZARDOUS MATERIALS.

It was not a very good hiding place, given that whoever had come out of the elevator was about to come upon them. Charlotte eyed the fleet of cars, looking for one to hide behind, and Zee went up to the door and tried the knob. "I guess they locked up the hazardous stuff," he mumbled.

A man in a business suit—too blond to be a Promethean—emerged from the elevator alcove and strode across the parking lot. A look of relief passed over Zee's face. But Charlotte had completely forgotten the danger.

"*Zee,*" she whispered, her voice full of portent. "Hector said, 'Don't do anything *hazardous.*' It was a clue." Zee blinked at her. "Do you know what's hazardous?" she continued, nodding toward the door. "*Fire!*"

Zee's eyes widened. Breathlessly Charlotte slipped him the key. Zee took it and tried it in the door.

The door opened.

The cousins looked at each other. "Thank you, Hector," Charlotte whispered under her breath. How much trouble was he going to get in for this? Why had he done it?

But when they entered the room, Charlotte's heart sank. There was no Flame at all in the room, just a boiler and some equipment and shelves and shelves of chemicals that were probably hazardous.

"I don't get it," Charlotte said.

Zee began to walk around the room, looking closely at the objects on the shelves. "There must be . . ." he murmured. And then he stopped and turned to his cousin. "Look!" he said, pointing at the wall behind him.

There was a door cut into the back wall, barely noticeable in the dark of the room. Zee grabbed for the knob, shook his head, and motioned to Charlotte for the key. The door opened and she followed him in, heart racing.

There was no fire in the room. And no hazardous materials. What there was was a bed, a sink, a chair, another doorway, and, sitting on the chair looking surprised, a teenage boy.

The cousins gaped. The boy gaped back.

"Who are you?" Charlotte finally asked.

"I'm Steve!" he said, as if it should be apparent. "Who are you?"

"Um," Charlotte said. "I'm Charlotte, and this is Zee."

The boy blinked. "Did they kidnap you, too?"

## CHAPTER 17

### Steve

Quite a number of odd things had happened to Charlotte and Zee over the past few months, but none surprised them quite as much as going through a door in the Prometheans' parking garage and finding a boy named Steve living there. As he gazed up at them with some combination of confusion and hope, Charlotte and Zee could only gape and stammer.

"Uh . . . kidnap?" Charlotte repeated dumbly. She stared at the boy. He was skinny and pale, with wide-set brown eyes and a thick head of curly black hair.

The boy frowned. "Are they holding you, too? Are we all going to live in here? Aw, *jeez*."

"Holding you? Who's holding you?"

"I don't know! They didn't, like, introduce themselves. Tall guys, dark-haired, surly, you know . . ."

"The Prometheans?" Charlotte asked incredulously.

"Who?"

Charlotte rubbed her forehead. "What do you mean, they're holding you here? You're staying here for a while? They're keeping you safe?"

"Yeah, they're keeping me safe," he said, his voice dripping with sarcasm. He lifted up his hands, and for the first time Charlotte noticed a slender chain linking his wrists to the floor. "I'm *real* safe here. Look, do you guys know a way out, or what? Do you have any idea how worried my mom must be?"

Zee spoke for the first time. "They're holding you *prisoner*?" he asked. "Do you know why?"

"No, they didn't exactly sit down and explain why they were kidnapping me." Steve was eyeing them like he had real concern for their obvious mental problems. "I went to sleep in my bed one night, next thing I know I wake up here."

Charlotte had never been so confused in her whole life. Was this boy evil somehow? He didn't seem evil—a little touchy, maybe—but that didn't mean anything.

Boys, in her recent experience, were all either she-vampires in disguise or pretending to like you just so you would help them turn their sea-god dads into toads. "Do you know anything about the Greek gods?" she asked.

The boy now obviously thought she was completely crazy. "Huh? The Greek gods? Like Hercules and stuff? Can we talk about this another time, maybe?"

"You don't have any idea why you're here," Zee said, his eyes narrowed. He didn't seem to believe him either.

"No!" The boy sighed, resigned to their stupidity. "I heard them say something about me being somebody's son, but my mom is a schoolteacher. She's never done anything wrong in her life!"

"I don't think that's it," Zee whispered, eyeing Charlotte, who had frozen at the boy's words.

*Somebody's son,* he'd said. Could this be Mr. Metos's secret son? And if so, why in the world was he locked behind the storage closet? Wasn't that taking secrecy a little far? He wasn't the most pleasant guy in the world, but still . . .

"What about your dad?" asked Charlotte carefully.

The boy's face darkened. "I don't have a dad," he said, crossing his arms sulkily—or trying to. The chains pulled back on his arms, and Steve let out a gargled scream, so loud that Charlotte jumped. "Can you get me out of these things?!"

"I—" Charlotte didn't know what she was about to say, but it didn't matter, for as soon as she started to speak there came the sound of footsteps pounding down a staircase, then the door in the back of the room flew open and Timon and the man from the security room burst through. Charlotte looked up and noticed a small camera in the corner of the room. *It's all the parking garage,* Zee had said. *And one bedroom . . .*

"What are you doing in here?" Timon yelled, his face looking murderous. Charlotte's stomach turned, and she found herself taking a step backward.

"We—," Charlotte started as Zee looked at her helplessly. "We were looking around, and—"

"How did you get in here? How? Have you been spying on us? Did someone send you? Who are you working for?" He took a great step forward and seemed suddenly to be the biggest person Charlotte had ever seen. She took another step back as the other man grabbed his arm. "Timon, they're just chil—"

The Promethean turned on his colleague. "Then how did they get in, Alec? Huh?" He looked back at Charlotte and Zee, his voice cutting into them. "What do you know and how do you know it?"

Timon was almost trembling with the force of his

own anger, and the very furniture in the room seemed to cower in his presence.

"Why don't you let Metos talk to them," the other man whispered, grabbing his arm again, more gently this time, as if to transfer calm to him. "He'll sort it out. Come on, you're upset. We're all upset. This isn't the time. . . ."

There was a moment of tense silence as Timon stopped and glared around the room. Meanwhile, the air around him hummed ominously. Charlotte half realized she was not breathing, but it hardly mattered if Timon was going to kill her anyway. Then, with almost a snarl, he backed off. "Fine," he spat, still looking murderous. "Metos can deal with them."

A few minutes later Charlotte and Zee were sitting in stunned silence in Zee's room, Charlotte's arm still aching from Timon's grasp.

"Are you all right?" Zee asked finally.

Charlotte nodded slowly. "That guy and Poseidon could be in the same anger management class," she muttered. She exhaled loudly; it was difficult to shake off the echoes of Timon's rage, but there were pressing matters before them.

She did not know what to think. The Prometheans wouldn't lock up a teenage boy in a basement without a very good reason, and it was certainly possible that he was not a teenage boy at all. He could have assumed that guise just to get their sympathy. But if he were a shape-shifter, you'd think chains wouldn't be that effective....

"Zee, why would they be keeping a boy? Is that Mr. Metos's son?"

Zee frowned. "Mr. Metos is pretty socially malformed, but I don't think even he would lock his own son up in the basement."

Charlotte pressed her lips together in thought. "But maybe he's evil. Or dangerous," she said. "I don't know how, but . . . Maybe there's a prophecy about him, or—"

Suddenly the expression on Zee's face changed. "A prophecy . . . ?" he repeated slowly.

"Yeah, maybe he has some kind of destiny, or . . ."

But Zee wasn't listening. He had gotten up and gone over to his bag, where he pulled out a library book and handed it to Charlotte.

"Read this," he said, his voice thick with import.

"What is this?"

"This is that play about Prometheus."

"A play? But—"

"Char," he said firmly, "read it."

Zee looked as excited as Charlotte had ever seen him. She opened up the book and started to read. "Zee, this doesn't make any sense. Why don't you just tell me—"

"Yes, it does," he said impatiently.

With an annoyed glance at her cousin, she began to skim through the play. It started with Hephaestus nailing Prometheus to the cliff wall and going on and on about how much he didn't want to do it. Then Prometheus went on and on about everything that had happened to him, and some other people went on and on about some other things. It was not a very good play.

"Zee, we know all of this!"

Exhaling impatiently, Zee grabbed the book. "You remember that Prometheus has the power of prophecy, right?"

"Yeah, Mr. Metos said—"

"Well"—Zee flipped through the book and settled on a page—"start reading here."

Charlotte glared at her cousin. She needed to remember to be equally annoying to him someday. "They're talking about the downfall of Zeus. . . ."

"Right. *And* . . ."

"And . . ." Charlotte skimmed along, wondering when Zee had developed such a sense of drama. And then suddenly her heart began to beat more quickly. Prometheus was saying that he knew how Zeus would be overthrown; he would marry a woman who would "vex him sore," the Titan prophesied. Charlotte's breath caught as she read the words that followed:

**She will bear to him a child,**

**And he shall be in might more excellent**

**Than his progenitor.**

With her heart fluttering, she read the passage again, then looked up at Zee and asked breathlessly, "Does this mean . . . ?"

"A son!" Zee proclaimed, eyes burning. "Zeus will be overthrown by his son, and Prometheus knows who he is."

The son who will overthrow Zeus. Zeus was destined to be overthrown by his son, just as he had overthrown Cronus and just as Cronus had overthrown Uranus. And—

"The 'secret son' isn't Mr. Metos's son, Charlotte," whispered Zee. "He's Zeus's."

"You don't think that boy is . . . Zeus's son?" Charlotte said slowly, barely able to believe the words that were coming out of her mouth. "The son of Zeus is named Steve?"

"This is Zeus, Char. You know what he's like with mortal women."

The son of Zeus. The heir of Zeus, destined to over-throw his father. In the myths, it was the only thing that had scared the god of gods. There was a prophecy that any son born to his first wife, Metis, would overthrow him, so he ate her. (Why these guys were always trying to get rid of their heir problems by eating people was beyond Charlotte.) He was about to marry another god-dess, but there was a prophecy that any son she bore would be greater than his father, so he married her off to a mortal. But other than that, the son thing just hadn't come up—at least, Charlotte thought it hadn't. . . .

Before they could say anything else, the door to Zee's room flew open and Mr. Metos came striding through, his face flushed, his eyes darkened. He slammed the door behind him. Charlotte's stomach flipped.

"What were you doing?" Mr. Metos gargled. She had never seen him so agitated. "Do you have any idea what you just did? Do you want to be set loose on the streets for anyone to attack you, is that it? And how on earth did you—"

Charlotte tossed her hair. "So you've found Zeus's son, huh?"

"What—How—?" He looked back and forth between them, utterly bewildered.

Until that moment, Charlotte had not been sure—it seemed so strange, so impossible. But there could be no doubt anymore; Mr. Metos's reaction had confirmed it.

"He is!" Charlotte exclaimed. "He's the son of Zeus, and he's going to overthrow his father."

Mr. Metos's mouth hung open slightly. He began to say something and then stopped. "How do you know this?" he asked slowly.

"We just do, Mr. Metos," Charlotte said, folding her arms. "We're very clever, you know."

"Listen to me," he said, his voice suddenly urgent. "You must not let on that you know. Do you have any idea—"

"Right, we know, Timon will feed us to a Hydra," Charlotte interrupted. "What are you going to do with him?"

Shaking his head and looking into an empty corner of the room, Mr. Metos said, "I can't tell you that."

"He's the weapon! You're going to use him as a weapon!"

"You want him to overthrow Zeus?" Zee interjected. "But why not just wait until he does? Why are you holding him hostage?"

Charlotte looked at her cousin. He was right; it didn't make any sense. If it was this Steve-person's destiny to overthrow Zeus, why not just let him? It was just like the mystery of the Flame, it didn't make sense, unless—

*Something that gives us power over Zeus.*

"You're going to use him as a bargaining chip, aren't you?" The words exploded out of Charlotte's mouth. "You're going to turn him over to Zeus to get what you want!" Next to her, Zee gasped. Even as the words came out of her mouth, Charlotte was horrified by them. "You're holding a boy prisoner and you're going to give him to Zeus! You can't do that. He'll kill him! Mr. Metos, he's a teenager!"

The expression on Mr. Metos's face traveled somewhere from shock to resignation. He sighed heavily and turned his face back to them.

"Sometimes sacrifices have to be made," he said, his voice now very quiet. "I told you that."

"But . . . that was *us* sacrificing. Not sacrificing somebody else. Anyway, what are you going to do? Give him to Zeus and ask him, pretty please, to be nicer? You think you can take him at his *word*?"

"Yes," Mr. Metos said. "If we ask Zeus, or any god, to make an oath on the River Styx, the oath is binding. It cannot be broken." He exhaled. "If you had the chance to sacrifice one person to save everyone else, what would you do? Like it or not, this boy is what Zeus fears most in the world. With him, we are extraordinarily powerful. Without him, we are"—he blinked—"nothing."

"But," Charlotte protested, "what about the Flame?"

"The what?"

"The Flame of Prometheus."

Once again Mr. Metos looked genuinely shocked. "How do you—" He stopped himself, exhaling. "The Promethean Flame is a myth. It does not exist."

Charlotte looked at Zee out of the corner of her eye. The Promethean Flame did exist, she was sure of it. Why else would they be having the dreams? For once, they knew more than Mr. Metos did.

"Why not just let him overthrow Zeus?" Zee repeated.

"We have no desire to replace the rule of one god with another. We are trying to secure the fate of humanity. Better to control the god we know rather than allow the rule of one we don't."

"But . . . is he even a god?" Charlotte asked. "His mother is a mortal, right?"

Mr. Metos frowned. "We don't know."

Zee exploded. "You don't know? You don't *know*? You're going to hand him over to Zeus and you don't even know if he's Immortal? You're just as bad as the gods! Treating people like pawns!"

Mr. Metos almost flinched at Zee's words. Charlotte had never seen him like this. He seemed to go back and forth from extreme agitation to something approaching blankness.

"What does it matter what you do?" she asked. "It's a prophecy, right? This boy . . . Steve . . . is going to overthrow Zeus."

"Do not take prophecies so seriously," he murmured. "The gods believe in them, in fate, in destiny, because they do not want to think that humans have wills of their own, have the power of choice. But when Prometheus gave us knowledge, that gave us choice. It gave us what makes us essentially human, and independent from the gods."

"Then why—"

"Because *Zeus* believes it! He believes in prophecy and always has. He believes that there is order to the universe. He needs to believe it. Because if there is not fate, if humans have choice, he has no control over them, and then what kind of a god is he?"

"So humans have choice, and you're *choosing* to sacrifice this boy," Charlotte said, her voice dripping with scorn.

"I'm sorry you're upset." Mr. Metos paused. "Know that this is something . . . we're not taking lightly. We have an opportunity to change the world, to ensure the very survival of the race—"

These last words distracted Charlotte from her anger. "What do you mean?"

Mr. Metos stiffened. "I am saying that it is worth a

great deal to have some power over Zeus. Worth, even, the sacrifice of one person."

"That's funny," Charlotte sniped, "because I thought it was people you were sworn to protect."

After his outburst, Zee had been sitting in silence, staring at Mr. Metos, but as Charlotte's words hung in the air, he opened his mouth to speak. "What if it were us?" he asked quietly.

"What?"

"What if you had to sacrifice us? To save humanity. What if Zeus said, 'Fine, I'll do whatever you want, just hand me Charlotte and Zachary.' Would you?"

For the third time that day, Mr. Metos looked taken aback. He regarded Zee for a few moments, trying to formulate an answer. He opened his mouth but nothing came out.

"I guess that's our answer," Zee muttered.

Mr. Metos let out a long exhale and shook his head slowly. His posture sank and his eyes fixed on a spot on the ground. "Listen," he said, his voice quiet and flat. "There is something I must tell you. I was looking for you earlier. I am needed in Greece, and I will be going soon. I want to stay here with you, but—you see, I am needed."

Charlotte felt another flare of anger. Wasn't Mr. Metos needed to keep them out of the way so he could give innocent boys to Zeus to be murdered?

"I think you should know," he continued, his voice completely devoid of affect, "our satellite office there was destroyed."

Charlotte froze, everything in her growing numb all of a sudden. She stared at Mr. Metos. The office was destroyed—just the office, right? No one was hurt, right? But his expression told her the terrible truth. He was gray, his eyes dark, his whole manner like someone who had lost everything he knew.

*"What?"* Zee whispered, his face white.

"Yes, I'm afraid the building was caught in the crosshairs of a godly spat. It was an accident. Our losses were . . . great." Mr. Metos straightened, and his tone grew businesslike. "I will be going, and several others. A few are staying—some junior Prometheans, Teodor, Timon, Alec."

"And Hector," Charlotte added softly. Hector was in the infirmary; they would not send him yet.

Mr. Metos gazed at her, blinking. "Charlotte, I'm sorry. Hector . . . did not survive his injuries."

A wave of horror smashed into Charlotte, knocking the wind out of her. She opened her mouth, but there was no air.

"What?" Zee said. "He said he was all right."

"He would have said that. Hydra poison is insidious,

I'm afraid. He knew that. There was never much chance," Mr. Metos said. His face was completely devoid of emotion. "It's a dangerous business."

No, no. Hector, who had been kind to them. Who was going to face his first Hydra. Who probably wouldn't have been sent had most of the Prometheans not been in Greece, fighting the chaos the cousins had helped create. Hector, floating toward some nondescript door somewhere in London, headed for an eternity of nothingness. Or worse.

"He knew what he was getting into," Mr. Metos continued. "They all did. This is our charge. I know it must seem hard, and cruel. But Steve is all we have now. I hope you can understand someday."

A wave of hatred flew up in Charlotte, and she could feel it manifest in her face. A dangerous business . . . he knew what he was getting into . . . I hope you can understand someday. The world was falling apart, and all he could give them were platitudes. Mr. Metos was dedicated to saving humanity and at this moment seemed barely human.

After that, there was really nothing left to say. His voice quiet and resigned, Mr. Metos gave them another warning about letting on what they knew, and about staying out of trouble, because he could not protect them anymore. Charlotte and Zee did not say anything, merely sat in silence as the world changed for them, yet again, and they made themselves, yet again, adjust.

Charlotte felt tears spilling down her cheeks. There was too much, right now. So many Prometheans, gone. It was too much. And Hector . . .

Time moved, but the cousins did not; they just sat thinking of life and what came after. Finally Zee said quietly, "Hector wanted us to find Steve, to help him. He knew he was going to die, and he wanted Steve to be saved." He closed his eyes, then looked at Charlotte. "Listen. You heard Mr. Metos. Steve is all they have now. Charlotte, they're going to give him up to Zeus. Soon. That means—"

Charlotte finished Zee's thought. "We have to help him escape."

# CHAPTER 18

## The Great Escape

Timon had agreed not to throw them out on two conditions—that they stayed in their rooms, and that he could place a guard outside their doors. Timon was apparently very big on imprisoning kids. The best thing to do, Charlotte and Zee decided, would be to lie low for a couple of days. They did not want to risk trouble, because they could not leave—not without Steve. The Prometheans were going to bring him to his death, but what was the point of protecting humanity if you'd forgotten everything it was to be human?

Their guard, a young Promethean named Leo, sat in

the hallway outside their rooms, reading. And whenever Charlotte or Zee needed to go to the kitchen or to the other's room, they had to knock on their door and Leo would unlock it and let them out.

Sometimes they saw one or another of the Prometheans in the kitchen, and they all seemed to have the same expression on their faces—shock and resignation. Every time Charlotte felt sorry for them, she thought of what they were prepared to do. She had thought they were so noble, fighting the good fight.

They did not see Mr. Metos, and Charlotte could not help but wonder if he was avoiding them, or if he'd already left. She didn't really mind; whenever she thought about him, her throat tightened and her stomach began to burn.

And then there was Hector. The door to his office was closed, locked. Was he across the Styx now? Was he fading already, or was there still some Hector left?

They spent their time in near silence, Charlotte sitting on the bed while Zee worked on translating the book about the Promethean Flame. But it was not going well—it took him hours just to do a few pages, and there were lots of blanks for words he did not know. The book, so far, was not that illuminating—it was the story of the author's quest for the Flame, and he seemed more interested in the details of his journey than anyone really should be. So the first chapter was all about the things he was packing. And on the second afternoon of their confinement, Zee was sitting on the floor, working, when he swore and slammed the book shut.

"This is rubbish! This stupid git is telling me what he had for breakfast. Who gives a—"

"Maybe you should skip ahead?"

"I don't know why I'm bothering. We know he doesn't find it. All this book will tell us is where *not* to look."

"Well, that's more than we know now."

"Right," Zee grumbled. "Whoever this dream-girl is, she sure is stingy with her information." He sighed and began to flip through the book aimlessly. "I mean—"

And then he stopped, sucking in his breath.

"Char, look!"

With round eyes, he handed her the book. Charlotte looked down. On the page was a sketched-out map. Frowning, she studied it carefully. There was an ocean, a town, some mountains with a kind of structure on them—

She gasped. "The map!"

Charlotte had forgotten all about the map Zee had gotten in the mail, but it was of a place much like this one. He went rummaging through his backpack, then pulled out the scroll triumphantly. "Here!"

They looked at the two side by side. There was no

question; it was the same landscape. Suddenly Charlotte remembered something.

"The last time I had the dream," she said, "the girl said, 'Do I have to draw you a map?'"

Zee's face darkened. "I'm beginning to really dislike her," he said, his eyes scanning the page next to the map. Then he stopped, pointing to one word.

Charlotte frowned. *"Delphes?"*

"It's pronounced 'Delf,'" Zee said. "Delphi. The map is of Delphi, Char."

She blinked, letting this sink in. "Well, how in Hades are we going to get there?"

At that moment they were interrupted by Leo's voice echoing through the hallway.

"You're ready to go?"

Another man said something inaudible.

"I can come to the meeting, right?" Leo asked.

The other man said something in reply. His voice was growing closer, but they still couldn't make out his words.

"Oh, come on!" exclaimed Leo. "I don't want to miss this!"

"I'm sorry," the other man said, his voice now audible. "Timon says—"

"Why doesn't Timon come down here and play nursemaid for a while—"

"Shh."

"Oh, who cares if they hear? They're not going any-where. Today's the day, right?"

Charlotte looked at her cousin, who nodded slowly. It was time to act.

*"Ahhhhhhhhhhhhhhhhhhhh!"*

Charlotte let out the highest-pitched scream she possibly could. Within moments, the lock was turn-ing and Leo had burst through the door. Zee, who had poised himself next to the doorway, whirled around and slammed a thick book on his head.

Time seemed to stop along with Leo. Charlotte froze, unable to move. The Promethean's hands flew to his head, and he yelled, "What the—!"

The cousins exchanged a panicked glance. He was supposed to pass out. Why didn't he pass out?

Zee grimaced and, his face contorting, squeaked, "Sorry, mate!" and slammed the book into his head again, while Charlotte darted out of the room.

"The keys are in the lock," she called as the Promethean fell to his knees from the blow, his head in his hands. He started swearing loudly, and, looking quite unhappy, Zee pushed him, grabbed his backpack, and ducked out of the door.

"He was supposed to get knocked out!" he com-plained, locking the door and pocketing the keys.

"It works in the movies! Hey, he deserved it. Look what they're about to do."

Zee just shook his head. "That was horrid."

They ran into Charlotte's room, and she hastily threw some clothes into her backpack.

They could hear Leo yelling next door. How long would it be before somebody heard him? The cousins hurried out of Charlotte's room and ran up the two flights of stairs to the top floor.

Creeping past the security room where Alec still sat in his spot, drinking from his mug, they hurried into the weapons room. This time the door was locked—convenient, then, that they had Leo's keys. Charlotte tried three before the door gave way.

While Zee looked over the weapons, she went to the wall of herbs, hastily grabbed the jar of sleeping potion, and poured some of the powder into one of the little envelopes that sat on the shelves.

"Ready?" she asked Zee. He was holding a large silver sword and, standing there in his jeans and T-shirt, looked like the hero in one of those stories where a modern boy falls through time and ends up in the fourteenth century, where he has to fight to save the princess and maybe the town.

"What?" Zee said, catching her look. "Fencing was compulsory in sixth year!"

Dropping off the bags and weaponry in the hall, the cousins headed for the security room. Charlotte tossed her hair and knocked on the door frame.

Alec turned around in his seat, and when he saw them, his eyes widened. "Aren't you confined to your room?"

"Yeah," Charlotte said, shrugging. "We were getting pretty bored, so Leo took us to the library."

"Oh," said Alec. "I don't blame you." He had the same numb expression on his face as the rest of them, and Charlotte felt a wave of guilt for what she was about to do.

"Anyway," she said, taking a step into the room, "we wanted to thank you. For the other day. I don't know what Timon would have done if you hadn't been there."

Alec nodded. "I'm not sure either."

Charlotte's eyes traveled to the security monitors. She could see Steve sitting on his bed, flipping through a book. Next to her, Zee had moved toward the desk and was now leaning on it casually.

"So where is everyone?" she asked, eyes full of innocence.

"Oh, some meeting," Alec said, taking a sip of his coffee.

"Don't you get to go?" Alec didn't look any older than Leo—or Hector.

"Nah," he said, putting the cup down. "They fill me in."

"Uh-huh," said Charlotte. "And—" She looked up toward the monitors and said, "Oh!" her face contorting in surprise.

"What?" said Alec, turning quickly to the monitors. Charlotte could sense Zee fidgeting next to him.

"Oh, nothing!" she said. "Sorry, I just didn't realize what you were looking at." Zee nodded at her very slightly.

Alec frowned. "Oh," he said.

"Anyway, Leo's waiting for us in the library. Come on, Zee!"

As soon as they were out of the room, the cousins ducked around the corner, pressed themselves against the wall a few feet from the room, and waited. And waited. And waited.

Zee turned to her. "You got the right stuff, right?"

Charlotte pursed her lips. Now that she thought about it, she wasn't absolutely, positively, 100 percent sure she'd grabbed the right bottle. She'd been in a hurry and hadn't been careful. "Oh, sure!" she said brightly.

There is very little in the world more exasperating than an adult with a cup of coffee. You're waiting to go somewhere, and they've got half a cup left, and they tell you they just want to finish drinking. And then they sit. And sit. And sit. And every once in a great while they lift the mug to their mouths and take the teeniest, tiniest sip, and then set it down again, ready to sit some more.

Charlotte was not entirely sure they would even be able to hear any sign that the powder had worked—they were waiting for a clunking sound, like a head hitting the desk, or the sound of someone falling out of a chair—but what they heard, finally, was something else entirely.

It began as a slight groaning sound. Then, there was a distinct troll-like grunt. Then the sound of a chair being pushed back hurriedly, then a retching, then a giant splash.

A distinctly green Alec burst out of the room, his hand over his mouth. Charlotte's stomach flipped, but he had no eyes for them—he turned the other way and stumbled down the hallway, disappearing behind a door. The sound of retching came echoing toward them.

"Maybe I didn't get the right powder," Charlotte murmured.

"Come on," Zee said grimly.

Grabbing their things, they went to the emergency exit stairs and rushed down the five flights to the basement.

There was no time. How long would it be before the meeting ended? Before someone found Leo? Before Alec recovered and returned to his post?

They hurried to the HAZARDOUS MATERIALS door and unlocked it with Hector's key, then went through the boiler room and into the other door. There was Steve, sitting on the bed, flipping through some British fashion magazine. When he heard the door open, he looked up and beheld the cousins with their full backpacks, Zee holding the sword. His eyes popped.

"Are you going to kill me with that?" He didn't look scared as much as skeptical.

"No!" Charlotte said. "We're going to rescue you!"

The boy frowned and looked behind the cousins to see if they'd brought anyone else with them.

Zee had moved next to Steve and started pulling on the chain that attached him to the floor. Nothing happened. Biting his lip, he wrapped the chain around the sword blade and heaved up on the handle, using the sword as a lever. With a mighty grunt he pulled against the bolt holding the chain to the floor. The sword bent, there was a great cracking sound, and the chain came out of the concrete, bolt and all. Zee tumbled backward, and the boy blinked rapidly.

"There!" Charlotte proclaimed. "You're free!"

"Free?" Steve said. The boy took a few steps, the

chain dragging loudly behind him. He looked at it. "Does this look free to you?"

Charlotte folded her arms. "You want us to put that back in the ground?"

"Char," Zee said warningly, glancing pointedly at the security camera in the corner.

"We've got to move," she said. "We don't have much time!"

"Move?" Steve asked blankly. "How do you expect me . . ." He raised his wrists.

"Wrap it around your arms," Charlotte snapped. "Come on, let's go!"

As Zee wrapped the chain loosely three times around the boy's arms, Charlotte ran through the boiler room, glanced out the door, and surveyed the parking lot.

There was no one there. The car exit was across the garage, and a few feet away was a door that Charlotte dearly hoped was a pedestrian exit. With a nervous glance toward the stairwell door, Charlotte ran back and motioned the boys forward.

"Hurry, hurry. Shh . . ."

Zee and Charlotte took off at a run as Steve, his chained wrists raised, bumbled awkwardly behind them, swearing the whole way. Zee darted back to him and supported his arm.

Across the garage they went, the lights around them

flickering atmospherically, Charlotte leading the way, Zee pulling Steve along. They kept low, ducking behind cars as they moved, aware all the time of the door that led back up to the Prometheans.

And then they hopped up onto the walkway and were at the exit door. Charlotte pulled on the knob to no avail, and then tried her keys. Nothing.

"Some fire exit this is," she grumbled. Zee and Steve pulled up next to her, as Charlotte noticed a keypad on the door. An image flashed in her mind of Teodor typing something into a keypad on their way into the garage.

"Did you see Teodor's code?" Zee asked.

She looked up. Whether it was her imagination or her senses being sharpened by fear, she could hear thudding footsteps above them.

"No," she said, racking her memory. Teodor had said something, what was it? "It didn't make any sense. Teodor told Mr. Metos it was about eating pies."

"Huh?" asked Zee, eyes bugging.

"I don't know!" Charlotte exclaimed. She could hear the footsteps more loudly now; it sounded like a giant was pounding toward them. "He ate pie?" What was it exactly? "I think . . . 'Pie, first ate'?"

"*Pi!*" The word burst out of Steve's mouth. "He means *pi!*"

"What are you talking about?" she yelled.

"Not P-I-E," he said impatiently. "P-I. *Pi.* The ratio of a circle's circumference to its diameter! Geometry! Pi!"

"Oh!" Charlotte breathed. Well, sure, that made sense.

Zee exhaled. "I only know the first three. Three point one four . . ." The cousins looked at each other wildly. They couldn't get out. They were trapped.

And then, across the garage, the stairwell door burst open.

Timon.

*"Stop!"* he bellowed, his voice filling the garage. Then he took off toward them, each footfall seeming to shake the whole building.

Steve was muttering something quickly, but Charlotte could not hear over the pounding of her heart. Timon, still yelling, was halfway toward them, and Charlotte took a step back toward the wall, as if that would help at all.

"THREE ONE FOUR ONE FIVE NINE TWO SIX!" Steve yelled.

"What?"

"Pi! I memorized fifty digits for Quiz Bowl! Hurry!"

"Oh!" Charlotte whirled toward the keypad and began to punch in the numbers.

*"Stop right there!"* Timon hollered. Sucking in his

breath, Zee brandished the heavy sword. Then there was a beeping noise, and the door unlatched.

Charlotte's hand was on the knob when Timon pulled up ten feet away from them and yelled, *"Don't move!"* And then he reached into his jacket and pulled out a gun.

"Don't touch that door," he growled.

Everything was still. Everything Charlotte had ever done or felt or thought left her—her entire life was this moment, staring into the barrel of a gun. The door behind them had opened slightly, and the sun streamed in toward them, so close yet impossibly far away. She felt the contents of her stomach rise up, and her legs wavered under her.

"You do not understand," Timon said. "You know nothing. This boy holds the fate of the world in his hands."

Steve blinked. "What are you *talking* about?"

"Free him," Timon continued, leveling the gun at Charlotte, "and you condemn humanity. Is that what you want? Do you want more people to die? He is all we have!" He took a step toward Steve, eyeing the cousins.

"I understand you are upset," he said, his voice softening. "But you must trust us. We have kept humanity safe all this time. We have saved thousands of lives, tens of thousands, since your adventures in the

Mediterranean Sea. There are few of us now, but we will keep humanity safe nonetheless. Move away from the boy."

His chest heaving, Zee took a step forward and Timon pointed the gun at him. Charlotte sucked in air. "Put down the sword, Zachary," he said. "You look like a fool. Put it down now."

Zee did not move for a moment. Charlotte could not tell if he was being brave or had simply frozen to the spot. Then, his eyes fixed on Timon, he moved in front of Steve, sword poised. Behind him, Steve gasped.

Timon raised his thick eyebrows and lowered the gun slightly. "I do not want to shoot children," he said slowly. "But I will. I will shoot you, and I will shoot to kill. This is far bigger than you two. Do not doubt me."

Charlotte did not.

As she struggled to keep breathing, her eyes met Zee's. The sword was shaking in his hands. Was this it, then? Was this their moment? Were they going to let Timon shoot them to save this boy? Or would they save themselves, hope for another chance, and have to live with the consequences? Who were they? How would their story end? Was it their destiny to die here, to fail, to hope at least they died for what was right?

Mr. Metos had said there was no destiny, only choice. Well, then, Charlotte would choose. It was ironic, after all they had been through with the gods, that they would die at the hands of a human. With her entire body shaking, with tears blurring her vision, with her throat closing, she moved next to her cousin.

"If he shoots," she said to Steve, struggling to speak, "run."

"I see." Timon raised the gun.

"STOP!" Mr. Metos's voice came bursting through the air. "STOP RIGHT NOW!"

He came hurtling toward them, and Timon turned his head to him. "I'm handling this!" He looked quickly between Charlotte and Zee and the approaching Metos.

"Timon. *Timon!* Stop!" Mr. Metos called as he ran.

"Metos, what are you doing?" Timon took his eyes off the huddled trio for a moment, but left the gun fixed on them.

"This," Mr. Metos said, reaching into his pocket and bringing out a small dagger. He stopped running and began to stalk toward the group, holding the dagger by the point.

Charlotte did not understand, but Timon seemed to, and he looked at his colleague, incredulous. "What do you think you're doing?" The men eyed each other, sizing each other up. "You're willing to give up the world for them?"

Mr. Metos's eyes traveled to Charlotte and Zee, who stood rooted to their spot in front of Steve.

"Yes," he said flatly, taking another step.

"How long do you think they will survive without us?" Timon said. "How long?" He looked from Mr. Metos to the group by the door. His eyes hardened. "Kill me, then," he said, his voice a challenge. "I'll die for this boy."

"Very well," said Mr. Metos, and, turning his arm slightly, he flicked his wrist.

The dagger moved through the air, spinning balletically, and Timon let out something between a grunt and a yell as it pierced his thigh. He stumbled and grabbed his leg, the gun dropping to the floor. He seemed to be screaming curses, but Charlotte could hear nothing; the world had gone absolutely silent.

And then Timon had the gun in his hands again, and just as Mr. Metos reached for another dagger, he had leveled it at them, his face contorted in pain and rage. And then everything happened at once. There was an explosion from the gun, and at the same time Timon screamed and wrenched to the side. A bullet flew through the air, whizzing by Charlotte and hitting the wall. Timon fell to the floor, writhing, another dagger lodged in his shoulder. Mr. Metos strode up to him and slammed his fist into the side of his head. Timon collapsed to the ground, unconscious.

The cousins stood, rooted to their spots. If Charlotte hadn't felt the sweat drenching her face, hadn't sensed herself shaking, hadn't heard her lungs struggle against the weight of her chest, she would have thought she had simply stopped in time and would spend the rest of her life standing there next to her cousin, frozen in a moment of absolute fear.

"Zee!" Mr. Metos shouted, tossing a small bag toward him. "Get out of here! What are you waiting for? Go, go!" He turned and drew the third and final dagger, then called back, "Zee, Cannon Street Station, it's around the corner!"

Somehow Charlotte began to move again, and she found herself in the doorway about to emerge into the bright day, when she looked back at Mr. Metos, her heart filling. He glanced at them, eyes full of words there was not time to say, and then from across the garage the stairwell door burst open and two Prometheans appeared.

"GO!" bellowed Mr. Metos.

And they did.

CHAPTER 19

Friends in High Places

Down the street they went, Zee with his sword, Steve with his chains, past all the well-tailored men and women walking out of the shops that lined the street. People gaped at them as they passed. Were they being followed? Had Mr. Metos held them off? Would he be okay? Charlotte's heart burned and tears filled her eyes again, but still they ran on.

They turned a corner, and, pointing off into the distance, Zee called, "There's the Tube station, there." They ran on, Charlotte's body, which had been feeling somewhat better since she'd stopped running for her life, protesting so loudly that she did not notice Zee had stopped in his tracks until she almost ran into him.

In front of him was a tall, dark-haired, athletic-looking girl of about their age. She was staring openly at Zee.

"What are you doing here?" she asked, shock on her face. Her eyes flicked to Charlotte and Steve.

"Um," Zee squeaked.

"He's just back for a visit," said Charlotte, the words tumbling out of her mouth. "I'm his cousin from America, and this is, um, Steve. . . ."

Silence, as the girl's mouth hung open.

"Er, this is . . . Samantha Golton," Zee said in a choked voice.

Charlotte stared. This was the girl, the girl Zee had liked so much before he came over, liked so much that he had never even spoken to her. She was looking at Zee as if he had come back to life.

"But," she said, shaking her head, "I hear you're *missing*!" She took a step toward him.

Charlotte's heart sank.

"No, no, we're all right," Zee said, taking a step back. "Please tell everyone we're all right. Samantha, I . . . I'm sorry, we have to go." And as Samantha stared after them, the trio rushed toward the stairwell to the Underground station. They reached the long escalator that would take them underneath the city, and Zee suddenly turned back and shouted, "Samantha! You're the best football player I've ever seen!"

Charlotte looked at him in utter confusion. Steve leaned in to whisper, "Football is British for *soccer*." She turned and glared at him.

As they descended out of view of the street, Zee turned back, looking pleased with himself.

When they disembarked, he went to the ticket machine and bought three tickets with the money that was in the bag Mr. Metos had thrown at him. Charlotte surveyed the lobby, seeing dark, shadowy men everywhere, while Steve bobbed up and down on his feet, looking very nervous.

They went through the turnstiles, still attracting people's curious gazes, and hurried to the platform. They only had to wait three minutes for the train to come, but it felt longer than an eternity, longer than math class. Steve said nothing, just stood there, pale and shaking slightly. When the train finally pulled up, the trio hopped on and looked around nervously, waiting for the train to leave the station.

It did not.

*"This is the District Line train for Ealing Broadway,"* said a pleasant, canned voice over the speakers. *"Change at Earls Court for Richmond."*

Charlotte closed her eyes and counted to thirty, and when she opened them, they still had not left.

"What's going on, Zee?" she muttered thickly.

"Just because I'm English doesn't mean that I have a psychic relationship with the Tube, Char," Zee muttered back.

"Don't look at me," said Steve. "I'm Canadian."

And still they waited. A few more people got on, glanced at Steve (who glared back), and moved to another car. Charlotte could hear one whisper, "Hoodlums."

And then Charlotte saw them. Leo and Teodor, running along the platform, looking into the windows.

"Zee!" She pointed, and they ducked down. Charlotte's mind flitted to Mr. Metos—how had they gotten past him? An ill feeling washed over her.

Charlotte peeked out the window. The two Prometheans were talking to a man who was pointing toward their car. Across the platform, another train was just pulling in.

"They're coming," Charlotte whispered. Zee gasped a little, and then motioned them all into the next car as the doors to theirs opened. Down the length of three cars they went. And then there was a loud noise, and the train began to stir.

*"This is the District Line train for Ealing Broadway,"* repeated the voice. *"Change at Earls Court for Richmond."*

"Come on," Zee said, motioning them forward. They jumped out of the doorway—*"Please stand clear of the closing doors,"* said the voice—and the doors shut behind them. "Quick, quick," said Zee, and he led them off the platform, into a hallway, and down some stairs. Their rapid footfalls echoed all around them. They ran up another set of stairs that led to the other side of the platform. Zee reached the other train first and caught the closing doors. Several people in the car gave him dirty looks as the doors opened again and Charlotte flung herself inside—*"This is the District Line train bound for Upminster"*—not daring to breathe until the train opposite them began to pull away.

"We did it," breathed Zee.

"We did it," said Charlotte.

Silence. The cousins looked at the seat next to them. It was empty.

"Um, where's Steve?"

They pressed themselves against the window and saw a chained form disappearing up the stairs in front of them. They both yelled at once and lunged toward the door, just as their train started to pull away.

Charlotte turned to Zee, jaw hanging open, as their train took them away from the station.

"That little git!" Zee exclaimed.

"What do we do?" Charlotte asked, panting. "Where's he going?"

Zee's face contorted in a grimace. "I have no idea. There's another line up there. He could be going for it."

"We'll get off at the next stop. Go back."

"Char," said Zee, still breathing heavily, "we can't. By the time we get back he could be anywhere, on another train, or—"

"But what if the Prometheans—"

"He can't be stupid enough to go back there. Char, Samantha saw us. She could be telling the police right now. We have to get away."

He was right. They couldn't get caught now. Steve had a plan, apparently; it just didn't involve them. Still, it might have been nice if he'd said thank you.

The two sat for a while, trying to catch their breath. Charlotte closed her eyes, trying to will away the tightening of her ribs. She'd been feeling much better—but sprinting for her life did not help. "What are we doing?" she asked finally.

"Char"—Zee leaned in—"we have to get to Delphi."

Charlotte nodded again. The Prometheans were near destroyed. It was all up to them now. If the Promethean Flame was in Delphi, they needed to go there. That was their next step, it was clear—find the Flame, and then use it. Give humanity knowledge. Mr. Metos said people were unique because they had the power of choice, but they didn't, not really. They couldn't make any choices without the truth. This was their mission now—not fighting the gods, but giving everyone else the ability to.

"What do you think we do with it?" she whispered. "Once we get it? Present it to someone, or . . ."

Zee grimaced. "Oh. Well. Right. Well, that's the thing."

"What?"

He shifted. "Well, I just read it. To use the Flame, well, we have to go up to Mount Olympus."

Charlotte stared at her cousin, waiting for him to burst out laughing at his own joke. This would be uncharacteristic for him—telling jokes in the first place, of course, and then bursting out laughing at them—but stress made people do strange things sometimes.

But he wasn't laughing.

"You're not laughing," Charlotte said.

"Yeah, well, this is what the book says. There's a hearth on Mount Olympus, and you put the fire there."

"And how are we supposed to do that exactly?" Charlotte's voice sounded several octaves higher than normal. She had ventured—rather bravely if she did say so herself—into two godly realms in the last six months and only survived by the skin of her teeth. It seemed that that should really be enough for one lifetime. She'd gotten attacked by a Chimera just for going to history class; she couldn't imagine what could happen if she waltzed up to Olympus carrying Prometheus's fire. It did not, after all, go that well for Prometheus.

Of course, it was all leading to this, all leading to Charlotte and Zee making the climb up to Mount Olympus, home of the gods, home of Zeus. It would not end any other way. She was marked for danger, just as her father had said, and there was no more dangerous place.

Charlotte's heart felt like it was going to run off the rails. She put her head in her hands and closed her eyes. *One foot in front of the other,* she told herself. *Find the Flame. That is all.*

"How much money did Mr. Metos give you?" she asked Zee finally.

"Um . . ." Zee opened the pouch and began to count. "About three hundred pounds."

Charlotte didn't know anything about British currency, but that didn't sound like enough. "You don't have any friends who are superrich and don't ask a lot of questions, do you?"

"Alas, no."

She put her head in her hands again and sighed. She needed to remember to collect rich friends along with foreign language dictionaries.

And then she sat up, beaming at Zee. "Yes," she said. "Yes, you do."

Thirty minutes later they had arrived at a modern business district overlooking the river and were standing in front of two tall skyscrapers of steel and glass. The scene looked nothing like the old-fashioned stone facades of London highbrow streets Charlotte had seen in movies, but she supposed London, like the rest of the world, was allowed into the twenty-first century.

A uniformed, white-gloved doorman let them into the special elevator to the penthouse apartment, which took up the entire top floor of the building. Charlotte found her heart rising along with the elevator as they traveled upward, and when the doors opened and she beheld the thin, pale, light-haired man in a dinner jacket in front of her, she found tears were streaming down her cheeks.

He held out his arms, exclaiming, "Miss Charlotte!" and she fell into them.

"Hello, Sir Laurence," said Zee.

"Sir Zachary the Brave!" he replied, bowing. "Smashing sword!"

Charlotte beamed at her friend. She had loved Sir Laurence as a giant squid, and now that he was human again she loved him even more. It was nice to have one person in the world whose very existence made you feel better about things. (It also did not hurt when that person was extremely wealthy.)

"My manners are beastly," Sir Laurence said, motioning them forward. "I suppose it's spending all that time as a beast, what! Please, come in."

As they stepped into the huge flat, Charlotte's eyes widened. She had been expecting to see something out of a Victorian design magazine, like Hades's Palace only much less grim, with intricately patterned flowered wallpaper and ornate trim and elegant high-backed chairs and something called a settee, whatever that was.

Instead Sir Laurence seemed to have gotten his hands on some rather unusual design magazines. The room was circular, with floor-to-ceiling windows that looked out onto the river. The center of the room was sunken, with three platform-like steps leading down to a furnished area lined with a big, curved, white leather sofa and two chairs that looked like some combination of Tilt-A-Whirl chairs and space pods, if the Tilt-A-Whirl chairs/space pods had zebra print cushions. The walls were lined with blue velvet, and the floor was covered in thickly tufted two-inch-high white carpet. Off to one side of the cavernous room was a spiral staircase made out of stainless steel steps that hung in the air as if suspended. In the center of the ceiling hung a giant mirrored globe, and in one corner proudly stood a black, Charlotte-size lava lamp.

"Wow," murmured Charlotte.

"Blimey," murmured Zee.

"Do you like the place?" Sir Laurence beamed at them. "I only wish the Lady Gaumm were alive to see it. She did so like zebras. Such a grand creature, the striped horse of the Serengeti! Now, what might I get for you? Tea?"

Soon Charlotte and Zee were sitting in the space pod chairs (surprisingly comfortable), drinking lemonade and eating funny little cucumber sandwiches while Sir Laurence sat on the giant albino cow couch and appraised them.

"Now," he said brightly, "Miss Charlotte, Zachary, has anyone tried to kill you today?"

They exchanged a look. "Well, actually—"

"Par for the course, what! But you outwitted them, didn't you? No one can defeat my Miss Charlotte!" He beamed at her. "Now, what might I do for you? I have rooms for the both of you. You may stay as long as you like. You will be under my protection."

Something squeezed at Charlotte's heart. How she would love to stay with Sir Laurence, in his weird velvet space palace, how she would love to eat strange little sandwiches and watch his lava lamp and be under his protection. Maybe just one night . . .

"Sir Laurence," Zee said quietly, "we really appreciate the offer, but we have to go. We have something important to do."

Sir Laurence leaned in, his pale blue eyes growing wide. "What?"

Charlotte did not know where to begin. It was all so odd—the dream, the book, this sudden sense of purpose. They really did not have that much to go on, except the utter conviction that this was what they were supposed to do.

"It's—"

"Sir Laurence," Zee said suddenly, "do you have any more of these sandwiches?"

"Oh! Quite!" said Sir Laurence, and he disappeared into the kitchen again. Charlotte turned to look at her cousin.

"Char," he whispered, "I don't think we should tell him."

"What? Why?"

"Because I don't think anyone else is supposed to know."

"But this is Sir Laurence!"

"I know, but"—Zee shook his head—"I just don't think we should tell anybody. I think we're supposed to do this ourselves."

Charlotte frowned at him. It was just like Zee. He

always had to keep everything to himself, not wanting to burden the world with his existence. And he had to do everything himself, to prove whatever it was he needed to prove. But Sir Laurence wasn't just anyone, he was the only person in the world (other than Zee, who was so obvious he didn't even count) whom Charlotte trusted completely. And it would be so nice, for once, for it not to be the two of them against the world.

And yet . . . and yet. Somewhere in her heart, Charlotte knew he was right. No one else had been able to find the Flame. Whoever was sending them the dreams had picked them. Charlotte had read enough books to understand: The Flame was their quest, and it was theirs alone.

When Sir Laurence returned with more sandwiches in hand, Charlotte looked at him sadly. "Sir Laurence," she said softly, "we can't tell you what we're doing. But . . . well, Zee's right. We have to go."

"Go? Go where?"

Charlotte looked at Zee, who nodded imperceptibly. "Delphi."

Sir Laurence straightened. "My dears, don't you think that danger seems to find you easily enough without you going to look for it? Have you seen what's been happening over there?"

"We have to," Charlotte said. "There's something we have to do."

He frowned. "And I suppose your quest is not one a gallant erstwhile giant squid might accompany you on?"

Charlotte looked at the ground. "I don't think so."

"All right," said Sir Laurence, looking resigned. "But you must promise me that you will be very careful. I am quite fond of you, you know. And if you need me, you just ring, and Sir Laurence Gaumm will be right by your side."

Charlotte nodded, unable to speak for a moment. She gathered herself and then, her voice thick, said, "Sir Laurence, our friend, Mr. Metos. He saved us. He's in trouble, and . . ."

"Say no more!" said Sir Laurence. "I shall rescue him! Fear not, my lady. Sir Laurence is on the case!"

Next to her, Zee had cleared his throat and was shooting her furtive glances.

She looked at him. "What?" Flushing, he stared at her, trying to communicate something he was clearly too embarrassed to say. Then it hit Charlotte. "Oh, yeah." She turned back to Sir Laurence. "Can we have some money?"

They had discussed nothing, had planned nothing. They were going on a dream, on an unlabeled map, on a book in French that concluded that their quarry did not exist. They did not know precisely where they were going or what they would do when they got there. But the next morning, Charlotte and Zee found themselves on Sir Laurence's private jet bound for Greece, the home of the gods.

CHAPTER 20

# The Kindness of Strangers

STEVE COULD NOT SAY WHY HE DID IT, EXACTLY. But when Charlotte and Zee reached the platform and hopped onto the other train, he found himself heading the other way. It was nothing but instinct, the sort of instinct that gets you to be captain of the Quiz Bowl team when you're only a sophomore. Impulse, his mother would call it—as in, try not to be so impulsive, sweetie, as in, when you punched the opposing team's captain at the regional finals, you might have found other ways to express your frustration.

They were better off apart than together, that was

the thing—he could make his own way. Those kids were willing to die to rescue him, and he'd never even met them before. It was quite a thing. He didn't know how to feel, how to react. He should have thanked them—he should have said something. But the best thing he could do for them, really, was stay away. He didn't want them getting shot for him.

He wanted to go back, that's what he wanted. He wanted to find those—what, Prometheans?—which sounded to Steve like a bad metal band who liked to light things on fire, and punch them. A lot.

But he did not want to get kidnapped again, and those guys did seem to have a lot of weapons at their disposal. Whatever they were planning on doing with him, it didn't sound good.

As he made his way up the escalator toward the sunlight, it finally occurred to him that he was free. Or at least as free as you can be with your wrists still chained. He did not know how long he'd been gone for—it felt like weeks, but he couldn't say for sure.

He still did not understand why those men were holding him. They never hurt him, never did anything to him except chain him to the floor and bring him food three times a day. At first he thought he was being ransomed, but his mother surely would have gotten them whatever money they wanted, somehow. That's how it had always been, just the two of them against the world. That's why he had punched Joe Koskie—after they'd soundly trounced Anola High, Koskie had said something completely inappropriate about her. That's the sort of thing that gets a guy punched.

That's what got to him about this—he'd heard those people say something about him being "the son." It didn't make any sense. Were they trying to get to his mom somehow? Or did they know who his dad was?

The thought sent a chill through Steve. His mother never said anything about his father, just that she had made a mistake once, that she had met someone who had promised the world and then disappeared—*poof*—in a puff of smoke. Then she'd gotten a teaching certificate and raised him on her own.

She was happy now, but when he was a kid he would hear her crying herself to sleep. He would go in and comfort her, again and again, "It's okay, Mama, it's okay."

He'd thought, at first, that maybe one of the creepy guys was his father, that maybe they had kidnapped him to bring him home. But his father never appeared. Which was good, because if he ever met the guy . . .

As he left the Tube station and turned down the street, Steve noticed passersby eyeing him and then moving hurriedly on. He was rather surprised that no one stopped to ask if he needed help. This was the problem with a big city like London. In Winnipeg if you saw a teenage boy walking down the street with his wrists chained up, you'd ask if he needed assistance. And maybe he wouldn't, maybe he was going to a costume party or was doing some elaborate piece of performance art or just liked wearing chains, but at least you'd *ask*. Or at least you would if you were Canadian.

There was a phone booth outside the station, and he ducked into it. He had to call his mom. He had no money, no calling card, nothing, but they had to let him call his mom, tell her he was safe.

The operator, though, the operator didn't believe him. He told her the whole story and she wouldn't do anything. She thought he was a liar. It was hard for Steve not to scream at her, but—*step back, calm down, consequences*—he did not. She finally offered to reverse the charges, and soon Steve heard the familiar ringing tone. His heart leaped. It rang once, twice, three times, four. Then the voice mail picked up. At least he could leave a message.

"Mom, I—"

*Click.*

"Why didn't you let me leave a message?" he yelled at the operator.

"No one agreed to pick up the charges," she said.

And then Steve did not step back, did not calm down, and certainly did not think of the consequences. He screamed into the phone, slammed it down—once, twice, three times—and left the phone booth.

A police officer. That's what he needed. He expected the police, in their funny hats and buttoned-up coats, to be all over the streets, twirling their nightsticks and whistling "chim chim-in-ey" or some such. He did not particularly want to ask anyone for directions to a police station, not any of these perfectly tailored Londoners hurrying off to their meetings and their shops who didn't have the time to see if he was okay. He did not want to give them the satisfaction.

In fact, Steve could not deny that he was feeling a little hurt. He didn't ask much of his fellow man, just a little courtesy, a little concern. Was it too much, after his ordeal, to expect a little kindness? If he ran the universe, people would be a lot nicer.

He could not say why, in particular, he turned down the street he did—it looked promising to him, and he did not realize it was just a narrow brick side street that was entirely deserted.

Well, not entirely.

A tall man appeared, as if out of nowhere, dressed for a costume party, and he was about to pass him right by just like the other ones. Steve wanted to turn and yell something, something hurtful, like, "Nice cape," except he would say it in a way that showed he didn't think his cape was nice *at all*.

But then something happened. As the man's eyes flicked casually over him—and were those special contact lenses he was wearing? The costume was kind of cool, really—his face suddenly registered concern, even distress, at Steve's plight. The man stopped dead in his tracks and asked, his voice soft and sincere, "Why, are you all right?"

His concern was so strong, so genuine, that it made up for every single person who had passed him by, that it made Steve's heart lighten and even a little lump rise up in his throat, though he would not have admitted it if you asked.

"No," he said. " No. I've been kidnapped, and—"

"Kidnapped!" replied the man in horror, his long-fingered hand flying to his chest. "Goodness me. That must have been awful."

"Well," said Steve, "yes. Yes it was." He held up his wrists. "I can't even get these chains off."

"Oh!" gasped the man. "You poor, poor boy! Well, maybe I can help you with that!" And then, before Steve's eyes, he pulled something out of his cape, something far too big to have been there in the first place. It was a three-pronged spear, a trident, like the kind mermaid kings always have, and frankly, it did not go with his costume at all. With a flourish, the man touched it to Steve's wrists.

And then he was free.

Steve looked up at the man—who, upon reflection, did not seem much like a man at all.

"Wow," he said, eyes wide. "What else can you do with that?"

"Oh, my boy," said the man-like man, "let me show you."

# PART FOUR

Air

## CHAPTER 21

### Greece Is the Word

CHARLOTTE EXPECTED THAT WHEN THEY ARRIVED in Greece she would feel awed, stunned, awash in the momentousness of it all. And, had her mission been ordinary, had she been on a trip with her parents, she might have been. But as they got off the plane and stepped into this country with its cartoon sun and Magic Marker sky, she felt only a sort of grim determination.

As they walked down the stairway to the tarmac, Charlotte found herself looking surreptitiously around. She expected the sky to be roiling and black, with monsters swooping in from above, shooting fireballs, but apparently that sort of stuff happened only at Hartnett.

Still, she could not escape the feeling that something was off. The very air felt anxious, unsettled, as if threatened by something it did not understand.

They got off the stairs in silence, nodding to the driver Sir Laurence had arranged for them, then climbing into the big black car. The driver got into his seat and pulled out of the hangar, and then they were off on the long, winding road that would take them to Delphi.

Zee got out the map, the book, and the French-English dictionary Sir Laurence had procured for them. The night before in Sir Laurence's flat they'd sat up trying to get through as much of the book as they could. The author had tracked the Flame to Delphi, somewhere on the grounds of the Sanctuary of Apollo, where the Oracle was, but he had searched everywhere and come up empty. Their map was no help. It lacked the essential feature that had made treasure maps so functional for centuries on end—the $X$ that marked the spot.

Translating the book with the dictionary proved even slower than without, and despite the hours they had spent the previous evening and on the plane, Zee still had half of the book to go. It would have helped if the information had been in any kind of order, but whoever this French guy was, no one had ever explained to him the benefits of making an outline.

So Zee worked while Charlotte found herself staring out of a car window at a new country for the second time in a week. But this was nothing like England. They drove out of the new glassy Athens airport into the countryside and found themselves in the mountains overlooking lush green valleys with groves of olive trees and, off in the distance, a strip of dark sea. They drove up and up, and the road grew more and more narrow. As they sped around steep curve after steep curve, Charlotte began to wonder if the gods weren't going to need to finish them off.

They came around a bend to behold a great valley. Charlotte had expected it to look like the others—thick with blooming olive trees—but anything that had been alive in this valley was gone. The entire place was black and charred now, with scattered shards of blackened tree trunks littering the ground. It looked violently desolate, as if Death himself had blown through the valley.

Charlotte nudged Zee and pointed out the window toward the scene. Zee inhaled, then shook his head slowly.

"What happened there?" Charlotte asked, leaning toward the driver.

The driver paused. "No one knows," he said.

She and Zee exchanged a look, and Charlotte turned away from the window. She didn't want to see any more. She got out a guidebook to Greece that Sir Laurence had given them and flipped to the section on Delphi. The Sanctuary of Apollo was on the slope of Mount Parnassus, near the southern coast of Greece. The Sanctuary was an archeological site, and a lot of the artifacts found were in the Museum of Delphi—lots of statues and stuff, and a fancy stone that was supposed to be the center of the Earth.

This is all they had now—weird, rambling French travelogues and tourist guidebooks. Before, there had always been Mr. Metos and the rest of the Prometheans in the background. They were the army behind Charlotte and Zee, the tough guys with all the secret intelligence and fancy weapons and millennia of practice. Charlotte and Zee were just eighth graders, yes, but eighth graders with an ancient secret society of god-fighting part-Titans behind them. And now they were all alone.

*How long do you think they'll survive without us?* Timon had said.

They drove on. At one point Zee leaned in to her and whispered, "Listen." He tapped the page before him and began to read, "'After giving the Flame to humanity,

Prometheus hid it in a place no Immortal could see. He gave the secret of the Flame to an ally, one who also had cause for anger toward Zeus.'" Charlotte's eyes widened. The girl!

"Anything else?" Charlotte whispered back. "Does it say who she is?"

With a glance toward the driver, Zee shook his head.

One who also had cause for anger toward Zeus? That hardly narrowed it down. But there weren't any little girls in the myths that Charlotte knew about—unless she was the daughter of a woman Zeus had wronged. There had to be about a jillion of those.

And then, finally, they were pulling into a vast parking lot lined with cars and tour buses.

"The Sanctuary is up ahead," said the driver, handing them some Greek money. "There's a ticket booth. You can buy admission to the Sanctuary and the museum both, and then you can just go look around. I'll be waiting here."

Charlotte and Zee looked at each other. "Oh," Charlotte said, "you don't have to wait."

The driver looked unmoved. "The man paying me says I do," he said flatly.

"Ah, well, we might be awhile," said Zee.

"That's all right," said the man, picking up some knitting. "I can wait."

They were in a paved clearing on the side of a mountain, surrounded by groups of tourists of various nationalities. They could see for miles around, and despite herself, Charlotte could not help but notice how beautiful it was. The air was clear, and the day was brighter than any Charlotte had lived before. The mountain kept rising sharply behind them, surrounded by its rounded green brothers and sisters. There was a village clearly visible on the plains below, and beyond that the Mediterranean Sea.

Charlotte stared at it. The waters were choppy and agitated, the color had gone from wine-dark to just plain dark, and just looking at it made her feel queasy. It was angry, tormented, wrong.

She turned her gaze away, but the uneasy feeling remained with her. It wasn't helped by the group of soldiers standing in the clearing, eyeing the crowd, extremely large guns hanging ominously off their chests.

At the edge of the clearing were some wide, steep stone stairs framed by a crumbling stone wall. Above them was the Sanctuary—a collection of ruins in the steep mountain wall placed here and there on a long, winding path. There were people milling everywhere, chattering and laughing. Charlotte had to fight the urge to evacuate them. They seemed like movie extras, oblivious to the danger that was around them, the danger that was silently approaching.

Well, soon they would all know, wouldn't they? If Charlotte and Zee could find the Flame, that is.

"I told you to stay with the group!" A voice came booming through Charlotte's reverie. A fat, sunburned man in tight shorts was storming toward them. Behind him was a group of American-looking high school students, watching him. Charlotte looked behind her to see who he was yelling at. There was no one there.

"Come on, let's go!" the man bellowed, motioning to the cousins angrily. Zee shrugged at Charlotte. It was as good a way to explore as any.

"Mr. West," said a boy as they moved toward the group, "they're not—"

"When I want to hear from you, Oliver Posner, I will ask! Now, this is your tour guide, Rosina. I want you to give her your undivided attention. The first person who steps out of line is back on the bus, you understand?"

As a round, dark-skinned woman stepped in front of the group and began to talk, the boy shrugged at Charlotte and Zee, who shrugged back. A few of the students eyed them with the same open wariness you might show the crazy person mumbling to herself at the grocery store.

They all moved toward the stairs, Rosina's voice

carrying through the air. "Once," she was saying, "Zeus, god of the heavens, released two golden eagles from the opposite ends of the Earth to determine the Earth's center. They crossed at Delphi, and Zeus placed there a stone called the *omphalos* stone, now on display at the museum. *Omphalos* means navel. For the ancient Greeks, Delphi was the center of the world, the navel of the Earth, the place where heaven and earth met. Delphi was the place where man was closest to the gods."

*Oh, great,* Charlotte thought.

The group ascended the stairs and found themselves on a wide path made of crumbling stone that wound back and forth up the mountain, framed everywhere by ruins. Charlotte craned her neck upward, but the mountain was so steep she could not see much. "We are now," said the tour guide, "on the Sacred Way. The visitor to the Oracle would travel along this path, lined with offerings. . . ."

Up they went along the path, stopping at ruins and piles of rock as the tour guide talked on and Mr. West glared at the group.

"On the column behind this rock stood a statue of the Naxian Sphinx, a gift from the citizens of Naxos to the Oracle. We'll see that statue later in the museum. . . ."

They'd arrived in front of a large wall made of polygon-shaped stones, with plants growing out of the cracks. In one corner was a small opening, like a crawl space. Above the wall loomed the columns of some decaying structure. Zee had taken out the map and began to unroll it. One of the schoolboys was looking at him like he was nuts.

Two girls next to them let out a loud giggle suddenly, and Mr. West exploded. "Back to the bus," he yelled at the pair. "I mean it! Go!"

As the girls left the group, giggling the whole way, the tour guide led them up the path to a ramp and onto the ruins of the Temple of Apollo, the home of the Oracle of Delphi.

They were on a rectangular structure about the size of a house. Most of the columns that had lined the sides were gone, though a few stumps were scattered here and there. Sections of stone wall of varying heights framed the structure, and a few students settled themselves down on the piles.

"Here was the *pronaos*, or lobby," said the guide. "It had inscriptions in the wall of some common aphorisms, like 'Know thyself' and 'Nothing in excess,' and over here was inscribed the Greek letter epsilon, or *E*. To this day, no one knows what it was supposed to signify.

"Now, here," she went on, stepping forward, "was the Altar of Hestia, where an eternal fire burned—"

Charlotte perked up. Could it be that easy? "Excuse

me," she said, raising her hand. The students all looked at her in surprise and confusion. "I'm new," she whispered to them.

"Yes?" asked the tour guide, looking at her.

"An eternal fire? Is it . . . uh . . . still here?"

The tour guide frowned. "Well, no. This is a ruin." A few students giggled.

"I know, but . . . it's eternal, right?" Zee was nudging her, but she motioned him off. "So it's got to be somewhere. What happened to it?"

"Well," said the guide, "I guess I don't know."

"Huh," said Charlotte, biting her lip. Mr. West looked at her suspiciously.

"Char," Zee whispered urgently, clutching the map.

"You!" shouted the chaperone, pointing at Zee. "Back to the bus! I warned you!"

"But—," said Zee reflexively. He looked startled, and Charlotte reflected that he had probably never gotten in trouble before. She wanted to remind him that this wasn't actually their teacher, but it didn't seem to be the time.

"NOW!" said Mr. West.

Zee shrugged and muttered to Charlotte, "I'm just going to look around. Come find me when you can get away." And then he was gone.

As the tour guide talked on, giving the history of

the Oracle, Charlotte scanned the ruins, trying to imagine the temple in its glory days. People came from all over to the Oracle at the center of the world to hear prophecies. Somehow the place felt odd to Charlotte, as if some remnant of all of those hopeful travelers lingered on.

She sighed and backed up toward a stone at the end of the temple, waiting for her moment to escape and meet Zee. When she sat down, she was surprised to find she was not alone. A woman in a white dress with long black hair was sitting there, filing her nails and looking bored. She glanced up at Charlotte casually, then started as Charlotte looked back at her. The woman looked all around, then back at Charlotte, who was watching her curiously.

"Can you see me?" the woman whispered in surprise, her oddly yellow eyes wide.

"Um," said Charlotte, looking around, "yeah." The woman was very beautiful, except for an extremely large zit festering in the middle of her forehead.

"Oh!" said the woman, putting away her nail file. "Okay. Um . . ." She tossed her hair and straightened. Putting her hands to her temples, she closed her eyes and began to hum. Charlotte eyed her.

After a few moments of this, the woman opened one eye. "Don't you have a question for me?"

And then it occurred to Charlotte just who this was. "Are you the Oracle?"

The Oracle's face contorted in derision. "Um, duh! Who are you?"

Charlotte raised her eyebrows. "Shouldn't you know that?"

"Oh, cute, are we? Fine, do you want to know your future? Want to know the name of the man you're going to marry? Will he be rich and have lots of goats?" She put her hands to her temples again.

"Wh-what?"

"Goats!" said the Oracle, as if Charlotte had a very annoying hearing problem. "Don't you lie awake at night and dream of marrying a handsome man with lots of goats?"

Charlotte straightened. "Not particularly, no."

The Oracle raised her eyebrows. "I see."

She knew what Mr. Metos had said. There was no such thing as fate. Still, this was the Oracle. She could not help but ask. "Um, do you know my future?"

The Oracle sighed, squeezed her eyes shut again, and hummed for about half a second. "Yes. You will meet a handsome and mysterious stranger."

"Oh, come *on*."

One eye popped open. "You will inherit a great fortune?"

Charlotte crossed her arms.

"Fine," the Oracle said, sounding extremely annoyed. She shifted on the rock. "What's your name?"

"Charlotte Mielswetzski."

The Oracle nearly slipped off the rock. "Really!" she exclaimed.

"Um . . . yes."

"You want a prophecy?" she said, leaning in, her eyes narrowing. "I'll give you a prophecy. *Get out of here.*"

"What?"

"Get out. Now. Go back to your parents and your mortal life and forget everything."

Charlotte's stomach turned. "What happens if we don't?" she said quietly.

The Oracle leveled her eyes at Charlotte. "We start all over again."

She watched the Oracle for moment, waiting for her to explain. But the Oracle closed her mouth and would say nothing else.

Well, whatever she meant, it didn't matter. They were not going to turn back. They had their quest. Charlotte set her jaw.

"We know the Flame is here," Charlotte said. "Do you know where it is?"

"If you haven't been chosen to find the Flame, you won't find it," muttered the Oracle, looking back at her nails. "If you have, you don't need any help from me."

"And you don't know whether or not we've been chosen?"

"Don't you?" said the Oracle, leveling her gaze at Charlotte.

"Is that all? You have nothing else to say to me?"

She raised her hands. "Don't look at me. I'm not part of this."

"Charlotte!" The voice seemed to emerge from the very rocks, and Charlotte nearly jumped off her perch.

But it was just Zee, standing by the wall below, eyes ablaze. "Come on," he called in a whisper.

"Oh, boy," she heard the Oracle say. "Here we go." Charlotte turned to look at her, but she had disappeared.

Charlotte looked around. The school group was heading out now, and Mr. West was surveying the temple, looking for stragglers. She ducked behind one of the segments of wall, only to see the Oracle crouching down next to her. The Oracle blushed when she saw Charlotte and cleared her throat. "You can see me, can't you," she said. Charlotte nodded, and the Oracle mustered her dignity and walked off.

Rolling her eyes, Charlotte stayed in her crouch and waited until she couldn't hear the students' voices anymore. She peeked up over the rock and then, seeing the group disappearing up the hill, slipped out of the temple and went to join her cousin.

He was standing by the polygonal wall, brandishing the map, which he thrust at Charlotte when she appeared next to him. "Look," he breathed.

The map had changed. Next to the illustration of the Temple of Apollo was a mark that had not been there before. A big letter *E*. Charlotte looked at Zee and remembered what he had mumbled in his sleep on the Prometheans' jet.

"*E* marks the spot," she said.

"What do you think?" Zee said.

There was only one place in the temple they hadn't been. Charlotte pointed to the small opening in the temple's foundation, and Zee nodded.

"Let's go," he said.

CHAPTER 22

# Seek the Belly Button

WHILE GROUPS OF TOURISTS MOVED AROUND THEM, Charlotte and Zee hovered by the polygonal wall, waiting for their chance. A tour guide eyed them suspiciously, as if he knew full well what they were up to, and together the cousins moved to the wall and began studying it as if there were something exceptionally fascinating about it. They were so convincing that a French couple appeared next to them to see what they were looking at.

And then finally they saw their chance. There was a break in the stream, and the cousins moved as one to the wall. Charlotte pulled herself up and climbed in, followed closely by Zee.

It was dark. It was wet. It was stinky. As Charlotte jumped down from the perch onto the slimy floor, she felt herself being pulled back by the daylight behind her. It didn't seem possible that such a place could exist in a world of so much sun.

Zee landed behind her with a thud. The cousins stood, letting their eyes adjust to the darkness. Not that there was much to see. They were in an underground chamber that seemed to be about half the length of the temple. The floor was littered with pieces of large stone brick. And that was all—there was no passageway, no cave, no Flame.

"It's got to be in here somewhere," Charlotte said. Her voice boomed through the chamber, and from the temple above they could hear someone yelp.

Oops.

The cousins moved slowly around the room, examining the walls, stepping in puddles, over rocks, and on squishy things Charlotte chose not to examine too carefully. At the far side was a large structure that proved to be the remnants of a staircase that led up to the temple. Muffled voices and footsteps emanated from the temple above, and narrow beams of light shone through the cracks in the walls. The stone walls were covered in two millennia worth of graffiti, from etchings to markers to spray paint. Charlotte frowned at some of the more recent additions—you're under the Temple of Apollo and all you can think to write is D.B. + L.W. in a heart?

"Maybe there's an *E* somewhere," Charlotte whispered. Zee nodded in agreement, and they scanned the walls up and down. It took forever. People wrote all kinds of things in secret places, swear words and confessions and love notes and dirty poems, but no one, in the long history of the place, seemed to have scrawled the letter *E*.

"I'll try the other side," said Charlotte. She hurried across the room so quickly that she did not notice the three-foot-wide stone brick in front of her until she was tripping over it. Time slowed just enough for her to reflect that she did not want to fall on this particular ground . . . and then she landed in a pile of goop.

She growled, and her face scrunched up as the decay of the ages assaulted her nose. Her hand flew over to the offending stone for leverage, and that is how she saw it. As she pulled herself up, her eyes traveled over the side of the brick, where one very large capital *E* was etched quite clearly.

"Zee," Charlotte whispered urgently. "Over here." As her cousin made his way over, she began to scan the large stone mass, looking for whatever mechanism would open the trap door or whatever it was that would lead them to the Flame.

"You try," she said, when Zee arrived. He crouched down and ran his hands over the brick, but found nothing. Charlotte couldn't believe it—they were so close now. What were they missing? She let out a grunt and gave the stone a soft, chiding kick.

And it moved.

The cousins looked from the brick to each other. Zee leaned down to push it, and it slid so easily he lost his balance. "That was lighter than it had any right to be," he muttered.

Charlotte thought of what the Oracle had said: *If you were chosen to find it, you won't need any help from me.*

The brick had been covering a hole in the ground about the size of a large pothole. Crouching down, Charlotte peered into it and saw only blackness—no light, no flickering, nothing. She put her hand inside it and moved it around, looking for a ladder or stairs or something. But there was nothing. She remembered her dream.

"Zee," she whispered. "I think we're supposed to jump for it."

"Can you tell how far down it is?"

"I think it's far," she admitted.

Zee nodded resolutely. "I'll go first. If it's all right, I'll call for you. If not, well . . ."

"Don't be an idiot," Charlotte said. "I'll go." Her cousin's gallantry always annoyed her enough to distract her from however terrifying the situation was.

But before she could react, Zee had jumped.

Charlotte froze. The world stopped. She was alone, entirely, perpetually. There was nothing at all, nothing but the dark hole and the silence Zee had left behind. It was as if the air he had displaced while jumping had solidified as a monument to Zee's rash act, and it and Charlotte would remain there for the rest of time.

Shouldn't she be hearing something? Should the whole universe have gone quiet like this? Shouldn't she be able to move? Shouldn't she be hearing Zee calling up to her, telling her he'd landed safely, that it was okay to jump, that there was a large, soft mat down below and a whole herd of kittens waiting to greet them?

And then everything started again. The footsteps, the voices, the air—but still no Zee. Heart racing, Charlotte did the only thing she could think of doing: She jumped.

It was just like her dream, except without the comfort of knowing that you'd wake up in the morning. She plunged into absolute darkness and kept falling. The air was thin and cold and oddly empty, as if the entire world had vanished and all there was was this endless space.

Down, down she fell, into silence, into cold, into deep, unending, unyielding blackness, her only companion the sensation of falling. She must be falling to the center of the Earth, beyond—

And then it was over. Like that. Charlotte never felt herself land, did not feel anything—at one moment she was falling and the next she was standing upright and still.

She stood there, sucking in the air, wondering how she had survived, wondering if she had survived. She could see nothing except a very dim, flickering light source off in the distance. Around her was a whooshing, pulsing sound, and she thought it was the Earth's heartbeat. And there was something else, something very familiar, something very close, the sound of rapid breathing next to her—

Zee?

She looked wildly around and saw in the darkness the very still form of her cousin. He was not alone. In front of him was a tall, broad mass, and there was something long and thin and pointed that bridged the gap between it and Zee. Charlotte squinted at the form, trying to make it out, but there was no need, for just then there was a clanking and a creaking and a six-foot-tall bronze figure with a bucket-like head and a barrel body appeared in front of her. Slowly, smoothly, it lifted up a long bronze spear and held it against her neck.

The point pressed against her throat gently, but with a promise of menace, and Charlotte froze. She tried to glance at her cousin, but could not move enough to see him.

"We're supposed to be here," she squeaked. "We've been chosen. The girl sent us, the girl in the white dress. . . ."

The bronze figures did not move. They were defenders, not attackers, and it seemed that as long as Charlotte and Zee didn't try to go forward, they would not kill them. But the cousins could not exactly go back the way they had come.

"We're supposed to be here," she repeated, panicking. "Zee and I—"

The pressure on her neck lessened slightly.

"What? Zee and I? I'm Charlotte and this is Zee. Zachary. We've been sent—"

In perfect, eerie unison, the automatons lowered their spears and took three clunky steps backward. The creatures backed right into a shadowy wall and, as one, lifted their spears upward to form an arch, framing a passageway Charlotte just now could see in the flickering light.

Rubbing her throat, Charlotte looked at her cousin.

"Friendly," Zee said in a tight voice.

"Come on," Charlotte murmured. "Let's go."

Their way was clear. The fire beckoned them through the long passageway, just like in their dreams. They arrived in a cave chamber, in the center of which flickered a fire—small, but dazzlingly bright. Shadows danced against the wall amid drawings that seemed to move in the firelight. Barely able to breathe, Charlotte let her eyes pass over the walls until she saw the tall form of Prometheus.

There was nothing to say. They had arrived. They had done it. Together, Charlotte and Zee stepped toward the fire, the silence of the ages embracing them. And then, suddenly, Charlotte turned to her cousin. "Um, how do we take a fire, anyway?"

Zee frowned at her. "Um, I guess a log or something? We could make a torch. Or—" Something seemed to strike him. "Or," he said, reaching into his bag, "I wonder . . ."

Zee produced the small silver lighter that had come in the package with the map. Charlotte stared at it with wide eyes.

"How . . . ?"

Zee went over to the Flame, wielding the lighter. He flipped the switch and the top half of it opened, revealing a small wick.

"Won't it go out when you close it?" Charlotte whispered. Fires need oxygen—she had paid some attention in science. One day.

"I don't know," said Zee, bending down and holding the open lighter out to the Flame. "But we'll just take a bit, and if it doesn't work—oh!" A little bit of fire had danced onto the wick and Zee closed the top of the lighter. Just as he did, the entire room went dark.

Silence. Charlotte stared at the spot where the ancient Flame of Prometheus used to be. A low groan came from Zee, and he muttered, "Oh, brilliant, we killed it."

"Open it," Charlotte urged, trying to keep the panic out of her voice. She didn't particularly want to be responsible for destroying the last hope of humankind.

But then a flicker of light appeared on Zee's face, and relief washed over Charlotte. He closed the lighter again, then flicked the switch, and the Promethean Flame sparked up, just like any ordinary lighter. In the dim light Charlotte could see Zee shaking his head.

"What?" she asked. "You didn't kill it!"

"It's too easy, isn't it?" he said.

"What was easy? We fell about six thousand miles and were attacked by Bozo and Buckethead!"

"I don't know," he said. "Do you think this will

work? We put this in the hearth, knowledge of the gods spreads among humanity, and they all magically rise up? Won't there be chaos?"

"It would serve them right," Charlotte said, determination swelling inside her. "They hid themselves from humans because we were too much of a *bother*. They're supposed to be our *gods*. They have the ability to help people, and instead they just sit around on fancy yachts and watch surfers getting eaten by sharks. They *deserve* this. Anyway, knowledge is power, right? Mr. Metos told us the truth, and look at us! We're marching up Mount Olympus to our certain deaths!"

A grim laugh emanated from Zee.

As Charlotte spoke the words, their import washed over her. She could not put off worrying about it anymore. They had the Flame; it illuminated the path before them, up to Olympus, up to the hearth. Except for one problem.

"Zee, how are we supposed to get there? Do we just find Mount Olympus and start climbing? Do we stop at Socrates' Suicidal Mission Mountain Supply and suit up?"

The people who lived next door to the Mielswetzskis were always going off camping and mountain climbing and the like, and their garage was filled with all sorts of strange-looking equipment. It seemed to her an insane way to pass the time. If mountains wanted to be climbed, they wouldn't be so high up.

Zee looked around uncomfortably. "I think I know how. I mean . . . I don't know how. But I have an idea. It was something in the dream. Did the girl ever say anything to you about, well, a belly button?" He grimaced as he said the words.

"A . . . what?"

"I don't know if it was just something she said once. I was in the room—this room—and then she said, 'Seek the belly button.'"

Charlotte remembered Zee talking to himself on the plane; she should have known then that he had completely lost his mind. "So, in other words, I stare at my belly button and then Mount Olympus pops out? Don't you think I would have noticed by now?"

Zee did not answer, and with a heavy sigh, Charlotte sat down on the hard ground. Another strange clue, another mystery, another struggle. It was the metaphor made perfectly true—they had another mountain to climb. Except they had to find the mountain first.

So—find the mountain they would. Charlotte pulled out her guidebook and searched the index. Surely someone had identified where Mount Olympus was supposed to be. They would go back to Sir Laurence's driver and drive around, climbing every single mountain in Greece if they had to. Though she would really prefer not to.

"Well," she said to Zee, "there is a Mount Olympus. It's in northern Greece. And from Delphi, that's—" She flipped back to the Delphi pages and then inhaled sharply. She looked up at her cousin. "Zee," she whispered. *"I found the belly button."*

There was the matter of extricating themselves from the bowels of the Earth. Whoever had constructed the chamber was not, apparently, so big on exit strategies. Charlotte and Zee walked around the dark chamber, looking for a magic ancient Greek elevator, with no luck. Then, rather nervous to be encountering the robot twins again, they headed back the way they had come, Zee holding up the lighter to guide their way.

But when they reached the antechamber, they saw no sign of their bronze friends. What they did see, in the wall directly opposite the passageway from which they had emerged, was an industrial-looking steel door. So, with a nod to each other, the cousins went through.

They found themselves standing on the clearing of the mountain just below the Sanctuary of Apollo. They were in front of a small nondescript storage shack with a heavy steel door and a sign in Greek that Charlotte was pretty sure read NO ADMITTANCE.

"We couldn't have gone in that way?" she grumbled.

They turned away from the Sanctuary and followed a path that curved around the mountain and led to their destination: the Museum of Delphi.

They found themselves in front of a modern-looking building made of white stone bricks. In front of the museum was a large, paved clearing filled with tourists. Zee nudged Charlotte and pointed up ahead where Mr. West, Rosina, and the school group were moving into the museum. The group had suffered from some serious attrition since they'd left them at the Temple of Apollo, and it seemed there were probably more students on the bus than off at this point.

"Maybe you should put that away," Charlotte whispered.

Zee looked at his hands. He was still holding the lighter clenched in his fist. But before he could, a young man sidled up to them and nodded toward Zee's hand. "Hey, man," he asked in a thick, undefinable accent, "can I have a light?"

A panicked look crossed Zee's face, and Charlotte opened her mouth to explain that the lighter did not work, when Zee said, "Uh . . . I don't speak English!"

The man blinked at Zee in utter astonishment, and Charlotte took the opportunity to grab her cousin and steer him into the museum door.

"You know you said that in English, right?"

"Yeah, I know," muttered Zee.

On the inside the museum was cavernous and white, with large, open rooms holding artifacts and Greek statues. Groups of tourists walked from one station to another, and in one corner a security guard surveyed everything. And, right in front of the entrance, in a roped-off square, was the omphalos stone, the navel of the world.

It turned out the world had a very big navel.

The stone was a three-foot-tall dome covered in a net-like pattern with a small square opening at the bottom. It looked like nothing more than a very old stone beehive.

The picture in the guidebook hadn't shown the stone next to anything, so Charlotte thought it was small, something she could stick under her shirt and run off with. She was going to need a bigger shirt.

A German family appeared next to them and studied the stone. The school group was off in a corner, listening to Rosina. One boy was looking around aimlessly when his eyes fell on Charlotte and Zee. He poked his friend and whispered something.

"Do you think you can lift the stone?" Charlotte whispered to Zee as the family moved off.

"Um, I think so, but—"

"I don't know," Charlotte said. "I'll . . . create a diversion and you can, you know, slip out the door—"

"Char," Zee said under his breath, "I don't know much about Greece, but where I come from, they really frown on people nicking artifacts from museums."

"I know, but—"

"What are we supposed to do with it when we get it, anyway?"

Charlotte shook her head. "I don't know. The tour guide said it used to be in the Temple. Maybe we bring it back . . . ?"

"I'm sure no one will stop us before we get there."

"Do you have a better idea?"

Zee sighed. "No."

"Okay," Charlotte said, taking a step toward the security guard, unsure exactly what she would say when she got there.

It didn't matter. Because before she got very far, Mr. West's voice came booming across the room. "You!" he yelled. "I told you to get on the bus!"

"I—" Zee looked around wildly. The security guard was staring at Mr. West.

"I don't know what's wrong with you kids," the chaperone said, grabbing Zee by the arm. His voice reverberated through the museum, and everyone stared.

"Sir," said the security guard, stepping toward the group, "I must ask you to keep your voice down."

Charlotte looked around. The group had moved a few feet away, and everyone was staring at them. There was her diversion, but it didn't work out exactly as planned.

Trying to be as invisible as possible, she moved next to the velvet cordons. She heard Mr. West say, "I will control my students in my own way," and, with a glance toward the group, she ducked underneath the cords and stood next to the stone.

Quickly Charlotte put her arms around the stone. Biting her lip, she began to lift up, realizing to her relief that it was hollow.

Everything happened at once. The security guard hollered something in surprise and exploded toward Charlotte just as an alarm shrieked through the museum. Terror coursed through her. Zee looked at her wildly as Mr. West, still clutching Zee, shook his head and covered his eyes with his hand. Not knowing what else to do, she began to back away as tourists from all over the world looked at her in astonishment.

She had had better plans in her life.

A threat—yes, a threat would be good. She had to use the only leverage she could: this sacred, three-millennia-old stone, more valuable than many small countries, and probably some big ones, too.

"Don't come any closer or I'll drop it," she said. Or at least she meant to say it, but before she could get the words out she kicked over a stanchion. It fell with a mighty clank just behind Charlotte's heel. She stepped down and her feet flew out from under her.

Time can behave so strangely sometimes. It will move so slowly at just the moments when you would like it to speed up. Charlotte fell backward, slowly, slowly, like a feather falling its way to the ground—while the omphalos stone hovered in the air for a while, as if bidding the world an extended adieu, a silent soliloquy to bring down the house, and then plummeted to the ground, shattering into dusty pieces.

Silence. Even the alarm seemed to stop in shock, or else Charlotte had lost her power of hearing. Then the security guard went entirely white, tottered, and passed out. That seemed to awaken everyone. Someone screamed, Mr. West hollered, and Zee wrenched himself from his grasp and gave him his best soccer kick in the ankle. As the bull-faced man howled in pain, Zee took off for Charlotte, who had unconsciously begun scampering on the floor for pieces of the stone, grabbed her by the arm, and pulled her out of the museum door.

Out of the museum they ran, Charlotte clutching a shard of stone so tightly her hand was cutting into it, expecting at any moment to be chased, caught, thrown into Greek prison. From behind them they heard shouts, and they burst onto the clearing as yelling exploded behind them.

They were going to keep running, down the path, past the Sanctuary, to the awaiting car, but when they got outside everything had changed. At the edge of the clearing, which previously had looked out onto the valley below, was now a tremendous marble staircase lined with columns that rose up, up, up into the clouds. None of the tourists milling around seemed to notice the enormous structure that had suddenly appeared in their midst, but it was not for them. There was no time to discuss, no time to even be nervous. Without a look back, Charlotte and Zee dove across the clearing and toward the stairs that could only lead one place.

Olympus.

CHAPTER 23

# Heart-to-Heart

In a small café in an out-of-the-way street in London sat a teenage boy who looked as if he was having an intense conversation with an imaginary friend. As he spoke to the empty chair across from him, stopping at times to listen and nod emphatically, the few other people in the café stared and giggled to themselves. One even got up and left.

But the boy did not even notice, so focused was he on the conversation with his imaginary friend. Who was not, of course, imaginary at all, as much as it would be better for the world if he were.

Steve was drinking hot chocolate and describing his ordeal to the not-quite-a-man named Phil Onacron who had helped him in his time of need. With Mr. Onacron's help, he'd left a message for his mother—at least, he was pretty sure he had. There was something about the hot chocolate, something comforting, something wonderful, a special taste that warmed him, soothed him, made him want to spill his secrets.

Phil was appropriately appalled by his story, gasping at all the right times, sometimes shaking his head with the horror of it all. And when it was all done, he leaned in, red eyes full of compassion, and said, "That must have been so awful for you. You were so brave."

"You think so?"

"Oh, yes . . . Say," he added quickly, "the children who rescued you, do you know what became of them?"

"No. I left them on the Tube."

"Oh," said Phil. "Pity . . ." Steve looked up at him questioningly. "It would be nice to thank them."

"Yeah. My mom will be mad that I didn't."

"Oh, your mother," said Phil, putting his elbows on the table and resting his chin on his hands. "Tell me about her."

Steve took another sip of hot chocolate. He felt so warm. "She raised me all by herself. Without any help from anyone. She wanted to be a singer, but she gave it all up for me."

"Oh, she sounds like a *marvelous* woman! She must be so proud of you."

"Do you think so?"

"I do. Why, if I had a son, I would want him to be brave like you."

Steve blinked. "Really?"

"Oh, really. I almost had a son once, but he . . . well, he got away. And"—Phil looked at him cautiously—"your father?"

Steve's eyes traveled to the ground. "I don't have a father."

"My boy," said Phil, "everyone has a father. My father was a demon."

"Oh, I'm so sorry!"

"No, no, I mean he really was a demon. You don't know anything about your father?"

"My mom never talks about him. My aunt told me once that he said he would marry her. And then she got pregnant and he just left her."

"My goodness! How appalling!"

"She was just twenty-two, she didn't have anything. Her parents left her to deal with it on her own." Steve did not know what was happening, but he felt so emotional all of a sudden, like he might cry at any moment. Steve did not cry. He punched things. He did not want to cry in front of this man, this man who thought he was brave.

But Phil only leaned in to him. "It's all right, my boy. It's all right. You must let out all your emotions, do not keep them pent up inside. It's not healthy."

Steve wiped a tear from his eye and nodded. All this therapy and finally he'd found someone he could talk to.

Phil let out a long sigh. "Stephen, I must tell you—I have not been entirely honest with you."

Steve sat up. "What?"

Phil put his hand to his heart. "I am sorry. But it is no accident that I found you today."

"What do you mean?" Steve asked, looking suspicious.

"No, I am afraid it was Fate that brought us together. For, you see—and I have been hesitant to tell you this— I know who your father is."

Steve stared at Phil.

"I do. And I can say for certain that he is as vile as you think, and that he used your mother most ill indeed. I must tell you, when he met your mother, he was *already married*."

"What?"

"Yes. I'm afraid your father likes to play around. It's . . . sport for him. Your mother is not the only woman to have suffered in his hands."

There it was, the anger, rising up inside of him.

"I *knew* it," he hissed, slamming his fists down on the table.

"He had no intention of staying with her," Phil continued. "He left her, young, broke, and—bereft."

"Bereft? What do you mean?"

Phil just shook his head. "She recovered, didn't she? She had you, such a fine boy, a boy who would protect her, who would avenge her! Your father, you see, that is what he does. That's what he's still doing today."

"You mean . . . ?"

"Oh, yes. Your father has not changed a bit since your birth. While your mother was struggling to raise you, he has been having fun, breaking other women's hearts." Phil paused a moment, as if to collect himself. "And they are not all as strong as your sainted mother."

Steve gasped. "Someone has to stop him!"

"Oh, yes, I couldn't agree more!" said Phil, looking extremely earnest. "I have always thought so. But . . . your father is a very powerful man, and it would take someone very brave indeed." Phil shook his head. "Well, my boy, we should get you to the police." He stood up and walked out the door.

"No," said Steve, following. "Wait!" He ran out of the café and found Phil standing on the street corner. "I want you to take me to my father," he said firmly.

Phil looked shocked. "You do? But don't you want to go home?"

"Yes. But after. I want to go see my father now. I have to!" He stomped his foot on the floor. "I have to stop him!"

"My goodness," said Phil. "I could tell what a brave boy you were. So honorable. This is a great thing you are doing. But—whatever will you do when you see him?"

Steve's eyes narrowed. "I'll think of something," he said through clenched teeth. "Now, where are we going?"

"Well," said Phil, clapping his hands together, "that is a bit of a long story. . . ."

## CHAPTER 24

## OLD SCHOOL

As soon as Charlotte's foot landed on the smooth white staircase, everything changed. The clearing, the crowd, the museum, the whole mountain disappeared behind her, and all there was in the world was the staircase and deep blue sky. Above them hung a thin, shimmery layer of clouds.

The cousins stopped and stared up at the blanket of clouds. They had done this before, hovered on the threshold of a realm, lingering in the moment before they crossed it. There was always the choice, every time—they did not have to go, they could turn back.

But of course they would not, could not, did not.

"I guess we should go in," Charlotte said, nodding to the clouds.

"Let's go," Zee said.

And they grabbed hands and climbed the stairs.

It happened very quickly. One moment Charlotte was just below the clouds, the next she was completely surrounded by them. Long, wispy tendrils that were nothing like what she learned about in science class wrapped around her, and she saw, smelled, tasted only this strange whiteness. And something was missing, something important, something that was right there with her, something she needed very much—

Zee?

Her hand was empty. She whirled around, fighting against the sticky tendrils. She tried to call out for her cousin, but as soon as she opened her mouth, the cloud invaded her lungs. Her chest felt as if it had filled with cotton candy, and she struggled to breathe. Her sense of direction was gone; she could not feel the stairs below her feet, and all she could do was struggle ahead. The cloud resisted, pulling her back, and it took every bit of her strength to push ahead. She shut her eyes tight and thrust herself forward. She was a fly caught in a web, and she had no desire to meet the spider.

And then, just like that, almost as if someone had

commanded it, the cloud let her go and she burst through into the open sky, gasping. She bent over, her lungs taking in air greedily, and it took her some time to notice her surroundings.

Nothing had changed. She was still on the staircase and another cloud blanket lay ahead. Only this time she could see something behind it, the lurking shadow of a large structure. And this time she was alone.

She looked around frantically, as if her cousin might be right next to her and she just hadn't noticed. He was not. She turned back to the clouds below and called:

"Zee? *Zee?* ZEE!"

But there was no response. Charlotte began to shake with panic. What had happened to him? Was he still trapped in the cotton-candy arms of the cloud? Was he struggling to get free, struggling to breathe? She'd have to go back in, have to find him, have to free him—

She was about to dive back into the clouds, with no idea what she would do when she got there, when a voice stopped her.

"I wouldn't do that if I were you."

Charlotte whipped around. A form had materialized a few steps above her. Actually, "materialized" was the wrong word, as the figure Charlotte saw did not seem to be entirely material. Standing before her was a diaphanous, violet-hued, vaguely woman-shaped creature that was about seven feet tall and not much more than six inches wide. Long violet hair curtained around a face that had only the barest impression of features.

Charlotte drew back.

"Why not?" she asked, glancing from the woman to the clouds below.

"It won't like it."

A shiver ran down Charlotte's back. *Where's Zee?*

"Don't worry about him."

"Don't *worry* about him? Where is he? Do you know where he is?"

"The journey to Olympus must be made alone," the woman said. Her voice was thin and whispery, as if the air itself were talking.

"Is he *okay?*"

"That is not your concern," said the woman impatiently. Her hue had changed slightly, and now she seemed more red than purple. "You have business at Olympus?"

"Um . . ." Charlotte looked around again. She could feel a lump rising in her throat. Zee was okay, she had to believe that. She would know if he was not okay. They had simply separated in the clouds, and he would be emerging at any moment, coughing and gasping and looking for her, and Charlotte would make some kind of comment about killer clouds and Zee would mutter something under his breath and then they would continue on their journey to Olympus, carrying the Flame, together.

"You have business at Olympus?" the woman repeated, now bright red. Charlotte looked at her uncomprehendingly, feeling as though she were falling off the staircase into the open sky.

The woman let out an annoyed sigh. "You will see your companion at the top. Should you both get there, that is. Now, mortal"—she cleared her throat and returned to her previous shade of purple—"you have business at Olympus?"

"I—uh, yes . . ." But what? Zee had the Flame. She had nothing. What was she going to do, give Zeus a good talking-to?

"What is the nature of your business?"

"Uh—justice."

The word just popped out of her mouth, as if someone had reached inside and pulled the truth out of her. She wanted to grab it and shove it back in, but it was too late.

But the woman only nodded. "Very well."

Very well? Was that it? Some sticky spiderweb cloud attack and then she announces she wants justice and the gates to Olympus pop open and she trots on in, and—

"We'll see how you fare."

Charlotte's stomach turned. That did not sound promising. And, just like that, the woman's color began to change from purple to blue, and then she dissolved into the sky.

Suddenly the world shifted, and a wave of nausea passed over Charlotte. She closed her eyes, trying to steady herself, and when she opened them her knees buckled in surprise.

Everything had changed. She was no longer on a stairway in the clouds, making her way to Olympus; rather, she was standing on the concrete stairs that led to the front door of Hartnett Middle School.

She stood there looking frantically around at her utterly familiar, utterly strange surroundings. Surely it was a hallucination, surely the scene would dissolve soon, surely in a moment she'd be back on the stairs above the clouds, heading up to Olympus.

But the scene did not shift. She closed her eyes and shook her head slightly, as if that might lift whatever spell she was under. It did not. She stood on the stairs frozen as her fellow students swarmed in around her, some talking and laughing, some trudging up dutifully. It was a scene she had lived hundreds of times before—but she could not understand why she was living it now.

She felt disoriented, seasick, as if she'd woken up to

find that someone had sucked out half of the world's oxygen. She wanted to run down the stairs and across the street and as far away from here as possible, but she could not move. This unexpected normalcy was perhaps the most frightening image she could conjure.

"What's with her?" she heard someone ask.

"Psy-cho," came the response.

A voice called, "Hey, Char," and she whipped her head around to find Jasper Nix standing next to her, giving her a friendly smile. "You're back!"

She blinked. "Back?" she repeated.

"You're back! I heard you were on a trip to save the world. How'd that go? Are you feeling all right? You seem a little green."

"Uh—" She closed her eyes and opened them again. "How did—have you seen Zee?"

Jasper shrugged. "No. Is he back too?"

"I—I don't know." She looked all around at her surroundings. However they did it, they had done a very good job of making this seem real.

He blinked back at her. "Are you sure you're okay? You seem kind of . . . weird."

"Yeah. No. Um, what day is it?"

Jasper frowned. "Maybe you should see a doctor, Char. Ooh, there's the bell!"

And with that he was off.

The stairs around Charlotte emptied out as she stood, waiting for something to happen, waiting for something to make sense. She looked at the building in front of her, and then the street behind her. She was about to go down the stairs, into the street, to test the boundaries of this illusion—when the doors to the school opened and Mr. Principle appeared.

"Charlotte? Are you coming?"

She looked around. "I—I . . ."

"School's started," he said, coming down the stairs. "Come on in." And the next thing Charlotte knew, he was steering her inside the building.

"So," he said cheerfully as they stepped into the lobby, "when did you get back?"

"Um—just now." She eyed Mr. Principle. He seemed to be himself—he had not grown any extra tails or fangs, but she couldn't help but notice that today's plaid suit, usually a muted yellow or green, was purple. His face was a mask of pleasantness.

"Oh," he said. "Terrific. Jasper said you saved the world."

"Well—"

"That's great. You must feel really wonderful about that. We'll be sure to remember you on awards day. You and Jack Liao, of course, who constructed that whole Ecuadorian village out of cheese."

"Uh-huh," Charlotte mumbled, looking around nervously.

"He used a combination of American and English cheddar, which I thought was a particularly interesting commentary on imperialism. Almost *piquant*, if you'll forgive the pun." Mr. Principle had passed the front office and was leading her down the main hallway now. If the school had indeed been reconstructed, someone had done a heck of a job. It looked exactly as it had on the day of the fire, down to the notes on the blackboard and the posters on the wall. And Mr. Principle was exactly as artificial and vapid as he always was—maybe even more so. And Charlotte noticed that his expression had not changed at all during their entire conversation.

"Mr. Principle, um, have you seen Zee?"

"No. Isn't he with you?"

"Well, no . . ."

"You lost your cousin? That was careless of you. Hey, did you know the Greek gods are real?"

Charlotte stopped. "What?"

"I know, who knew, right? It just came to me, all of a sudden. Well, I had a clue when half the seventh grade got eaten by a Minotaur."

"What?"

"Yeah, there's monsters all over the place. I don't

know how we didn't see it before. Don't worry, most of the city is still alive."

Oh, Charlotte saw now. She was supposed to think she had failed—made things worse, condemned humanity by trying to save it. All right, that was the game—

Suddenly she stopped in the middle of the hallway. Up among all the familiar inspirational posters was one that had decidedly not been there before. Under the headline, HAVE YOU SEEN ME? was Charlotte's own face.

"Oh," said Mr. Principle offhandedly. "Yes, well, your parents insisted. There are signs all over the place. We all knew you were off saving the world, but you know parents."

Charlotte's chest tightened. This was not real, of course, but the poster might as well be.

"I have to tell you," continued the principal, "I don't know if I'd have the courage to leave my family like that, even to save the world. It must have been very hard. Especially given how they reacted—"

Just then someone called to Mr. Principle from inside one of the offices, and he smiled at Charlotte officiously and excused himself.

She stood alone in the middle of the hallway. If this were real, everyone would be in homeroom now, but there should still be a few stragglers. Unless they'd all been eaten, of course. Everything was utterly, totally quiet, and Charlotte felt as if she were all alone, not just in the school, but the universe.

Well, whatever was planned for her, she had no intention of walking into it willingly, and she turned around and headed back for the front door. She didn't know what she would do then—try to find her way back to Olympus somehow—but she would figure it out when she got outside.

But when she got to the lobby, she found there would be no escaping for her. For the school no longer had a front door at all—there was an empty doorway, and outside she could see only clear blue sky.

Charlotte went over to the edge and then quickly jumped back. It seemed Hartnett Middle School was floating in the air—there was nothing around them but sky and clouds, and there was no sign of any ground anywhere below. She had no plans to fall a jillion feet today.

She went back to the edge, holding on to the wall for support, trying to see some sign of something, anything. Just when she thought the sky was completely empty, a white winged horse flew into view.

In a better world, Charlotte would call to the horse and he would fly over and gaze at her with his beautiful horse eyes, and they would bond, because she was a girl and he was a horse, and then he would he offer his back and she would climb on and they would fly off together to safety and she would say, "Good horsey."

But this was not that world. The horse looked at her, whinnied derisively, and flew off.

As Charlotte stared into the boundless sky, she shuddered and her heart began to race. Never had she wanted to get out of her school as much—and that was saying quite a bit. There must be a way out somewhere, something that led to *something* else. Something where she didn't feel like a mouse in a psychological experiment.

Grimacing, she turned away and stepped back into the main hallway.

It had changed. The entire hallway was papered with missing-Charlotte flyers, there must have been hundreds, and she shivered seeing so many copies of her own face staring down at her. She saw a brief image of her parents solemnly hanging up the posters, a ghost in time, and then it disappeared and she was alone again.

Then a great flapping noise, and an all-too-familiar screeching that shook the posters on the wall. She instinctively ducked as a Harpy appeared—with its giant vulture wings and sneering old woman face and rotting smell—flying down the hallway, singing:

*Charlotte had a little quest*
*Little quest*

*Little quest*
*Charlotte had a little quest*
*And it destroyed the world.*

The Harpy buzzed right over her head, grazing her with its claws as it passed. She stayed down, covering her head, until the flapping disappeared down the hallway.

She headed down the hall again. All the doors around her were closed, and she tried a few of them as she went by, but they did not open.

The main hall, about fifty feet long in real life, was taking her an eternity to walk down, and with every step the missing-Charlotte posters multiplied.

Ahead of her, where the hallway branched off into classroom wings, Charlotte could see an open door, so she went toward it, planning on trying a window. It didn't seem like the door that happened to be ajar would handily lead to her escape route, but she had to try.

But when she got there, she found the class was not empty at all. Standing at the billboard, giving a talk on dramatic irony, was a green-faced, snake-haired, red-mouthed Gorgon. One of the snakes turned to Charlotte and hissed, and before the Gorgon could turn its gaze upon her, she ducked out of the way, but not before noticing that the students sitting so placidly at their desks had all been turned to stone.

"Typical," she muttered.

Suddenly she felt a firm hand grab her shoulder. "Miss Mielswetzski," said a disapproving voice.

She sighed. She should have known. "Hi, Mr. Crapf." She turned around to find the math teacher glaring at her. She nearly started when she saw him—he was very thin with angry eyes, more like Charlotte always thought of him than he actually was.

"What are you doing out of class?" His grip on her shoulder tightened, and she felt a pang of fear. The real Mr. Crapf couldn't do her any harm—other than psychological—but who was to say about Olympus Crapf? Didn't things have to get threatening here soon? Indeed, as he squeezed, a shot of pain traveled from her shoulder through her body, and suddenly all her muscles began to ache in response.

"Get your hands off me," she yelled, squirming.

The teacher turned a bright, blinding red. "How dare you, you little ungrateful malcontent," he spat, squeezing her arm. "I am a *teacher*. You will *respect* me. I've seen kids like you before, you will make nothing of yourself—"

"Let go of her!" The voice reverberated down the halls. Charlotte wrenched herself from the math teacher's grasp and whirled around.

Mr. Metos!

But was he real? He strode down the hallway toward them, full of purpose and Mr. Metos-ness. He looked ... the same, human, like the Mr. Metos they had left in the Prometheans' garage. Her heart started to beat so loudly she thought the whole fake-school could hear.

"Let go of her, Crapf!"

"Easy, Metos," muttered the math teacher, backing away. As Mr. Metos approached, Mr. Crapf dissolved into the shadows.

"Mr. Metos?" she said questioningly.

"Charlotte. Are you all right?"

"You're not real."

"Of course I'm real. I was looking for you. I was on the stairs to Olympus, and then—"

She gasped. "You ended up here. Why? Why am I here?"

"I imagine they are trying to find ways to stop you."

"But, it's totally stupid. It's math teachers and, you know, *middle school*. I don't care about this place."

He blinked. "You don't?"

"Well ... no."

"Huh. That's funny," he said, in a genuinely puzzled voice that Charlotte did not understand. "Anyway, I know a way out. We can find Zee and—"

"Metos!" The word came as an explosion that shook the school. Charlotte jumped, and Mr. Metos spun around. Timon! Had he followed them? "I knew I'd catch you."

And as Charlotte watched, Timon lifted his gun and shot Mr. Metos three times.

Charlotte screamed as the Promethean collapsed in a heap on the floor. Timon stormed off, and Charlotte dropped to her knees next to the Promethean.

"Mr. Metos? Mr. Metos? Are you okay?" Tears flooded her eyes as she shook him, but he did not respond. Blood pooled from his back onto the floor, and he took one great, rattling breath, and then was still.

"No!" Charlotte yelled.

"Don't worry, it's not real," said a smooth voice.

"Wh-what?" She looked up. Crouching at the end of the hall, filling the entire space, a giant lion-like creature with great eagle wings and a woman's head stared at her levelly. A Sphinx.

Charlotte drew herself up. She knew all about the Sphinx. In the Oedipus story, a Sphinx stood guard on a path outside a kingdom and would not let anyone pass unless they answered a riddle. Everyone who answered it wrong she ate. The riddle was, "What goes on four legs in the morning, two in the afternoon, and three at night?" Oedipus got it right: Man, who crawled as a baby, walked upright as an adult, and walked with a cane when he got old. The Sphinx was devastated and fled, the whole kingdom rejoiced and made Oedipus their king, and he married the queen (who was actually his mom but he didn't know it). It was a long story.

"It's not real," the Sphinx repeated, blinking its cat-like eyes lazily. "But it could be, right?" It flicked a paw toward Mr. Metos's body. "They may well have killed him, right? Because he saved you? You don't know what happened to him, do you?"

Behind the Sphinx was not a stairwell but open sky. It was guarding the way out.

Charlotte wiped her eyes and stood up, trying to keep her eyes away from the sight of Mr. Metos's lifeless body on the floor. Fake as it might be, the Sphinx was right. It could be real. The thought was more horrifying than anything Charlotte had encountered so far, and if they meant to unnerve her, they did a good job.

"Do you know?" she asked weakly.

The Sphinx smiled and licked its paw, a long cat tongue emerging from its mouth.

Charlotte closed her eyes and tried to piece herself together. "What's my riddle?" she asked flatly. Of everything they could have used to block the way to Olympus, a Sphinx was probably what she would have picked—not a test of strength or dexterity but a test of wits. A riddle she could figure out; it might take her awhile, but she could do it.

The Sphinx continued to bathe itself. "Yes, of course. A riddle. Your riddle, Charlotte Mielswetzski, is thus." The Sphinx fixed her with a haughty stare. "Does humanity deserve to be saved?"

Charlotte stared. "What—that's my riddle? . . . I don't get it."

"Answer the question. Does humanity deserve to be saved?"

"Of course it does!"

"Look at what you see every day," the Sphinx said, indicating the Hartnett hallway. "You hate this place. And this is nothing. This is just day-to-day pettiness, it does not touch on humans' capacity for evil. This is not cruelty, avarice, murder, war. You act like you are so noble, you act as though you are so much better than the gods, but have you read a newspaper lately, Charlotte Mielswetzski?"

Charlotte took a step back. "It's not all that way. It's not! Not everyone's like that."

"I see. And you think you are above the pettiness, the cruelty? Do you think you are worth saving?"

"Y-yes. Yes, I do."

"Hmmm," said the Sphinx. "That's surprising, given what you've done." The creature flicked a paw, and the doorway next to Charlotte flew open to reveal her own living room. Her parents were huddled together on the floor, among a pile of missing-Charlotte posters, her mother sobbing and her father, eyes red, holding her and staring dully at the ground.

"This," the Sphinx said, "is real."

It was too much. Every bit of Charlotte wanted to pass through the doorway, to go to them, but she could not move, so frozen was she by the sight before her.

"And humans aren't cruel," the Sphinx added.

It was real, she knew it was real. She could step through the door and be home again. Zee had the Flame, he would go, she had nothing, nothing but her parents, who loved her with the immensity of the sky, whom she had nearly killed from grief.

"If you go on, if you go to Olympus, they will know. They will know they have lost you forever. Because you are giving up your life when you cross this threshold."

Charlotte stared. The Sphinx began to lick its chops. One way was Olympus, her quest, perhaps her death (if that was what the creature was saying?); another was her parents, broken, whom she could put back together again with one step, whom she could destroy with one step.

The Sphinx lifted its immense body up and stretched, then took a languid step forward, its eyes fixed on her.

"Aren't you going to answer?" it cooed.

No. She could not. She was absolutely still. She would die this way, devoured by the Sphinx.

Just then a sound came from the living room—like fifty snakes all hissing at once. Charlotte and the Sphinx both turned their heads, and the Sphinx crouched down. Charlotte's parents noticed nothing, but Charlotte saw. Mew was bounding through the living room toward them.

She leaped through the door, landing on all fours between Charlotte and the Sphinx, her ears flat against her head, her fur standing straight up along her spine, her mouth fixed in a menacing hiss.

The monster narrowed its eyes. "What are you?" it said, frowning. "You are not right. You are a riddle."

Mew poised on her haunches, a coiled spring.

Suddenly the Sphinx frowned. "This is not a fight you can win, riddle."

A sound from Mew, like the scream of an eagle, and then she pounced.

Starting, the Sphinx reached out a defensive paw but was too slow. Mew sprang toward the beast's face, claws out, a flying puffball of doom. The Sphinx shrieked as Mew landed, grabbing onto its face with her claws. A flurry of motion and fur and paws and the Sphinx was screeching, swatting at the cat attached to its face.

Then Mew leaped off. The Sphinx's face was covered in blood, and Charlotte looked away. The creature yowled and lunged around wildly, swatting this way and that.

With a glance at Charlotte, Mew bounded back through the door, and as she did, the room disappeared—there was nothing left but shadow. The Sphinx screeched and hurtled blindly toward the blackness, and Charlotte seized her chance and ducked behind it into the open blue.

## CHAPTER 25

# Bread Crumbs

"Y̶OU HAVE BUSINESS AT OLYMPUS?" THE PURPLE woman asked.

Zee looked around, bewildered. He had no business at all now except finding his cousin, who had not come out of the clouds. "Pardon me," he mumbled to the nymph, and had turned around to dive back into the clouds when a long arm grabbed him and pulled him back.

"You have business at Olympus?" she repeated.

"I—" He looked back behind him. "I need to find my cousin."

"Very well," said the woman.

A sudden wave of nausea brought Zee to his knees. He felt as though the world was swirling around him, and when he finally recovered he found himself alone in the dark. It took a moment for his eyes to adjust from the sky-brightness, but when they did he realized he was no longer on a marble staircase in the clouds, but rather standing in a dark forest. The trees around him were enormous, thick, and shadowy, with great limbs that contorted as they reached out to one another. A heavy cover of dark leaves obscured the sky. The whole place was eerily quiet, with no wind or rustling or anything to let you know the forest was alive, was of the Earth—yet Zee still felt with eerie certainty the presence of creatures lurking in the shadows. It seemed like he had landed on the very expensive set for a film version of Hansel and Gretel.

"Charlotte?" Zee called weakly, looking around.

He was conscious of a tightness in his chest and a thinness in the air and a slant to the ground. He was high, and going higher.

A flash of memory hit him—tendrils of cloud wrapping around him, pulling on him, infesting his lungs, filling him with the bizarre and terrifying sensation that he was going to drown in the clouds. Was Charlotte still trapped there?

He had to get back. He didn't know how—since

he'd apparently been dumped here by the random skinny purple lady—but he had to help her.

He looked around for some sign, some indication of the way out. But there was nothing, just this endless fairy-tale forest, and he was out of bread crumbs.

Taking a deep breath, he tried to dull the panic inside him. It could not be that he had lost Charlotte after all of this. It could not be that after everything they had been through, after everything she had survived through her very Charlotte-ness, she would get trapped inside some malevolent cloud-thing.

No. Of course not. How had he gotten out? He'd struggled through. He'd pushed against the encroaching wisps and gotten free. It was nothing Charlotte could not do, nothing she had not done many times before. Encroaching wisps had nothing on Charlotte. She had gotten out. She was fine. The random skinny purple lady had asked what his purpose was, and he said to find Charlotte, and she'd sent him here, to what could only be the slope of Mount Olympus. Very helpful, the random skinny purple lady.

"Charlotte?" he called again, taking a step forward. Something seemed very wrong to him, and it was not until he took another step that he realized that when his feet hit the falling leaves, they made no sound at all. Everything was entirely silent.

"If a Zee falls in the forest and no one is there, does it make a noise?" he muttered to himself.

A flicker of movement near a lithe, graceful, skinny tree caught his eye, and he whipped his head around, trying to find the source. It was not something near the tree that was moving, but something within it—a shadow that shimmered slightly just under the surface of the tree, and then was still. He stopped and stared, not trusting his eyes. And then something separated from the tree—a tall, willowy female form the color of bark. She was a shadow, a ghost, transparent and insubstantial. Zee took a step back and she froze, then melted into the next tree, and all was still again.

Zee set his jaw. There was nothing to do but go forward. Charlotte was here, in this forest, looking for him and making her way up the mountain. He would do the same. And then—

Oh! Zee had forgotten entirely about the Flame, and he reached his hand to his back pocket to see if the lighter was still there. When his hands felt the familiar rectangle, he exhaled in relief. It would be just like him to lose the Flame of Prometheus—hidden by the great Titan five millennia ago, sought for centuries, faded into legend, and then found and irrevocably lost by Zachary John Miller, age thirteen.

In truth, Zee was uneasy about the whole thing. Mr. Metos had said that people did not necessarily want to know the truth, and Zee understood. People, he'd noticed, were fairly attached to their own beliefs. He'd caused enough trouble in his life without unleashing worldwide chaos. Charlotte seemed to think that because someone had led them to the Flame, they were supposed to use it, but Zee had been led a lot of places in the past year—none of them good.

But, as Charlotte said, the gods wouldn't like it at all, and that alone was worth a good deal. He wished, though, that they had come up with something else.

Like Steve. It isn't often that the thing that Zeus fears most in the world appears in front of you. Perhaps they should have talked to Steve, explained, had him overthrow Zeus (how exactly? Challenge him in Quiz Bowl?) and then install some benevolent Canadian rule over the galaxy.

Or something.

But Steve had fled, and this was all they had.

As Zee walked, he began to sense some kind of presence behind him, something as silent as the forest, and he looked again to the trees. But this was different— there was something, something at the edge of his field of vision, some strange, diffuse glow that quickly disappeared into the darkness. Something nudged at him—it was so familiar, but he couldn't place it, nor could he understand why he suddenly felt so cold.

"Charlotte?" he called again helplessly. His voice seemed to be swallowed by the unyielding silence. She could be a few feet away and not hear him.

And then, suddenly, noise—loud, ominous, closing in. The ground trembled beneath him, and the trees seemed to bend slightly to make way. Then, bursting into view, came a pack of white wolves the size of bears. Their fur gleamed like sun on new snow, their eyes were gold, their red mouths grinned as they sprang across the forest floor. Zee did not understand how they could be making noise—they seemed to almost fly as the forest parted around them—but he did not have time to consider the situation too carefully, given the pack of enormous wolves heading right toward him.

Something in his head was telling him to move—and quickly—but the sight of the wolves was so beautiful, so dazzling, he could not really pay attention.

The wolves were not alone. Galloping behind them was a tremendous black horse ridden by a goddess-size woman with black hair and skin of blue-tinged white. On her head was a thin diadem with a small crescent moon in front, and she carried an elegant moon-tipped bow and a quiver of silver arrows. Everything about her seemed to shine—not like a jewel, but like a single star in a black sky. She was the only light in a world of absolute blackness.

That voice in Zee's head was more urgent now, yelling something, and Zee wanted it to stop, be quiet, it was distracting him from the sight before him. The gleaming hunting party grew closer and closer and Zee stood in its path, watching, waiting, his whole body tense with anticipation. If he could just see this goddess's face, look into her night blue eyes—

A large hand grabbed his shoulder and yanked him backward. He found himself on his bottom on the ground behind one of the massive trees as the hunting party passed him by. They flew off into the distance, and when they disappeared, the trees closing behind them, it was as if the whole forest let out a breath.

Zee's heart raced, and he felt like he had just awoken from sleepwalking to find he'd almost walked off a cliff.

"Artemis really doesn't like it when mortals see her," a low voice said behind him.

He whirled around to find himself staring up at a creature with the torso of a man, the legs of a goat, a young man's face, and small goat horns. A satyr.

"You are fortunate. Those wolves are trackers. If Artemis asked them to find you, you would have no hope."

The satyr was a little taller than Zee, with gray skin and fur and big eyes so dark they were almost black. He carried a very large backpack, as if he was on a long journey. There was something very pleasant and open about his appearance, and Zee found himself feeling oddly comfortable.

"Th-thank you."

The satyr bowed. "Always a pleasure to help a traveler," he said in his low, soft voice. "It is not very often we see mortals in here these days, and you are the second today. . . ."

At these words, Zee straightened. "Was the other a girl? My age, smallish, peach skin, red hair, freckles?"

The satyr's eyes widened in the picture of surprise. "Why, yes! Do you know her?"

Zee exhaled. She was all right. Of course she was; she was Charlotte. "Where is she? Where did she go?"

"She went ahead, to the gate to Olympus. She was looking for her cousin—is that you?"

"Can you show me?" he asked, not even trying to mask the urgency in his voice.

"Of course," said the satyr, bowing again. "Follow me, my friend."

Just then Zee noticed the strange glow he'd seen before, again just out of the corner of his eye. He looked toward it, but still could see nothing. "Did you see that?"

"Must have been a nymph," said the satyr. He straightened, and a look of pain flashed over his face. "My friend, might I trouble you for a favor? This pack I carry is a little heavy, and it is getting difficult to walk. It would make our journey easier if you wouldn't mind helping me a bit with my burden."

Zee nodded. "Of course!" The large pack bulged on his back, and Zee suddenly noticed weariness in the satyr's expression. He felt a pang of guilt—he should have offered.

"Thank you," said the satyr, lifting the large pack carefully off his back. He opened it and pulled out a white, disc-shaped stone about the size of a dinner plate.

"It's a rock," Zee said, surprised.

"Yes," said the satyr simply. "Thank you, my friend. I am so grateful." He handed Zee the rock—which was heavier than it looked—and without prying any further, Zee wedged it under his arm.

"Much better," said the satyr, and he hoisted the pack back up and began to walk forward through the trees. Zee followed him uncertainly, conscious of the feeling of eyes on him as he moved. Which was probably because there were—as he passed through the trees he noticed shadows moving within the bark, and while everything was as silent as death, he could almost feel them whispering to one another about him. He got the strangest feeling he would not like what they said.

And there was something else, too, something that lurked at the edge of his perception, something that felt familiar and yet entirely wrong, something that made him put his head down and focus only on the path straight ahead.

"If I may ask—," said the satyr.

"Anything!"

"You and your cousin, well—are you the ones . . . that is, we have all heard tell of the mortal children who went to the Underworld. . . ."

"That's us," Zee said, his jaw clenched a little.

"Well," said the satyr, nodding his head in a bow. "It is an honor."

Zee squirmed a little. "My cousin," he asked, "did she say anything?"

"Oh," he said offhandedly. "Not really. She was worried about you. She'd tried to go back for you and then found herself here."

"Oh," said Zee. He could empathize. They walked on quietly, making their way through the silence. Zee realized his chest felt tight and he was laboring to breathe, and he wondered how high up they were. He got the distinct impression they were getting higher. Which, he supposed, was the point.

"Olympus is ahead?" he asked.

"Yes," said the satyr. "We're heading to the entrance."

"And can I just, you know, walk on in?"

The satyr paused. "The gods have their ways of trying to stop you," he said. "But in the end, the choice is yours. There is a goddess there, Hecate, the goddess of the crossroads. If you still want to pass when you get there, she will let you in."

"What do you mean, still want to pass?"

But before the satyr could respond, Zee felt a rush of motion just behind him and stepped out of the way just as a white stag came running by. It was tremendous, magnificent, so white it glowed against the dark trees, and as it leaped along it seemed to almost float in the air. Time slowed for a moment in deference to the creature's graceful strides, and Zee could see every muscle ripple through its flank as it moved. He let out a gasp as it passed, beautiful and as quiet as the night, as the forest itself.

"Wow," he muttered.

He turned to the satyr, ready to ask about the stag. The satyr was bent over, his hands on his knees, breathing heavily.

"Are you all right?" Zee said. "Can I carry something else for you?"

The satyr looked up at him, uncertainty flashing in his eyes. "Are you sure?"

"Of course!" Zee said.

Sighing in obvious relief, the satyr unbuckled his pack and handed Zee another smooth white stone. Zee frowned at it but did not ask questions, merely tucked it under the other arm. His back and arms protested, and Zee eyed the satyr's pack wonderingly. It still looked quite full, and he didn't know how the satyr had made it this far.

"Thank you, my friend," said the satyr. "Shall we?"

They moved forward again, Zee keeping one ear open for approaching giant stags or drooling tracker wolves or whatever else the forest might hold. The air seemed to thin with every step, and the stones seemed to grow heavier and heavier.

"How much farther do we have to go?" Zee asked, trying to make it sound like he was only curious.

But before the satyr could answer, the forest ahead began to glow. And then, all of sudden, a line of faceless, glowing, human-like forms appeared across the way. The Dead.

Even from a distance, Zee felt the chill of their presence. He looked around instinctively, as if he could just turn in another direction and forget they were there, but through the leaves and thick trunks he could see that they were everywhere, surrounding him in a vast circle, still and watchful but somehow menacing, like the ghosts of past misdeeds that linger at the edge of consciousness.

Zee could barely stand to look at them. The Dead, ignored and abused by Hades, who was too consumed with the reluctant Queen Persephone to care for his subjects, the ghostly manifestation of everything that was wrong with the gods, left to rot in the emptiest corners of the Underworld. He and Charlotte had wanted to save them, had been desperate to do something for them, but there was nothing they could do. He had thought of them so much since they'd returned from the Underworld—but it was nothing like seeing them.

"What is it?" asked the satyr, looking bewildered.

"What are they doing here?" breathed Zee, glancing around. The Dead did not move.

"Who?"

"*Who?* The Dead!" Zee motioned to the vast circle around him.

The satyr lowered his pack and looked around. "You see the Dead?" he asked, blinking. "Where?"

"What do you mean where? You don't see them?"

"No!" The satyr's eyes narrowed thoughtfully. "There are no Dead here. But . . . the forest can do funny things to mortals. Sometimes if there is something weighing on your conscience, it can manifest itself here—I believe it is the gods' way of distracting people from their quests for Olympus. It's just an illusion, though. Best to ignore it."

Zee blinked. "My conscience?"

"Yes," said the satyr. "Because you left them. You were so concerned about the Dead, but you left them down there. That must eat at your conscience—"

Zee's jaw dropped. "I—uh . . . no, I—"

"Oh, well," the satyr said. "Good." Closing his eyes, he exhaled heavily and adjusted his pack.

"There was nothing we could do," Zee continued, his voice suddenly tight. "What could we do?"

"Did you try? You had an audience with Hades. You saved his reign, right?"

"I—" Zee's throat tightened. It was true. They had had an audience with Hades, who should, after all, have been a little grateful to them. And they had not said any-thing. Here they were, telling themselves they were the sort of people who saw injustice and could not sit still, and it was exactly what they had done.

He looked around at the circle of Dead, and they looked back at him blankly. He took a step forward, as if to say something, though he did not know what.

And then one of the Dead broke ranks and stepped toward him. It should have been ominous, but it wasn't—there was something about the presence that signified something quite different. Zee's breath stuck in his chest as it took another step, and then he blinked, and suddenly they were all gone.

Zee stared at the space where the Dead had been, feeling at once relief and a great sense of loss. That was not—it could not have been . . .

"It's all right," said the satyr, stepping toward him. "It's not real."

"One of them moved toward me," he said quietly.

The satyr's horns twitched thoughtfully. "Do you know someone who has died recently?"

Pursing his lips, Zee gave a short nod.

"As I said," the creature continued, his voice kind, "the forest is a strange place. It can do things to you."

Zee looked down. Had he seen his grandmother? If it was his own mind doing this to him, well, then it didn't matter. It was not real. And if his conscience was burdened over the Dead, well, nothing like seeing Grandmother Winter as one of them to make it worse. She was down there, wandering aimlessly, being harassed by Harpies, losing all her Grandmother Winter-ness, and he had blown his one chance to save her.

"Are you all right?" asked the satyr softly.

Zee nodded slowly. There was nothing to do now but keep going.

The satyr let out a great grunt as he hoisted up his

pack again, and Zee eyed him. His steps were slow and labored, and after some time he was able to convince the satyr to give him one more stone.

"If I may ask," the satyr said as they walked, "how did it come to be that your cousin is accompanying you on your quest? It was you who inspired the usurper's plan, right? That is the story I have heard, at least."

Zee flushed. "Um, yes. My cousin, well, she got involved and—she's not the sort of person you can leave behind."

"Mmmm," said the satyr. "That must be hard, though, knowing she is in danger. This is really *your* quest, isn't it?"

"Um"—Zee looked down—"well, I suppose. But she would say it's hers, too—Poseidon tried to kill her, and—"

The satyr's eyes widened. "He did? Because of what happened in the Underworld?"

Zee nodded.

He shook his head. "You must be so relieved he did not. I am sure you do not want that on your conscience. . . ."

"No," he said quietly. "I don't."

Suddenly the satyr stopped and stared at Zee as if something had just struck him. "Your cousin," he said carefully, "is there anyone else who might hurt her?"

"Why?" Zee asked, his throat catching. A chill passed through him and he was taken to Exeter, to the moment when his mother said his grandmother was not feeling well. He was standing on a precipice, about to be pushed off.

The satyr inhaled sharply. "I—I didn't think anything of it at the time. There was a half-breed god here, not of this realm. He had the stink of demon on him. He asked if I'd seen a mortal girl."

Zee could not move, could not breathe. Philonecron. He was back. He was after Charlotte.

"She had not come by yet," he continued, dropping his pack, "and even if she had I would not have said anything, for I did not like the look of him at all. He was not one to help a satyr with his burdens. But, my friend, he was not alone." The satyr looked at the ground, as if to gather himself. "He had a wolf with him. I believed it was just a companion, but now I realize—it was a tracker. Oh, my friend, oh—"

The satyr's reaction was enough to tell Zee exactly what that meant. He was looking at Zee with some combination of pity and horror, and Zee could only stare back, mouth hanging open slightly, absolutely unable to move or speak. His stomach roiled, his blood was ice, he felt as if he were plummeting through the air.

"We . . . we have to find her," he said when he could speak. "We have to save her."

The satyr looked at him sorrowfully. "I do not think there is any hope."

"We have to try," Zee said. "We have to try! Philonecron hates her, he wants her dead."

"Very well," said the satyr. "I understand how you must feel. For what it's worth, I will guide you."

His words cut Zee. Of course. It was his fault. If something happened to her—

Just then the ground began to tremble again, and Zee looked around in a panic. The wolves were coming. And—a flash of white ahead of them and Zee saw the great stag, still as a statue. He was going to yell, clap, do something to startle the magnificent creature.

It happened so quickly. The satyr pushed him behind a tree, just as three moon-tipped arrows came singing through the air. The stag fell. The wolves appeared from the shadows and pounced. The forest filled with the sound of snarling and clacking of teeth and some other noises Zee did not want to think about. His stomach clenched and turned and it was only through great will that he did not lose its contents.

He did not have time. They had to go. They had to find Charlotte. One of those creatures was after her. He looked around frantically for the satyr, trying desperately to block out the noises so near to him.

It took a moment for Zee to find him. The satyr blended in with the tree next to which he stood, and it took some searching for Zee to recognize his form. The satyr stood utterly still as the wolves finished their meal and the hunting party took off again, leaving the remnants of their prey, another being Zee had failed to save.

"We have to go!"

The satyr nodded and lifted his bag with a mighty grunt, and then stumbled. His face went white and his knees buckled under him.

"My friend," he said in a breathless voïce. "I am sorry. I do not think I can go on—"

"I'll take it! I'll take the whole pack!"

"No, no, I—"

"Come on!" Zee said.

Reluctantly the satyr stripped himself of his pack and handed it to Zee, but he could not hide the relief on his face. Quickly Zee opened the pack, placed the three stones he had been carrying inside, and hoisted it onto his back.

He groaned and felt he might topple under the weight. It was as if he was carrying a mountain on his back. His knees began to quiver, and sweat flowed out from every pore.

"Can we leave this and come back?" he asked the satyr through gritted teeth.

The satyr was grinning at him, a grin that changed his whole face. "Now, my friend, the burden is yours. You must carry that until you find someone else to take it."

Zee gaped at the satyr, who gave him a huge, theatrical wink, then darted off, quick and carefree.

He could not move. Charlotte, the wolves, the stag, the satyr, the pack—it was so much at once that his body threatened to collapse in on itself like a dying star.

He was alone. He had no idea how to find Charlotte—if she was indeed in trouble. But there was nothing he could do but keep looking.

He set down the pack and set off in the direction they had been heading. And then he slammed into a wall. Or felt like it anyway—there was nothing at all in front of him, but he could not go any farther. He glared at the pack and tried another direction, with the same results.

Zee half screamed, half gargled out a stream of expletives as the tree nymphs stared at him, then he darted for the pack, hoisted it on his back, put his head down, and barreled ahead.

Ah, it was heavy. His back screamed, his muscles ached, but there was no choice. With it he was slow, unsteady, hopeless, but he had to go on, so go on he did.

So much had been happening that he had not noticed that the forest had been thinning and bright light was starting to appear in between the trees. He did not really notice, in fact, until he saw a signpost in the path. He stopped, glad for the chance to rest, and stared. On it were three ebony arrows, one pointing straight ahead, the other to the right, the other to the left, with words engraved on them. The first read OLYMPUS, the second WAY OUT, and the third WAY BACK.

Zee stared at the sign, bewildered and wondering how it came to be written in English, when a goddess materialized in front of it.

She had three heads, one facing straight ahead, the others to either side. Her skin was white, and her hair and dress were as black as the ebony sign. She was wisp-thin, seemingly made more of shadow than substance. Next to her sat two large dog-shaped shadows. Hecate, goddess of the crossroads. She stared levelly at Zee.

"Look," she said, through the face that looked at Zee. She pointed off to the right, and, as she did, the trees split to reveal Charlotte, about fifteen yards away, looking around as if she had no idea where she was or how she got there.

Zee's heart nearly exploded. She was there, she was okay. "Char!" he called.

His cousin's head whipped toward him, and her face melted in relief. "Zee!" she yelled.

"Char, we have to go, Philonecron, he—Wolves! Bad wolves!"

Just then Hecate pointed in the other direction. There was a low growl, and the forest around him seemed to tremble. Then a flash of white, and the mighty wolf was in front of Charlotte, crouching and growling and ready to pounce.

She screamed, and Zee tried to run to her but suddenly could not move. The goddess pointed at him, then the road sign.

"You must choose," she said.

"Zee! Help!" Charlotte said. "I can't move!" As she recoiled, the wolf gave a great snarl, then leaped at her. Hecate snapped her fingers and the wolf froze in the air.

"Zee! Please!" Charlotte screamed.

"You must choose," said the goddess again, her voice sounding like it was amplified by a megaphone.

"Choose?" Zee said. "Choose what?"

"That way is Olympus, the way forward. That way is the way out. And that way"—she pointed in the direction of the third arrow—"is the way *back*. You can change it all, go back to the beginning, make new choices, and it will be as though you and your cousin never knew about

the gods. And then you—and she—will never get here."
She pointed to Charlotte again, who was trying desperately to break free of whatever held her. The wolf hung in the air, inches from her throat.

Zee stared at Hecate, then his cousin, then the road sign. He could do it—he could go back to the beginning, keep any of this from happening, keep Charlotte from danger, he could—

"Zee!" shrieked Charlotte. "Do it! Please! Do it!"

Of course, of course. He turned to the goddess and opened his mouth, ready to go back, then suddenly looked at his cousin again.

"Wait, what?" He tilted his head questioningly.

Her eyes filled with terror, with pleading. "Zee! Please! Do it!"

Zee straightened under the load of stones. He stared at the scene around him, at the goddess, at the woods, at the sign. "You're not Charlotte," he breathed.

"What?" she shrieked. "Of course I am!"

"No, you're not! This isn't real! None of this is real!" And with that, he threw down the pack and strode past the goddess toward the light ahead.

## CHAPTER 26

## Sacrifice

Suddenly Charlotte found herself on the same wide staircase in the sky as before, in front of the same cloud, with the same dark structure looming behind it. She whirled around, but the school was gone. It was as if none of it had happened.

"Good kitty," she whispered.

As she looked behind her, the thought occurred to her that she could head back down, pass through the cloud unharmed, go all the way down the staircase, and find herself in front of her house, where her parents would be waiting for her. She knew, somehow, that it was true, that she was being given a way out.

She had to hand it to the gods—or whatever it was that designed that vision for her—they sure knew how to mess with a girl. Charlotte had seen monsters, had faced her own death, but never had she faced anything like that.

The imaginary guilt-tripping Sphinx was right. She was cruel. The Prometheans wanted to sacrifice Steve for the greater good, and here she was sacrificing her parents. Was it worth it? Was it worth hurting the two people who loved her best in the world for this quest? For—justice?

If that's what it was. Before, when they went to the Underworld, they were saving kids' lives. They had no choice; they were the only ones who knew the truth, the only ones who could do anything. But what about now? What did Charlotte really want?

Charlotte carried the Underworld with her wherever she went; the Dead always lingered behind her eyes. Behind her eyes, she saw them as they parted for her and Zee after they stopped Philonecron. Charlotte and Zee were the only people in several millennia who had done anything for them, and now they were alone again—except a few Prometheans richer. Including Hector. And in danger.

She had to go on ahead. She had to go on, to find Zee, to use the Flame, and then—

And then her parents would know, wouldn't they? And she could tell them what she'd done, tell them everything that had happened, explain why she'd left them. And they'd understand and forgive her and—

And they would all live happily ever after? Because that was how life always worked, right?

And where in the world was Zee? *Don't worry about him,* the rainbow-lady had said. *The journey to Olympus must be made alone.* Probably wandering through the hallways of Hartnett or his old school or some bizarre, guilt-plagued Zee-verse while Olympus did its best to stop him from heading forward.

Well, it wouldn't stop Zee, and it wasn't going to stop her, either.

"I'm ready," she shouted at the cloud in front of her. "Let me in!"

The clouds parted, and Charlotte was standing below a marble temple with a mammoth wall of six-foot-thick columns that stretched up into infinity. She quavered a little, feeling suddenly like a flea about to dive into the ocean. And then she crossed the threshold into Olympus.

Charlotte was standing in a vast atrium surrounded by a series of balcony-lined floors that stretched up as far as she could see—there must have been hundreds of them.

Everything looked as if it was made of crystal or glass of a delicate light blue—the floor, the huge Grecian pillars that lined the room, the arches and columns of the balconies above. The building was made for giants; the room she was in was four times taller than anything on Earth. The balconies were each a shade lighter than the one below until the building disappeared into the white beyond. A soft yellow light emanated from somewhere above, giving everything a blue and gold glow.

While everything was distinctly there, present, real, somehow Charlotte felt a diffuseness and impermanence to her surroundings. And, while she was supposedly inside somewhere, the air around her was open, warm, fresh, sweet-scented, like she imagined it would feel if you stepped off an airplane into a tropical world. She didn't feel like she was in a building at all, merely some illusion carved out of the sky.

There was also something familiar about the place— the open atrium, the arcs and columns of the balconies, the vaguely bank-like architecture—it looked like a very large sky-version of the Prometheans' headquarters.

There was even a desk in the center of the room, shaped like half of a pillar and made of the same blue crystal as everything else, and at the desk sat a woman with smooth white skin and pinned-up white hair, with great feathered blue wings tucked primly behind her back.

She was not alone. The lobby was packed with Immortals, none of whom showed any interest in Charlotte. A god and two goddesses stood a few feet away from her, arguing loudly with one another. The god was heavily tanned and dressed in a sequined gold suit. One of the goddesses was very pale, with a long white dress that matched her skin and a small, luminescent crown on her head. The other had pink cheeks and hair and wore a neon orange toga. A bit away from them, two blue-skinned sea nymphs were rolling on the ground, scratching and pulling each other's long hair. A few paces behind them, a tall skeletal goddess who was ink black on her right side and pure white on her left was screeching and kicking a pillar repeatedly. A short, naked, muscular god with bright yellow skin was hurling flames from his hands at a tall, naked, muscular god with bright blue skin, who shot water back at him. A female goddess with Harpy-like wings and greenish skin was running in circles around the lobby, cackling madly and hurling rotten apples at everyone. In one corner, an Olympus-size giant with a hundred arms sat slumped over, muttering to himself and weeping loudly. When the Harpy-winged goddess tossed an apple at him, he reached out one of his arms, grabbed her, and threw her so she sailed all the way through the lobby out the door.

There were Immortals everywhere, gods and

monsters and combinations thereof, fighting, yelling, sulking. Charlotte stood and gaped.

Through the cacophony, she heard a pleasant female voice emerge from somewhere overhead, its tone completely incongruous with the scene before her. *"The weather today is sunny and warm, thanks be to Zeus the Stormbringer. Today's activities include Book Club at Hestia's Hearth . . ."* Charlotte frowned. She did not expect Olympus to have a PA system. *"Wine Tasting with Dionysus, and War-Mongering with Ares. Today's Cuckolded Wife Support Group will be led by Hera, and the all-wise Zeus will be resolving disputes for your edification and amazement in the evening."*

Groans and boos from the crowd. A harp came whizzing by Charlotte's head, and she had to jump away.

"May I help you?" A soft voice floated in the air toward her. Charlotte turned to find the receptionist looking at her curiously. She cleared her throat and stepped forward.

"Um, hi," she said, her voice sounding high and strained. "I—"

The receptionist's bead-like eyes widened as she approached. "Are you *mortal?*"

"Um," Charlotte had heard this one before. "Yeah."

"Heavenly Zeus on a pogo stick!" she gasped. "Huh. It's been a while." She reached down under the desk and grabbed a huge binder. "I just need to . . . ," she muttered, flipping to the end and scanning a page. Leaning into the book, she whispered, *"What do I do?"*

Charlotte sensed suddenly a presence behind her, and she turned her head to find that a centaur had appeared in line behind her, arms crossed over its chest. She stared up at the creature, who had a pinched, thin face, a scrawny forest green torso, and a skinny brown horse bottom. She noticed something glistening behind him and peered around to see a large silver arrow sticking out of his butt. She raised her eyebrows.

"Do you *mind?*" he asked pointedly.

She turned back around to the receptionist, while the centaur began tapping his hoof impatiently. A very large human-headed slug slithered in line behind him and let out a slug-like sigh. "You'll want to take those elevators to the tenth floor," the receptionist said, pointing to a bank of large pillars behind her. "You'll find altars there. And, uh . . ." The woman glanced back down at the book. *"Okay, what?"* she murmured to it.

"Hurry *up,*" grumbled the centaur.

"Just follow the instructions!" finished the woman brightly.

"Okay, thanks. Um, bye."

"Have a wonderful day!" said the receptionist. She started and looked back down at the book. *"What, too friendly? Oh, sorry."* Her voice changed to one of haughty dismissiveness. "Thank you for visiting Olympus."

"Sure," said Charlotte. She left, as the centaur muttered, *"Finally,"* and headed toward the elevators.

And then stopped. What was she doing? Here she was at Olympus with no direction, no plan, no Flame, no Zee, nothing but a spacey receptionist, a lobby in chaos, and a centaur with an attitude problem. She needed to find Zee, put the Flame in the hearth, and get out of there.

"Excuse me," she called, heading back to the receptionist.

"Oh, great Stygian gods!" muttered the centaur, stamping his foot.

"Um, is there, like—oh, an empty hearth somewhere? And nobody knows what it's for?"

"Huh," said the receptionist thoughtfully, putting a long, bird-like finger to her chin. "Well, now that you mention it, there is! *What?*" She glanced back toward the binder on her desk. *"Just a second! I'm being helpful!* Floor forty-five," she said brightly. *"What?"* she whispered to the book. *"Oh, I'm not?"* She looked up again and called to Charlotte. "Wait a second!"

But Charlotte had taken off toward the elevators.

The elevators were built into three of the pillars and dotted with small, pentagon-shaped call lights, which Charlotte had to jump up to hit. Had she not been through the Underworld and Poseidon's yacht, she would have thought it odd that she could just waltz into Olympus and call the elevator with nothing but a snippy centaur with an arrow in his butt to stop her. Elementary schools had better security. But she knew that was the way of the gods—humans were nothing, not worth considering.

The pillar opened, and Charlotte stepped inside to find herself in a blue-silk-walled elevator. She was not alone. A four-foot-tall man with goat horns and black goat legs was sitting on a small pillar, strumming a lute. When he saw Charlotte, he sighed. "What floor?"

"Um, forty-five, please."

"Fine. Any requests?" He nodded to his lute.

"No, thank you," she replied as the elevator door shut.

"Okay," trilled the little man. Then he strummed the lute a couple of times and began to sing:

*Mortal girrrrrl*
*Without a song to hear*
*Mortal girlllll*
*Who thinks she has no fear*
*Plucky little redhead*
*With just a touch of bedhead*
*Has your skin ever seen the sun?*

Honestly! "Do you mind?" asked Charlotte.

"Just doing my job," said the goat-man. "Oh, hey," he added, perking up, "watch this."

The elevator stopped and the floor trembled. There was a sound of pounding hoofbeats, and Charlotte instinctively stepped away from the elevator door. In a flurry of motion, a tremendous black chariot pulled by two giant black horses rolled in. The elevator grew to accommodate them. Standing on the chariot was a red-skinned god wearing a large black helmet and very little else. The color of his skin flickered and changed, as if there were fire just underneath the surface. He looked as if he had once been very muscular, but his skin was loose and flabby. A black iron mace hung limply in his hand. His face was stubby and pockmarked, and he looked at Charlotte and belched.

"What are you looking at?" he growled in a slurred voice.

"Uh," said Charlotte, willing herself to be smaller.

"Hello, Lord Ares," said the goat-man brightly. "Any requests?"

"Shshuuddup!" drawled Ares.

"Very well, then." He punched a button, the elevator door closed, and he began to strum and sing:

*WAR! (huh, yeah)*
*Good gods y'all!*

*What is it good for?*
*(Absolutely nothing)*

"Why, you little—" Ares jumped out of his chariot, grabbed the little man, and hurled him right through the floor, sending blue crystal shards everywhere. Charlotte gasped and recoiled, her hands flying up to protect her eyes. She was breathless with shock and revulsion—until she heard echoing through the shaft:

*WAR! (huh, yeah)*
*Good gods y'all!*
*What is it good for?*

The voice got more and more distant. There was a loud crash, and then a squeal of, "I'm freeeee!" and the sound of goat hooves pattering off. One of the black horses belched fire down the elevator shaft.

Charlotte stared at the hole in the elevator floor while Ares started pounding his fists on the elevator buttons.

He roared in anger, then turned to Charlotte, eyes blazing. "Do you know how to run this thing?"

"Um . . . ," she said, "actually, I'm getting out here." This seemed like an excellent time to take another elevator. She pressed a button, the doors opened, and she slipped off.

So focused was she on getting out of there that she did not notice the smell emanating from the room until the doors had closed behind her and the elevator moved on.

And then she noticed. Charlotte had stepped out of the elevator into a large pile of cow manure. She was in a vast green field, surrounded by hundreds of moon-eyed, snow-white cows, who were all staring at her in surprise and what seemed very much like terror.

"What?" Charlotte asked, as the cows near her began to slowly back away. Something about their fear made her heart begin to pound. It was like they were mistaking her for some kind of bovine serial killer.

"I'm not going to hurt you," she protested, feeling slightly sickened by their fear. "My parents eat ground turkey!" She looked around wildly for some explanation. It was a field like any other—perhaps the grass was a little greener, the sky a little more blue. She could see a simple white fence penning them all in and a brown barn in the distance. The only other structures were the pillar elevator behind her stretching to the sky and, off to the right, twelve pedestals.

Keeping one eye on the cows, who looked as though they might snap at any minute, Charlotte went over to the pedestals to investigate.

On each was a word written in Greek, but as Charlotte's eyes landed on them the letters altered into English. ZEUS, read the first one. HERA, the next. POSEIDON, then DEMETER, then ARES. Twelve pedestals, twelve Olympians. Behind each pedestal was a small fire pit, and at the top was a large knife with a bone handle and curved blade.

Charlotte picked up the knife and stared, bewildered, and then as it dawned on her she swore loudly.

She was supposed to sacrifice one of the cows.

*"Hello, mortal,"* said the pleasant loudspeaker voice. *"Welcome to Olympus. Please select your sacrifice."*

*You'll want to take the elevators to the tenth floor,* the receptionist had said. *You'll find altars there.* It seemed that every mortal who came to Olympus was supposed to make a sacrifice to the god she wanted to see. A flame of rage shot up through her chest, and tears burned in her eyes. Oh, how she hated the gods, she hated their cruelty, she hated their vanity, and if she ever got back home she was totally going to become a vegetarian.

"Hey," she said, turning to the cows, her voice softening. "I'm not going to do it. It's okay!"

One of the cows mooed balefully.

"Seriously!" Charlotte said.

*"But you have to,"* said the loudspeaker voice, sounding more surprised than bossy.

"No, I don't," said Charlotte, looking up.

*"You're on Olympus, missy. You have to make a sacrifice.*

*It's the way it works."* From up above she heard an ominous cawing noise.

"You want a sacrifice?" Charlotte breathed. "Here." As the cows looked on, she stomped over to the fire pit, grabbed a log, scooped up some manure, and plopped it on the altar marked ZEUS.

*"Oh my goodness, oh my goodness,"* said the voice. The sky above Charlotte darkened suddenly. She turned to the cows, who were all watching her with a rather dazed expression, looking like—well, like cows.

Charlotte set her jaw and stomped over to the elevator and pressed the call button. Lightning flashed in the sky, and some sort of rumbling passed through the cows.

The elevator door pinged open, and sitting there was a brown-legged little goat-man, who had a small electric guitar and an amp.

"Can you fit them all?" she asked, motioning to the cows.

"Er," he said, "I think so. . . ."

*Thank goodness for expando-vator technology*, Charlotte thought. "Take them to the lobby and point them to the exit, okay?" She got a mental image of several hundred white cows descending the stairs into Delphi. That school group was in for a surprise.

The goat-man looked at Charlotte appraisingly, and

then his eyes flicked over the giant herd of cows. His face broke out in a grin. "Awesome!"

*"Security, please, to the tenth floor. Security."*

"Come on," she shouted to the cows, standing aside as the great mass of them poured into the elevator. There was a rumble of thunder, and Charlotte glanced up at the sky. The goat-man followed her gaze and muttered, "I wouldn't come this way. There's an exit in the barn back there." He nodded to the distance.

Then, as the cows tramped onto the elevator, he picked up his guitar and began to sing:

*Go down, cow Moses*
*Way down in Olympus land*
*Go down, cow Moses*
*Let my Holsteins go. . . .*

"*Go,*" he hissed. Another bolt of lightning clapped overhead. Charlotte ducked away from the stampede and ran as fast as she could in the direction of the barn.

*"A storm front has moved through the middle floors of Olympus,"* said the voice on the PA. *"Gee, I wonder why."*

Charlotte tightened her grip on the knife, which she still held in her hand, and kept running.

There was a cawing noise, and three giant eagles appeared in the black-clouded sky. The clouds opened up, and water poured down on Charlotte. One of the eagles saw her and began to dive, and the other two followed.

She raced for the door of the barn and pulled it open. She heard one thump on the roof, then two more.

In front of her an impossibly old man-like man in overalls was moving hay with a pitchfork. He looked at Charlotte, bewildered.

"Hi," she said, wiping the rain off her face. "Is there, um, a way out of here?"

Still confused, the man pointed behind him. There was a wooden ladder leading to a hayloft. Up above, the eagles' claws began to tear at the roof.

"Do you know what that racket is?" asked the man slowly, leaning on his pitchfork.

"No," said Charlotte innocently, trying to mask her heaving chest. "Um, I gotta go!"

"I hope the cows are okay," he murmured as Charlotte scaled the ladder to find a small door in the wall with an exit sign just above it. She lunged toward it. There was a screeching whine as a roof board was peeled away. A dripping, scaly claw about the size of Charlotte burst through the opening and starting swiping blindly. The claws were between her and the exit. Then, a blur of motion too fast to follow, and she felt a ripping pain, then hot blood streaming down her cheek.

A great shudder passed through her body, and tears stung her eyes. The claw made another grab for her and she lunged toward it, nearly blind with tears and blood, flailing with the knife. She'd only intended to ward off the eagle arm for a second so that she could dive for the door, but the knife had other ideas, and before her eyes two of the long, razor-like talons were cut clean off. The eagle shrieked, the barn shook, and Charlotte reached for the small door and hurled herself through.

CHAPTER 27

# Dream Come True

And then Zee was on the great staircase in the sky again, staring at a sheet of clouds with a large structure looming behind it. He did not need anyone to tell him what that was.

Zee's fists were clenched and his teeth seemed to be welded together. He had the distinct urge to punch someone, except there was no one to punch, and even if there were it probably wasn't a good idea, considering. He looked behind him, as if the vision might still be there so he could shoot it some kind of nasty look. It was horrible, cruel, and even though he knew it wasn't real, the image of Charlotte with the great wolf inches from her throat still haunted him. And that satyr—Zee wanted to devote his life to a crusade against not just that satyr, but satyrs everywhere.

Zee felt different—and it wasn't just the clenched fists or the lockjaw, not to mention the burning in his stomach or the vaguely psychotic murmurs of his brain. He felt light, focused. Everything around him was sharp and clear, and despite being however high in the sky, he had never breathed more easily.

He reached into his back pocket and patted the lighter, then looked at the structure ahead.

"Let me in," he called.

And the clouds parted.

He was about to step forward when a clear, strong voice rang through the sky. "Wait!"

Zee whirled around so quickly he almost toppled off the stairs.

Standing two steps down was the girl from the Flame dreams—white dress, dark hair, white ribbons—looking up at him with fire in her green eyes.

"Took you long enough! Do you have it?" she breathed.

Zee gaped at her. It was so strange to see her in the flesh that he half wondered if he had fallen asleep somewhere and this was a dream after all. But of course he knew it wasn't. And what exactly had become of his life when he could be standing on a giant staircase in the sky and know it wasn't a dream?

"Who are you?" he asked.

"It doesn't matter," she said, her childlike voice firm. *"Do you have it?"*

He didn't have to ask what *it* was. His hand unconsciously reached for his back pocket.

"Let me see it!"

Zee narrowed his eyes. He wasn't really in the mood to be bossed around by someone in an overstarched white party dress. "Where's Charlotte?"

"She went in already. She's fine. Now let me see the Flame!"

He wasn't going to get anywhere with her. With an annoyed, Charlotte-like sigh, he reached into his pocket and brought out the small lighter. The girl grabbed for it, and then suddenly yelped and dropped it onto the marble staircase.

"Get it!" she shrieked, clutching her hand.

Zee had already lunged for it—he'd gone through too much to get the thing to let some spastic faux primary-school student plummet it off Olympus. His hand was on it just as it bounced and skidded toward the edge.

"I can't even touch it!" the girl said, wide-eyed, still holding her hand.

"No, I guess not," muttered Zee, tucking the lighter back into his pocket protectively. She was making him anxious. "Do you want to tell me who you are?"

She glared at him. "There's no time. Let's go."

"I think I'll just wait here," said Zee, folding his arms. He had the lighter. She would have to give him some answers.

Then, in an instant, the sky around them turned dark, and there was a flash of lightning. Zee glanced at the girl, who was looking around nervously. A noise shattered the air, a great cawing sound, and three enormous eagles appeared on the horizon, heading right toward them.

"Uh," said Zee, his heart speeding up.

"I think we should go in," she hissed, looking nervous.

"Right, then."

The girl led the way, trudging up the stairs and through a wall of tremendous columns and into what looked like a giant glass bank lobby. Everything was the same color as the sky—this dark, stormy blue-black. Every once in a while there was a flash in a pillar or the floor or running down the balconies, like lightning within the building. Zee could feel rumbles through the floor. The lobby was filled with strange-looking Immortals who seemed completely unaware of the rumblings around them. A white-skinned woman-like creature was sitting at a reception desk arguing with a giant man-faced slug. As they passed, the receptionist glanced over at Zee and the girl, raised her eyebrows, and said, "Is it spring already?"

The girl shot her a look and walked on, Zee following her.

One foot in front of the other—Charlotte always said that was the trick to getting through the godly realms. But while his heart was pounding and he found himself looking this way and that for stray oncoming Zee-eating monsters, he was not as nervous as he might be walking through the atrium of Olympus. Perhaps because this was his third realm, or because he was following someone who was certainly some kind of god—despite her weird fashion sense—or because they had a plan that, if it worked, meant he might not confront anyone at all. Or perhaps because he was very, very stupid. Still, there was one thing—

"Where's my cousin?" he asked.

"I don't know," said the girl offhandedly, glancing around. "I'm sure she'll meet us at the hearth."

Zee pursed his lips. He did not like this at all. How was he supposed to know whether or not she was all right?

The girl stopped in front of a bank of giant pillars

and pressed a button, and Zee realized they were waiting for the lift. The gods might not think much of mortals, he'd noticed, but they sure like their stuff.

And then something very unusual happened. The lift door opened and out burst several hundred snow-white cows. The girl gaped as the herd kept pouring out, streaming through the lobby and out the front door.

The Immortals around them stopped what they were doing and stared. A couple of them screamed and ran/flew/galloped/slithered out of the room. The receptionist stood up, her vast blue wings unfolding in surprise, while the slug cowered as cows swarmed around them. She looked around the room wildly and, catching the equally bewildered eye of the girl in the white dress, exclaimed, "What's going on?"

A smooth female voice rang out from overhead. *"Will the mortal who freed the sacrificial cows please report to floor thirty? Will the mortal who freed the sacrificial cows please report to floor thirty?"*

Zee looked at the ground quickly, trying to hide his smile. Charlotte, it seemed, was fine.

And then it was all over, and the cows were gone. The girl hesitantly peeked into the elevator, then wrinkled her nose and muttered, "We'll take the next one."

When the next one arrived, they stepped in to find glass shards all around and a great big hole in the floor.

The girl examined the scene with a distinctly puzzled expression on her face and eyed a pillar-like stool in the corner. "There's supposed to be . . . ," she murmured. "Ah, never mind."

And then they were off, traveling up, up, up in the glass column. The lighter in Zee's pocket began to feel warmer and warmer. The girl's face was flushed, and she kept tugging at her ribbons nervously. Standing so close, Zee could feel the nervousness and excitement radiate off of her, and his own heart began to thump in his chest so hard that he had to close his eyes and try to quiet it.

"You know," he said, exhaling, "you could have been a lot more helpful."

"Hmm?"

"With the Flame. I mean, you gave us these barmy dreams and sent us a map with no names. You could have been more helpful. Like sent us a letter with instructions, maybe?"

She looked at him levelly, her childish manner suddenly dropped. The force of her gaze caused him to take a step back. "No, I couldn't," she said simply.

"What are you *talking* about?"

"I was given a charge," she said. "The bearer must find the Flame for himself. That is the rule. I helped you as much as I was able."

Zee could barely restrain himself from rolling his eyes. "Couldn't you at least have labeled the map?"

"*Labeled?*" she said, as if Zee were the greatest idiot in all of human history. "Who needs a label for *Delphi*? It's the most sacred place on Earth!"

Zee really, really hated the gods. "I still say you should have done more."

"Well"—she gazed at him haughtily—"you're here, aren't you?"

Zee had nothing to say to that. The elevator pinged and stopped, and the girl sucked in breath and began to bounce on the balls of her feet, looking suddenly very much a little girl again. Again his heart began to speed and a wave of dizziness passed over him.

The door opened slowly, and Zee and the girl were standing in front of what looked like a great castle hall cut out of dark crystal. The room went on and on as far as he could see, with vast tapestries lining the walls and a long crystal table that was taller than Zee, with what seemed like a hundred intricately engraved giant-size armchairs pulled up to it.

It was made of the same material as the lobby, but, where that was pristine and shining, this whole room was covered in a thick layer of dust, casting a gray tinge over everything. Zee looked at the girl in surprise—it did not seem Olympus should have a housekeeping problem.

"This used to be a banquet hall," she said in a low voice, "but they haven't used it in about a thousand years. Come *on*."

She burst out into the room, and immediately Zee's head began to clear. Still, he could feel the energy crackling off of her, and he was loath to get too close.

She darted ahead and Zee followed slowly, eyes darting this way and that. Walking next to this high table with chairs meant for people three times his size, he felt like a midget man, and it wasn't helping his confidence. The tapestries along the wall seemed to shimmer as he passed, and he looked at one only to see that the gods and beasts embroidered on it were all looking at him.

"Yeesh," he said.

"Come *on*, slowpoke!" the girl said again.

Zee felt a flash of irritation so strong he knew it didn't come from him. The girl was radiating so much energy now that the room was thick with it. As she motioned to him, bouncing up and down rapidly, he could see her form flicker and then solidify again, as if she was having trouble holding it. The lighter was growing hotter still, and Zee wondered if it was literally going to burn a hole in his pocket.

On and on they walked; there seemed to be no end to the hall, and the girl's agitation was getting more and more tinged with trepidation. Zee could not see why, but he did not like it one bit. It didn't help that he was beginning to feel like he might burst apart as well.

"Where is this thing?" he called, his jaw clenching.

"Just a little farther," she said.

The smoky blackness of the glass rolled and roiled, interrupted only by flashes of electricity. Another low rumble reverberated through the walls.

Where was Charlotte? Was she off leading meetings for the Bovine Liberation Front? Wasn't she trying to find him? He needed her here, now—he needed to regain control of this situation, he was not going to be someone's puppet. He'd had enough experience with that, thank you very much, and if Charlotte were here she would tell the girl off and—

Well, she wasn't here.

"STOP!" he yelled. "Just STOP."

"What?" She turned, eyes blazing. Zee felt a surge of heat rise up inside of him.

"I'm not going any farther," he said. "I want to know what's going on."

She let out a snort of exasperation. "What's going on," she said slowly, as if he were very stupid, "is you have the Flame of Prometheus in your pocket. I have picked you, above all mortals, to be the one who finds it and uses it to give humanity knowledge of the gods again."

"*Why?*"

She looked at him like he was an idiot. "Then Zeus would have to deal with humans again, wouldn't he? He thought he was being *so* clever. We'll see how he likes it when people start asking for things again, and when everyone sees that one of his stupid plans failed."

Zee noticed she said *Zeus* not *the gods*.

"*Why?*"

"Because he would *hate* it! Poseidon would hate it, Hades would hate it! They would all *hate* it! When people pray to you, you can't just ignore it. They'd have to pay attention, and they'd *hate* it. It would serve them right for playing with people's lives!"

"So . . . ," he said carefully, "this is just *revenge?*"

"It's justice!" She blinked rapidly. "Isn't that what you want? Poseidon tried to kill your cousin. Philonecron tried to take over the Underworld and throw all the Dead into Tartarus, and all anyone cares about is punishing you for interfering."

Zee frowned. "And what has Zeus done to you?"

The girl flushed. "That's not important. What is important is that Prometheus gave me the task of finding a mortal worthy of bearing the Flame, and after waiting for millennia for the right person, I chose you. Now, shall we?"

She pointed ahead of her, and Zee saw a dusty

fireplace set into the wall. The wall was covered in engravings, and he could tell without too much examination that they told the story of Prometheus. The fireplace was covered by a thin, intricately woven grate made out of something that looked like spun silver.

Zee's heart flipped. He stared at the fireplace, and at the girl, who was practically vibrating with excitement. Then suddenly she shook her head and whispered, "I can't do this."

In an instant the girl was gone, replaced by a goddess in a simple hooded cloak, with thick curly hair of the darkest of blacks, olive skin, and deep green eyes. It was as if the whole room took a breath—but Zee's breath stopped. He had never seen anyone so beautiful. And he did not know why, but he suddenly felt an intense, unyielding sadness.

"Persephone?" he whispered.

She did not speak, merely gazed at him, and he believed he would do anything she wanted.

He had not seen her in the Underworld—it did not seem she was around Hades very much, and he could not blame her. She was magnetic—the whole solar system should be orbiting around her—and Hades was a black hole, pathetic, nothing. He could not imagine her life, wandering around in that horrible, lifeless place.

*He gave the Flame to an ally,* the French book had said,

*one who had cause for anger at Zeus.* Well, Persephone had that, all right. It was Zeus who gave Hades permission to kidnap her, Zeus who came up with the compromise that stuck her in the Underworld six months of the year.

And then something occurred to Zee, and he gasped.

"It was *you.* You knew what was happening in the Underworld. You sent Charlotte the dream of the Footmen last fall. And me the dream of Charlotte in trouble on the sea."

She nodded.

"But," he said, "I don't understand. Why did you warn *me* about the sea? Why didn't you warn Charlotte?"

"Then she would not have gone," she said simply.

Zee was missing something. "Well . . . right. Wasn't that the point of warning me?"

"The point of warning you was that you would follow and understand Poseidon's nature and be motivated to act. I did not know of Philonecron's plans to kidnap you, but it still worked."

"It still worked? It still *worked*?" Zee could not believe what he was hearing. "She could have died! Poseidon could have killed her!"

She nodded. "True. But he didn't."

Zee could only shake his head in shock and disgust.

"Mortals die. You are specks in the spectrum of time. It is the way of things."

"Not to us!"

"This is far more important than the span of one mortal girl's life. I needed to see if you were truly worthy of the Flame," she said matter-of-factly. "And I needed you to be motivated."

He took a step backward in horror. "You're just like the rest of them!"

Narrowing her eyes, she spat, *"Take that back."* Zee felt her anger like a punch.

"No. You're playing games with people's lives for your own end! You just want revenge on Zeus for sending you to the Underworld!"

"Yes. And?"

*"And . . . ?"*

She glared at him and whispered, "If you knew what I'd done for you."

He stopped. "For me? What have you done for me?"

But he never heard the answer. A loud rumbling interrupted them, not thunder this time, but something else, something approaching. . . .

Persephone hissed, "There's no time! Come on! Use the Flame."

"No." It took all his will to say it.

"What?"

"No!" he exclaimed. "I'm not going to!" It was not right. It was not their quest, they were being used, that was all. And for what? Revenge.

It wasn't rumbling, it was footsteps pounding, and whatever belonged to those footsteps was almost there.

"Foolish mortal!" she spat. Her head whipped in the direction of the noise, and real fear passed through her eyes. Zee's stomach turned. "They can't see me here," she breathed. "If they knew, they would lock me up. The Dead need me. I'm sorry."

And with that she was gone, and all Zee saw was a small green and black bird disappear up the hearth.

He looked around wildly for something to hide behind, but it was too late. The wall next to him burst open, and a white bull the size of a truck charged through. He saw Zee, snorted, and slammed into him. Zee fell backward into the hearth, into darkness, and began to fall.

## CHAPTER 28

---

# Zeus on High

CHARLOTTE WAS HUDDLED IN A SMALL STAIRWELL LIT
by a flickering fluorescent light. It looked like the fire
exit staircase of a 1964-era office building, one that no
one had used in a decade. It was small—human-size,
in fact, and quiet except for the eerie buzzing of the
dim light. It gave the impression of a set for a horror
movie, in which one of the young heroines bravely
fights off her attackers and then makes her way to the
exit stairs, bleeding and bruised, where she has one
moment of respite before the villains burst through
and stab her.

In other words, Charlotte was not feeling very comfortable.

She was soaked, shivering, covered in blood-tinged rain. Her face burned in a pain so intense she started to see black. She felt ill, clammy and shaky, and her stomach shifted violently. She blinked furiously against the tears in her eyes, because she imagined it would not be fun if those tears crossed the gash in her face.

She clutched her fists to her face and let out a gargled scream that echoed up and down the stairwell. A flash of anger and hatred seared through her, almost as intense as the pain. She was so sick of getting attacked, scarred, bruised, beaten. She'd just started to feel better, and now this happened. She was in eighth grade, she was supposed to be complaining about math and worrying about her balance beam routine, not fleeing from giant god-sent eagles with extra bonus poison juice in their claws.

*"Will the mortal who freed the sacrificial cows please report to floor thirty? Will the mortal who freed the sacrificial cows please report to floor thirty?"*

Her stomach turned again, and suddenly its meager contents were on the stairs next to her. Charlotte hated throwing up. In seventh grade she lost her lunch suddenly right in the middle of the Hartnett hallway, and Chris Shapiro called her "Miels-puke-ski" for a month.

She gargled another scream, trying to will herself to overcome the pain in her face. She had no choice; she'd already bled and vomited on this gross staircase, she was not going to die here. She clenched her jaw, wiped her face (a little too hard), and hoisted herself up.

Her legs were shaking underneath her, and she felt gray-green all over. Plus she smelled like vomit, which didn't help matters.

*"Will the mortal who freed the sacrificial cows please report to floor thirty? Mortal to floor thirty, please."*

"Um, no," Charlotte muttered. Her path was clear—she needed to go up to the room with the hearth, where Zee, she hoped, would be waiting for her. (Because it was always that easy.) And that was floor forty-five . . . and she was on the tenth floor.

She swore and began trudging up the stairs.

She kept hearing the oddest noises. More thunder and lightning crashes, and then something that sounded like an earthquake going through the whole building. She was sure that something was going to burst through the walls and come toward her, but whatever it was seemed to pass by, apparently heading for someone even more unlucky than she.

Up she climbed, into the sickly fluorescent glow, while the pain in her face subsided from excruciating to burning. Her head still buzzed, her stomach still swam, her legs still wobbled, and she focused all her concentration on putting one foot in front of the other, because that is how gods are best fought.

She counted each stair as she went, thirteen per flight, up and up. Thirty-nine, fifty-two, seventy-five. Her chest heaved and her legs began to burn as well as wobble. She'd been exhausted going to the Underworld, but at least that was going down. Eighty-eight, a hundred and two, a hundred and—

From somewhere down below she could hear a door opening, then the sound of heavy, plodding footsteps echoing through the stairwell, moving upward. Her heart stopped. Then, from above, another door opening, and another set of footsteps, now coming downward.

This was probably not a coincidence.

Charlotte froze and looked around, deciding at once that she was very sick of exit stairwells. She'd find another way to forty-five. Suddenly getting a second wind, she ran up steps one hundred thirteen, fourteen, and fifteen, pulled open the door, and ducked out.

Charlotte had stepped outside again, into some kind of lavish terrace framed by the same large columns that decorated the lobby. Inside the columns thunderclouds roiled, but the sky around the terrace was clear and blue, with white cotton-ball clouds that looked like they came from the set of Charlotte's elementary school production of *Peter Pan*. Scattered around were fruited trees and lush green potted plants with beach-ball-size flowers of hues so intense she could barely look at them.

She had emerged from a small door in one of the columns that disappeared as soon as she passed through it. Right in front of the column was a couch-size planter that masked Charlotte's entrance.

Which turned out to be rather fortunate, as lounging on the terrace were five Olympian gods.

Zee was sprawled on a cool, smooth floor. He gasped and pushed himself up. He found he was still holding the Flame in his hand—its warmth seemed to give him strength, and he clutched his hand around it.

He could not see. The room was pulsating with the full spectrum of light, as if sunbeams were being refracted through giant crystals. He squinted his eyes, trying to see through the assaulting brightness.

He was alone. As his eyes adjusted to the light, he could tell that. He was in a great pillar-lined room with twelve semitranslucent stormy crystal chairs. There was no other decoration or ornament, but it was still the most beautiful room Zee had ever seen. The light was everywhere, pouring out of the crystal, covering the room in diffuse rainbows. Zee felt as if he had fallen into a diamond.

He could see no door, no means of exit. Just endless crystal walls. He had no idea how he'd gotten there, but he was pretty sure it would be a good idea to get out as soon as possible. He moved to get up; he didn't want to wait around for—

"Zachary John Miller."

The voice was all around the room, vibrating in the floor, the walls, coming from every direction—so strong and resonant that something inside Zee began to hum.

He felt, suddenly, the impossibility of breath. His lungs would not work, might never work again. He could see no one, just the prisms around him, and as dazed as he was he began to see the shoots of light as weeds or vines wrapped around him, threatening to strangle him.

He was not supposed to be there. It was wrong, all wrong—he was wrong. The world was not made for him, with a heart that needed to beat and lungs that needed to breathe—he was too fragile, too fleeting. He was not supposed to be there.

"Get up," said the voice. He obeyed; he had no choice but to obey. Something inside urged him to revolt, but once again, Zee was not his own master.

"Who are you?" he breathed. But he knew the answer. It had come to this, at last.

Zee could feel himself shaking, so hard that he thought he might just come apart, little bits of Zee flying everywhere, and all that would be left would be a pile of bones.

"What are you doing here, mortal? Did you come to apologize for your hubris?"

Zee could not speak. Did Zeus really not know why he was here? That was probably a good thing. He had to come up with an answer, something extra convincing, something that would make Zeus apologize for capturing him, plus the whole bull-thing, and come to see the error in his ways, and agree (cheerfully) to wave his thunderbolts and solve all the world's problems, *and* give Zee a biscuit.

"What is that in your hand, mortal?"

Zee's eyes fell on his clutched fist, where he was holding on to the Flame like his last breath.

He closed his eyes. "It's just a lighter," he whispered.

"A lighter? Why do you bear it like gold? Let me see."

What could he do? His palm opened to reveal the small silver lighter. It was humming in his hands, seemingly conscious of what was about to pass.

Then, out of the brightness, a shape. A god. The god of gods. Zeus, great and terrible—and, frankly, a little bit paunchy. He was ten feet tall, with a well-manicured sky blue beard and big, wide-set eyes the color of a storm cloud. In his hand was a long, curved, wickedly jagged metal thunderbolt that he grasped like a scimitar. He wore a silvery laurel wreath and a simple toga that revealed loose, flabby flesh that was still haunted by the ghosts of muscles past. His stomach rounded under the toga as if it was a planet to itself, and Zee was reminded of the bully in grammar school who based his power entirely on the threat that he might sit on you.

Zeus gazed down at Zee and smirked, and rage boiled up in Zee's stomach. He got the urge to grab Zeus's thunderbolt and shove it down his throat—but that would probably not go according to plan.

"What is so special about that lighter?"

"Um," Zee said, "it gives me protection." There, that was good, wasn't it? That would explain why he was clutching it like that, why it didn't seem like the sort of thing a thirteen-year-old displaced British boy would be carrying around. It might not get him a biscuit, though.

Zeus raised a blue eyebrow. Something very like lightning flashed in his eye. "Protection?" he said thoughtfully. "Hmmm . . ."

With one deft move he swung his thunderbolt into Zee's wrist.

The pain blazed up Zee's arm, and his mind went white. His back snapped straight, his arms flew up uncontrollably, and he heard somewhere a distant roar of agony. The next thing he knew, he was on the floor holding his wrist, which he was amazed to find was not on fire. The lighter lay some distance from his feet.

Eventually the burning subsided into a throbbing and Zee came to himself again, enough to notice that Zeus was staring at him with an expression of mocking curiosity.

"Hmm," Zeus said. "Doesn't work very well, huh? You should probably—"

As Zeus talked, he bent down to pick up the lighter. When his great hand touched it, he let out a terrible scream that shook the room. His eyes flashed yellow and then turned back. He drew himself up and fixed his gaze on Zee.

"What," he spat, "is this?"

Charlotte crouched behind the planter, willing herself to be very, very small. She knew she should creep away, but she could not seem to will herself to move. She should at least be hiding, but somehow she could not help but peek around the planter at the scene in front of her.

On a purple chaise lounge across from her lay a gray-eyed goddess in a pantsuit and pearls with a large gray owl on her shoulder, working on what looked suspiciously like a book of Sudoku puzzles. A few feet away an overly tanned goddess in a kimono lay snoozing, while a cherub-like little boy ran in an orbit around her, shooting arrows randomly into the distance. In one corner a violet-skinned god with a long, purple, crazy-guy beard and a hot pink toga sat in a pile of vines, picking off grapes and sucking on them. In another a stern-looking, steel-haired goddess in a glittering cocktail dress was absentmindedly stroking a peacock and thumbing through a French fashion magazine, while a shiny-skinned god in gold lamé shorts and T-shirt roller-skated around the perimeter, picking at neon lute strings.

No one seemed to notice the intruder in their midst—they all kept on complacently doing their things. The owl and the peacock, though, were looking around suspiciously. You might not think a peacock could look suspicious, but you would be wrong.

"How's that sun going, Apollo?" muttered the goddess in the kimono, plucking an earphone out of her ear. The cherub dashed by her and shot an arrow into the sky. From somewhere in the distance came a gruff, growly, "Ow!"

*Aphrodite,* Charlotte told herself, goddess of love and beauty (and, apparently, suntanning). She had silver-white hair, blue-green ocean-colored eyes, and a burbling voice like the sea. The Cupid-like boy was her son, Eros, who cackled as he ran around recklessly. Charlotte could not help but notice that the arrows he was shooting looked quite a bit like the one that had been sticking out of the centaur's butt.

"This isn't good enough for you?" snapped the roller-skating god. "Somebody's having a tantrum, haven't you noticed?" He pointed to the stormy columns.

"What else is new?" Aphrodite mumbled sleepily.

"Anybody know what that's about?" asked Apollo. He sped up, and a moment later the scene grew brighter by a few degrees.

"Someone freed the sacrificial cows, I guess," said the owl-woman. *Athena,* goddess of wisdom.

"Ha! Wish I'd thought of that," muttered the steel-haired woman with the peacock. *Hera,* Zeus's wife.

"Who?" asked Aphrodite, looking up.

"I guess a mortal," said Athena with a shrug.

Hera looked up. "There's a mortal on Olympus?"

"Doesn't anyone listen to the PA?" muttered Athena.

"Who cares?" slurred the grape-sucking god.

"I do, Dionysus," said Aphrodite, now sitting up.

"And you should too. Do you want mortals bothering us all the time? Do you want to give all this up?" She waved her hand around. Charlotte did not, honestly, see anything that great about "all this"; they all looked bored to death. But no one seemed to want her opinion. "What if it's those cousins?"

Charlotte sucked in her breath, then clamped her hand over her mouth. The peacock whipped its head in her direction, and she crouched down and pressed herself against the planter.

"The *children?*" said Athena scornfully. "Who cares?"

Charlotte bristled, but this was probably not the time to stand up and yell, *I am not a child!*

"They took Poseidon's trident," said Aphrodite, standing up. "What if they're coming to overthrow us?"

"Mortals can't use the trident," scoffed Athena.

"One of us is helping them," Aphrodite continued, not listening. "They have to be. How else would they have survived Poseidon? Do you see everything that's happening? Someone destroyed my *temple!*" She stomped her foot.

"They destroyed mine, too," said Athena. "Quit whining."

"Come on," said Hera, "Poseidon versus two pea-brained mortal whelps? He doesn't have a chance!"

The gods cackled.

"Yeah, maybe they stunned him by using a three-syllable word!" said Apollo.

"Or made him add two one-digit numbers together!" said Athena.

"This is serious!" said Aphrodite. "Somebody's using those mortals to get to us. Maybe we're all going to be sea cucumbers. Maybe Cronus is coming back! Maybe the Titans are going to break free."

The Titans! Well, that would be interesting if it were true. After the Olympians had overthrown Cronus and the other Titans, they'd locked them deep within the bowels of the Earth. Of course, in that war every living thing on Earth had been destroyed, so it probably wasn't something they'd want to repeat.

"Come on." Hera waved her hand dismissively. "The mortal children have been lucky so far. Perhaps they have grown arrogant. But if they are caught on Olympus, my ever-so-wise husband will finally get off his fat behind and do the right thing."

Charlotte's heart began to race. Whatever the "right thing" was, it was probably not good. What was he going to do to them? The whole thing was more than creepy—the other gods were nodding like this was something they had all discussed, all knew about. No one had to say, "Well, gee, Hera, can you remind me what the 'right thing' is again? Because I haven't been devoting all my time and energy to thinking about how to destroy these two eighth graders, so it's just slipped my mind."

"I don't believe it," said Aphrodite. "We've been begging him for centuries. Why would now be any different?"

*Centuries?* Charlotte thought. That was a bit of an exaggeration. Although it looked like a year up here might *feel* like an eternity.

"I appealed to his sense of justice," said Hera, with a smirk.

All the gods laughed, and something about the laugh sent a great shiver through Charlotte.

"Well, then," said Aphrodite, "I hope they are caught."

This, Charlotte reflected, would be a good time to make her exit, as sitting in the same room with five Olympian gods who are salivating at the thought of your capture is probably not a good road to self-preservation. She'd have to go back into the stairwell and duck out on another floor, and then find Zee and—

So focused was she on creeping toward the small doorway that she did not see the arrow flying through the air, did not even hear the small humming noise it made as it came toward her. She noticed nothing until it burst through the skin on her back—which,

it turned out, was incredibly painful, painful enough
that it caused Charlotte to shriek.

Zeus stared at Zee with his storm-dark eyes, and Zee
could not think of a thing in the whole world to say. All
language, all thought, left him, and he was just empty,
meaningless, nothing, the void before the birth of the
universe.

"Pick it up," Zeus said.

Zee wanted to say no, to cross his arms and stand
tall and firm—but what good would it do? There was
no way out of there, out of this. Zeus was running his
finger along his scimitar-like lightning bolt, and Zee
felt his heart flutter a little. In films he had seen heroes
stand strong in the face of torture, squaring their jaws,
uttering snappy comebacks through gritted teeth, and
Zee had always thought, *Yes, indeed, that is what I would
do, that is the right thing to do, that is the only thing to do,* but
it is one thing altogether to see it in films and another
to have Zeus's thunderbolt searing your skin. He would
like to pass the rest of his life—as brief as that might
be—without ever feeling that again, and in fact would
go to great lengths not to. And if by some chance he
failed, if Zeus touched him with that white-hot stick of
burning death again, Zee would find himself very short
on witty comebacks.

He thought, suddenly, of his cousin, wandering around Olympus. Was she up in the hearth room now, standing bewildered among the wreckage, wondering what had become of him? Would she figure out that he had been captured, realize that she was in terrible danger, and run from Olympus?

Well, Zeus might torture him, he might kill him, but it was Zee's job to stay alive as long as possible. Because if Zeus was focused on him, he would not be looking for Charlotte.

"Pick it up," Zeus repeated, his words sharp as the scimitar he held.

There was nothing else to do. Zee slowly bent down and picked up the lighter.

"That's better, mortal," said Zeus, a terrible smirk crossing his face.

Zee gritted his teeth and felt his fists ball up. He did not know what he had been expecting from Zeus; Hades had been inept and dithering, Poseidon had been—according to Charlotte—a narcissist with serious anger issues, and Zeus, Lord of the Universe, was just an overgrown, smirking bully.

There was nothing divine about the gods, nothing noble, nothing that made them worthy of their power—except their power itself. They were just a bunch of immortals who happened to overthrow the previous batch of immortals who ruled the universe, that was all. Zee could not believe anyone had ever worshipped this worthless band of petty tyrants and spoiled brats.

"Now," said Zeus, eyes full of dominance, "light it."

Zee allowed himself to feel a small glimmer of hope. The Flame didn't look different or special; it looked like an ordinary fire, the sort an ordinary boy might be carrying, even in this very unordinary place. Trying to keep his face impassive, he pressed down on the lighter.

The Flame burst upward, flickering gently, commonly. Its yellow and orange dance was reflected in the crystal around him, tiny Flames everywhere, telling Zee he was not alone, he had an army of mortals with him, all burning with the fire of Prometheus, protecting him—all with their ordinary, extraordinary flames.

Zee stood, brave and strong, bearing his worthless mortal trinket for the almighty Zeus, feeling suddenly that he might survive this.

Zeus looked at the Flame, his face impassive, then confused. And the Flame flickered on, its reflection mirrored in Zeus's stormy eyes. And then, suddenly, his eyes turned black, and then flashed red.

"What," he spat, "is that?"

"Just a lighter," Zee repeated, his surety gone.

Zeus eyed the Flame carefully, steadily, the only motion the fire flickering in his eyes.

"Where," he said, his voice as quiet and final as death, "did you get *that?*"

## CHAPTER 29

### Consequences

CHARLOTTE COULD HEAR HER SCREAM HANGING IN THE air like a big flashing neon arrow. Her heart started beating so fast it seemed it might run right off the rails. Everything seized up, and she was ready to burst off running somewhere, except her whole back stung with pain, and she felt something cool and deadly begin to spread where the arrow had joined with her flesh. She went green, her skin turned cold, and still she tried to crawl away, toward where the exit door used to be.

She was too late. Eros had come running behind the

planter and was staring down at her with his cherub eyes full of panic.

"I didn't do it," he called to the room around him, hiding his bow behind his back.

"What is it?" called one of the goddesses. "Who is it?"

Footsteps, then behind Eros came Aphrodite, Hera, and Athena. All three gaped down at Charlotte.

She could not move anymore. There was an intruder inside her, sharp and deadly and wrong. Something cold was pouring through her veins, and everything in front of her was bright and fuzzy. Blood mixed with some other substance she probably needed was spreading on her side and back, and she realized with great clarity that the warmth that was flowing out her body at the puncture point was her own life.

She saw black spots in front of her eyes and vomited again on the floor, and somewhere in the distance she could hear Aphrodite say, "Ew."

Charlotte had faced her death so many times in the past few months she knew it like her own reflection. Yet it had never gotten easier; she could steel herself, try to be as brave as she could, but there is nothing welcome about death, and it wasn't just that she had failed, that everything had come to nothing after all, but she did not want to die, not like this, not at all, she wanted to live her life and have lots of cats and what if it hurt and she did not want to be one of the Dead and she was cold and scared and she wanted her mom. . . .

There was a pressure on her, a hand, but it gave no warmth at all, and she could not even lie to herself that it was comforting. There was a shape bending over her, something glittery and sharp-featured, then she heard Hera's voice, steely and cool:

"Charlotte Ruth Mielswetzski."

Aphrodite pointed and screamed.

"Oh, for the love of Zeus," muttered Athena. "She's dying. What are you scared of?"

"I didn't do it!" Eros said again.

"It's all right," said Athena. "Zeus will be glad. This will be the end of it."

A moment of silence, then Hera called, "Heal her."

"What?" Apollo stopped roller-skating.

"Heal her, Apollo!" she repeated. "I want her alive."

"Are you sure?"

"Yes, you nitwit. Heal her."

"As you wish, but I'm not responsible for this."

He rolled over to her and placed his hand on her wound, and Charlotte felt suddenly warm again, like stepping out of a cold, dark house into a summer's day, and she smelled something bright and meadowy and sweet. Then, pain again, like nothing she had ever felt before—which is saying quite a bit—like someone plucking her heart with their hands. She screamed, and the scream seemed to shake the very air, and then the arrow was gone. Her whole side throbbed. Apollo stood over her, crumbling some kind of plant between his fingers and thumb, sprinkling it along her back, placing his hands on the wound, and it was like being touched by the sun itself.

And then Charlotte knew nothing.

When she came to, she found all pain was gone, and she felt with incredible clarity the beating of her heart, the blood in her veins, the rise and fall of her chest. It all seemed like such an amazing thing, that lungs could expand with air, that blood could course, that a heart could beat. She was awake, aware, alert, alive.

And she was being carried by Hera.

They were in the elevator, Charlotte draped in Hera's arms like an old curtain. The brown-legged goat-man was strumming his guitar and humming something mournful. It was the saddest song Charlotte had ever heard; it filled her with a profound sense of something lost. The melody went through her skin, into her veins. Tears blurred her eyes, and her heart felt like it might break in two. Despite everything, there was suddenly nothing left in the world but that song.

"Something a little cheerier?" asked Hera wryly. She had not noticed that Charlotte had awakened—or if she had, she did not care.

The goat-man glanced up at her, then put his head down and kept playing the same song. The tune moved into Charlotte's heart and settled in for a long stay.

Then the elevator door opened, and Charlotte was assailed by bright, glimmering light. Her hands flew up in front of her face as Hera tightened her grip, strode forward, and called, "Oh, honey, I have something for you!"

And then she dumped Charlotte on the floor.

Zee stared as his scarred, blood-soaked cousin was dropped on the floor a few feet away from him. She was covering her eyes against the light and had not yet noticed him.

The steel-like goddess who had borne her into the room made a great show of wiping off her hands. Then her eyes turned on him.

"Zachary John Miller." Her voice was like the sharp end of a knife.

Zeus nodded.

"You see," she said to her husband. "I told you they would come." She looked him up and down, and Zee felt his heart turn cold. Her eyes landed on the lighter, and something flickered inside them.

"And what is that he has?"

"That, my love," said Zeus, sounding pleased with himself, "is the sacred fire. See, I finally found it!"

Charlotte was staring upward, blinking. Zee's heart was spinning in his chest; he did not want her here, did not want her in danger, and yet—he realized with a stab of guilt—he could not help a feeling of great relief. They were better off together; that much he had learned.

Hera was staring at the lighter in shock and disbelief.

"Were they going to use it?" she whispered.

"I believe so."

"This is your fault," she said in a low, cold voice. "I've been telling you and telling you, and you would not listen. Do you see what happens?"

"*I told you to stop nagging!*" said Zeus. "I'm in charge!" He turned to Zee and said, "The child was about to tell me where he got it when you so rudely interrupted."

This was where he was supposed to stonewall, of course. Zeus could threaten him, do whatever he wanted, but Zee would never give up the name of the goddess who had led them, manipulated them, nearly let Charlotte go to her death, abandoned Zee to his fate. . . .

Oh, wait . . .

*Persephone,* it was on the tip of his tongue to say. She used them for her own revenge? Well, let Zeus deal with her, and then perhaps she might regret having played with them like pawns. She just left Zee there, saying, what? *The Dead need me.*

*The Dead need me.*

Zee stopped. Did Persephone, in all her lust for revenge, care for the Dead, too? Did she feel sorry for them, trapped there as she was?

"No one sent us," Zee said. "We read about it in a book and then we found it."

"You're lying, mortal," said Hera with a sneer.

Charlotte was sitting up now, still blinking rapidly, but looking from Zee to the pair of gods. Their eyes met. There was a huge gash on her face that made him sick to look at.

"Tell them the truth, Zee," Charlotte said, her voice weak and pained.

He stared at her. What was she getting at? Her eyes were trying to communicate something to him, but he could not tell what.

"It was Cronus," Charlotte announced.

"Charlotte," said Zee quickly, "don't tell!" He didn't know what she was doing, but he would play along. That was what they did, they worked together.

"We have to!" said Charlotte. "He'll kill us!" She looked back to the gods. "Your daddy's coming. He wants his universe back. And the mortals are going to help. It's not like they have any loyalty to you."

Zee understood. They were going to bargain, that was it. They would pretend they had the power to speak for all of humanity—and the power to sway them. Charlotte was going to talk the two of them out of this.

"Ridiculous," said Zeus. "We defeated the Titans before. We are stronger. Hades has his helmet, I have my lightning bolt."

"And the trident?" Charlotte finished pointedly.

There was a moment of silence, then rage crossed over Zeus's face. "Where is it?" he spat. "What did you do with it?"

"We gave it to Cronus," Charlotte said. "When we went to see him under the Earth. The Titans are metal-workers, aren't they? He said they'd be able to use it."

Hera was looking from the cousins back to Zeus. Zeus was studying them both. "I don't believe you," he said slowly. "If Cronus was coming, he would not use mortals. You have no one coming for you. You have no one to help you. You are all alone, and you are noth-ing."

Hera straightened. "Sweetie," she said, her voice oozing, "these mortals have invaded the Underworld, the Sea, and now Olympus. They have brought the sacred fire that Prometheus stole from us in order to destroy what we have built. Only you are discerning and just enough to come up with the right thing to do."

Zeus nodded slowly. "Yes, yes. That is true."

"Well," she said, "I'll leave you to it, O wise one." And she turned and floated out of the room.

Zee and Charlotte exchanged a panicked look. Zeus turned on them.

"She was being sarcastic," Charlotte said, her cheeks flushed. "Trust me. The gods all think you're stupid. They think you can be manipulated. I heard them." Zee shot her a look. This might not be the time for Charlotte's temper.

Zeus straightened. "Mortals," he said disdainfully, "do you know what separates you from a mangy dog?"

Charlotte tossed her hair. "Not being mangy?" Zee closed his eyes. He really needed to have a talk with her.

"This fire," Zeus said, reaching for the lighter. As Zee watched, the god grabbed the lighter from his hand. When it touched Zeus's flesh, his eyes went black and a flash of pain crossed his face. But he squeezed his hand around the lighter and did not let go. "This simple fire. If Prometheus had not given it to you, you would be animals, stupid and dirty. Quite an insubstantial thing that keeps you from crawling on the floor, barking and whimpering, isn't it?" He pressed down the button, and the Flame shot up. "Except dogs were better than you, dogs have fur and sharp teeth and could hunt and survive. Humans had nothing. Humans would have gone extinct in the blink of an eye."

"And you didn't care," Charlotte said coldly.

"No. Why should I care?"

"You're awful!"

"Mortal, do you know how many species have gone extinct? I didn't cry over the dodo bird or the spectacled cormorant, did I? And they could fly!"

"But—"

"And what about you? I didn't see you fighting to save the Western black rhinoceros. And what about the polar bears? Stopped using cars and air-conditioning, have you?" He raised his eyebrows. "You do not understand anything. You are nothing. You could not march up here and seek to take me on. There is a way to the Universe. Now, mortals"—Zeus took a step back and appraised them—"it is time for justice. You two have declared war on the gods with your actions." As he talked, Zeus strode over to one of the crystal walls and placed his hand on it. The wall disappeared to reveal bright blue sky. Out of the corner of his eye, Zee noticed a small bird floating in above Zeus's head, but he was too focused on the terrible god to process it.

"What would you have me do?" Zeus continued. "Another flood? How about a plague this time? Or a great fire sweeping through the Earth?"

"Huh?" Zee and Charlotte said together.

"You may choose," said Zeus with a smirk. "That is what you mortals like, right? Choice? Choose the method of humanity's destruction."

The words took some time to make their way into the cousins' minds, to take shape, to blossom into meaning. And even then, they hung there for a few moments, inert, as Charlotte and Zee refused to see them for what they were. It could not be. It could not be.

Zeus took a step toward them, his eyes terrible. "You do not think I would let humanity live, do you? You two know your history, you know what happens when mortals are given the gods' sacred fire. You must have known this would happen."

"No!" Zee didn't even know which one of them had shrieked it. Charlotte stumbled backward as if she had been hit.

"I gave you one more chance!" Zeus said.

"What?" Zee exclaimed.

"I did!" Zeus insisted. "Hera wanted me to destroy humanity when you disrespected my brother, but I said, no, no, they have one more chance."

"You didn't tell us that!" yelled Zee.

"Really, it's only just. And it is your own fault," Zeus said, clearly enjoying himself. "In fact, I think I will keep you two alive so you can see what you have done.

You can wander around the Earth all alone, with no one but the polar bears to keep you company. I'm sure they'll be grateful for all you've done for them."

Panic choked Zee, and he could not breathe. Charlotte yelled and ran at Zeus, fists flailing. Zeus smirked before swinging his thunderbolt, hitting her with the flat of the blade. She let out an inhuman cry as she was flung backward, and she landed in a heap on the floor. She did not move.

Zeus smirked and went over to retrieve the thunderbolt. "Ah, mortal fortitude." He turned to Zee, who was staring at his cousin in wide-eyed horror. "She's alive," Zeus said. "Don't worry. There's only so much pain the human body can take before it shuts down. Now . . . a plague, I think." He gestured to the open sky. "I will send my thunderbolt down to Earth and spread plague around the whole planet. I think there should be some suffering, don't you, after what you have done? It will be a terrible bother, but I think it's worth it."

Zee could not breathe. He closed his eyes, trying to find the ability to make words. This was what the Prometheans had been saying. *We're trying to secure the fate of humanity,* Mr. Metos had said. *This boy has the fate of the world in his hands,* Timon had said. They knew. They knew Zeus would do this. It was Steve, not the Flame, that was humanity's last hope.

*Would you sacrifice one person for everyone?*

This was not real. This was a nightmare, and soon he would wake up and Mew would be sleeping on his chest and purring gently, and everything would be all right, and he would stroke the cat and feel the gentle peace of knowing that there was a creature next to him that was perfectly happy.

In the silence of the next few moments, Zee could feel what it would be like, lying perfectly still, with the humming of the cat against his chest. That was peace, that was happiness.

Before his grandmother died, so many long months ago, she said, *I will watch over you.* He would see her again. It would be all right.

And then Zee opened his eyes. Everything was clear. "Why are you punishing the world for what I did?" he said in a low, calm voice.

"Why not?" said Zeus, as if he legitimately did not understand the question. "You're a mortal." He held out one open hand. "Ergo . . ." He motioned with the other.

"But just punish *me.*"

Zeus blinked. "Punish you?"

"Yes. Don't punish everyone else. Kill me."

"Zachary Miller, would you give your life to save humankind?" Zeus looked curious, almost amused.

"Yes, of course!" Of course. It was an easy choice. He could have died senselessly so many times over the past few months; at least now he would die for something.

"Mortals," Zeus said under his breath. He looked at Zee carefully, then strode over to where Charlotte lay.

"Would you give hers?" he asked slowly.

"W-what?"

Zeus nudged Charlotte's body with his foot, and she slid across the floor to the edge of the room, just in front of the open blue sky. One more inch and she would be over the edge.

"You heard me. Would you give hers?"

Zee took a step back. "No!"

"Push her over the edge. That's all I ask. I pledge right now on the River Styx that for the sacrifice of your cousin, I will not destroy humanity. That is your choice. Choose."

What Charlotte knew first was pain. Pain had colonized her entire body, so that she was no longer a creature of flesh, blood, and breath, but only of nerves and synapses.

And silence. Absolute, eternal, desolate. There was nothing, no one, nothing.

Then, from somewhere inside, somewhere among

the nerves and synapses that were once Charlotte, came a humming noise. A melody. Someone was humming the saddest song Charlotte had ever heard.

She could feel the melody under her skin, in her veins, settling into her heart for a long stay. Because suddenly she had skin, veins, and a heart again—she had eyes that teared up and lungs that gasped and arms that wrapped themselves around her chest.

And still there was the song—so tragic, so beautiful, so fragile, so fleeting—and yet it was strong and clear, too, growing stronger every moment, asserting itself against the unyielding, everlasting silence. It would not, could not last, but for these few beautiful moments, it was here, present, for these few moments it had conquered the terrible quiet of everything.

And the pain, too. The song was everything, stronger than the pain, better than it. She held on to each note like an old friend until the pain was gone.

And then, quiet again. Charlotte found herself at the edge of a crystal cliff, surrounded by endless blue sky.

She heard shouting, as if from far away, loud and urgent, so strange to hear shouting in such a beautiful place—

Zeus was standing over her cousin, his face in a terrible smirk. Zee looked as if he was going to crack apart; the agony in his face made her lose her breath.

"I can't do that!" he said, his voice thick with horror.

"No?" Zeus said. "You will not sacrifice your cousin for all of humanity? You would rather have the whole world die?"

"I can't," Zee whispered, so quietly she could barely hear him.

"Well, then," said Zeus, lifting up his thunderbolt.

A feeling of great warmth and peace came over Charlotte. And then she rolled off the edge of Olympus into the infinite blue.

CHAPTER 30

# Forced Entry

On the great staircase up to Olympus, Isadora, the nymph of the Gate, sat feeling rather sorry for herself. After having spent a good couple of millennia not having to do any work at all, she had had to deal with two, count 'em, two mortals in the same day.

It was a little much.

Oh, she was tired. She hurt from the strands of her purple hair down to her purple tippy toes. In fact, as she sat she was fading slightly, less purple than blue-violet. And there was nothing she disliked more than being blue-violet. It was better not to try at all.

It had taken her a long time to be such a brilliant, beautiful hue. You did not turn yourself into the world's lushest, richest purple just by wishing it so—it took study, concentration, will. Other sky nymphs were content to be some ordinary, common shade of blue, but not Isadora. It took centuries of stealing from rainbows, bit by bit—sure the rainbows didn't like it, but who in Hades were they? They weren't sky nymphs, privileged with one of the most important jobs in the whole Universe—manning the doorways to Olympus, testing the mettle of any mortal who dared approach.

And now she was going to have to start all over again.

So bad was her mood, so tragic had been her day, that she was barely surprised when the cloud moat in front of her began to pulse. She muttered a few choice curses to herself and then waited.

A boy burst through, a mortal boy, if you could believe that, dressed in the same ridiculous manner as the others had been, slightly older perhaps, but no less annoying. Isadora heaved her blue (barely) violet self upward and stood waiting.

"You have business at Olympus?" Her voice was still beautiful at least. If clouds could speak—well, how boring would they be? But still, that is what they would sound like.

"Um, yes, I guess so," the boy said. He was looking all around, as if he could not believe where he was.

If she had eyes, she would roll them. There were procedures, you know, there was a way this worked, and "Um, yes, I guess so," was decidedly not it. She could feel herself turning red.

"Could you state your business, please?" Moron.

"Um," said the boy, now gaping at her. "I guess I'm . . . here to meet my father."

Well, she'd heard that one a lot before, but not in a number of years.

"Very well," said the nymph, raising her hand. She was ready to plunge the mortal into a vision, something to test him, something to stop him, but as she readied the spell to sink him into his own mind, the cloud moat in front of her pulsed again. Once. Twice. Then it exploded.

She gaped as little quivering pieces of cloud littered the staircase around her.

"Hey!" she said, as out from the wreckage emerged someone who did not belong on the staircase at all.

A red-eyed, overdressed half-breed, with skin a sickly shade of white—as if that was attractive.

"You have business at Olympus?"

"Yes," said the half-breed. And then he poised something in his hands, something that was supposed to be missing, something that should not have been found, something he should not be able to use, except there he was, and there it was—

A burst of light came out of it, toward her, and when it hit her she felt herself begin to dissipate like smoke in the wind, but in the millisecond before she did, she turned the most beautiful shade of purple the world had ever seen.

CHAPTER 31

# An Unexpected Assist

ZEE COULD NOT BREATHE. HE COULD NOT THINK. HE was stuck in time. He did not want to go forward, because if time moved, Charlotte would be falling, falling from Olympus, miles down to Earth, and if he could just keep everything perfectly still, she would still be floating in the bright blue sky, alive and well and full of Charlotte-ness.

Zeus was staring too, his eyes wide and dull. His mouth hung open slightly, and he seemed as unable to move as Zee.

"That was unexpected," he said finally.

And with Zeus's words, time started again.

A rush of feeling crashed into Zee, knocking him backward. It did not happen, no, no, it did not happen. The thoughts screamed themselves in his head, so loud as to let nothing else in. It could not happen like that—one moment Charlotte was there, the next she was falling to her death. It was a trick, a lie, a plan. She had a plan—that was Charlotte, his Charlotte, she always had a plan. A winged horse waiting to fly her away—that was it. Beautiful Pegasus with his angel-white wings waiting just under the missing wall, like in a movie. Charlotte knew what was going to happen, knew everything, had prepared. So clever, she was.

She was still there; Charlotte was still there.

Zeus continued to look out the window, his brow knit in puzzlement, as if he was thinking very hard and he was not used to the feeling. He shook his head.

"I thought she hated people. . . . Hmmph." Zeus shrugged, then turned on Zee and said cheerfully, "Well, too bad it was all for naught." And he raised his thunderbolt again.

*No. No.* Zee shook himself. He needed to focus now, there was no time, there was no time.

"Wait! Stop!" His voice came out so thick he did not even know if Zeus could understand him. He was either being very quiet or very loud; he could not tell. "You swore! You swore by the River Styx!"

"I said you had to push her off the edge. You refused. Therefore—"

"No," Zee whispered. Zeus's words rang in his head as if he were speaking them right then. "You said you swore by the River Styx that *for the sacrifice of my cousin* you would not destroy humanity. My cousin was sacrificed, wasn't she? She sacrificed herself."

His own words cut into him. He could feel his stomach burning, setting his whole insides alight; he was going to vomit fire, he could feel the tears streaming down his cheeks. *My cousin was sacrificed.* It was not true. How could it be true?

Because she was Charlotte, that was how.

Zeus stopped, his thunderbolt poised. He looked at Zee, then the blue sky, then back at Zee. His brow furrowed even more, as if he was trying very hard to add two numbers together and was not entirely sure of how one went about doing that. Then he lowered his thunderbolt slowly.

"Well," he said. "Well."

Zeus stared at Zee, blinking rapidly, and through his haze of grief and shock and denial it took Zee several moments to define the look in the god's eyes, because it was not what he was expecting; Zeus looked panicked and blank, an actor who has forgotten all his lines.

He didn't know what to do, Zee realized slowly. He was Lord of the Universe, and he had no clue what to do now. Zee had imagined Zeus as mighty, omnipotent, and terrifying; he had certainly acted that way at first. But it was all bluster. Zee hadn't realized that the only thing worse than an all-powerful god is an all-powerful god who has no idea what he's doing.

He seemed to be waiting for someone to appear, Hera or another god, someone who would tell him what to do now. And Zee was waiting too, waiting for Charlotte to come back, and she would tell Zee about her secret plan, and then they would turn their backs on Olympus forever.

Zee felt the beauty of the lie he was telling himself; he wanted to wrap himself up in it, live in it forever. And even as he knew it was a lie, he would not let go.

He did not particularly care what happened to him now. Zeus seemed unsure himself. But he was not going to wave cheerio and let Zee wander back to Earth. He seemed the type who would probably kill Zee, for lack of anything better to do, to make some sort of point to himself if no one else—and there was really nothing for Zee to do but wait.

There was no way out of this, here, now. And it didn't matter, anyway. Their work was done. They had not known it, but their task all along had nothing to do with the Promethean Flame—no, no, it had fallen on Charlotte and Zee to secure the existence of humankind.

And Charlotte Mielswetzski, in one act, had done just that.

You have a lot of time to think as you tumble miles through the sky toward the very ragged, very hard mountains below, and one of the things you will think is, *Boy, I hope I don't feel that,* and another thing you will think is, *Mom and Dad, I love you,* and another thing you will think is, *I should be very, very afraid, but I had no choice and thus I am only a little afraid.* And you might think about the Dead, and meeting them as one of their own, and finding ways to keep your very Charlotte-ness in all that bleakness, and if you do then perhaps you can help the others, too, and maybe after all you will have done something for the Dead.

And you are, indeed, a little afraid.

It should have been very loud. Charlotte could feel the wind whipping around her hair, could feel its bite on her skin, its whooshing in her ears, but she did not hear it. It was drowned out by the beautiful song of the goat-man that accompanied her as she fell. She was glad not to be alone.

Her family was with her, though, her family who would now live. Her mother, father, Mew. Well, Mew was never in danger; Zeus was going to destroy all of humanity, but he couldn't be so evil as to kill kitties, too.

And Zee. Her cousin, who was always with her. Zee

was still up there with Zeus; she could picture him staring in utter disbelief at the empty space where she used
to be. She could do nothing for his grief; she could only
tell herself that he understood. She hated the pain he
would feel, but it was not as though her death was meaningless. He would know that, and he would be all right,
eventually. It is a wonderful thing, to have a cousin.

She did not know how Zee was going to get out of
there, but he would. She had faith.

And Zeus, Zeus was even worse than she had imagined him. She had misunderstood. She had no business
being angry at the gods, for they did not deserve her
notice. There was no hope they would be anything but
petty and worthless. They were pathetic, cruel, horrible,
and it was best to forget about them and let humanity
try to struggle on for itself.

After some time, she began to see a large shadow below,
a shadow that was moving toward her at a rapid pace, and
she realized with some trepidation that it was the ground,
and she, in fact, was moving toward it. It is one thing to
contemplate hitting the ground from miles up in the air—
and, she guessed, another altogether to actually do so.

She was more than a little afraid now, for she was
only human. She closed her eyes and, as the goat's song
comforted her, she thought of Zee, and of Mew, of
Maddy and her mother and father, of Mr. Metos, of

Hector, and how she would see them again, how she would make a better Underworld for them, somehow. She would feel nothing, it would happen too fast, she would fall and fall and then find herself being carried by Hermes the Messenger to the banks of the Styx.

She wondered if the bridge was still there. She wondered what Charon would say when he saw her.

She did not want to lose herself.

With her eyes closed, with the image of her loved ones burned on her brain, she could no longer see the earth coming toward her, so it was quite surprising when she realized she was no longer falling. Her heart turned a somersault—had she landed? Was this it?

But—she realized, perhaps more slowly than she should have—had she landed, surely she would have noticed. Right?

Charlotte carefully opened an eye and found she was moving through the air on a parallel line to the ground below. A slow burn of comprehension passed through her. It was over. She had died and was being carried by Hermes to the Underworld. She hadn't felt a thing, hadn't even noticed hitting the ground, but her life was over now, and the eternity just begun.

It seemed odd to Charlotte, then, that she could still feel the pounding of her heart, that she had breath to catch, that her hands in front of her looked just as they had a minute ago. Perhaps this was what it was like, before the long fading, or perhaps it was all an illusion born of death and desire. It was a nice illusion.

Charlotte craned her neck upward to her bearer, wanting to say something—though she did not know what. But any words stopped in her mouth, for she was not being carried by a god at all. She was in the claws of a very large, purple-bellied, bird-like creature with broad, powerful wings, soaring with the wind.

Several thoughts occurred to Charlotte at once—one, that she was apparently not dead. This took some getting used to. Two, that she was being borne through the air by some genetic-engineering experiment gone horribly awry. Three, that as much as she found her body trembling with the relief of the reprieved, she had intended to sacrifice herself for humanity, and now she was going to have to kill herself all over again.

"Let me go!" Charlotte shouted at the bird. But it did not waver, merely kept flying. Charlotte twisted, trying to free herself from the bird's grasp.

There was a mountain moving toward them (or, Charlotte supposed, vice versa), and the bird began to descend slowly toward it. Its wings beat against the air, and then Charlotte was being placed gently down, and the bird alighted next to her.

The bird looked like a purple and green sparrow,

but a hundred times the size, and it was regarding her intently, if sparrows could do such a thing. A wave of panic crashed over Charlotte.

"Why did you do that?" she screamed.

The bird blinked twice, and then there was no more bird, but a goddess—black-haired, green-eyed, impossibly beautiful, impossibly sad. Something about her looked familiar to Charlotte, but she could not place it.

A goddess, then, one who would bring her back to Zeus, one who wanted the world destroyed. Anger made Charlotte feel like she was choking.

"You guys won't even let me kill myself!" she yelled, tears blinding her eyes. She was going to have to jump off the stupid mountain now.

"No," said the goddess, raising her hand. Something about the gesture stilled Charlotte, and she could not seem to avert her eyes from the woman before her. "I have to take you back to Olympus."

Oh, how she had had it with these people. Charlotte folded her arms and set her jaw. "You can't stop me," she said.

"I don't understand," said the goddess. "Don't you want to be saved?"

What? "No! Zeus will kill everyone, he said!"

"But you already sacrificed yourself. It is done."

Charlotte stared dumbly at the woman.

"Yes. I was there, I heard it." Somewhere in Charlotte's mind, the image appeared of a small sparrow flying into the throne room. "Zeus asked for your sacrifice, and you gave it."

Tears poured unbidden from Charlotte's eyes, and she wiped them away roughly. It is quite something to think you are going to die and then find yourself very much alive.

"Wh-why?" Charlotte asked finally. "Why did you save me?"

The goddess appeared to think for a moment. "I made a mistake," she said. "I have recently been made to see that in my own quest for vengeance I treated you as I was once treated."

"I don't understand."

The goddess looked at the ground for a moment. "It was I who led you to the sacred fire. Your cousin will explain to you later. He has a way of explaining things. . . ."

And then the goddess gave Charlotte her name, and Charlotte could only stare. She could not be surprised anymore.

"You two saved my people once. All I did in the face of the threat to them was send visions of the Footmen to their quarries—including you."

"Your people?" Okay, Charlotte was a little surprised. "You mean the Dead?"

Persephone's eyes grew sad. "They are condemned to that place, as I am. I cannot do much. Little things, here and there, for those who seek me out. But"— she turned her eyes toward Charlotte, and the gaze was so powerful Charlotte nearly took a step back—"I am not brave, like you. I have never risked myself for them, for anyone." Suddenly her faced darkened. "Listen, there is no time. The half-breed is on Olympus."

"The—who?" Charlotte had the distinct feeling her brain might explode.

"The usurper called Philonecron. The demon who would torment the Dead. I saw him go through the gates."

Charlotte gasped. Acid poured through her blood. She should have known. They would never be rid of Philonecron, never. Charlotte and Zee will be in a nursing home playing checkers and he'll show up and overturn the board. That is, if he could be kept from taking over the universe.

"But . . . it's Zeus. Philonecron can't defeat Zeus!"

Persephone shook her head. "The demon has Poseidon's trident. And, apparently, he has found a way to use it. He and Zeus will be closely matched. And if Zeus is separated from his thunderbolt . . ."

Charlotte felt dazed. Philonecron had the trident? Wow, that couldn't have worked out any worse. It would have been far better for humanity if Charlotte had just let Zeus destroy them than whatever Philonecron had in mind. And Zee, Zee was up there. Philonecron was heading toward Zee.

"I have to go back up," said Charlotte. Persephone nodded, and Charlotte got the odd feeling that she thought Charlotte and Zee had a better chance against Philonecron than her fellow gods.

"There is something else," Persephone said. "He is not alone. There is a mortal boy with him. Do you know who he is?"

A what? Had Philonecron enchanted another little pet? Charlotte shook her head. A mortal boy was the least of her worries.

"Come," said Persephone. "There's no time." And just like that, the goddess was a bird again. There was a great fluttering of wings and billows of dust, and then talons wrapped around Charlotte's shoulders and they were in the air again, soaring back up to Olympus.

As Zeus looked around uncomfortably, and Zee waged his inner struggle between truth and lies, something very unusual happened. It began as some noises, far off in the distance, like thunder. The refracted light in the room around them flickered and went out like an old lightbulb, leaving only clear, colorless crystal. Zee assumed it was just another effect of Zeus's anger, but the god was suddenly looking even more uncertain than before.

From somewhere below came a scream, and the sound of shattering and crashing, like a great chandelier falling to the floor. And another scream.

From above came an announcement: *"Security to the main lobby, please, security."*

Zeus turned on Zee. "Is this your doing?"

"What? No, mate!" Zee couldn't put his finger on why, but he began to feel very uncomfortable.

*"Security, where in Hades are you?"*

"Is it Cronus? Is he free? Tell me the truth, mortal!" Zeus raised his thunderbolt to Zee, his hand shaking slightly.

"I don't know!" Zee cried, as the walls around him rumbled.

*"Would the half-breed who destroyed the lobby please report to floor thirty? Thank you."*

"Half-breed?" Zeus muttered, shifting a little. He turned on Zee, spitting, "Who did they send? Who?"

Zee was growing weary of this. *"I don't know!"* he repeated.

"It doesn't matter," Zeus mumbled. "Cronus does not overthrow me. There is a prophecy. . . ."

*"Half-breed to security, half-breed to security. . . ."*

"I am beloved," Zeus said firmly to Zee. "My family will rise up to protect me. That is the benefit of being a great leader."

Suddenly the elevator door opened with a dainty *ping*.

"Ah, there they are now!" Zeus said, with a self-satisfied look at Zee. "You see? You mortals understand nothing about—"

But whatever it was they did not understand, Zee would never know. For just then something went flying out of the elevator doors. Zee and Zeus followed the object with their heads as it sailed through the room. It was difficult to make out anything in the blur—but as it whooshed past them Zee saw a face, goat legs, and a guitar. In fact, the object—who was clearly not an object at all—seemed to be playing the guitar and singing, rather cheerfully. Indeed, as the guitar-playing, singing, goat-legged non-object soared through the room and out the opening from which Charlotte had jumped, Zee could make out some of the words:

*That's the ballad of Phil-o-ne-cron*
*and Steeeeeeeeeeeeeeeeve. Wheeeeeee!*

But that made no sense, no sense at all, and it didn't even register in Zee's head, not until there was a blast of green light through the room, and out strode the very being Zee wanted to see the least in the whole wide universe.

And . . . Steve?

CHAPTER 32

# The Ballad of Philonecron and Steve

Up through the air Charlotte and Persephone went, soaring past the great marble staircase, through a strange mass of wispy white tendrils that had the appearance of shattered cloud, and through the giant pillars into the front lobby.

Or what was left of it.

Gone were the elegant crystal atrium, the desk, the receptionist, the arrow-butted centaur, the clusters of Immortals. All had been replaced by blown-out ruins. There were crystal shards everywhere, knocked-over columns, and great craters in the wall and floor of a deep, empty, endless black. A pall of smoke hung in the air. It looked as if a bomb had hit the lobby. Philonecron, for all his pretensions to decorum, had proven to have a serious appetite for destruction.

The great bird's wings flapped furiously to come to a halt, and it gently released Charlotte. In a blink of an eye, Persephone was before her, tight-lipped and pale.

"I don't know if Zeus can stop him," she whispered.

"The other gods—Apollo, Hera, Athena—they're all in the same place," Charlotte panted. "Some terrace. Or they were when I left. Maybe they've all gone to help, though."

"I doubt it," Persephone murmured. "They don't pay much attention to things around them."

"Well," said Charlotte, "we could go get them!"

Persephone shook her head slightly. "I don't think that will help."

What did she mean, it wouldn't help? Six gods were a lot better than one and two mortals. "Well, at least it's something!"

"Very well," said the goddess, looking reluctant. "We will try. But we must hurry." And she led Charlotte through the wreckage to the elevators.

The elevator rose up slowly, creakingly. There was no goat-man in it, no sad song to keep Charlotte company now, just her and Persephone and this apocalyptic fear. Philonecron with the trident was too much. He would see her and turn her to ash. He would set the whole world aflame, then flood it, then set it aflame once more for good measure.

When they arrived at the terrace, Charlotte expected to see the gods in a panic of some kind. But as the elevator door opened, the scene was almost the same as before. Only now there were flakes of ash falling from the sky, and Apollo was moving so quickly on his roller skates now that he was just a blur.

Persephone stepped out of the elevator first, and Charlotte heard Aphrodite drawl, "Oh, you're back?" She didn't sound too happy about it.

Charlotte followed, and as she emerged Aphrodite pointed and screamed. Hera narrowed her eyes and muttered something quite rude about her husband.

"It's all right," said Persephone to Aphrodite. "We need her—"

"Need a mortal?" Hera sniped. "Why, is the Minotaur hungry?" Charlotte narrowed her eyes. She did not like Hera.

"The half-breed Philonecron is here! On Olympus. He has the trident and he's blasting his way to Zeus."

"Oh, is that what that's about?" Athena mumbled, distractedly brushing off a small pile of ash from her Sudoku book.

"Yes!" cried Persephone. "He destroyed the lobby!

Didn't you hear anything? And what about this?" She waved her hands in the air to indicate the falling ash.

"Philonecron!" snorted Dionysus, his mouth full of grapes. "Didn't he get defeated by mortal children?"

Hera snorted. "Even my pathetic husband is more powerful than mortal whelps. Though apparently"—her eyes flicked over to Charlotte—"not by much."

"He has the trident!" Persephone repeated.

Charlotte was trying hard to stay focused, but the very air around Persephone was thrumming with anxiety. Charlotte was anxious enough on her own.

"He can't use it," dismissed Athena.

"Yes, he can. I saw him. Remember, he is the grandson of Poseidon. Perhaps he—"

"Well, perhaps it's time we had a real leader, then," Hera said, picking a piece of ash from her peacock.

"What?"

"It would serve Zeus right, don't you think? Anyway, at least Philonecron has goals."

"Goals? *Goals!* Do you think he's going to just let us go on as we are? He's going to depose us all. He'll lock us in with the Titans!"

"Why would he?" Hera replied. "We'll be no threat to him."

"Besides," said Aphrodite, "if he has the trident, he'll kill us if we fight back."

"She has a point," slurred Dionysus.

Charlotte couldn't take it anymore. She had been watching the conversation with her mouth hanging open, but it had gotten too absurd.

"You're not going to do anything?" she cried.

Persephone shot her a warning glance. The peacock hissed, and Hera's head snapped to look at her. "Don't tell us what we should do, mortal. . . . And what are you doing with *her*, anyway, Persephone? Don't tell me your time in the Underworld has turned you into a mortal-lover."

The goddess rolled her eyes. "A mortal-lover? Like your husband?"

The peacock hissed again, and Hera drew herself up to her full height, the whole room trembling with her rage. Persephone scoffed, and then suddenly the goddess was gone, and Charlotte was being borne aloft in the air again, flying across the terrace into the open blue sky, up toward Philonecron.

Before Zee or Zeus could react, there was a great blast of light from the trident that slammed into Zeus. His thunderbolt fell from his hands, and Zeus flew backward into the wall. As Philonecron cackled, thick steel-like ropes sprang from the trident and began winding their way around Zeus like snakes. The Lord of the Universe struggled and shouted, but could not break free.

"Philonecron, you evil, scheming half-breed!" roared Zeus. Philonecron raised an eyebrow and lifted the trident again, and a thick red velvet gag wrapped its way around Zeus's mouth.

"Whoa," breathed Steve.

Zee watched in horror. Philonecron had told him, once, back on Poseidon's yacht, about an attempted overthrow of Zeus by Hera and Poseidon. They'd done just this—bound him up, separated him from his thunderbolt—and the only thing that saved him was the intervention of another goddess who sent a giant to free him.

Zee saw no giant here, no one to intervene. The Lord of the Universe had been trussed like a cow, and instead of being brave and defiant, instead of showing the cocksure attitude of the more powerful, Zeus was looking at the trident in utter terror.

"Is that really him?" whispered Steve, eyes aflame, as the ropes continued to bind Zeus up. "This is incredible—" He glanced around the room and noticed Zee and gaped. "What are *you* doing here?"

Philonecron turned his head toward Zee very slowly, and when he saw him, his red eyes flared. "You!" he hissed, clapping his hand on his chest.

"You *know* him?" Steve asked Philonecron.

Philonecron looked from Steve to Zee, then sighed languidly.

"Well, this is awkward," he said. "Zero"—he turned to Zee and took a deep, reluctant breath—"I've met someone."

"How do—," Steve began. But whatever he was going to ask went unsaid, for Philonecron gracefully swung the trident so it touched Steve, and the boy was still.

Philonecron turned back to Zee, took a few tentative steps toward him, and clasped his hands together over the trident as if he was about to break it to Zee that there was no tooth fairy. "It's better if we discuss this alone," said Philonecron gravely.

Zee did not, could not respond. In his shock and anger and hatred, every muscle had seized up. He was planted there, a board stuck in the mud. Philonecron's voice insinuated itself in his brain, his blood, moved through him like poison, curdling everything inside of him, changing Zee from the inside out.

"I'm sorry you had to find out like this," Philonecron said, his words an ooze. "I never meant for it to happen this way. I know it must hurt, but rest assured, it's not me, it's *you.*"

Zee's jaw was actually going to fuse closed, his hands

would remain clenched for all of eternity. He would never move again; he would have to stay here for all time in his own metaphorical Tartarus with Philonecron driveling at him.

"Now, Zero, don't look at me like that. I gave you every chance, didn't I? You were my protégé, you were like a son to me, and how did you pay me back? You ran off with that sour, scheming little cousin of yours."

Zeus's thunderbolt lay on the floor about fifteen feet from Zee. If only he could get it, if only he could move—

"You know, Zero, the first time you betrayed me I was ready to forgive you. Yes, I know, it is impossibly noble of me, but I am impossibly noble. I forgave everything! I welcomed you back with open arms! I offered you a place, a home, family. I took you under my wing, I gave you the finest of everything! I was ready to give you the world, Zero! The Universe!" Philonecron's voice cracked with emotion, and he bit his knuckle to control himself. "And what did you do? How did you pay me back?" He shook his head despondently. "You have no one to blame but yourself, Zero, no one!"

In his corner, Zeus grunted through his gag. Philonecron whipped his head to the god and snapped, "Quiet! I'm having a moment here!" He took the trident and blasted a hole in the ceiling. A pile of crystal came tumbling down on top of Zeus.

"Now," he said, turning back to Zee, "I will admit to being a little . . . hurt. I am a very feeling soul, you know. But it was all for the best, of course, for if you had not committed such a foul and despicable act of betrayal, I never would have made the acquaintance of my friend here." He stroked the trident lovingly.

Zee's head spun. How did it happen? How could it have happened? He hurled the trident into the Ketos's mouth, that was all. How had Philonecron gotten it? Was this his fault too?

No, no. It was not time for Zee to be crushed with his own burdens. It did not matter. Philonecron had the trident. Philonecron was going to take over the universe. He had the trident, he had Zeus in chains, and he had—

*Steve.*

The realization smacked Zee across the face. Everything became clear: Steve was prophesied to overthrow Zeus. Philonecron had found out somehow and had brought him up to fulfill the prophecy. Steve would overthrow Zeus, then Philonecron would kill Steve and turn the whole universe into his sick little playground. It would have been better just to let Zeus flood the place.

"Ah, yes," said Philonecron, eyeing Zee. "And my

other friend too." He squeezed Steve's shoulder pos-
sessively. "Oh, Zero. He is not you, I must admit. He
does not have your bravery, your nobility, your *je ne sais
quoi*, and all he talks about is some magical place called
'Canada.' But he is wonderful in his own very special
way. And I have you and your fiendish spot-faced cousin
to thank for leading me to him. The first time I saw you,
I knew you would lead me to greatness. I just did not
understand how." Philonecron's head began to twitch
as if a fly were buzzing around it. "Ah, I can't stand it
anymore!" Philonecron hoisted the trident again and
blasted the wall behind him. A dark spot appeared
where the spell had hit, and blackness began to spread
through the walls like a stain. Soon the whole room was
covered in black marble—except for the missing wall
and the blue sky Charlotte has dived into.

Philonecron exhaled. "That's much better. What
did happen there?" he murmured silkily, nodding to the
place the wall used to be. "Careless. Well"—he turned
back to Zee—"speaking of your cousin, my moment of
triumph has arrived. Where is she, off destroying other
people's dreams? Hmmm? Is she planning on swooping in here at the last minute for our final apocalyptic
battle?" His voice rose to a screech. "Does she think she
is going to stop me? Where is she? I want to squash her
like the tacky bug that she is!"

Zee could not fight off the wave of despair that crashed into him. Charlotte was not coming. She was never coming again.

Philonecron's head snapped toward him. Eyes on fire, he strode up to Zee and grabbed him by the shoulders, staring penetratingly at him. Zee's stomach turned in revulsion.

Philonecron sucked in air. "No? No!" He tilted his head and watched Zee's face carefully. "Where is she? Not . . . *dead*, is she?" His eyes sparkled as if someone had just told him a most marvelous secret, and his wide mouth turned up in a terrible grin.

Zee tried to keep his face impassive, but it was too hard, too much.

Philonecron threw his head back and cackled. "Dead! Ha! Dead!" He threw his arms up in the air giddily. "Ha ha ha ha ha! Why, it's too marvelous, too marvelous for words! Tell me," he breathed, turning back to Zee, "was it painful? Tell me it was painful!"

"No," Zee hissed, struggling with all his might to say the words. "Stop it."

"Was it at least slow? Oh, let me believe it was slow." He squeezed his eyes shut and grinned, as if imagining something most wonderful. "It is too bad, really, for I so would have liked to kill her myself. Ah, well, the Universe does not always make sense. And she fulfilled her purpose, didn't she? She brought me here. If it weren't for your cousin I never would have sought the Universe." He beamed at Zee. "And, Zero, my boy!" He danced over to Zee and grabbed his chin. "Don't you see? There's nothing standing between us now! I will take you back into my warm bosom, yes, even after everything! We can be a family again! Really, Zero, there is no joy like the joy of fatherhood!"

Zee narrowed his eyes and, mustering all his strength, spat on Philonecron.

The god yelped and jumped backward. His red eyes narrowed. "That," he hissed, "is a very expensive dinner jacket. I am very disappointed in you, young man. I know your cousin's venom is still in you. We will have to find a way to get it out. Now"—he whirled around to Zeus—"as for you, Stormbringer. *It is time.*"

Zeus was moaning beneath the gag and squirming in his bonds like a kidnap victim in a movie. His behavior did not inspire confidence.

"What is that?" Philonecron said, cupping his hand to his ear. "I can't understand you. Oh, wait!" He slid over to Zeus and tore off the gag, the force causing the god's head to bang against the inky wall. "That's better!"

Zee looked around the room frantically. It was all on him. Everything that had happened—the shadows, Hades's Palace, the cruise ship, the Flame—it had all led to this. The gods were no help. They could have stopped Philonecron—in the Underworld, after the Underworld, anytime before he got his hands on the trident, on the heir of Zeus. But they didn't—all they cared about was the two thirteen-year-olds who had dared to interfere with them. Zee wanted to scream at Philonecron, attack him, spit on him some more, but he could not indulge his vengeance. There was nothing else but him between Philonecron and the universe.

Oh, how he wished Charlotte were here.

Zeus's thunderbolt lay halfway across the room. He didn't know if he could use it even if he got to it. But he could give it to Zeus. Somehow . . . He had to be careful; Philonecron had shown in the Underworld that he could control Zee with just his voice; he made him do all kinds of things against his will, and that was not a feeling Zee ever wanted to experience again. Carefully he took a step closer to the artifact.

"You vile, trident-thieving, half-breed scum," growled Zeus. "You are not worthy of carrying that."

"Oh? Really? Goodness. That hurts my feelings," said Philonecron, looking aghast. "Not worthy? That's too bad, I really wanted to—" He aimed the trident at Zeus. There was a flash of light, and Zeus screamed so loudly it rattled Zee's soul.

Zee stared at Zeus in horror. His arms were gone. Smoke poured from their stumps.

"There," said Philonecron, as the ropes bound more tightly around Zeus. "That's what you get for hurting my feelings. Hard to lose appendages, isn't it?"

Zeus roared, his face a mask of rage. "You will pay for this, demon! You will not overthrow me. You cannot. There is a way to these things."

"You're right, I can't," purred Philonecron. "But he can." He turned and indicated the motionless Steve.

Zeus peered in Steve's direction. "A mortal boy?" he sneered. "I think not."

"Oh," said Philonecron, dancing over to Steve and stroking his hair. The very air in the room was buzzing with Philonecron's unabashed glee. Zee truly had never seen anyone so happy. "He is not just any mortal, my Lord. Do you remember the Titan's prophecy?"

Everything grew very still. Zeus's eyes, which had been a deep black, turned suddenly white.

"Prophecy?" he repeated.

"Yes, you see, I had thought that I would kill you myself, but it is not fated to be. I am not foolish enough to toy with fate. Though you are, aren't you? You tried to get Prometheus to tell you the name of the son who was destined to overthrow you so you could kill him, but he would not give it. You tortured him on that cliff face for it, but he never wavered. Having an eagle gnaw on his ever-regenerating liver, now, that was very clever"— he raised his hands in Zeus's direction—"praise where praise is due. But it didn't work, did it? You never found out. But *I* did. Zeus, meet your destiny."

With that, Philonecron touched the trident to Steve. "Wake up, son," he cooed. "It's time." As Steve blinked dumbly, Philonecron tilted his head toward Zeus. "Do you even know him? Do you remember his mother? You don't, do you, you vile cad. You care nothing for anyone but yourself. Ah, well." He exhaled philosophically. "The son overthrows the father. Isn't it always the way of things? Steve is young, of course. He will need someone to help him with the Universe, a mentor of sorts, to show him the way."

"It will not work," Zeus breathed. "Not if you've enchanted him. Not if it's not his own will."

"Oh," said Philonecron, pacing dramatically, his cape billowing behind him. "It will be. This is a fine young lad, very loyal, as you will see."

Philonecron was standing between the thunderbolt and Zeus now. There was no way to get it.

Steve's eyes unclouded, and he began to look around the room. "Wha—what happened? I was—" He looked up at Philonecron, confusion and doubt on his face.

"Oh, nothing, nothing!" sang Philonecron. "Just

momentary befuddlement, could happen to anyone, but you're better now, aren't you? Now—" He grabbed Steve by the shoulders and steered him to Zeus. "Steve, meet Daddy."

Silence in the room, thick and expectant. Zeus stared at Steve in utter horror while Philonecron watched rapturously. The Lord of the Universe was terrified. Steve looked at Zeus, disbelief and pain and anger and shock on his face, and Zee took one more step toward the thunderbolt.

"Is it really true?" Steve asked.

"No!" said Zeus quickly.

"Yes," cooed Philonecron.

"You're *Zeus?*" Steve asked.

"No!" said Zeus.

"Oh, yes," cooed Philonecron.

Steve gaped at Zeus. "You broke my mom's heart! You said you would marry her, that you loved her! She gave everything for me, she gave up her life!"

"No," said Zeus again. "It was not me."

"Self-centered and a liar, too," sneered Philonecron. "You won't even own up to your own son. There is nothing you can do, Zeus. It has been prophesied." He turned to Steve. "He takes the shape of a mortal, seduces women, leaves them devastated. This is what he did to your mother. Didn't you always know? Didn't you know there was something different about you? You know the truth now, don't you?"

"Yes," whispered Steve, face flushed, unable to take his eyes off Zeus.

"No!" said Zeus.

Philonecron put his hand on Steve's shoulder comfortingly. "You poor boy. It must be so hard, imagining someone treating your mother this way. She's always been sad, hasn't she? And you never knew why."

"Yes!" said Steve.

"Yes, yes," dripped Philonecron. "He hurt her. And she is not alone. A real heartbreaker, that Zeus. He has done the same thing to countless women through history. Used them and discarded them." Carefully he placed the trident in Steve's hand. Zee could almost see it humming, still charged with Philonecron's power.

"Do you know who my mom is?" Steve asked Zeus, his voice trembling.

"Who—?"

"Do you remember her? Do you know her name? Tell me her name!"

"Um . . ." Zeus's mouth hung open. "Beverly?"

"NO!" yelled Steve.

"You can do whatever you want to him," said Philonecron in a low musical voice. "You can turn him into the lizard he is. You are destined to, for abandoned women and sons everywhere. You are their champion. Someone must stop him. You can make the Universe better, Steve."

Steve was staring at Zeus with a mixture of indignation and contempt. He clutched his hands around the trident as Zeus trembled like a cornered mouse.

"Steve!" said Zeus. "My son! You can rule by my side. And your mother, uh, Melinda!"

"No!" yelled Steve, the trident shaking in his hands. "You're pathetic. You're awful. You're a god! What are you doing with human women anyway?"

"I—"

"You could have made things better for her at least. Why didn't you make things better? Why?"

"You're right, son," said Zeus, "of course you're right. I should have, and I will. I'll give you whatever you want—"

"*No!* You're lying to me. You're scared of me. You're Zeus and you're just a lying, scared, pathetic nothing."

"*Steve,*" whispered Zee.

"You be quiet!" hissed Philonecron, whirling on Zee. His voice softened. "Now, now, Zero. Jealousy does not suit you. This is a great moment, isn't it? Can you believe you are going to witness it? I only wish your little cousin were alive to see this."

Steve turned his head. "Charlotte? What?"

"She's dead, my boy," said Philonecron, eyes twinkling with wonder. "Dead!"

"Dead?" Steve blinked.

"Yes! You don't have to worry about that meddling miscreant anymore. She won't bother us. Your path is clear! Now, go!"

"What happened?" said Steve, eyes wide.

"Oh, she can't hurt us anymore, my boy. I promise you. You see, it is fated to be! I'm sorry, I would have liked to have killed her myself, but—"

"What do you mean?" said Steve. "She risked her life to save me. She was just, what, thirteen?" He stared uncomprehendingly at Philonecron.

Zee held his breath. He dare not move, not one inch.

Philonecron goggled at Steve. "A trick!" he said. "A mere trick. Nothing that sniveling succubus does is for the good."

Steve turned his head to eye Philonecron. "How can you say that? She saved me. I never even thanked her."

"No, no, she is my nemesis, do you understand? Whatever she did, it was just to thwart me! Come now, Stephen, do it." Philonecron motioned to Zeus. "Make him pay!"

Steve looked to Zee, eyes wild. "Would she want me to do this?" he asked, his voice loud and trembling.

Zee shook his head slowly, his whole face a mask of

pleading. "He wants to use you. He wants the universe for himself—"

Philonecron turned on Zee, eyes blazing, "Nothing out of you, Zero!" he shrieked. "I will kill you!"

"What?" Steve exclaimed. "No! What's wrong with you?" And with that, he took a long step back, exhaled, and turned the trident on Philonecron.

"Attaboy, son!" said Zeus.

"Shut up!" yelled Steve.

*Yes, yes,* thought Zee. *Shut up.*

"Stephen!" gasped Philonecron, "what are you doing?"

"Charlotte saved my life," Steve said, anger in his eyes. "She was going to let that crazy guy shoot her for *me.* And now she's dead. And you're being horrible. It's not right."

"But—"

"Why do you want me to do this so badly, huh? Why do you care?"

"I just want what's best for you," cooed Philonecron. "You need a father figure, and—"

"No, I don't! And if I did, it wouldn't be you. You're creepy and weird and . . . creepy. He's right. You want me to overthrow Zeus so you can rule the universe, don't you?"

"At your *side!*"

"I don't want to rule the universe. I want to go back to Canada."

"My boy! You can turn the whole Universe into Canada!"

"No. I want to go back to my mom. I don't need to do anything to him." He nodded his head toward Zeus. "He's a pathetic coward, scared of a fifteen-year-old boy. He's got to live with that."

"That's right, I do," agreed Zeus.

"You have to!" Philonecron was almost shouting. "You are fated to. It is foretold!"

Steve let out a yell and a torrent of curses, then stepped back. He closed his eyes a moment, then turned to Philonecron and said, "I don't have to do anything I don't want to do."

Philonecron screeched and dove for the trident. Steve stumbled and collapsed backward. Zee saw his chance. He threw himself across the room toward the thunderbolt as Philonecron and Steve wrestled, Philonecron screeching insults at the boy.

And then Zee had it. Zeus's thunderbolt. It was cold, lifeless, there was no power for him to use. But there was nothing else to do. He was the only one left with hands. "Philonecron!" he yelled, aiming the thunderbolt at him.

Philonecron was on top of Steve, trying to wrench

the trident from his grasp. He looked up at Zee and his eyes narrowed. "Zero, you bad little boy," he hissed. "You cannot stop me. Remember, Zero, you will always be mine." And then Philonecron's voice turned soft and Zee's blood chilled. *"Zerooo,"* he cooed. *"Zero, freeze."*

And there was the feeling again, the one he hated most in the world. Control was gone from Zee; his body stopped of its own accord. He could not move.

With a great grunt Philonecron wrested the trident and aimed it at Steve. Zee stared in horror, unable to speak.

And then, out of the corner of his eye, Zee saw movement coming from the sky beyond the blown-out wall. Flapping wings, a flash of purple and green, then of a very familiar red. His mind sharpened, his heart leaped, warmth spread through his body, and Zee felt suddenly in perfect control of every muscle.

As Philonecron screamed at Steve, Zee aimed the thunderbolt and ran toward him, thrusting the sharp point into the god's back with all of his might.

Philonecron screeched and arched backward, the trident falling out of his hand. Zee dove for it as Philonecron fell to the ground. And then Zee was standing over him, trident and thunderbolt poised, as his tormentor howled.

"Zero, no! Zero, my boy! *Zerooooo.*"

Zee could sense rather than see his cousin—his brave, marvelous cousin—climb into the room. Philonecron's voice insinuated itself in his mind, but it no longer mattered. Zee's blood was no longer listening. If Charlotte had defeated death, Zee could defeat Philonecron.

Zee had felt the trident before, cold and dead. It was different now; fresh out of the hands of Philonecron, it was humming with life, with possibility. Zee felt a surge of power, of the world being his.

"Destroy him," Zeus cheered. "You can with the trident. You can blast him into bits."

Standing there, the trident in his hands, Zee saw himself saying the words, he saw Philonecron exploding in front of him. And then he thought about justice, and he thought about revenge, and the difference between the two. And then he made his choice.

## CHAPTER 33

# The End, the Beginning

Everything happened so quickly. One moment it looked to Charlotte like it was all over—Zee frozen, Zeus bound (and armless), Philonecron about to use the trident on someone, she could not see who. And then suddenly Zee was running at Philonecron, Philonecron was on the floor and Zee had the trident at his neck, and then two giant black birds swept in above her, picked up Philonecron by the jacket, and carried him off.

And then Zee was staring at her, eyes alight, face bright and open as the sky, and she thought how very happy she was to see him again.

And then he was next to her, his arm around her shoulders, squeezing her into his chest protectively. And no one spoke.

And then another voice was exclaiming, "You're alive!"

Charlotte turned in surprise to find someone she had decidedly not expected to see.

"I'll explain later," Zee whispered.

And then, from his place on the floor, Zeus coughed slightly.

Charlotte and Zee turned to him, wary. He was sitting there, trussed like a cow, armless and looking very much like he was struggling for dignity.

"Hmmm," said Zeus. "I would have prevailed, you know. I had him right where I wanted him."

"Oh, we know," said Zee earnestly, nodding.

"And you," he said, turning to Charlotte. "My pledge will not hold if your sacrifice was not sincere. If you knew you would live . . ."

"Your pledge will hold," Charlotte said quietly. She could feel Zee's eyes on her.

"And you," Zeus said to Steve. "I am very proud of you. Indeed, you are worthy of being my son. It is a shame that I have to end your life. Mortal"—he nodded to Zee and the trident—"give me my arms back!"

"What?" said Zee, taking a step back. "No."

"No?" Zeus repeated, blinking.

"Not if you're going to kill Steve."

"Yeah!" said Steve.

"I have no choice," Zeus said matter-of-factly. "There is a prophecy. He will overthrow me."

"No, I won't!" said Steve.

"So?" Zee straightened. "Do you want your arms back or not?"

There was silence as Zeus furrowed his brow, trying very hard to think.

"We'll just go," Charlotte said, tossing her hair and taking a step toward the elevator. "I'm sure someone will come for you eventually. Maybe we'll go tell Hera you're here, all bound up and helpless without your thunderbolt. . . ."

"Hmm," said Zeus. "Well . . ." He looked around the wreckage of the room uncertainly. Then he clucked his tongue and thrust his jaw out like a child. "Fine," he snapped. "I swear no harm will come to this boy."

"Swear on the Styx," said Zee.

"I swear on the River Styx. Now can I have my arms back?"

In a few moments Zeus was standing in front of them, whole and unbound, thunderbolt in his hand. Zee stood slightly in front of Charlotte and Steve, trident raised, just in case.

"There," said Zeus, brushing himself off. "Just how I planned it. Now"—he nodded to Zee—"do you still have the Flame?"

Zee nodded slowly.

"Show me."

Zee glanced at Charlotte, and she shrugged. He reached into his pocket and produced the lighter. Zeus's eyes flashed, and he lifted his thunderbolt and blasted the Flame. Zee yelped as the lighter skidded across the floor. There was a burst of fire, and then—

The lighter was still there, unharmed.

Zeus frowned, muttered something to himself, and then blasted it again, with the same result.

"You cannot destroy it, Zeus," said a voice. "Only its mortal bearer can."

Charlotte turned her head. Persephone was standing in a corner, face impassive.

Zee whipped around and looked at Persephone in utter confusion. Charlotte squeezed his wrist gently. *It's all right.*

Zeus looked no less confused. "What are you doing here? And how do you know?"

Persephone simply shrugged. Zeus frowned at her. "You were always contrary," he said. "You should be grateful to me. I arranged your marriage, made you a queen. . . ."

"Oh, I *am* grateful," said Persephone, wide-eyed, her tone dripping with insincerity.

"Brat," Zeus sneered. Then his face turned questioning. "But the Flame? You're telling the truth?"

Persephone nodded. "I am. If you want it destroyed, you will need them to do it."

"Well, then—" Zeus turned to Zee and raised his thunderbolt. "Mortal, destroy the Flame."

Man, he was bossy. Charlotte opened her mouth to say something lippy, but before she could, Zee scoffed, "Why should I?"

Zeus frowned. "Do it. I command you!"

"No," Zee said simply.

"I am Lord of the Universe!" bellowed Zeus. "Do it or I'll destroy you both!"

Again Charlotte opened her mouth, but Zee had already begun to speak. "If you kill us, who is going to destroy the Flame?" he asked matter-of-factly. Charlotte glanced over at her cousin. He was standing as straight as she'd ever seen him, and he looked almost as if he were enjoying himself.

That seemed to throw Zeus for a loop. He frowned and thought carefully.

"Hmmm . . . ," he said. "What if I promise *not* to kill you if you destroy the Flame?" He looked at them questioningly.

"No good," said Zee.

"Arrrgggghhhh!" Zeus threw up his hands. "What do you want now? Eternal life? Wealth? What?"

It took Charlotte a moment to realize what had just happened. Her breath caught in her chest. The air around them hummed. She looked over to Zee, and, eyes flashing, he nodded at her imperceptibly. There was only one answer possible.

"The Dead," Charlotte said, struggling to keep the excitement out of her voice. "You must give them a better afterlife. Build a city for them. Get rid of the Harpies. Take care of them. So people don't fade."

Charlotte could feel a wave of excitement from Persephone so strong her heart fluttered with it. She struggled to keep still. Next to her, she sensed Zee doing the same.

Zeus eyed them thoughtfully. "For the destruction of the Flame."

"Yes," they said at once.

The god's eyes flicked over to Persephone. "I suppose you'll whine about this, too. After all, you are Queen down there."

"Well," said Persephone, "it will be a *great bother*, of course. But we will make do, for the destruction of the Flame. This is very wise of you, O Zeus."

Zeus blinked. "It is?"

"Oh, yes. Only someone with your great wisdom could come up with a solution like this." Charlotte looked down, trying to suppress a smile. She could learn a thing or two from Persephone.

"Well." Zeus nodded slowly. "That is true." He turned to Zee and Charlotte. "Very well, mortals. If you destroy the Flame, I swear by the River Styx the Dead will be well treated."

Charlotte squeezed her eyes shut, letting the words wash over her. She struggled not to squeak, sob, squeal. She was there, in the Underworld, Zee next to her, an honor guard of Dead lining their path.

Zee looked as if he was struggling to keep the emotion off his face too. He exhaled, then picked up the lighter and looked to Persephone questioningly.

"Anything," she said. "It will work."

So Zee placed the lighter on the floor and, with a great breath, stomped on it. There was a small crackling noise, and the air was suddenly filled with a tremendous sense of loss. The three mortals in the room all shuddered at once. Then Zee bent down and picked up the small silver lighter and flicked the switch. Nothing happened. The Promethean Flame, kept hidden for centuries, the mother of the mortal soul, and its savior, was gone.

"Now," said Zeus, "would you all please go away?"

The cousins eyed each other. *Gladly,* Charlotte thought.

"And I strongly suggest not coming back," Zeus added. "Remember, it is only through my great wisdom that you live."

"Wait," said Charlotte. "What about the Mediterranean? The gods? They've all gone crazy, and—"

A pained expression crossed Zeus's face. "Oh, bother. Is there still life in the trident?" he asked.

Zee felt it and nodded.

"Very well," Zeus said, looking relieved. "Poseidon will put it all right. I have a feeling that as soon as he returns everyone will fall in line quite quickly."

Charlotte did not doubt it. But was he going to return? "Poseidon? You know where he is?"

Zeus nodded toward the back of the room. A large aquarium sat in the corner. Inside, a sea cucumber was watching them intently.

Charlotte and Zee exchanged a look. Was that . . . ? It couldn't be. But if it was, it was time to leave. They began to back out of the room, slowly.

"Oh, Steve?" called Zeus, sounding uncomfortable.

"Yeah?" Steve asked.

"If you should see my wife," Zeus said, "it would be best not to tell her who you are."

• • •

The three mortals wasted no time traveling down to the ravaged lobby and out the door, where they were met by a great purple and green bird that bowed when it saw them. They climbed on its back, first Charlotte, then Zee, then Steve, and they headed back to the mortal realm.

Charlotte found herself shaking slightly—from relief, from exhaustion, from residual terror, from joy. There was so much inside of her she could not contain it all, and it was only the feel of her cousin seated behind her, holding on to her back, that kept her from exploding.

She could not see Zee, but she imagined his face set in a sly, quiet smile. They'd had an obligation to the Dead; they had been bound with them ever since the cousins set foot in the Underworld and saw their plight. And now it was over.

Soon they were on a mountain clearing, with the holy beauty of Greece surrounding them. The bird became Persephone, and every person within a hundred miles felt a flash of pleasure but did not know why.

The goddess smiled at the trio. "You will find the Temple of Apollo half a mile away," she said. She looked at Charlotte and Zee, eyes full, and neither had ever seen anything as beautiful in their lives as the goddess before them. And then she shook her head and muttered to herself, "Mortals."

She took a step back. One moment she was there and the next she was a bird, but somewhere in between she told them, "Send my regards to your cat."

And then she flew away.

The cousins exchanged a glance and shrugged, and then the trio made their way along the path, reveling in the sun and the air and the sea and the earth. The cousins began to tell their stories. Zee told Charlotte of the imaginary forest, the fake Charlotte, the hearth room and Persephone, his confrontation with Zeus, his cousin's appearance and beautiful, horrible disappearance, the arrival of Philonecron and Steve, the moment when the universe might fall, then the flash of red that let him know that they were going to get through this.

And Charlotte told Zee of the dream-Hartnett, the Sphinx's curious riddle, the cows and the eagles and the lounging gods, being borne to Zeus in Hera's bitter arms, the pain and the darkness and the moment of light and truth, the beauty of the endless sky, the great bird and Persephone's apology, and the sight of her cousin, trident raised over Philonecron, and the knowledge that they were going to get through this.

When they arrived at the clearing below the Temple, they looked up to see the great mass of tourists winding their way as tour guides rattled on about the dead religion of the ancients. A family stood a few feet away from them, the mom and dad wearing big, ugly straw hats, the dad thumbing through a guidebook, a high school girl tapping her feet and rolling her eyes, and a little boy running in circles around the group, singing a song about bodily functions at the top of his lungs. Charlotte looked at the ground and grinned.

Zee nodded to the parking lot. "Uh, do you think he's still waiting for us?"

It had been a long time since Sir Laurence's driver had left them to wander off to Delphi. Charlotte hoped he had had a lot of knitting to do.

But when they followed the path to the parking lot, the driver was gone. The car was still there, and huddled in front of it in earnest conversation were two very familiar, very welcome faces.

"Mr. Metos! Sir Laurence!" Charlotte yelled. Bursting into a run, she tore over to them. She could feel the elation that radiated out from them at the sight of her as if it were coming from Persephone itself. And she fell into their arms.

"My dear friends," said Mr. Metos, his voice thick with emotion. As Charlotte hugged Sir Laurence, he slapped Zee on the back enthusiastically.

"Miss Charlotte, what happened? You're injured!" Sir Laurence eyed Charlotte's scarred face and bloody shirt.

"No," said Charlotte, "it's all right. I feel great."

"Hi, I'm Steve," Steve said to Sir Laurence, holding out his hand.

"Capital, capital," enthused Sir Laurence, shaking it vigorously.

"You're safe," Mr. Metos said, shaking his head.

"Mr. Metos, what happened?" Charlotte asked, wiping a tear away from her eyes. "We thought they were going to kill you."

"Well," Mr. Metos said, a wry smile creeping across his face, "it is very funny, but just at the key moment, the police came."

Charlotte blinked. "To rescue you? How did they—"

"No. To arrest me. It seems I was wanted for your kidnapping."

"Oh," said Charlotte. "Oops."

"Yes, apparently someone recognized you and the police came to the Import/Export offices. I will say I have never been so happy to be arrested."

"After you two left me so mysteriously," added Sir Laurence, "I set about to track down your friend. It appears that if one hands the police large sums of money, they are very happy to let one go!"

"Thank you again," said Mr. Metos.

"Glad to do it!" exclaimed Sir Laurence. "Any friend of Miss Charlotte and Sir Zachary the Brave is a friend of mine."

"He told me you were going to Delphi," Mr. Metos continued gravely, "and I had a good idea where you were headed. Are you all right? What happened?"

Charlotte and Zee glanced at each other. Tears filled Charlotte's eyes, and she looked down. "Mr. Metos, we'll tell you everything," she said, her voice choked. "But can we do it on the way home?"

First they went to the Canadian Embassy, where they made their phone calls and said good-bye to Steve—the angry young man who held the whole universe in his hands and gave it back, for the sake of the mother who had raised him and the strangers who had saved him. Then they went back to the airport hangar to Sir Laurence's jet, which was all ready for the long flight across the Atlantic.

There, Charlotte and Zee told their stories, each filling in details for the other. Mr. Metos listened gravely. When Zee haltingly told the story of Charlotte's sacrifice, he stared at the floor, eyes burning. And Charlotte told of Zee's defeat of Philonecron, of his talking back to Zeus, and together they explained their great bargain with the Lord of the Universe.

"We wanted justice," Charlotte said. "We got a compromise. But—"

"My dears," said Mr. Metos, grabbing their hands, "I am so proud of you. Do you know what you've done?

Generations of Prometheans have not been able to do what you did. You are truly the most extraordinary people I've ever met."

They sat in silence for a long time, watching the world go by. They slept some, letting themselves be embraced by dreamless quiet. As they began their descent, Charlotte turned to her mentor and asked, "Mr. Metos, what will you do now?"

"The Prometheans will need to regroup. We will see how necessary we are now. In the meantime, I would like to teach English. Maybe get a cat. And a real home. I did have a long-term offer from Hartnett that I hope is still valid. If I can get my criminal record cleared, that is. I don't have the same contacts I used to. . . ."

"Fear not, old chap!" said Sir Laurence, clapping him on the back. "Sir Laurence to the rescue!"

And then they were landing, and a car was waiting for them in the night. Charlotte had no idea how long they'd been away, but the car could not drive fast enough. And then finally they were pulling around the block to her house, to her parents and her cat, and as it approached Charlotte felt her heart was as open and endless as the universe. Charlotte and Zee had accomplished quite a lot in the past few months, but they were about to do the very best thing they had done yet— come home, safe and sound.

EPILOGUE

## A Suitable Finish

Deep in the middle of the country, there is a clothing store like many others. In fact, you could find a branch of this particular store in just about every major city in the whole country, and even a few in Canada. The typical customer for this store is a man who is required to dress in a way he cannot afford. It is lined with discount suits, jackets, ties, and shirts, which are all very good replicas of the real thing. Many people cannot tell the difference.

At this clothing store was a customer just like any other, looking for a suit for a job interview. "I need a job," he had told his girlfriend, "before I can afford the suit." It was for people like him that this store existed.

On this particularly day, this customer was being waited on by a new employee of the store, a man who was, frankly, not very much like any other man the customer had ever seen. He was thin, gaunt, slightly taller than average, with black, spiky hair and black, beady eyes.

This employee, who was in fact exactly like a man, had recently had an odd experience. He had awoken, like a newborn babe, to find himself at this particular store in this particular cheap suit, selling another man gaudy imitation cuff links.

The customer picked out a brown suit coat and held it up to the employee questioningly. A strange look passed over the employee's face, some mixture of disgust and despair. The employee shook his head slowly.

"You don't want this."

"Why not?" The customer blinked.

"It's atrocious." The salesman diverted his eyes from the suit as though he could not possibly look at it anymore.

"I like it."

"No, no, you can't *possibly*."

"I do!" protested the customer.

"My gods, you cretin," said the salesman, voice full

of emotion, "have you ever felt a natural fiber in your life?"

The customer frowned and eyed the salesman's name tag. "*Phil*, do you have a manager I could speak to?"

The employee named Phil sighed languidly. "If you must." *This again,* he thought. His eyes surveyed the room as he wondered what he had done to deserve this. And then he saw something that made him stop.

"Excuse me," he asked the customer, "are they with you?"

"No," said the customer, walking away.

Phil looked toward the doorway. Standing there were a boy and a girl, both dressed appallingly, both whispering and staring at him. There was something about them he did not like, not at all. In fact, he might say he was filled with an inexplicable loathing.

"Security," Phil called. "Those children are loitering."

"Whatever," said the security guard, ambling toward the children.

"We were just leaving," muttered the boy. And the two turned and left.

The employee named Phil did not have time to reflect on them, though, because as soon as they walked out the door, the manager appeared next to him, a short man with oily hair who clearly bathed in cheap cologne every day before work.

"We need to have a talk," said the manager.

Soon Phil found himself in the manager's office. The desk in front of him was covered in porcelain cats and other knickknacks. Phil could not remember anything about his past, but he knew he loathed knickknacks. Even the chair he was sitting in was horrible, squeaky and squishy and wrong.

He had heard the manager's tirade before—you must not insult the customers, you must not degrade the merchandise, I should be firing you, I don't know why I'm not, I can't seem to—

Phil did not listen. The manager was weak, he knew that. His employees had no respect for him. He let them take long breaks, leave early, dress sloppily. What this store needed was a change in leadership. What this store needed was Phil.

As the manager droned on, Phil rubbed his hands together and looked around the office greedily. Oh, yes, he thought. Someday this would all be his.

# BESTIARY

## Automatons
Animate bronze statues. Not much for conversation.

## Chimera
An enormous beast with the head of a lion, body of a goat, and tail of a dragon. Has an extra goat head sticking out of its torso. Cannot be manipulated or controlled—except, perhaps, by an evil genius.

## Centaur
The head and torso of a man, the body of a horse. A convivial and erudite creature. Prone to irritability, especially when having an arrow stuck in its butt.

## Cyclops
Big, mean, cave-dwelling monsters with one eye and a taste for human flesh.

## Eurynomus
Underworld demon with blue-black skin the color of flies and a cloak of vulture feathers. Has some personal hygiene issues.

## Giant
Humanoid monsters, often with many arms. Fought

against the gods in the War on Cronus. Very large, as you might imagine.

## Gorgon

Hideous female demons with serpents in place of hair, golden wings, stringy beards, and hands of claws. Best not to look them in the eye, unless of course you want to be turned into a statue.

## Harpy

Massive flying creatures with the body of a vulture and the face of a nasty old woman. Mean and very, very stinky.

## Hydra

A dragon-sized serpent with nine heads. If you cut one head off, two grow back in its place.

## Ketos

A massive sea monster. Its belly is an excellent place to find tridents, should you be looking for one.

## Minotaur

Legs of a man and head and torso of a bull. Often can be found at the center of labyrinths, which is why it's better to go around.

## Pegasus

Flying horse. Never there when you need it.

## Satyr

A creature with the body of a goat and torso of a man. Musical and mischievous.

## Scylla and Charybdis

Sailors who pass on one side of the Strait of Messina will be devoured by Scylla, a giant female beast with a pack of dogs below her waist. Those who pass on the other side will be sucked into the horrible mouth of Charybdis. It's what you call a dilemma.

## Siren

A female nymph whose irresistible song enchants passing sailors who then dive off their ships and drown. A good reason to carry earplugs.

## Sphinx

A creature with the body of a lion, eagle wings, and the head of a woman. On the plus side, knows a lot of great riddles. On the minus, will eat you if you get them wrong.